FIND ME IN THE SHADOWS

THE APEX DUOLOGY

ANNABELLA LOWE

INDEPENDENT PUBLISHING NETWORK

First Published in Great Britain in 2024 by the Independent Publishing Network
Text Copyright © Annabella Lowe
Cover designed by Maldo Designs
All rights reserved.

No part of this publication may be reproduced, stored or transmitted in any form or by any means, electronic, mechanical, photocopying or otherwise, without the prior written permission of the publisher.
The right of Annabella Lowe to be identified as the author of this work has been asserted by them per the Copyright, Designs and Patents Act 1988.

This is a work of fiction. Names, places, events and incidents are either the products of the author's imagination or used fictitiously. Any resemblance to actual persons, living or dead, is purely coincidental.
A CIP catalogue record for this book is available from the British Library.
Ebook ISBN: 9781805179962
Print ISBN: 9781805179948

For those who stand beside the dreamers and help them reach for the stars.
Thank you.

PROLOGUE

Mint with a hint of orange.

The discordant flavours assaulting my tastebuds were really quite off-putting. Micah's tongue made another clumsy sweep of my mouth, and I peeked my eyes open, a quick glimpse of long dark lashes—highlighted pink in the light of a passing strobe—just to remind myself that he was hot. Getting here had taken considerable effort, and though it wasn't quite how I'd imagined my first kiss to be, at least it was happening.

A warm, clammy hand slithered down the small of my back. I didn't flinch or pull away, despite our teeth awkwardly clacking together.

This was far more invasive than I'd thought it would be.

Heat crept into my cheeks, and as the drum and bass that had been reverberating through my body came to an end, it felt like the natural time to break our encounter. I gave Micah a flirty grin, which he reciprocated, dark brown eyes glazed with desire. I pulled away, turning on my heel before he could request another dance and discreetly wiped my mouth.

My neck was stiff from leaning down into the kiss, a hazard of being so tall; all the boys my age hadn't quite caught up with my ridiculous growth spurt. Not that I knew any boys personally; these were all Penny's school friends. I looked around the crowded, sweat-soaked room and spotted her still entangled, her chestnut hair spilling down her back in ringlet curls and hiding the wandering hands underneath. I left her be and shuffled to the edge of the dance floor, slipping past the press of teenage bodies and out into the corridor. I needed to find the toilets.

It didn't take long, it was a small-town community centre so they were not particularly glamorous. I closed the battered stall door and grabbed a piece of tissue to twist the lock shut then hovered above the seat. I glanced down and my stomach lurched, dread and embarrassment swept over me, like a scurrying plague of insects.

Not now. Oh God, this could not seriously be happening to me.

This was not a first that should be happening tonight.

Why did the universe hate me? No doubt it was my penance for lying to my parents—I knew I shouldn't have listened to Penny.

I bit back my tears, and with no other option, I lined my underwear with a wad of tissue, hoping it wasn't noticeable through my short navy dress, and made my way back into the main hall.

I found Penny at the edge of the dance floor with a different boy and pulled her away from him.

"Olivia I was in the middle of something," she yelled over the blaring rock song that had been most recently requested.

"I'm sorry! Please, can I borrow your phone? I need to make an urgent call, and I left mine at your house so my parents couldn't track it," I shouted back, my voice almost lost against a chaotic guitar solo. My pleading eyes won her over. She relented and rummaged through her glittering purse, unlocking it before she dropped it into my hand.

"Thank you," I mouthed and headed for the door, already

pulling up location maps. Perfect, there was a local Spa shop five minutes away and still open. Hopefully, I'd be back before she even noticed I was gone, and I could still salvage some of the night. Micah might have been my first kiss, but he certainly wasn't going to be my last kiss tonight.

∼

I stepped onto the street, and the bitter autumn wind immediately pulled at my hair. The long dark strands blustered around my face, and I fought against them, tugging them from my mouth while trying to pay attention to the glow of the map.

It wasn't late, but the evening was drawing in fast. I had only the streetlights, along with the faint glow of homes set back behind quaint gardens, to guide me. It wasn't long before I saw the shop. The brightly lit interior overlooked a small car park bordered by tall silver birch trees swaying angrily in the wind. I hurried across, relieved to fling myself into the warmth of the store. The sudden blast of heat brought sweat glistening on my forehead, and my stomach dipped with embarrassment now that I was here. At least I was alone, and at least I had realised before I'd made a spectacle of myself.

It could have been so much worse.

I browsed the scant range of products, quickly selected the least daunting, and paid, my cheeks burning bright red. I didn't dare look at the attendant but patiently waited for my change, and as soon as the metal hit my palm, I was rushing for the exit.

The biting cold had every inch of my skin puckered in unforgiving goosebumps, and as I crossed the car park, I was hit with a wave of nausea. Was this normal? I paused, wondering if I was going to vomit right there, and in the absence of my hurried steps, I heard another set.

A glance over my shoulder confirmed a dark lean figure

headed in my direction. I stumbled forward, my nausea overshadowed by a more imminent threat. I needed to get back to the shop—to safety—but he was blocking my path, and something told me I should not go anywhere near this person.

I reached the far edge of the car park and sprinted diagonally across it, intending to put as much distance between us as possible. I heard the echo of pounding steps behind me, the sound driving my heartbeat to an even wilder gallop, but no matter how hard I pushed my legs, I wasn't fast enough. Fingers snatched at the material of my dress, halting me so fast I struggled to remain upright. My breaths were sharp and began to fog in the cold air, my heart beat harshly against my ribs as though ready to burst out, and the sound of my pulse roared in my ears drowning out all other noise. My hands flung out, wildly hitting and scratching with every ounce of my strength. A hand clamped on the crease of my elbow, painfully tight and restrictive, and the other grabbed my wrist, leaving only my feet to defend me as I struggled to break his hold.

I kicked hard.

The grip faltered, but I was off balance and suddenly weightless. Everything slowed. Dread filled every facet of my body as I fell. I hit the ground hard, gravel biting at my skin, and I was cast in wretched shadow as my assailant pinned me to the ground. I drew breath to scream, but a hand clamped over my mouth. The cold clammy skin covering half my face reeked of metal, grease, and smoke, and I gagged. My head was forced into the concrete, and a searing pain burned against my throat, my flesh torn and stinging. A muffled shriek escaped me. There were needle-sharp teeth, embedded in my skin. I cried hysterically, gagging and screaming against the hand that pinned me. Then, just as quickly, the teeth wrenched painfully free. For the briefest of moments, my eyes met those of my assailant. A flash of eery ice blue, visible even against the cloak of darkness, and a gurgling, choking sound erupted from its throat—covering me in blood and spittle. Whatever this creature was, it collapsed against me, its full weight crushing the air from my lungs as it thrashed and wretched. My skin tore as I was pressed into the sharp concrete beneath me. My assailant gagged and writhed until the last of its stuttered breaths ebbed away entirely.

Everything went still.

The neighbourhood—the very darkness pressing in around me—seemed to hold its breath in what was the most surreal and utterly terrifying moment of my life. I gathered enough strength to push, and my assailant rolled off of me. He hit the cold floor with a sickening thud.

I shook so hard I couldn't stand. I crawled instead, hands and knees scraping on dirt and the occasional loose stones that sank into my flesh, making my way to a lonely vehicle a couple of metres away. I slumped against it, drawing my knees up and hugging myself.

This couldn't be real. Blood trickled down my legs, but I could only sit and sob.

I glanced up, half expecting the scene to dissolve as I woke from a bloody nightmare, but there was still a body lying prone. In the moment of quiet, I heard an unholy noise. I stared at the creature, trying to make sense of the sound. An unsettling gnawing, like that of a thousand rats demolishing a carcass. I crept close enough to see my attacker in the dim light, and I froze. Its skin was shrivelling away. There were no longer eyes on its face. A concave pit where the nose had been. Tissue and flesh were decaying at an alarming rate, revealing tendons and ligaments, muscles, and then finally bone.

I retreated to sit against the car, my body trembling as I begged the creator—begged anyone who might listen—to make it stop. But it didn't stop. Crack after ear-splitting crack echoed around the car park as I remained, rooted in fear. I couldn't tear my eyes from the sight, even as the body caved in on itself, and finally, there was nothing but a pile of clothes and unearthly silence.

"Are you okay?"

I startled, looking up to find a middle-aged lady hunched over. Her long dark hair was flying around her face as she watched me, concern crinkling her brows. I hadn't heard her approach, my muffled cries had masked her steps. I wasn't sure how long I'd even been sitting there. I pointed a quivering finger at the pile of clothes.

"A man attacked me. He bit me," I choked out around my tears.

She glanced at the clothes, the frown on her face deepening. "What's your name, little love?"

"Olivia. Olivia Blake."

"Okay, Olivia, can you try and tell me the extent of your injuries?"

I stretched my legs out; some cuts were still bleeding, stones were still embedded in my skin, and parts of my skull and face were sore from being scraped against the concrete. My backside was the worst, having taken the impact when I fell—it grew stiffer the longer I sat. My fingers made their way to my neck, expecting to find torn flesh but the skin was impossibly smooth and dry.

"I fell," I said uncertainly. "I've got cuts, and I'm sore."

She stepped closer and crouched. "Does your head hurt? Did you hit it when you fell?"

"No."

"Okay, I'm just going to shine my torch over you for a second." The light from her phone flared so brightly that I had to shield my eyes as she did a quick sweep of my body and turned it off.

"Olivia, can you tell me how you got here?"

The reminder sent a jolt of crippling panic through me. I didn't know how long I'd been gone, whether Penny had noticed my absence yet or if she was still enthralled by the boys that had been swarming around her all night.

Oh God. My parents would find out that I had lied. The air seemed to chill at the prospect, settling against my skin with sickly dread.

"Olivia, take a deep breath. You're safe now. I want to help you," she said calmly. I followed her advice, sucking in long deep breaths and with each step closer to calm—my body screamed louder in pain.

"Were you at the local school disco, Olivia?" I nodded, still focused on breathing through the panic. "I'm going to ask you a question that might be very distressing, but it's important. Was the assault of a sexual nature?"

I stared at her in shock "No," I said brashly. "Why?"

She gave me a sympathetic smile. "I'm relieved to hear that. I just thought it might have been a possibility given the clothes over there and some of your injuries. I think it's best we give the police a call and obviously your parents. Do you know their contact details?"

"Please don't call my parents. Can you take me back to the disco?" I felt sick at the thought of facing them—of admitting my duplicity. My life was sheltered enough without giving them a reason to lock me away.

Despite my pleading, twenty minutes later, my parents were en route and the car park was lit with flashing blue lights. Pockets of people gathered to nose at the commotion, and the low hum of speculative chatter floated across the car park as I stared numbly at the tarmac. I sat perched on the back of an ambulance, a blanket draped around my shoulders keeping most of the biting wind at bay. A paramedic had assessed and cleaned my wounds; thankfully most of them had been superficial. The kind lady—Isobel was her name—had found and gathered my things and stayed faithfully by my side throughout, a quiet encouragement while I gave preliminary statements to the police. She departed once Penny arrived with her parents in tow.

Penny stood before me now, gaping at my battered and bruised legs, her eyes glassy with concern. My neck caught her attention. She took a step closer and stooped to get a better look.

"Did Micah give you that?" My fingers pressed to my throat, surprised that she would accuse him of hurting me.

"Is there a bruise? It wasn't Micah. No—it was the...the man."

She flinched, her brows tugging down and the seriousness made her look far older than her fourteen years. "He gave you a hickey? Did he try and..." She trailed off, horror lining her features as she didn't dare utter the unspeakable words.

"He bit me," I said under my breath, not quite sure if I remembered everything correctly. Maybe I was wrong. Maybe his teeth didn't penetrate. Maybe he just sucked on my skin. But that couldn't be right—I could still remember the echo of pain as I felt my flesh tear. I'd heard the slurp of blood as he sucked it into his mouth. Or was it saliva?

"Who stopped him?" Penny asked, disturbing my internal hysteria.

"No one. He choked on top of me and died." My voice came out shrill and scared, and she moved to my side, draping an arm around my shoulders.

"At least the police don't have to catch him though, right? Did they tell you what killed him?"

"He disappeared. I don't know what happened." Tears spilled onto my cheeks and dribbled towards my chin, leaving the taste of salt on my lips. I licked them away. I could feel the distrust growing in the mounting silence between us as I waited for her to reply.

"Did you leave the car park?" she asked carefully. I could hear the disbelief in her question. The rational part of her trying to work out a plausible explanation.

"No, I watched him disappear. LITERALLY disappear. Like he was eaten alive by some invisible creature."

I felt her tense, and then she stood, releasing me from her grip as she stared ahead, another look of horror shadowing her pale face as my parents marched towards us.

My mother, ever the businesswoman, was dressed in her trouser suit, her dark hair swept into a graceful bun that even the wind couldn't disturb. She ignored Penny and held out a hand to me, squeezing my fingers when I took it.

"Let's get you home. You're probably in shock and need to rest."

My father squeezed my shoulders and at least had the decency to nod at Penny as he steered me forward. His towering form was almost a head taller than everyone we passed. He opened the car door for me, his expression tight as he waited for me to get in and carefully pushed it shut. He halted before getting in the car, whirling as an officer came dashing across the car park.

"We'll take it from here and be in touch tomorrow," he told them with an air of authority that the officer wasn't keen to question.

My mother gracefully swung into the seat next to me, one leg delicately crossing over the other as she monitored the scene outside. Neither of them spoke for several minutes. The only noise in the car was the soft click of the indicator as my father manoeuvred us out of the town and back towards home.

"You're not to see Penny again," my mother said as she stared out the window, her tone suggesting she would take no argument, and so I sat quietly, my heart breaking and silent tears streaming down my face.

"The police gave me the gist of your statement. Are you sure you didn't hit your head when you fell? They think you may have passed out during the attack," she said, her sharp brown eyes now scrutinising my appearance.

I wasn't sure how to answer that. It was certainly very clear that everyone thought I was mad. The paramedic had checked my pupils after I told her, worried I might have a concussion. Isobel had breezed past most parts of my story, asking several more times in one way or another if I had been raped. The police had me take a breathalyzer test and requested I provide a urine sample. Not one person, not even my best and only friend, had listened to me. The trembling grew worse as another wave of fear rattled through my body. What would happen if they thought I was insane? Oh God. This couldn't get any worse.

I was wrong. It could get worse. I stood in my living room the following morning staring at the stranger sitting demurely on our brown leather Chesterfield. Every limb ached, my head throbbed, and yet my mother had still insisted I get up and get dressed. I thought she hadn't cancelled my tutor, but no, a study session would have been a kindness compared to this.

The blonde woman smiled and stood, her green silk skirt fluttering around her ankles as she straightened. She was a decade younger than my parents at least, a sophisticated beauty, her age only just beginning to show in the fine lines around her deep blue eyes.

"It's nice to meet you Olivia, I'm sorry to hear you had a difficult day yesterday," she said as she gestured to the twin sofa opposite her. "You went through something deeply traumatic, and I think it shows just how much your parents love you—that they asked me to come and talk to you today."

I thought it showed exactly how little they loved me, but let's not pull at that thread. I dragged my feet across the carpet, nausea creeping into my stomach, and dropped awkwardly onto the sofa. She sat gracefully, an empathetic smile sweeping across her perfectly shaped lips, and picked up her notebook and pen. As she tilted her head, appraising my bruised and battered appearance, I realised I had a decision to make. I could tell the psychologist the truth, which I expected would not end well for me at all; my sanity would be called into question, and who knew what measures my parents would take to fix me? Or, I could lie through my teeth, accept a temporary punishment for my disobedience, and hope this all became a distant memory once the dust settled. I tapped my fingers on the high arm of the sofa, the hard, rich leather clacking under my nails, and my knees started bouncing as I pulled together a realistic story in my mind. I would throw myself under the proverbial bus to protect my sanity. To protect myself from being held under a bright and traumatic spotlight. Did it make me a coward? Probably. Maybe some people were born to be heroes—but I was born a survivor.

So let the lies and parental disappointment begin…

1

TEN YEARS LATER

The smell of burnt garlic hit my nostrils a second too late. The wail of the smoke alarm blared through the apartment, setting my teeth on edge, and the apprehension I'd been feeling turned to anger as I lifted the sizzling pan off the heat.

"Shit. Noah, can you please press the button on the alarm?" I shouted through the apartment.

His muffled reply carried from the living area, and moments later, the horrid din ceased, and I blew out a breath of relief as I turned off the gas ring. The return to quiet felt like a feather-soft caress against my mind.

I scraped the garlic into the bin, wiped out the pan, and set it back on the hob to rest. Taking another deep, calming breath, I braced my hands on the cold quartz worktop, stifling the urge to punch something. How had my mother even managed to sap the enjoyment from my cooking? She wasn't even here yet. On top of everything else I had to deal with, why couldn't I have a normal family?

The creak of a window sliding open had me jolting across my shoebox-sized kitchen, panic driving all thoughts of my parent's impending visit from my head. Racing across the living room, my legs scraped the low coffee table, almost tripping me as I launched myself at the sash window and fervently tugged it down. It snagged on the pulley system, which was stiff with disuse, and sent my heart into a chaotic beat. No, no, NO! I had to get it closed. Noah's hands joined mine, the added strength overcoming the resistance, and it soon clanged shut.

"I didn't think you'd want the apartment smelling of burnt garlic," Noah said warily, pushing his round-framed glasses more snugly onto his cute button nose. His chestnut eyes were pinched with concern and he cautiously took my hand, his thumb gliding over my knuckles as he waited for me to catch my breath. I inhaled long and slow, reminding myself that Noah didn't need to keep his windows closed as a matter of life or death, and that to him, I was probably looking a little crazy right now. I winced, I hated the term crazy and was especially annoyed that I'd let it creep into my thoughts. I forced a smile.

"The air purifier will sort it. It's far too cold to have the windows open."

It was a partial truth. Spring came later and later each year, and even in late March there was no sign of winter letting us out of its clutches anytime soon. Last week had seen Nottingham decorated with inches of crisp white snow. The schools had closed, and Noah and I had spent the days off organising homeschool lesson plans which parents promptly ignored. It had been nice though, having him snowed in at my apartment. We'd watched the city while trapped behind my window, the flurry of snow falling thick and wild like a snow globe.

I stood on my tiptoes, my fingers combing through the short lengths of hair at the base of his neck and our lips softly met. His wariness melted away, hands confidently winding around my waist as his kisses stole my breath. He pulled away too soon, his fingers pushing his blond curls away from his glasses as he gazed at me with a lazy smile.

"I wouldn't normally advocate for getting on your parent's bad side but...time is running short, and I was just imagining how funny it would be to see the spectacularly prim Diana and Benjamin Blake eat fish and chips! What do you think? Shall we bin off cooking and make them eat *street food*?"

My mouth stretched into a devious grin. "You, Noah, are an evil genius!"

"I'll even tell them it was my fault," he said with a wink.

I laughed. All the tension was cut loose, my breath coming easier as if the laces of an invisible corset had been sliced open.

"Oh, I also have a gift for you," he said. "I left it in the hall. I'll be back in a mo." His long legs carried him swiftly out of the room, and he was back before I had time to dread the possibilities.

He handed me a small rectangular parcel. I ripped away the brown paper wrapping, not caring that it crumpled to the floor, and stared at the framed picture of us. We were sitting by our favourite spot along the River Trent, snuggled together in our winter coats. The fiery touch of autumn was still visible in the distant trees. It had been my twenty-fourth birthday, and he'd surprised me with a picnic lunch. Hot soup canisters to warm our fingers and bellies and a flask of hot chocolate for a touch of sweetness. One of my favourite days last year. Probably my favourite birthday ever.

"Thank you so much," I murmured, trying to keep tears locked tightly away—smudged makeup would only give my mother more ammunition to goad me. He teased the frame from my hands and looked about my scantly furnished room.

"The real question is, are you putting this on the bookshelf or the coffee table?"

I could see the triumph in his eyes—he had finally gotten me to accept a gift that was considered an ornament. He found my place strange for its lack of embellishment, a sentiment shared by my parents. I pointed to the bookshelf, its top bare like most surfaces in my apartment because I cared little for decoration. It took longer to clean and longer to pack. The only exception to my rule was my book collection, and even that was kept to a minimum. Three shelves worth of mystery novels I couldn't bear to part with. It had been one of the things connecting us when I started teaching at the same school last April.

He set the black frame in the centre of the bookcase, a satisfied smile on his face that had ideas forming in my mind, but they would have to wait until later.

I let Noah answer the door when my mother's brisk knock signalled their arrival. She breezed through the apartment and stopped in her tracks when she saw me loitering at the window where I'd been watching the street below for signs of trouble. She scanned me head to foot, taking in my ripped jeans and knotted white T-shirt.

"Do you go out in public dressed like that?"

"Do you ever pay attention to fashion?"

Her eyes narrowed, and she straightened, glancing around my hideously bland, beige apartment and immediately spotting the picture frame. She was drawn to it, her fingers clutching at the frame as she scrutinised our happy moment.

"This is nice," she said and gently placed it down. I said nothing, surprised that her heart of stone could offer such a compliment. Perhaps she saw something in our candidness that she secretly longed for.

Mercifully, my father and Noah entered, the former crossing the room to kiss my cheek in greeting.

"Noah was just telling me about his cooking disaster," he said, his smile so genuine, it showed in the creases near his deep brown eyes. "We've all been there. I haven't had a takeaway in years—it feels quite exotic!" A short distance away my mother stared at him in horror before turning an obnoxious glare on me.

"Why was Noah cooking?" Typical that she would still find a way to make it my fault, despite her being staunchly feminist.

"Olivia had a lot to organise for the Easter event at school, so I offered to give her some extra planning time," Noah cut in, smoothly defending my honour with his lie.

It seemed to placate her. She perched on the edge of my only sofa, clasping her hands around her knee. My father sighed, drawing my gaze. He stood with hands in his pockets, resigned to the tension undoubtedly about to fill his evening. It was a miracle he hadn't turned completely grey. His almost-black hair was only lightly peppered with silver—just visible in the shortest lengths near his temples and the nape of his neck. The rest was well hidden within thick waves that were neatly combed and waxed to one side.

"You're looking rather tanned, Dad. Where've you been?"

He was always tanned—as was I, carrying his olive skin tone and freckles. I was my father's daughter through and through, but now his skin had a deeper, richer hue to it. His freckles were more pronounced, having been kissed by the sun.

"Oh, I was in Brazil last week, and thank God too as I missed all that ghastly snow." He sat down next to my mother and accepted the collection of takeaway leaflets Noah handed him. "What do you fancy Diana?" He fanned the leaflets out in front of her, giving a pointed look that broke through her bruskness.

She pulled out the Thai menu. "I suppose I could stomach a Massaman curry"—she glanced up at me—"so long as I'm not eating from my lap."

An hour later we sat around the fold-up table and chairs that I kept for such occasions, the fragrant smell of spice and grease saturating my apartment. I liked it that way. Spice was no stranger to my kitchen. I deliberately cooked pungent and flavoursome meals to drown out my scent. Whether it be cooking or using cleaning chemicals, I spent my time at home trying to eclipse the one thing that brought on the hunt.

"Yes, that's exactly why we spent tens of thousands on the best private tutors; so that you could spend your days cleaning up piles of vomit." The comments from my mother were no less barbed as we ate.

"It's just that time of year. At least I didn't catch it this time. And it wasn't piles it was one small bit—"

"Olivia, we're eating. This is hardly the appropriate time," she seethed, placing her fork down on her plate far too dramatically and readjusting in her seat to make a show of her discomfort.

"You asked," I said petulantly under lowered brows.

Beside me, Noah stared awkwardly at his plate, avoiding all eye contact as I continued to stoke the fire of my mother's anger.

"Yes, and you know it infuriates me. You could be so much more. You could be doing something that stretches you, that earns you enough that you wouldn't have to live in a hovel and have actual furniture. It's not like you spend your summers travelling, is it?"

She wasn't wrong. My travel was limited to wherever I could fly during daylight hours—it was too much of a risk to be out after dark. That's when they found me.

"Right, I could be chained to a desk for twenty hours a day helping rich people get richer. No, thank you. I enjoy my work, and at least I can sleep without a guilty conscience."

My father's shoulders drooped, and any pretence of looking cheery fell from his expression. My mother's haughtiness remained, however, and she tapped a fingernail on the table with irritation.

"You are young…and so very naive," she said sharply before turning to Noah. "Please understand, I was not insulting your career choice, it's just not the path we expected Olivia to take; it's not what we trained her for or where we know her capabilities lie."

He shrugged, his face brightening with a composed smile. "No offence taken," he said and turned to my wilted father, with determination in his eyes. "Where are you off to next Benjamin?" he asked in a lilting tone, breaking the mounting tension.

My father cleared his throat, some of the warmth coming back to his face, and he rubbed a hand over the back of his neck. "Oh, I'm all over the place for the next few months. I'm in New York, Jakarta, Paris, Abuja, and then Beijing towards the end of the year I think."

Noah's eyebrows quirked. "Wow, it must be nice to see so much of the world."

"You'd think. I'm getting too old for it now. My back doesn't appreciate the time away from my bed, and I'd much rather be sipping a mojito on a beach in Turkey if I had to travel anywhere."

My mother gave him a fleeting glance, a sharpness in her expression that she quickly masked.

"Are you going with Dad on any of these trips?"

"I'll be going to New York and Paris, but I've got a lot to oversee here." She hesitated and then pulled her expression into something resembling warmth and charisma. "Why don't you two come and stay over the Easter break? I'm sure it would do you good to get out of the city for a few days?"

I nearly choked on my wine.

Noah squeezed my leg under the table and offered her a sincere smile. "We'll see if we're free. I'd love to see where Olivia grew up."

Noah did his best to facilitate conversation for the rest of the evening, and when they finally left, I sank against the door, fighting a yawn, my head ready to explode. It was only the third time they'd met Noah, and it already felt like my mother preferred him. It did make the visits slightly more bearable with their attention split between us. But it was never pleasant.

"See, they're not so bad," Noah mused as he leaned against the wall, his arms folded as he watched me slither to the floor in exhaustion.

"Sure, let's swap parents if you like them so much. I'm sure they'd be thrilled to have a son who might actually listen to them."

His laugh echoed around the small hall of my apartment. When I looked up from between my fingers, he extended a hand and hauled me to my feet, the promise of a better evening ahead captured in his smile.

2

JINXED

"That will be £32.67. Are you paying by card?" The cashier's polite, melodic voice brought my frayed attention back to the present, and I nodded absentmindedly while carefully stacking my carton of eggs in the top of a shopping bag.

It had been a long, long day of teaching, a parents' evening on top, and then a traffic accident on the outskirts of the city had delayed my journey home considerably. It was far too late to be out shopping, and typically I'd have been more organised and arranged a delivery robot, but I didn't know what I wanted and needed to browse to see the possibilities. At this hour, the store was eerily quiet without the steady thrum of customers keeping the checkouts busy, and the low, constant hum of the refrigerated shelves was the only ambient noise. I found myself longing for a crowd.

Looking back at the till, I found the cashier patiently smiling at me as I checked the total.

"Sorry it's been a hard day; my brain is frazzled," I told her and tapped my watch, holding it over the machine. As the payment was authorised, the shrill confirmation beep cut through the quiet, and the hairs on the back of my neck stood on end. Fuck. This was really bad timing. I glanced around the almost empty store. Chills shuddered down my spine, making my hands shake. The checkout lady gave me a warm parting smile as she handed me the receipt, and I snatched it along with the bag, rushing for the exit.

As the doors slid open, I darted left instinctively, running as fast as the shopping swinging at my side allowed as it repeatedly crashed into my legs. I skidded clumsily into an alley on my left; it led to the bin storage for several shops along the street. Discarding the shopping on what was hopefully a clean patch of concrete, I forced myself further into the dark. Not that it mattered where I hid. They would always find me. The reek of the bins wafted towards me, adding to the nausea already curdling in my gut, and it was an effort to breathe through it and not retch. I was so damn tired, it took everything in me to keep my trembling limbs upright.

The scrape of shoes sliding on concrete signalled it was here. I pressed my back against cold bricks, readying myself, trying to grasp an ever-illusive measure of calm. It had taken ten years to cultivate this pathetic and rather peculiar form of courage. If you could call it that.

The warm glow of distant street lights revealed a tall wiry silhouette in the mouth of the alley and a flash of unnaturally bright eyes had mine snapping tightly shut.

Brisk footsteps echoed around the walls, closer and closer. My stomach turned, like the tides of the sea, and feverish chills spread throughout my body—leaving every hair on end. The footsteps abruptly stopped, and I could feel its presence before me. The putrid smell of oil, metal, and smoke gathered under my nose. Cold hands pinned my shoulder and clutched under my jaw exposing my neck. My heart was a raging beast in my chest, my body rigid with fearful anticipation, and then came the intense sting of teeth plunging into my throat and the pull of my blood being violently sucked from my body; the sound was amplified in the depths of the alley and grated against my ears. I counted in my head. One. Two. Three. Four. The teeth predictably ripped away.

My assailant struggled, clumsily stumbling to the ground, and my fingers flew to my ears, blocking the sounds of growling and gargling as it choked on my poisonous blood, a fitting end for a monster of the night. The hunter unknowingly the prey.

When the last breath left its body, it thudded heavily on the floor. I opened my eyes and edged towards the alley entrance. This part was always the worst. I located my bag and grabbed my headphones, shoving them in with shaking fingers, and hurriedly loading my music. Indie rock blasted in my ears, filling the silence while I waited.

Even with the distraction of music, my brain still dredged up old memories. There were some things you could never, ever unsee. It was that first time that haunted me. The night that changed my life forever. Hard to believe it was a decade ago—hard to believe I'd kept my secret for so long. Sometimes I thought it would be easier to curl up and die, then I'd never have to endure this again. I'd never feel the sharp, brutal sting of loneliness either. Few would miss me—nobody truly knew me; my cowardice held them all at bay. But my survival instinct was remarkably strong. Or was it the overwhelming fear of death masquerading as the will to live? Either way, I'd acclimatised gradually, like a frog slowly boiled alive, I'd kept going and accepted my fate. I found ways to cope and told myself that even if I wasn't some powerful, badass hero, each one that poisoned itself on my blood was one less set of teeth to sink into somebody else's neck.

After three songs had cycled through, I went back into the belly of the alley and rifled through the pile of clothing—the only remnants of the creature's existence. I found a leather wallet, though, as usual, there was little in it. I pulled out the only bank card and pocketed it, then gathered the garments and stuffed them in the nearest bin. Still trembling, I retrieved my shopping and made my weary way back to my apartment. It was less than three minutes from the shop. The thought of one of them so near my home made my blood run cold, especially when I had been so careful these past few months. Evidently not careful enough.

Once home and certain I wasn't followed, I sat for some time, lamenting in the bottom of the shower. The feel of the water hitting my skin was one of the only things that helped me overcome the horror. It helped wash away the feeling of those repulsive, abhorrent fingers and the teeth lingering ghostlike on my skin—a purifying ritual.

Afterwards, I eyed the bruising in the cabinet mirror above my sink. It was already a deep purple-red. Arnica gel seemed to have a positive effect on the hickey-like marks, lasting a few days rather than a whole week when liberally applied. I sighed, all my plans would have to change. This was precisely why I decided to never get involved with people.

As I climbed into bed, my phone chimed. It was Noah, and my heart felt heavier for all the lies I would have to tell him. It was one of the reasons I had sworn off romance and relationships—until I was too weak to keep him at bay. His persistence had worn me down, and I'd decided I would chance a little happiness. It was hard work—juggling lies and truth and all the idiosyncrasies that came with my complex and nightmarish existence, but it was worth it.

Begrudgingly, I cancelled our plans, told him I wouldn't be at work, and snuggled down into my bed with my book, reading until exhaustion overtook me, and I fell asleep still clutching the pages.

The chiming of my phone dragged me from sleep the following day. It was Noah, and it would now be lunch break at school. "Hey, I've just woken up."

There was a long resounding sigh before he answered "Hey, you. I was getting worried, Emily said you didn't contact her?"

"Shit, I was all over the place last night, I meant to email her before I went to sleep. Was she mad?"

"Well, she wasn't exactly happy, but we managed to cover you. But more importantly—how are you feeling now?"

I sat up, my heartbeat calming, my skin warming at the timbre of his voice. The feeling of being cared for and wanted lightened the burdens of my soul.

"I feel better after all that sleep. I'm so sorry about our date. I'll make it up to you next week, I promise."

The last few months had required an enormous amount of strategic planning to stay clear of the vampiric beings that were drawn to my scent. Until last night, I had pulled it off. I knew how this could look—I was the girl at university who was labelled as promiscuous despite having a pretty modest list of sexual accolades. After attacks, I wore high-necked tops and summer scarves to hide my bruises and tried countless concealer brands over the years. But people always seemed to know they were there. People always judged.

"Hey, don't worry about it, you can't help getting sick. Do you need anything? I can drop by after work?"

Even though I wanted nothing more than to curl up in his arms, to breathe in the familiar and comforting scent of his cologne, I couldn't risk it. If he asked me directly about the mark, it would involve bare-faced lying, and Noah was smart. And he didn't deserve that.

"As much as I would love to see you, I'm really not up to eating anything. I think I'm just going to stay in bed and sleep it off. You don't want this anyway! I must have jinxed myself the other week when my parents were over."

It was enough to ward him off. We said our goodbyes, and I slithered out of bed. I had shopping still to put away and now I had a grovelling email to write to my boss.

~

I busied myself the rest of the day with emails, cleaning, religiously rubbing Arnica on my neck and willing the angry colour to reduce.

While my laptop was open, I retrieved the pocketed bank card from last night and added the name to my list. Mr. James Holly, sitting at kill number twenty-nine. I'd started the list at university when the attacks became more frequent, a way to discern whether these creatures were being reported missing. They wore clothes and carried seemingly fake IDs, which alluded to some humanity. They had some sort of life when they were not driven after my scent, but of the twenty-three I'd stolen IDs from, not a single one was filed as a missing person.

After the first attack at fourteen, it only happened twice more before I moved to Bristol to start my teaching degree. The second time had, in a strange way, felt validating. It was still horrifying, but there was a strange sort of relief to know I wasn't clinically insane. I kept it to myself, unwilling to relive the previous brutal betrayal. After the third time, I became obsessed with vampires, reading everything I could get my hands on to figure out what was happening to me. The poisonous effect my blood had on these beings was unchartered territory. There was nothing in any book anywhere about this phenomenon. Each time it ended the same way—after approximately five minutes the bodies were gruesomely disintegrated as if they'd ingested a lethal dose of sunlight.

As I sat and continued theorising how these beings kept

evading detection, there was a firm knock at my door. Snapping my laptop shut, I hurried to my room to grab a dressing gown that would cover my neck. To my immense relief, it was a delivery driver.

"Olivia Blake?"

I nodded, accepting the giant bouquet of pink roses and thanking her. I checked the card and swooned a little despite myself.

Dear Olivia,

Feel better soon, and don't panic, these already have a vase!

Much Love,

Noah x

I set them down, pride of place, on my coffee table and grabbed my phone, a huge smile spreading across my face.

"I just got the flowers. Thank you so much, they're beautiful :)"

"Not as beautiful as you ;)"

"Noah, YOU are the most beautiful being on the planet. I miss you. Picnic on Sunday??"

"I miss you too. I'll pick you up at 10.30 a.m. Already counting down the hours! xx"

It scared me to think that someday, my little bubble of happiness would undoubtedly burst. But not yet.

3
AN INVITATION

By Sunday, the bruising on my neck was barely detectable, a subtle yellow tinge further masked by my olive skin tone. It was too hot to wear a jumper, and although I briefly debated concealer, I decided against it. I let my long tousled waves fall about my neck instead and used smoky eye makeup to draw attention away from the remnants of the mark. Fortunately, Noah was fascinated by my eyes. They were hazel—a rich brown centre that bled into light blue around the rim of my irises. He claimed he'd never seen a more beautiful colour, and I'd often catch him staring when he thought my attention was focused elsewhere.

Despite the circumstances of the last few days, I felt giddy at the prospect of spending time with him. Whenever I saw him, I felt like a child walking into a toy shop. It was all so new and exciting —the romance magical—even though it was never set to last. I did my best to stay in that dazzling moment of possibility and refused to consider the future point when it would all fall apart. When I'd have to walk away empty-handed. There was no prospect of children—not while I was frequently attacked. Then there were the horrifying prospects of genetics that might be passed down. No one deserved that. But we were young. We had plenty of time to live in the moment.

At precisely 10.30 a.m Noah's rhythmic tapping signalled his arrival. I yanked the door open and my face stretched into a wide smile. He wore a white linen short-sleeved shirt and light jeans. His hands were stuffed into his pockets, and his shoulders hunched a little—he subconsciously tried to avert attention from his tall frame.

"Oh my God, I've missed you so much." My words brought a rosiness to his cheeks. He stepped towards me wearing his shy smile and delicately cupped my face in his slender hands. His eyes didn't leave mine even as he leaned in close and kissed me. His kisses were always soft and slow—always left me aching for more. As he reluctantly pulled away, I resisted the urge to haul him into my apartment.

Having never been attacked during daylight, I liked to make the most of adventuring out with him when I could. "I'm just gonna grab the picnic. I'll be back in a sec."

As I turned and skipped to the kitchen he followed me inside. He was quick to retrieve the rucksack from me, hoisting it onto his shoulders while I slid my feet into my flats.

He was always quiet when he first arrived. He'd confessed early on when we made the transition from friends to lovers that I made him nervous. It took him a while to relax around me as he could never quite believe that I wanted to be with him, despite my reassurances that I found him irresistibly sexy. Now I'd gotten used to his initial shyness, I gave him time to adjust, prattling on about the amusing things I caught the children in my class doing and saying. This week, Tristan had declared that his dad had a sex book in his bedside drawer, and last week, I'd caught Fallon sneaking a woodlouse into Evie's lunchbox because Evie had performed a better cartwheel in gymnastics. I'd missed out on all these things as a child, so their strange classroom politics and colourful ways of seeing the world fascinated me. When Noah pressed me for childhood stories I had very few. Happiness was an occasional feeling, an infrequent visitor that was largely overshadowed by the constant longing for things I couldn't have. Over time, my memories had faded like a sunset, all the colour gradually bled out until what was left was hazy and grey.

As we made our way across the city, hand in hand, I watched Noah's confidence slowly unfurl like a daisy receiving the sun's first rays of light. His shoulders straightened, his head held high instead of being tethered to the floor, and when we weren't chatting, his lips were fixed in a permanent secret smile. It would widen every time he caught me staring at him and the world would stop spinning as we halted in the middle of the street to steal kisses, oblivious to the people moving around us.

When we reached the river, we idled alongside it for some time, taking in its tranquillity before finding a worthy spot to relax in. The river had stone steps leading down to its edge where many people liked to sit but we opted for a spot further up the grassy bank nearer the trees. This was one of my favourite places to be. With the expanse of evergreens and newly budded oak trees that hid the chaos of the city from view, it was easy to forget where you were. We spread out the blanket, and Noah sat down, leaning back on his elbows as he quietly took in the view. I settled next to him, my long legs stretched out alongside his.

"You know, I'm starting to regret suggesting a picnic," I admitted, and he chuckled as he turned to face me. He ran a hand along my thigh and tugged at one of the frayed edges of my ripped jeans where a large expanse of my skin was exposed.

"Hmm. When I saw you in these, I wasn't sure I had the

willpower to leave your apartment." He held my gaze, that secret smile playing about his lips, making my breath hitch.

"Keep talking like that and you might end up in a very public display of affection!"

His smile stretched into a grin. "Define *very*?" he said, his eyebrows arching mischievously.

I liked this playful version of Noah. I liked every version of Noah, but this one was reserved for times when he felt particularly self-assured. I mostly saw this side of him within the confines of his home. It was one of the reasons I pushed for us to spend more time there, rather than my apartment. Well, at least until the summer hit, and then we would be forced to be at mine where the air conditioning kept my windows safely shut, my scent carefully concealed, and my sanctuary unbreeched.

"That sounds like an invitation." I leaned forward to kiss him and crawled astride his lap. This playful Noah wrapped me up in his arms, unrestrained and unbothered by passers-by. We exchanged tender kisses, only breaking apart when our smiles grew too wide. Neither of us had outright confessed that we were in love, but in those moments, I felt the unspoken words lingering under the surface. As much as I ached to hear them, those words would hurtle us down a dead end faster than I cared to get there.

While I stuffed away all the thoughts that tried to steal my peace and contentment, Noah's eyes narrowed.

"What happened to your neck? It's bruised."

Of course, he had to notice.

"I was mauled by a vampire, but by the time I was finished with it, it will NEVER fuck with anyone again," I said with a smirk on my face.

He rolled his eyes and shook his head "I don't doubt it you ferocious animal."

How easy it was for him to laugh away my truth, every part of him believing it a joke. He kissed me again and lowered himself down onto his back with a contented sigh.

Crisis averted, though I could hardly believe he didn't push for the 'real' answer. I moved off his lap and laid down beside him. "Did I tell you my parents are threatening to visit again?"

"No, did they say when? Do you need me to run interference?"

"Ha, you know me too well! I don't know when, but yes, please come and be my knight in shining armour!"

He rolled onto his side, a wry smile on his lips. With a soft kiss to my cheek, he whispered, "I'll always be your knight in shining armour."

4

A CHOICE

The following weeks were a monotonous grind as I doubled down on my efforts to remain invisible from those that both haunted and hunted me. It was still a shock that I had been attacked so close to my apartment, and in the back of my mind, I fought the urge to start packing boxes. Occasionally I found myself browsing the local listings, but I wasn't that desperate. Yet. One attack in five months was pretty good for city living. Still, I wasn't entirely free of them. My mind was constantly plagued with worry about the risk to other people. My blood may kill the vampires but what about those people whose blood fed them?

I spent carefully planned time with Noah as often as I could, my parents had dinner with us at his home. I was grateful when he'd suggested it. My sparsely furnished apartment made him feel uncomfortable, and I wanted them to see the sides of him that were confident and assured. My parents were forceful characters at the best of times, and their overwhelming assertiveness could saturate a room, but Noah held his own, and it had been one of the more successful encounters with my parents.

It was mid-May, and the summer had arrived abruptly, almost bypassing spring, making the air sticky and claustrophobic. Hot summers were so much easier to navigate in the remote places I had grown up. In the city, the heat multiplied and pressed in unbearably.

I pulled into the multi-storey where I kept my car, my mind full of planning for the last week of school before half term. Once that was over I'd have a whole week to be with Noah. It felt extravagant. Sure, I got to see him every day at school, but our time together consisted of fleeting coffee breaks, legs touching as we sat together in a staff meeting, and discreet hand squeezes when passing in the corridor. It was undeniably comforting to know he was just across a hallway, but it was also a tease. A whole uninterrupted week with him was a heavenly prospect.

I had an hour to shrug off the day before Noah arrived for a blissful evening together. I parked and gathered bags, my mind mentally curating my plans for the week as I strode across the car park towards the stairs. Halfway across, I felt *it* and stopped in my tracks. No. This could not be happening. It was still daylight outside. Had one of them gotten trapped in the car park at dawn? But how had I not noticed this morning?

I whirled around trying to find it, a dangerous mix of anger and panic rising. I could not let this ruin another fucking date. I formulated a plan and started running back to my car. On my right, a dark-haired figure emerged around the corner of the lower parking level and headed up the entrance ramp to my section. I sprinted for the safety of my car. It clocked me and accelerated up the steep ramp, giving chase. I reached the car just ahead of it and was grateful my keys were already clutched in my hands. I wrenched the door open and in my panic, slammed it on my ankle as I hastily scrambled into my seat. The pain was white hot and stole my breath, but I was in just as it hurtled for the door.

I clicked the locking button frantically on my key fob and felt temporary relief when I heard the mechanical whine of the locks sealing me in. There was no calming myself now; my breath was desperate and ragged, and my hands were shaking as I tried to put the key in the ignition. The vampire jerked at my door handle, and when it refused to open, it took a step back and launched its fist at my window, the glass shattered and poured over my lap.

Fuck fuck fuck.

A bloody hand grabbed at my hair, trying to haul me out through the window. I clawed at its arm, trying to untangle myself, and realised I was still clutching the keys. I unlocked the doors and snatched at the handle, pushing the door open with as much force as I could and as wide as it would go. The vampire stumbled back and lost its footing, falling against the neighbouring vehicle. I swung myself out of the car, glass flying and tinkling as it hit the concrete floor. I darted towards the rear trying to put the car between us, but I wasn't quite fast enough. The vampire yanked me back by the hair mid-leap and threw me into the side of my car. As I stumbled and tried to right myself, the vampire smashed my head against the passenger rear door. Everything blurred, and I fell to my knees. My head was pounding, and I could hardly breathe. I couldn't get back up. The vampire sank its teeth violently into my neck from behind me. I closed my eyes and tried to breathe. Four seconds, and it would be over. I could do this. As the teeth ripped out, I gathered what little strength I had, and pushed to my feet. The vampire was gurgling and choking on the floor.

"You fucking deserve that." I shakily gathered my things and half ran, half hobbled to the stairs. It was too public a place for me to linger. I just had to hope no one saw it.

I kept my head down, letting my hair fall over the bleeding wounds on my face and ignored everyone who passed. It was amazing how invisible you could be in a city. When I entered my building I was grateful for the use of a lift. My ankle throbbed, the pain pulsing up my leg with each step and almost crippling me.

As I neared my apartment, I willed myself forward every step, one hand clutching my belongings and keys and the other supporting me against the wall. From up ahead, I heard footsteps rushing towards me.

"Fuck. Olivia, what happened?"

Then Noah's arms were around me, almost as shaky as my own. I dropped my things and collapsed against him.

"Olivia, tell me what happened?" His voice was wild and frantic. I probably looked quite frightful. It was hard to conjure words as the adrenaline coursed through my body.

"Get my keys," I whimpered.

Once we were safely inside, he lowered me onto the sofa.

"Olivia, how did this happen? Do you need me to call an ambulance?"

I shook my head, resting my ankle on the coffee table with a grimace. He sat beside me and gently tilted my chin towards him to assess my face then scurried off to the bathroom to get a damp towel. Every line of his face was fraught. His hands shook as he delicately dabbed at the wound, and he took long, deep breaths in and out.

"Olivia please, tell me what happened?"

I closed my eyes, and leaned my head back against the sofa, it was too painful to keep them open with the throbbing behind my temple. I took a shaky breath and tried to get some words out. "I was attacked near my car."

"Fuck. FUCK. We need to call the police."

I shook my head as much as the pain allowed. "I just need to shower, and I'll be fine."

"Olivia, you're in shock. We need to call the police and report this."

"I don't want to call the police, I just want to shower and go to sleep."

"You don't have a choice—"

"I do have a choice, and I am not going to report this. There's no point anyway, I didn't see who it was."

"It doesn't matter. There has to be footage somewhere either from a dash cam or somewhere in the car park, somebody did this to you, and they cannot get away with it."

He was angry. I understood. If the situation was reversed, I'd be furious. I'd want to call the police too. But it would be a complete waste of their time and resources. I'd be sending them on a wild goose chase.

"I know you're angry, but I'm not calling them. I was assaulted when I was a teenager, and getting the police involved made everything worse. I am not going through that again, so please respect my choice."

"How could you even contemplate allowing someone to get away with this?" He was seething. His breathing was hard and fast, and his eyes were full of disbelief.

For a brief moment, I imagined what it would be like to tell him the truth. For some people, the truth would be incomprehensible. One night, during my early uni days, a drunken student stumbled across an attack and tried to stop it. While the vampire choked to death, I led the student away, trying to spare them the sight of the repulsive decaying body, but they escaped my grasp and went back to deliver their own brand of justice. When they returned to the scene of the crime and saw the empty pile of clothes on the floor, they laughed and thought they were stoned. It was an impossibility for them, their brain created a plausible rationale to protect them. The truth was too much for them to handle, and I had a feeling it would be too much for Noah. He was soft, gentle, and wonderful, and he deserved to live in a world where monsters didn't exist, other than the human ones he already knew about.

Noah still focused on the good—he had faith in humanity and hopes for the future. I was not going to be the one to shatter that illusion for him. Maybe I was a selfish coward, but I didn't see an absolute right or wrong. The truth could do an infinite amount of damage, so I kept tucking it safely away.

I started to weep. "Noah, can you please just help me in the shower?"

His face softened, and he wiped away my sullen tears. His eyes glistened too. I wasn't sure if it was helplessness or frustration or both that caused him to well up, and I felt sick with guilt.

"Let me take a look at your ankle first. It might be better to ice it for a bit and shower later."

I nodded in agreement, grateful he was listening to me but heartbroken that he had to deal with this.

~

He tended to me the rest of the evening, though he said very little. I couldn't help but feel he was disappointed in me, which was far more excruciating than any of the wounds I'd been dealt. Once the physical shock had worn off, it was easier to move around, and painkillers had taken the edge off the throbbing in my temple. Despite our disagreement, it was much easier to pull through the trauma with him beside me.

By the time we climbed into bed, I was only a little nauseous, which was not unusual. We settled down facing each other. Noah looked conflicted and remained quiet, his gaze frequently snagging on the wound above my brow. I traced his eyebrows with my finger, then slid it down his nose and over his lips, but they remained pursed and didn't kiss my fingertip like they usually would. For the first time since we'd been together, I longed to hear those unspoken words, but they didn't come. I snuggled against him, forcing him to cocoon me in his arms. I bit my lip, trying to keep the tears locked away, and focused on drifting off to sleep.

5

THE TRUTH

When I woke in the morning Noah was gone, the sheets on his side of the bed already cold. I threw on my silk dressing gown and limped into the living room, and to my relief he was on the sofa with a coffee in hand. He looked up and smiled, but it wasn't a real smile. It was the kind of smile that was rooted in sadness, that you gave someone out of pity. It was a smile that had never been directed at me, and my chest got a little tighter at the sight of it.

I stooped to kiss him on the cheek before heading to the kitchen. While I poured a coffee, I internally chastised myself for overthinking, but the mood felt ominous.

When I returned to the living room Noah was hunched forward, resting elbows on his knees and looking very serious.

He didn't wait for me to sit before he spoke "Olivia, tell me the truth, why won't you report this to the police? Are you in trouble with the law?"

I almost dropped my coffee.

"Excuse me? Noah, I'm a fucking teacher. They do detailed background checks. Don't you think that would have come up?"

He shrugged. "People use different identities. It's not an impossibility." He stared at me, carefully watching and assessing my reaction.

"So last night I told you that I had previously been assaulted and didn't want to go through that process again, and the conclusion you jump to is that I must be a criminal?"

His jaw clenched, and he looked away. He brought his palms together, resting his chin on his thumbs while he thought.

"Noah, you've met my parents. We work together every day. How can you possibly believe that I could be a criminal?" I asked incredulously.

He stood up, facing me defiantly. "Because there is so much about you that I don't know. Look at your apartment! You have no personal things—it's fucking weird! And you clean it so much, I bet there's barely any evidence that you live here. You move a lot. You have no friends. We never go out at night, and then you show up having had the shit beaten out of you and won't report it. You claim I'm your FIRST boyfriend, which, quite frankly, I just can't get my head around, because you're not shy, and you're a fucking supermodel, so I don't know what to believe." He turned away from me, clasped his hands behind his head and stared up at the ceiling.

"Wow. That's quite a list," I retorted to his back.

So many emotions were writhing within me. I wanted to cry for the betrayal, to shrink and shrivel away from the judgement that made me feel about an inch tall. I wanted to yell at him for being such an idiot and for misunderstanding what I did. I wanted to beg and plead with him to believe me and not be like all the others ten years past. I wanted to laugh at how stupid I had been to think this could work. I wanted to tell him the whole truth and hope he'd think I was a hero rather than a criminal or a coward. Instead, I cried, because I realised just how desperately I didn't want this to be over.

"So much for always being my knight in shining armour." I

turned and limped back to my bedroom and threw myself on the bed. Giant obliterating sobs burst through me, the sound muffled by my pillow.

Moments later I heard Noah's quiet steps and the bed dipped as he sat down.

"Olivia," he breathed, "tell me the truth."

This was one of those life-defining moments—a distant echo of the morning after my first attack, where a fork split in the road before me and two possibilities stretched out with vastly different consequences. Maybe it was time to try this a different way. Maybe the whole, unedited truth would take the responsibility out of my hands. Perhaps there was a way for the government to deal with this discreetly without the rest of the world being terrified and paranoid and mistrusting everything they'd ever believed to be true. That's if Noah didn't drag me to the doctors for a psyche evaluation first. I dried my eyes and sat up. His face was damp, and there were several wet patches around the collar of his T-shirt. I'd never seen him look so utterly defeated.

I took a deep rallying breath. I could be brave.

"The truth…is that when I was fourteen, my life changed. Forever. My parents failed me, my friend failed me, the law failed me, and I have never fully trusted another person since."

Noah closed his eyes, fresh tears streaking down his cheeks, and I swallowed back a whimper and tried to continue.

"I don't go out at night, because I don't want to be attacked. I clean my apartment obsessively, because it's one of my many coping mechanisms. You are the only person I have willingly allowed into my life." Noah looked stricken. He started to reach out to me but I continued, "the truth is…I will never marry or have children because there are deeper things about me that I cannot speak of or change, and I'll never be able to. I am broken and complicated and cursed." I wanted to add that I wasn't a criminal

41

but I couldn't in good conscience, because a part of me believed that I was. I had done things that I was afraid to face even now.

Noah reached out and pulled me against his chest, holding me tightly as we both cried against each other.

"I'm so sorry," he whispered over and over between sobs.

Not as sorry as me.

When our tears had lulled Noah took a deep breath. "Things can change. Maybe in the future when you've had more time to heal, you can think about having a family?" Ever hopeful.

"I can't, Noah. It's not about healing. That future is not on the cards for me, and you'll have to accept that."

He shuddered and swallowed thickly. "Do you not see us having a future? Do you not think about it at all?"

I couldn't lie to him. Not now. "I do. And I see us fizzling out when what we have isn't enough for you, and I can't give you what you want—what you deserve."

He scoffed. "Don't say that. You don't know that."

"But I do know that. You're already thinking it, Noah. You're already hoping that I'll change, and I won't." I pulled away from him. "Look at me."

Begrudgingly his eyes slid to mine. They were shining brightly with unshed tears, and he was worrying his lip with the effort of keeping himself together.

"Tell me the truth. What is in the future that you dream about for yourself?"

He shook his head and turned away.

"Tell me the truth," I pleaded.

He took a deep breath, his shoulders trembling.

Finally, he said, "I've always seen a wife and a family and a house somewhere in the countryside."

And here it was. The moment I knew would always come. The moment I was walking out of that magical toy shop empty-handed. It hurt so much more than I had ever imagined.

"I don't want this to end," he said remorsefully. "I care about you, but if a family is off the table—if you're really set on that..." His resolve broke. He wept into his hands and I sat behind him, my arms weaving around his body like vines pulling him together while hating myself for causing us both so much pain. My body heaved against his with great reverberating sobs.

Eventually, he pulled himself free and kissed the top of my head as he got up.

"I'm so sorry. I can't do this, I have to go."

6

LACE MARKET

The pain of loss was a monstrous thing. Calling into question every small and big decision, every memory a double-edged sword of bittersweet joy and deepest regret. Allowing even the smallest portion of my heart to be vulnerable when I'd caged it so long was now punishing.

I'd been alone for so much of my life, I'd thought it would be easy to go back again—like stepping into old familiar shoes that knew the shape of your feet. But it wasn't. In the few short months we'd been together, my life had grown, evolved, and changed shape, no longer was I able to slip back into old treads. I had to learn day by day how to adjust to life without him, and it was agonising. I thought I'd have so much more time with him before it came to this, and I was angry at the vampires for ruining this period of happiness. I was angry at myself for all the lies, the half-truths, the way those things had made him distrustful and shaken his confidence. He deserved so much better.

With all my battle wounds, I had taken the last week of the term off. I thought it best not to scare the children, and my car was being fixed, then sold. I needed a fresh start.

Everything from my kitchen pretty much fit in two large cardboard boxes, which I was currently packing. I was wrapping the last of my wine glasses in wads of brown tissue paper when there was a rhythmic knock at my door.

Noah.

I contemplated ignoring it, but the desire to see him outweighed the need to preserve the remnants of my shattered heart, and I braced myself and let him in. He looked despondent; there was no warmth in his eyes, and there were shadows creeping underneath them. The hunch to his shoulders was more pronounced than usual. Words stubbornly evaded me, and I gestured for him to enter.

"Where are you going?" He stared wide-eyed at my neat stack of boxes in the living room. His voice was panicked.

"I don't feel safe here anymore, so I'm moving further into the city. I found an apartment near Lace Market."

"Oh…are you coming back to school after half term?"

I suspected this was the reason he had stopped by. To ask me if the rumours were true.

"No, I'm not. I've switched to a supply agency."

"Because of me? Us? Can't we at least try to be friends?"

I hated the desperation in his voice. I wanted to go to him, to breathe in his comforting smell and never let him go, but I wasn't the future he wanted. It wasn't fair for either of us.

"At some point, yes, I would like that. But it's too difficult right now." Unruly, disobedient tears streaked down my face, and Noah raised a hand to catch them. I turned away before he could, knowing I couldn't stop myself from reaching out for him if he touched me. The silence stretched between us like a great chasm. The room saturated in our sadness.

"If you need me…" His voice trailed off, and he turned toward the door. "Bye, Olivia. I hope the move goes well."

I took a deep breath as he quietly slipped out of my life, and told myself that tomorrow would be better. Tomorrow would be a fresh start.

∼

Four days later, I stood on the street outside my new apartment, my most precious box of books heavy in my arms, breathing in the comforting smell of Italian cooking. My new home was a second-floor apartment above Piccolino's. There were various other restaurants along the street, and I hoped they would contribute to disguising my scent and keep my home off the vampire's map. The moving team had already deposited my meagre furniture upstairs, and this was the last box to carry in. It was time to start a new chapter.

It wasn't long before the apartment was clean, furniture set up, and I was putting the last of my books on the lonely bookshelf opposite my sofa. I had tucked the photo frame of Noah and me in amongst the books, not wanting to part with it but equally not ready to see it yet without crying. The bookshelf and sofa looked ridiculous within the generous proportions of this new place.

Not only was the living space bigger, but it was open plan, with very acceptable light-grey walls that perfectly complimented my sofa. It had high ceilings and two big sash windows facing the street below allowing me to people watch. A narrow galley kitchen fed off from my living room, and I could even fit a bistro table and chairs in if I wanted to sit and eat at a table. But I probably wouldn't—the empty seat would remind me of Noah.

The apartment had two bedrooms, the master included an en-suite, and the second bedroom I would conveniently leave unfurnished to deter my parents from lengthier stays. One evening was quite enough to endure their company. They would probably offer to furnish it to their luxurious standard, but I would refuse as I always did. Their money was never in short supply, but wherever possible, I denied them any control over my life. They'd already had too much in the past, and I never wanted to be indebted to them. They were named as guarantors on my rental agreement, but that was a worst-case scenario.

After watching the ebb and flow of the street for a while, I poured a glass of wine, grabbed my laptop, and slumped on my soft and forgiving sofa. I opened my vampire record and cross-referenced the names with the Missing People organisation. Then googled and checked against social media platforms. Still nothing. I checked the official Missing Persons List for potential victims of the vamps, but nothing new had been filed.

There was only one unidentified body posted for this current year, and the rest all dated back to previous years and didn't fit the situation. Next, I visited the official police website and checked the crime hotspots in my area. Statistically, over the last two years, there had been a minor decrease in crime within the city and a notable reduction in drug-related incidents. But I had never found a crime suspicious enough to be connected to a vampire. I'd never found a report that stated there were peculiar marks around a victim's neck or a body that seemed to be drained of blood. It drove me crazy. The conclusion I desperately hoped for was that they didn't kill their victims. Given there were no assault charges of a vampiric nature, they might have the power to alter people's memories after it happened. Like me, the victims would be left with a love bite and perhaps be led to believe that they had a fling with a stranger. Maybe they looked more appealing when they were not lusting for my blood. I highly doubted it, but I suppose beauty is in the eye of the beholder. Perhaps they had partners who willingly donated their blood? The other option was that they had help to cover up their existence. A possibility I didn't like to consider. I wished there was a way for me to follow them and monitor their activity, but it was impossible once they caught my scent. There were so many unanswered questions that relentlessly churned in my head, and I would stubbornly keep digging. I had to get to the bottom of this.

7

BITE ME

As the sun began its descent, it flooded my apartment with beautiful golden light and cast deep long shadows on the street below—stretching towards my building like they were chasing the rays of sunlight. It was late September. I had spent the remainder of the last school year working as a supply teacher, which gave me greater flexibility. On the two occasions I'd run into a vamp, I was able to take time off to let the marks heal and avoid any questions or accusations.

The long summer days had promised more freedom in the evenings, but despite being careful, the vampires had found me in the multi-storey car parks. Since then, I'd doubled down on my efforts to avoid them. It felt cowardly and selfish, but I'd needed time to grieve the loss of my fairytale relationship and slowly rebuild my fragile mental health. I'd worked through multiple self-help books, applying their strategies where I could, and finally reached a place where I felt my version of normalcy. I still carried a deep longing for companionship, made worse by my complete lack of consistent work colleagues and children to interact with, and my book club connections did little to alleviate that loneliness.

One of the hardest things was dealing with the guilt of my inaction. It terrified me that if I had friends or colleagues who found out what my blood could do—if they actually believed me in the first place—they'd be disappointed by my cowardice. That fear was usually enough of a burden to keep me safe and isolated, to stop me from developing connections. But not tonight. Tonight I felt like a caged animal slowly going mad in confinement. Restless and desperate to be on the other side of the looking glass.

The hustle and bustle of rush hour gradually dissipated, making way for a pocket of quiet before the flourish of evening activity began. People meandered up and down in small groups, drawn by the tantalising smell of French and Italian cooking along my street. They ambled through the city with so little to fear and such frivolity—it evoked a sharp pang of jealousy, and my chest ached to watch it. As the minutes and hours ticked by, the more claustrophobic I felt. Eventually, with a heavy sigh, I pushed myself away from the window and stalked to my bedroom.

I opened my wardrobe, my fingers trailing over the fabrics, hung in neat, colour-coordinated sections. As my hand skimmed to the end of the rail where only black remained, I pulled out a mid-length dress and scrunched it between my fingers. I closed my eyes and took a deep breath. I tried to remember just how many weeks it had been since I'd ventured out to live a little, but the weeks blurred together. I needed to feel alive again. Resolve steadily soaked through me, drowning out anxiety and filling me with the measure of courage I needed. I was going to risk it. Risk leaving my apartment to do something fun instead of living as a shadow. I got ready quickly, wanting to leave the security of my apartment before the light was completely gone. I grabbed my favourite clutch bag, and before I could talk myself out of it, I triple-checked that my door was locked and hurried down the stairs of the apartment.

As I stepped out into the evening, a warm breeze ruffled

through my loose curls, sending tendrils of hair across my face and sticking to my lip balm. Prying it from my mouth, I tucked my hair behind my ears and set out with grim determination. The breeze would usually send me scurrying back inside, fearful of where my scent would carry, but tonight I wasn't going to think of that. The desire to be among people was overpowering. I needed this.

I headed west along the main street and scooted around crowds of jovial people shouting and laughing with friends.

My preferred nightclub wasn't far away; if I maintained a brisk walk, it was less than ten minutes. There were closer venues, but the atmosphere at Eclipse was reliably exuberant and primarily known for being a student bar.

I rounded the final corner of my route and emerged onto the main road where Eclipse was situated. The boom of the bass beckoned, igniting me with anticipation. The building front was clad with wood and painted a rich dark blue, above the wide glass doors the signage was backlit in a deep shade of orange. The sight of it filled me with nostalgia for those first days at uni in Bristol, when I'd felt wild and euphoric outside the clutches of my parents. Every day had felt like an intoxicating adventure. Drinking, sex, companionship. It had given me a healthy dose of courage and curiosity that quickly burned out when I realised the city was full of vampires. But the club was one place I'd never been attacked. Neither here nor in Bristol. It was my sanctuary. I bounded up the wide semi-circular steps, and as the last dregs of golden light cooled to dusk, I slipped inside.

The night was young, but already the atmosphere was heady with the smell of sweat, alcohol, and the multitude of perfumes. I found comfort in it—I was safer amongst all those competing smells, disguising my own. Out of habit, I scanned the room, assessing what could be lurking in the shadows. The dance area was oval—the sunken hub of the room. The perimeter was marked with a mix of large white columns and sections of low walls where people sat to drink. It kept the dancing semi-contained, leaving the outer edges of the room as space to queue for drinks or thoroughfare to the corridor at the back corner of the room.

Couples gravitated to the pillars, leaning on them while their hands and mouths fumbled against each other. I wondered if I might be lucky enough to find myself against one later in the evening. To my left was a long stretch of bar that faced the dance floor. The lower half was frosted glass and reflected the blue LED lights that ran under the lip and along the bottom strip where it met the floor. I counted eight people staffing it and they were a constant flurry of activity. They worked around each other with surprising grace, dispatching drink after drink with an admirable efficiency that kept the queue to a minimum. After grabbing a couple of shots to loosen up my nerves, I wove through the crowd and headed down the shallow steps onto the packed, sunken dance floor.

Content enough that I was safe, I let the music wash over me, filling every dark corner of my mind with life and energy, my heart pounding along with the beat as I lost myself in it. I felt free. The tension in me slowly unfurled, and I revelled in the tantalising proximity to other people, space so limited bodies would frequently slide against mine. Hands finding their way to my hips and pulling me close, hot breaths sending shivers down my spine.

I danced and danced until my feet throbbed from being stepped on and finally took a break. I clawed my way through the packed bodies and headed away from the noise and down the corridor at the far corner of the room. It led to the toilets and then a second bar somewhat hidden in the far reaches of the building. The entrance was manned by security guards to keep the more inebriated patrons out.

It was refreshingly quiet here and the air was breathable. It was a dark, lamp-lit room that contained a few small central clusters of tables and chairs, and a couple of long leather sofas against the walls. A pretty blonde I had danced with on and off all evening was already at the bar and about to be served. She smiled flirtatiously and winked as I slid onto a leather bar stool next to her.

"Can I buy you a drink?" she asked with a suggestive flutter of eyelashes. Her lips curled into a saccharine smile, and I nodded in reply, noting how piercing her big blue eyes were. The barman was watching our exchange with hopeful intrigue. His dark eyes flickered between the two of us, a barely contained smile tugging at his lips.

I flashed her a conspiratorial grin, and she signalled for more shots before turning back to me, those penetrating blue eyes dropping to my lips. As she leaned closer, in the corner of my vision I saw the barman pause, mouth hanging open as he gaped at us. Her lips landed delicately on mine, small teasing kisses at first before her warm tongue brushed my upper lip and pushed deeper into my mouth. She playfully bit my lip as she pulled away, throwing a wink at the barman.

He was now leaning, elbows braced on the bar, unashamedly staring and chewing on his lower lip. He pushed the shots towards us, and with a wry smile, announced they were on the house. My blonde conspirator grinned triumphantly, and after slamming back her shot, departed with a quick wave. I watched her go, seductively weaving herself between a few loitering men. I wondered if I'd be seeing her again. In my limited pursuit of intimacy over the years, I'd found enjoyment with both men and women, and I had a feeling we would have a lot of fun.

As I turned back to my drink, I found the barman still staring at me. "Are you just into girls?" he asked as he peered at me with lustful half-lidded eyes.

I shook my head and downed my drink, enjoying the burn as it scorched my throat like lava and warmed my chest. I raised my glass and held it out for a refill, which he readily obliged. He eyed me as I drank. I could feel his stare and caught it lingering on my cleavage as I slammed the glass down on the bar. His lips pulled into a devilish grin as he dragged his eyes back to mine, and with a wink, he turned away to take another order.

As the burn of the alcohol subsided, I registered the goosebumps now prickling over my skin. Cursing my lack of diligence, my eyes darted around the room looking for the source of danger I was sensing. It wasn't the same sickening dread as usual but I couldn't ignore the unease. I scanned the room repeatedly but couldn't spot the typical pallid figure moving through the shadows. Just when I thought the alcohol must be distorting my senses, a flash of icy blue eyes caught my attention near the group of loitering men the blonde had passed through.

I hopped off the bar stool and darted back into the corridor, startling the security men, but before they could grab for me, I noticed a fire escape and sprinted for it. I burst through into a dark concrete square meant for bin storage. A narrow alley fed off to the left, leading back to the main road. I flung myself against the far wall and watched the exit intently, trying to get my fear under control with slow deep breaths. Just as I wondered if I'd overreacted, I heard the screech of the fire door hinges and the sound of steady footfalls approaching.

Out of the shadows emerged a tall, broad figure, and he slowly sauntered towards me. His hands were tucked into the pockets of his jeans and as he came to a stop less than two metres away his expression was one of curiosity.

"Do you make a habit of running into dark alleys?" he asked, eyeing my terrified stance against the wall.

"Do you make a habit of *following* women into dark alleys?" I spat back, shocked that he was capable of communicating with me and unnerved by what it could mean.

He let out a low chuckle and kicked a stone absentmindedly, sending it careening off a bin and making me jump. His pale glowing eyes flickered over me again, narrowing as he met my gaze and his head cocked to one side. He was not the usual vamp. From what I could make out in the dim glow of streetlights, his skin was not the least bit pale. I would swear it was actually golden, and his tousled hair was a lighter, warmer shade than the usual black.

He assessed me quietly, but his demeanour didn't appear threatening; more curious. I inched off the wall and forced myself to take a step toward him. I focused on the glint of gold at the base of his throat—a chain with a golden cross, visible where his dark shirt was left unbuttoned and went against the typical vampire myths.

"Are you even armed?"

His question threw me off guard, and I tore my gaze from the cross and met his eyes. It was the first time I'd looked in detail at those unnatural eyes in such proximity. Attacks usually happened in a dizzying blur of fear and revulsion. His pupils were fully dilated in the low light, but the band of colour around them glimmered eerily bright. I expected them to be cold and unnerving, but his beautiful warm features ensnared me, locking me in place, and I was fully at his mercy. It took me a minute to string a semi-coherent sentence together.

"Is it not hard for you...to be this close to me?"

One of his brows arched. "Modesty is obviously not your best virtue," he said with a smirk. "Why would I find it hard to be this close to you?"

To punctuate his question he stepped forward, so close now my chest grazed his with every ragged breath I took. My mouth was dry with nerves making it hard to swallow. I was utterly stuck. My body refused to move, and I couldn't tear my eyes from his.

The shots I'd just downed had started to take effect, my head swimming as he watched me with such intensity it was hard to think. I wanted to part his lips and see his teeth. I needed reassurance that I wasn't crazy—that he really was a mythical monster and not some figment of my alcohol-addled mind.

The thought seemed to take on a life of its own, my arm was reaching for him a moment later. His fingers snapped around my wrist, and he ushered me backwards until I was against the alley wall. The brick scraped against my bare skin. My bag dropped to the floor as he grabbed my other wrist and held me in place with one hand while quickly searching my body. Did he genuinely think I was armed? I struggled against him, trying to remember the self-defence from years gone by but only managed a hard stomp to his shin. He grunted and pressed his body against mine to keep me pinned.

"For fucks sake just bite me and get it over with" I hissed, my eyes narrowing on his as I seethed with fury.

I squirmed and strained against him, forcing him to press closer. I waited for my scent to overcome him and my blood to do what I could not but he snorted in disgust.

"That is not my kind of kink," he answered. He was now so close even his forehead pressed against mine, pushing my scalp into the wall to stop me from smashing him in the face as I struggled. The warmth of his breath mixed with my own; it was heavier now, and I felt satisfied that restraining me required at least some effort. I took a deep breath to counteract my rising panic, and with a start, realised he didn't have the same repulsive smell as the other vamps. No, it was fresh and comforting, barely detectable against the scent of his aftershave. Was that a good sign? Or a sign that they'd adapted—making him more dangerous.

"What the fuck are you, and what do you want?" My options were limited, I might as well make the most of his ability to speak to me since I couldn't overpower him. He drew back enough to comfortably look at me. His eyebrow arched as he waited with bated breath to see what I would do.

"What I am is fucking stressed, and what I *want* is answers.

Preferably not while in a seedy dark alley with you pinned against a wall—we need to talk privately. I don't want to hurt you, but I do need answers, so you're coming with me one way or another." The last words came out through gritted teeth, and a chill crept down my spine, spreading across my body with a shudder. He felt it, his eyes narrowing before he eased away fractionally.

"What's this about? And where are you planning to take me? And for how long?" I asked, stalling for time and weighing my limited options. Putting up a fight while being so spectacularly outmanned, risked the possibility of my blood being shed in a public place which was highly undesirable. The last thing I needed was to be mauled by a pack of bloodthirsty vampires in front of a crowd. That was a one-way ticket to being the world's biggest freak show and my worst nightmare.

He nibbled one corner of his lip before answering, drawing my attention away from his piercing stare as I tried to catch a glimpse of a fang.

"I don't want to talk about it here. I'm taking you to a small B&B on Mansfield Road. And for how long will depend entirely on you."

Ambiguous, but he sounded honest, and I hoped that meant he had a conscience. He loosed a long breath through his mouth and eased his body away from mine, gripping my wrist tightly as he bent to pick up my clutch bag and tucked it under his arm.

I stayed pressed against the wall, watching his every move like a hawk and trying to understand what in the hell he was. Despite the implied threat, I still felt no nausea as I would have with a typical vampire. It didn't seem like he wanted to hurt me, just that he was desperate enough to force my hand. He took another deep breath and tightly interlaced our fingers, locking us together so tightly, my fingertips instantly numbed. His skin was surprisingly warm despite the cool chill of night.

"What if I scream?" I blurted nervously, some idiotic part of me hoping he would see the futility in trying to take me so brazenly and change his mind. Instead, it gave away my only realistic option of escape, even if it caused a scene. His eyes bore into mine before flicking to my neck and our joined hands.

"Shit," he said under his breath, and I both felt and saw his body tense, readying to take action, and ensure that I couldn't make good on my threat.

"I won't scream! Please don't knock me out," I pleaded, utterly ashamed of my stupidity and lack of courage. Being rendered unconscious and completely out of control at night while out in the open was a risk I was not willing to take. "Please," I begged again, my body trembling with the onslaught of adrenaline, "I swear, I won't scream. I'll go with you willingly."

After several long seconds of further scrutiny, his expression wavering somewhere between relief and fear, he nodded and started pulling me gently away from the wall. With no better plan, and a deep-rooted hope that my blood was still my last line of defence, I followed pliantly.

8

NICE STORY

My captor led me through the alley, bringing us out along the side of the building. He briefly scanned ahead and then his attention avidly returned to me. There was a definite flash of distrust in his expression, like he was re-evaluating his actions and wondering if he'd made a huge mistake.

There were several small groups of people gathered along the street outside the club, and he clutched my hand even tighter as we wove through them. His face was taut with tension, and he monitored my every expression and movement. He was wary of me. Or perhaps wary of the scene I could cause in public. I considered my physical reaction to him, relieved that it continued to be far milder than it was with the usual vampires.

As we continued our route towards his B&B, we moved away from the city centre, taking some narrower, quieter streets that made me nervous. I shuddered at the prospect of facing off against a less friendly creature and fervently scanned every dark entrance and alleyway, checking over my shoulder repeatedly as we passed. A firm squeeze of my hand brought attention back to my captor. His brows were knitted together in an expression of both pity and intrigue.

"We're nearly there." He pulled me closer as we rounded a corner onto a dark, narrow street. This was even more disconcerting; a vamp not only talking but being concerned for my wellbeing. We took a left at the end and crossed the street heading towards a boutique B&B. He pushed open a low red gate and led me up the narrow garden path. At the end was a large, black wooden door with bay leaf trees on either side, each decorated with delicate twinkling lights. With a final glance over his shoulder, he pushed it open and ushered me inside.

Our feet scuffed over black and white chequered tiles as we emerged into a small reception foyer. Wall sconces cast a soft warm glow, and an elegant reception desk sat off to the right, crammed with leaflets and maps, but there was not a soul in sight. He led me up two flights, my hand still tightly laced with his. When we reached the last door on the second floor he rooted through his pocket and pulled out a simple brass key, a novelty given the hotel's boutique aesthetic. As we stepped into his room he finally untangled our fingers and pulled his phone out to text while locking the door.

The first thing I noticed was the open sash window across the room. I dashed towards it and heard him curse behind me and give chase. His arms ensnared my waist and started to tear me away just as it slammed shut. I struggled against him, self-preservation kicking in and knocking us off balance.

"Get the fuck off me," I hissed. "I'm trying to lock the window, you absolute dick."

He dropped me unceremoniously, sending me sprawling into a low chest of drawers, and sachets of coffee and sugar cascaded onto the floor. When I regained my composure I returned to the window, shakily slid the latch across and turned to glare at him. He was holding his hands up apologetically, his breathing was hard and fast, and his face the picture of guilt.

"Why would I make absolutely no attempt to escape from you

the entire way here and then throw myself out a second-storey window? That makes no fucking sense!" I shoved past him and headed to the only other door in the room, which revealed a small simple shower room. There was a narrow window, which I closed and locked and when I turned he was leaning against the door frame watching me with the same intensity he had all evening.

"I'm sorry," he choked out. As I drew closer, he flattened against the door jam to let me pass, and followed me back into the room.

I took a deep breath. The large wooden bed was unmade, and clothes were thrown haphazardly at the bottom end. A suitcase lay open by the wardrobe, still filled with a tangle of clothes suggesting he hadn't been here long and creases were the least of his concerns. In between the window and the bed was a small coffee table and twin leather tub chairs. A bottle of red wine sat unfinished on the table. Either he had a more refined taste or he'd had company. On a larger chest of drawers by the bathroom door, a few toiletries were heaped untidily. Perhaps he'd unpacked in such a rush he hadn't had time to set them upright or was he genuinely so stressed he didn't care. Even an untidy person wouldn't leave deodorant cans lying on their side! It hit me then how surreal this felt. I had often wondered what vamps were like when they weren't subjected to me, whether they had distinct personalities and tastes.

My analytical stare must have struck a nerve as he strode past me with scowling, stormy features and gathered his clothes. He laid them in the suitcase, flipped the lid shut, and turned to make the bed. I could only assume that meant he cared what I thought of him. That was a positive at least.

Before I could start throwing questions at him, there was a soft knock at the door. My heart raced and utter dread filled me.

He raised his hands apologetically. "These are my friends—I promise they mean you no harm."

He hurried to unlock the door while I tried to reconcile that a vamp could actually have friends, and in filed a short, petite blonde with long wavy hair. She was pretty in an understated way, dressed in a casual T-shirt and ripped jeans. Trailing behind, holding her hand, was a tall man with black hair hanging around his face in waves. He was also dressed in jeans and a plain white T. They both had the same pale eyes as my captor, and the blonde girl stared at me in muted terror.

"Callahan, what the hell! She's not even tied up," she hissed and ducked behind her partner. He was so tall, she looked like a child next to him.

My captor huffed a laugh in response. "Not necessary." He gestured to one of the tub chairs, beckoning me to sit. Stunned by their reaction, I obliged and cautiously sank into a chair.

"This is Isla and Fletcher. I'm Callahan."

His friends quietly sat on the far side of the bed, tentatively glancing at each other with pursed lips and narrowed brows. Nerves seemed to get the better of Callahan, and he paced in front of the window. His golden complexion had paled, and he dragged his hands through his tousled brown hair and blew out a breath. He retrieved my clutch bag from where he'd dropped it by the door and chucked my phone on the bed in front of Fletcher. He picked it up and turned it off, sliding it into the pocket of his jeans while Callahan pulled out the dinky purse I used for nights out. He took out my bank card and ID, glancing at them with raised eyebrows as he passed them to Fletcher.

"I don't have much money if that's what this is? I'm a primary school teacher living on my own. I do have about a couple of grand in savings but—"

"I don't want your money," he said tersely, cutting me off. He grabbed two glasses from the sideboard and poured two generous measures of wine. His face softened a little as he held out a glass to me. "I don't know about you, but I need a fucking drink." When

I didn't take it he sighed and placed it on the table in front of me. "It's just wine." He took a large sip from his glass and sank into a chair.

The room fell uncomfortably silent as we eyed one another. In my very limited experience, he didn't look like the terrifying torturous type but I supposed they never did. He was young and clean-shaven. I would have guessed he was around my age, but for all I knew he could be hundreds of years old.

"If you don't want my money, and you claim you don't intend to eat me, what the fuck do you want?"

There was a snort from across the room, and Callahan shifted in his seat, setting his wine glass down on the table and massaging his temples.

"Of course I'm not going to fucking eat you," he said under his breath. Ironically out of the two of us, he was the one who currently looked the most tortured.

Fletcher eased off the bed and approached. "Tilly, I can't find anything useful."

Callahan eyed him wearily and cursed under his breath, slouching back in his chair.

Fletcher dropped my ID cards on the table in front of me, and by the way he stared, I wondered if he was trying to see right through to the depths of my soul. "Are these fake?"

"No," I said exasperated, my hands bracing the arms of the chair. "Why the hell does everyone assume I'm a criminal? I'm a teacher."

Callahan sat forward, his brows narrowing. "Why did you run from me in the bar?"

Maybe I was reaping the consequences of ten years' worth of lies. What had started as a necessary survival tactic was now catching up to me. But then I remembered he had assumed I would be armed when we met and his friends were surprised I wasn't tied to a chair. My head was beginning to throb.

"What exactly do you think I am?" I countered and massaged the frown line between my brows as I waited for him to answer.

He exchanged an unsettled glance with Fletcher, who was perched on the edge of the bed, then his eyes flickered warily over me. Great. This was going to be a long night. I picked up my wine glass and sniffed it before taking a sip and fidgeting with the stem.

"For someone who claims to want answers, you're not asking a lot of questions," I said.

He glared at me. His shoulders were so tense I could practically see the fury rising from him.

"Funny, because the one question I did ask, you didn't fucking answer. So I'll ask it again, if you're not a criminal, why did you run from me in the bar?"

I took a shuddery breath in, trying to keep a lid on my fear and agitation. I made myself look in those unnaturally blue eyes —the eyes of every vamp I'd ever glimpsed. His eyebrows raised even higher, the right brow now partially hidden by the hair that fell messily over his forehead. He was waiting, and losing the very limited patience he had. I took another breath, my body trembling as every instinct battled against revealing any of my truths.

"I thought you wanted me dead."

"Why would you think that? And surely running into a dark alley on your own would be the worst possible thing to do if you thought you were about to be murdered?"

I shook my head. "Are we really doing this? Obviously, I thought you were something...other. Inhuman. Which I wouldn't want to expose to other people."

He took a sharp breath and gave Fletcher another fleeting glance. He sucked in his plump lower lip, a hint of panic in the fraught lines of his face, and he reached across to pick up his wine. He took a sip and then stared into the depths of the glass, his brows pinching together. His face eventually relaxed, and he looked up at me, his eyes bright with challenge and his lips twitched into a smirk.

"Are we really doing this?" he said wryly. "For someone who thought they were about to be murdered, you were remarkably ready to meet your end. You could have run back out onto the street and escaped but you stayed there. *And* I distinctly remember you requesting I hurry up and bite you. Why? What did you think was going to happen?"

I tensed. Maybe I needed to be the first to speak of what we were all dancing around. It was clear we were all connected in some way.

"I thought you were a vampire."

"You thought?"

I nodded. "You have the same eyes."

One brow hitched momentarily, but he kept the same steady expression. "I've never met one in person, so I'll take your word for it. What would you have done if I had been a vampire?"

"Nothing." It was the only word I could force out of my mouth. My pulse was erratic and so loud it seemed to echo around my skull and throb behind my eyes.

He shook his head and scoffed. "No. You had a plan. You walked right up to me in that alley, and if you thought you would die, or be seriously hurt, you wouldn't have done that. What were you going to do?"

"Nothing," I said again with more force.

"Bullshit. You wanted me to bite you! Was that to distract me? Are you pretending to be weak and helpless?"

"NO!"

"Have you ever killed a vampire?" he asked. The question seized my lungs and squeezed my heart. His gaze was fierce, his fingertips digging into the arms of the chair, like he was on the verge of an important discovery.

I stared back at him, painfully frozen in my seat. My brain

turned to mush, and long seconds passed before I managed to say, "not intentionally."

He glanced at Fletcher and exhaled a long breath before getting up to pace in front of the window. Was he here to deal with me? To punish me for the crimes I'd committed against his kind? Fletcher didn't take his eyes off me, his gaze traversing over me like he was assessing what level of threat I posed. My skin became a textured expanse of goosebumps as every hair on my body stood on end. Yes, I was pretty sure my death-inducing blood was about to catch up with me.

From her place on the bed, Isla's voice broke the stifling silence. "Can you just clarify for me? Are you saying you have killed a vampire, but accidentally?"

I stared at her wide-eyed and nodded. Shit. Why wasn't I defending myself and lying my way out of this? Maybe it was the shock of someone believing me—of having a serious conversation about vampires as if it were a normal part of life. Whatever it was, my body and brain had disconnected. There were so many things I needed to know, and yet my mind felt inaccessible. I rubbed my temples but my head remained an empty useless void. My legs were bouncing in a wild, urgent rhythm as the rest of me shook. The only response from my body was the readiness to sprint out of danger, but there was nowhere to run. The door and windows were locked. Barricading myself in the bathroom would be pointless, and I couldn't use SOS voice activation on my phone as Fletcher had turned it off. I was screwed. The bastard had promised they wouldn't hurt me. I was a fucking idiot.

Isla slid into the chair opposite, which gave me a small slither of hope. A female being present was surely a positive thing. Particularly one that had been concerned for her safety. Fletcher moved closer to me, no doubt ready to cut me off if I made any move to hurt her. I concentrated on my breaths, slowly in and out, trying to bring about a state of calm so that I could think unimpeded by shock.

"How do you accidentally kill a vampire?" she asked, her tone surprisingly kind. She crossed one leg over the other, leaning forward expectantly, her arms resting on her thighs. She was certainly no longer afraid of me.

Callahan stopped pacing, his hands sliding into his pockets as he watched me with a bemused expression.

"Are you planning to accidentally kill one yourself?" I asked.

Her lips twitched, and she pulled them into a tight line but failed to hide the hint of a smile. "No. I'm just intrigued, but I guess you never know when you might need that sort of information."

Perhaps she could be a useful ally if I played this right. My knees started bouncing again as I debated the merit of telling them a half-truth. It was probably dangerous to reveal it, but clearly Callahan was not going to settle for a lie. I could, however, spin this story to portray that I was merely someone mixed up in a stupid accident. That I wasn't the one responsible for all their disappearances.

I blew out a breath and looked her in the eye. "About three years ago, when I was at university, I was on a night out, and things got a bit wild. You know how it is. Anyway, I had to leave after slicing my arm open." It was a half-truth, I'd gone out deliberately hunting, thinking I was braver than I was. I'd never made that mistake again. "I was heading back to my car when three of the…creatures started following me. I tried to fight them off but they bit me, beat me up pretty bad, and when I eventually managed to get away, I made it back to my car just as another one arrived." I rubbed my face, wondering if I was insane for voicing any of this. The trembling was so brutal they could no doubt hear it in the breath I exhaled.

"What did you do?" she asked gently.

I couldn't bring myself to look at her. "I drove my car into it," I said, my tone soaked in my shame.

"I assumed it would be more...indestructible. I just wanted to give myself time to get away." Panic crept into my voice. "It was horrific...the way it landed when it rolled off my roof, the way it crunched when it hit the floor..." I grimaced at the memory and a wave of nausea rippled through my stomach. "I waited to see if it would move again, but it didn't. Eventually, I plucked up the courage to get out and check if it was alive but—" I shook my head and then looked at her with glazed eyes. "I'm a murderer. A cold-blooded fucking murderer. I never reported it. I even took its wallet to make it look like a mugging. I spent months living in absolute terror, expecting police at my door every single day." I exhaled another shaky breath and stared at the table waiting for judgement to rain down.

A slow deliberate clap resounded across the room and Callahan edged toward the table. "Nice story."

His disbelief was both heartbreaking and infuriating. Wounds that I had kept stuffed down and locked in the back of my mind for a decade burst to the forefront of my mind. My body propelled me to my feet and I rushed forward, ramming my palms against his chest.

"How fucking dare you! It's the truth, and I've never, ever told anybody else for fear of being turned in. I took a huge risk admitting it to you."

I shoved past him and hurried for the bathroom, noting with embarrassment that he'd barely moved when I pushed him. Tears were threatening to break, and I was embarrassed that I'd lost control so pathetically. I tried to slam the bathroom door shut, but Callahan halted it from the other side. We wrestled against each other but I was wholly unmatched and as he thrust the door open I stumbled, catching myself against the cold wall tiles. He slammed it shut and leaned against it, blocking off any exit. Tears spilled over and I hurried to wipe them away.

"I was telling you the truth. A truth that has eaten away at me for three damn years and—"

He cut me off before I could finish. "How did you get away from three vampires? You couldn't get away from me in the alley, you just pushed me in a blatant rage and I moved all of a foot. You couldn't even keep me from getting in here so how do you expect me to believe you got away from three vampires who had bitten you, presumably draining you of at least some blood and 'beaten you badly' while you struggled to escape?"

I was momentarily stunned—it wasn't that he didn't believe me, but that he'd seen straight through my deceit.

"What are you?" I asked through clenched teeth.

"Don't deflect. Answer the question. How did you get away? Why did you want me to bite you?"

My stomach dipped. He was so close to the truth. I struggled to control my breathing, to form any coherent thought that might help me out of this. It was strange, the cover stories usually rolled so easily from my tongue but now my mind was stubbornly blank.

"I can't tell you."

He edged forward, caging me with his arms, and I pressed myself back against the smooth tiled wall, my fingers finding a line of grout and tracing it to try and focus on something physical rather than fear.

"You can tell me, and you will." His face was steady and fierce, and I got the sense he was not going to yield easily. I started to tremble, the cold of the tiles seeping into my exposed skin on top of the stark warning my body was giving now that Callahan was so close.

"You promised you wouldn't hurt me," I whispered, appealing

to any honour that he might have—to the part of him that might be concerned for my well-being.

He snorted. "I've held to my word. Tell me how you got away."

"Why is it so important to you?" I countered, and he went still, even his breathing ceased for a few seconds until he swallowed thickly.

His mouth parted as if he would speak but whatever internal war he had raging made him close it and bow his head. He took a deep breath, and then suddenly leaned in, his nose grazing my neck and sending shivers skittering over my body.

"Well that's interesting," he muttered under his breath, so close I could feel the warmth of his words flutter against my skin.

I stood rigidly, wondering what effect my scent might be having on him and how he managed to control it.

He lingered, the soft warm skin of his cheek grazed my jaw sending my stomach somersaulting. He sighed heavily a moment later and pulled away. I exhaled a long jagged breath but didn't move from my rigid stance.

"We're getting nowhere. We both want and need information, so would you be willing to trade it? Exchange a truth for a truth?"

I opened my eyes. His face had softened and he watched me with a curious gaze. I nodded. "You're answering first," I told him. "You have far more explaining to do, and I've already told you something that could destroy me." He quirked a brow, and I tensed, waiting for him to argue with me but he nodded.

"Right." I took a deep breath. "Show me your teeth."

It sounded ridiculous but at least I would see some visible evidence. His mouth tugged into the beginnings of a smile, and he looked away to try and hide it. When he turned back his expression was steady, his tongue swept along his lower lip and he swallowed before pulling his lips back to reveal all his shiny white teeth. I leaned forward to get a closer look at his canines and his teeth snapped towards me. I jumped back, my head hit the wall with a thunk and my heart beat so wildly I expected he could hear it. He'd pulled his arms away from the wall and was chuckling at my reaction.

"Dick," I seethed at him.

"I'm sorry, I honestly don't know what came over me," he whispered around his chuckles. "It's just not what I expected you to ask." Eventually, he composed himself and leaned forward revealing his teeth once more. His canines were longer than average and thicker than I imagined the vampire teeth being, and though they tapered to a gentle point, they looked far too blunt to cut into anything. My hand was halfway to his mouth when his fingers snapped around my wrist. We both stared at my hand, held midway between us within his grip. He looked back at me, his eyes alight with recognition.

"In the alley, is this what you were going to do? Check for fangs?"

My cheeks heated at the absurdity of it, but I nodded. "I'm sorry, I didn't even mean to do it. Either time," I told him sheepishly.

He dropped my hand, straightening and folding his arms across his chest, back to his steady stare. Long canines. Maybe other beings were just as real as vampires.

"Are you...a werewolf?"

His eyes widened, his brows shooting high up his forehead, and he erupted into more sniggering chuckles, shaking his head. I supposed laughing at me was better than the many other terrifying alternatives. He wasn't a werewolf or a vampire, yet he possessed the exact vampiric eyes that haunted me and a rudimentary set of canines that were definitely suspicious.

"Are you an assassin?" he asked, his face once again gravely serious.

I tried to stop my snort of laughter but failed. "Is that what you think I am?" My voice pitched a few octaves higher than usual. "So that's why you thought I was armed and why your friend thought I should be tied up?"

He shrugged. "It seemed unlikely but it was a working theory."

That left a hell of a lot of questions. I supposed from the vampires' perspective, I was an assassin of sorts. My stomach churned with the possibilities. I looked up to find Callahan watching me, his face unreadable.

"I'm out of guesses. What are you?" I probably should have asked why he'd taken me, but I needed to know.

"I'm a farmer," he said with a wink. I shook my head, frustrated that I hadn't been more specific. Of course, he wouldn't make it easy for me. But being a farmer would explain his golden skin and his physique—his lean frame pointed to an active lifestyle. He was solid and muscular but not in a gym-bod sort of way.

"What were you planning to do to me in the alley?" he asked, inclining his head as he waited for my response.

"Nothing."

He sighed. "Truth for a truth, remember? I genuinely am a farmer. What were you planning to do?"

"I was being truthful. I genuinely planned to do nothing. I don't know how to fight."

He exhaled sharply through his nose, his eyes narrowing. "You should learn."

I thought about my next question. Of how I could phrase it so that he couldn't get around it on a technicality.

"For what specific purpose, did you need me to come with you and answer your questions?"

His eyes closed, and he took a deep breath. There was a long pause before he answered.

"The vampires have my family." His tone was low and raw, barely more than a whisper. For the second time tonight, I was utterly shocked. He moved to the sink, his fingers tightly gripping each side of the basin, head hanging in defeat.

"Were you hoping I was an assassin? So that I could help you get them back?"

He peered at me over the top of his arm. "Something like that."

9

HUMAN

I approached him slowly. "I'm so sorry. I can't begin to imagine how worried you are." And how much of a disappointment I must be if he was expecting a trained vampire assassin to help him. He shook his head and straightened, his hands sliding into his pockets as he turned to face me. His eyes were heavy with sadness.

"Tell me how you got away," he asked pleadingly. He looked so utterly defeated, I almost wanted to tell him.

"Tell me what you are, and I'll think about it."

He shook his head, a wry smile breaking through that sadness. "It's my turn."

I nodded, hugging myself, trying to rub some heat into my arms and stop them from prickling. "And my answer still stands."

He shrugged. "Fine. If you genuinely have no way of protecting yourself, why didn't you make more effort to escape??"

I raised an incredulous brow at him. "Oh, so not only did you assume I'm a criminal, you also think I'm dumb?"

He ignored my comment. Bastard. I bit my lip, debating how to frame my truth to my best advantage.

"I've been researching vampires for quite a while. You seemed to have more humanity than the ones I've come across in the past, and when you were willing to speak to me, I thought you might present a good opportunity to find answers to some of my questions. I thought it might be worth the risk but...I was, in fact, stupid."

Before he could answer, I threw my next question at him. "You might not be a vampire or a werewolf, but what is it that makes you different or otherworldly? What sets you apart from every other normal human?"

He leaned back against the sink, hunched over in silence, as if the weight of the world was pressing down on his shoulders. He ran his hands through his hair, tugging the longer lengths down over his forehead and brushing them back absentmindedly. I thought we might remain at our impasse, but after a few moments, he sighed and turned his face towards me.

"I don't consider myself a vampire. But I am a blood drinker." When my eyes widened he hurried to add, "Not by choice and animal blood only. Hence—the farm."

He may not consider himself a vampire, but he must be related to them in some way. Even if it was only distantly, which would explain the eyes.

He folded his arms. "I am human," he said defiantly. "You know, in Africa, the Maasai tribes drink blood from their cows as part of their diet. They enjoy it as a speciality, literally straight from the cow. And they're human." He sounded a little defensive and I realised I hadn't acknowledged his revelation. I nodded.

"Right so...what happens when you don't drink it?" I had a million other questions brewing, it was an effort not to spew them all out at once.

He stood, worrying his lip as he watched me intently.

"Technically, it's my question but...I would get sick. Flu-like symptoms and then eventually I would deteriorate and die."

At least he wouldn't turn rabid. Silver linings and all. I waited, bracing myself for the inevitable question. My stomach flipped and churned and my arms pimpled again. A knock on the door gave me a thankful reprieve and as it crept open, Fletcher's head appeared through the gap.

"Just checking you're still alive. And wondering if you ever plan to come out again?" He raised an eyebrow pointedly and Callahan sniggered.

"I very much doubt I'm in any danger. But yeah, we'll come out now." He gestured for me to move and my blood turned to ice.

"Please don't ask me that in front of your friends," I pleaded. The thought of speaking my secret out loud was horrifying enough but the prospect of sharing it in front of a small audience was infinitely worse. His sharp eyes assessed me before looking to Fletcher. "Just, give us a minute would you."

I closed my eyes, relief swelling in my lungs, and I exhaled slowly.

"Ignore truth for a truth for a moment, this is us having a mature adult conversation."

He opened the door a crack. "Can one of you grab a hoodie from my suitcase?" He thanked whoever came to his aid and closed the door, passing me a soft grey garment. "Here, put this on, I'm sick of watching you shiver."

I did so, recognising his very pleasant, fresh scent—like the forest after it rained. I tugged it down to find the hem reached midway down my thighs, it was so big.

"Why are you so reluctant to give me an answer? You've already confessed to a hit-and-run." He was leaning casually against the door, his hands in his pockets. A smile tugged at his lips. "I'm not sure if killing a vampire counts as a hit-and-run though. If anything, you should get a reward."

I huffed a laugh and moved to the sink, leaning against it and crossing one foot over the other to try and stop my feet from nervously tapping. I stared at my hands, brushing my thumb over each glossy fingernail as I attempted to calm myself.

"It's hard to speak about because it's a secret I've guarded for the last decade, and I guard it because every day I'm living a real-life fucking nightmare that most people would find impossible to believe."

His brows pinched together, a deep groove forming between them. "Well, given the circumstances, it's highly unlikely that I won't believe you. So what's the worst that could happen if you tell me?"

I laughed. "Well, you could use me against the vampires and sentence me to death."

I looked up to find him staring at the ceiling, his head thrown back. His hands slid from his pockets to rub his eyes.

"Could those things be mutually exclusive?" he asked and then eased himself to the floor, leaning back against the tiles, his long legs stretched out almost reaching the opposite wall.

"Maybe," I told him, feeling the urge to sit and take the weight off my feet. He scooted further towards the door and patted the space beside him as if he sensed my thoughts. I gave in to weariness and slid to the floor, leaving a healthy gap between us and pulling my dress and the hoodie down over my knees. The warmth was divine against my bare legs. Callahan looked as if he might chide me for stretching his hoodie but thought better of it.

"Humour me. My next question is related, I promise," I said.

He nodded in agreement, eyebrows quirked inquisitively.

"What was so interesting about my scent?"

He looked flustered, a dusting of pink flaring across his cheeks. "I don't know if I can explain it."

"Try," I urged him.

He stared at my neck for a long moment and cleared his throat. "Can I...?" He gestured to my neck, not willing to voice the awkward question. When I eventually nodded he shuffled himself closer, brought his face to the underside of my jaw, and took in another long deep breath. I stilled, my breathing ceased at the discomfort of having him so close, goosebumps rising along my skin and shudders reverberating down my spine. When he straightened he was frowning, wrestling with words.

"It's not that you smell of anything specific, well, other than your perfume. But it's like you're…addictive. There's this feeling of comfort and…and a sense of rightness." He avoided eye contact as he scooched back, putting more distance between us than before and leaning back against the wall.

"The vampires are drawn to me," I said softly. "I think I'm some sort of natural balance. Which is incredibly shitty."

His eyes narrowed. "In the alley, you asked if I found it hard to be near you. This is why, isn't it? What happens when a vampire finds you?" He drew in a sharp breath. "What happens when they bite you?"

I sucked in my lower lip and took a deep breath, stunned that I was about to speak the words aloud. My head throbbed, my hands clammy. "They die—horribly." The release was almost anticlimactic. I glanced at him briefly, as expected his eyes were wide with shock.

"My blood is poisonous to them, but once they catch on to my scent, they lose their minds. They aren't capable of reasoning once they get to me. They can't speak, they just have this insatiable need to bite me. I think even if they knew they were going to die, they wouldn't be able to stop themselves."

He was a few shades paler when I dared to look at him.

"How many times has that happened?" His voice was barely above a whisper as he stared at me, lips parted and eyes weary.

"Thirty-two, including the one I hit with my car."

"Fuck." He rubbed his eyes with the heel of his palms. He swore again and looked me over. "Do they hurt you every time this happens? You said the three the night you were at uni beat you?"

I shook my head. "Not always. After the first few times, I realised if I just let it happen they were less abusive. They still handle me roughly, and the biting always hurts, but if I don't fight them, they don't get vicious."

He stared at me, his eyes brimming with pity and I turned away, leaning my head back against the tiles. "How old are you?"

"I'm twenty-four," I answered softly.

He muttered more curses under his breath and then silence fell between us and with it—exhaustion hit. I had no idea what the time was, but I distantly remembered going to the bar for drinks around 11 p.m.

Callahan scooted closer and gently nudged me from where he sat, now an arm's length away.

"What do you do with the bodies? You said you were worried about the one that you hit, why not the others?"

I grimaced. "That's the worst part. My blood seems to speed up the process of deterioration. Their skin, their flesh, and their bones all get eaten away until there's nothing left other than their clothes. The sound is horrific."

He stared at me wide-eyed, his lips parted as if he would speak but the words stuck to his tongue.

"Yeah. I'm sure you can imagine what that does to your head when you're a fourteen year old who's been attacked, bitten, had your attacker choke to death while lying on top of you and then watched the piece of shit gruesomely disappear.

"Oh, and the icing on the cake is that no one believes you and thinks you're hallucinating or just fucking crazy."

His mouth closed, and he swallowed thickly, dragging his hands through his hair. "I'm sorry," he murmured.

The bathroom door opened, and Fletcher eyed us both solemnly resting on the floor. He shook his head as he glared at Callahan.

"Isla's making drinks. I think you need to get out of here." His tone was clipped, and Callahan nodded, grunting as he picked himself off the floor and held out a hand to me. I debated ignoring it, but I let him haul me to my feet.

"I need to tell the others," he said with a wince and then turned to leave.

Isla handed Callahan a coffee and turned to ask me what I wanted.

"I'll have a hot chocolate please, if there is any. I don't trust the coffee in hotels."

She smiled and pulled a sachet out of the cluster of packets haphazardly dropped on the side and then tidied the rest into their respective containers. She checked the kettle and disappeared into the bathroom for more water. I hovered by the chest of drawers, eyeing the pile of toiletries. Fletcher and Callahan were across the room by the door, deep in conversation, and while they were preoccupied, I righted the deodorant and cologne and screwed the lid back on his hair wax. I jumped when Isla flitted back past me and clicked the kettle on.

"How long has he been staying here?" I asked.

She leaned against the drawers, tapping her nail against the wood.

"This is his third night. We've been here two nights." She watched them talking for a minute and then turned back to me. "He looks even more stressed after talking to you. What happened in there?"

"He told me the vampires have his family."

The kettle clicked off, and she poured steaming water into a mug, the scent of cocoa drifting over as she stirred. As she handed me my drink, my brain flickered to life, and I turned to stare at him. Nausea stirred as I realised I hadn't asked the most significant question. I'd been so stupidly fixated on figuring out how they all related to the vampires. "Why do they have your family?" I asked.

Isla was at my side a second later, relieving my shaking hands of the mug filled with scalding liquid. "I'm putting this on the table. Why don't you come and sit down?" she said pleadingly.

I shook my head. Callahan and Fletcher were staring at me, pity written all over their faces.

"Tell me," I spat. Callahan grimaced at Fletcher before moving cautiously towards me.

"They're holding them for ransom." His voice was anguished and he reached for me as I swayed unsteadily on my feet.

"For me?" I choked out, my hands clammy and sweat beading at the back of my neck as my worst fears materialised. "They're going to kill me." My eyes pooled and hot tears rolled down my cheeks. "You promised me," I whispered. "What's the worst that could happen? This. This is the worst that could happen. You…"

He looked guttered. Good. Maybe I could fill him with enough guilt that he'd change his mind.

Isla laid a hand on my arm. "Olivia, come and sit down and talk to me. We honestly don't wish you any harm. Why do they even want you?"

I let her lead me to the chair, shaking incessantly every step. I was so disappointed in my decision. I should never have left the club but his eyes—I was so certain it was going to end like every other encounter. Isla handed me a wad of tissue.

"No offence, but you don't seem like an assassin. I don't understand why they want you?"

Callahan cleared his throat from where he hovered nearby. "She's not intentionally killing them. If we're concentrating, we can feel that distant pull to her, but they seem to hone in on her scent much more severely. Unfortunately for them, her blood is poisonous, so when they bite her—"

"They die," she finished for him. She turned back to me. "If you're bleeding, does that draw more of them?"

I nodded numbly, drawing my knees up onto the chair and pulling the hoodie over my cold-pimpled skin. I was vaguely aware of Callahan pacing back and forth, and I tried to break free from the fogginess in my mind—tried to keep myself from fracturing into a spectacular mess of tears.

The pacing beside my chair stopped.

"What alerted you to my presence in the bar?" He paused and then cautiously continued. "When I first walked into that smaller bar, I didn't know who I was looking for, just a general feeling in my gut of where to go. I saw you and your…blonde friend at the bar, and after she left, I moved closer and it was like a switch. One minute you were drinking, the next minute you were scanning the room utterly terrified."

I pushed my sleeve up to reveal my textured skin without looking at him. "It happens when I'm close to vampires. It makes me feel sick, particularly after they bite. It lasts for hours." I pulled the sleeve down and folded my arms around my legs, resting my chin on top of my knees. Callahan crouched so that I'd be forced to see his face in my line of sight.

"Do you feel sick now?"

I nodded, refusing to meet his eye. "But I didn't. That's why I agreed to go with you. I thought it meant I was in less danger."

His head bowed a moment then he got up and quietly moved away. I lifted my head to look at Isla, tears gliding down my face.

"Look, I'll be the first to admit my life is pretty shit, but I don't want to die. Especially not by them. There's got to be a way we can work together. I will do anything to help you."

She looked crushed, her eyes locked silently on Fletcher across the room but she didn't speak. Callahan was by the window, his head leaning against the frame. Shakily I got up and approached him.

"Callahan, please? I never asked to be this way. I one hundred per cent want you to get your family back, but can't we try and work together to do it? Maybe we can find them and rescue them?

You can use me to draw all the vampires out and away, and then you can go get them?"

He bit his lip but didn't speak, and I dropped to my knees—not too proud to beg for my life.

"Please. What if we could stage my death? You could tell them you accidentally killed me when I tried to escape, and I'll disappear so that you and your family stay safe?" I waited, tears puddling on the carpet where I leaned prostrate at his feet.

Quiet footsteps approached, and Isla's delicate fingers clutched my shoulders "If there is a way, I know Fletcher and Callahan will figure it out. Come on, let's take a minute."

She shook as she pulled at my shoulders. I didn't want to move, but I pulled up the hood and buried my face in it as Isla led me to the bathroom. She closed the toilet seat and motioned for me to sit, turning the sink tap on and testing the water. She retrieved a fresh face cloth from the complimentary basket of essentials provided and soaked it under the water. Once she'd wrung out the excess, she passed it to me.

I scrubbed at my face, black and beige streaks staining the crisp white cotton.

"He actually has face wash," she said surprised and popped the lid off to smell it. "It smells nice, and it would probably get the rest of your mascara off."

I nodded numbly and she ushered me to the sink, holding my hair back as I scrubbed my face clean. When the water ran cold, it snapped some life back into my exhausted mind. She handed me a dry towel and waited patiently for me to gather myself.

"Can you manage a fresh hot chocolate? How much did you drink when you were out?"

I snorted. "Not enough."

She gave me a sympathetic smile and headed back through the open door to flick the kettle on. I stared at my bare face in the mirror; the stress was leaching the warmer tones from my skin and dark shadows were forming under my eyes. If it weren't for my freckles, I could almost pass for a vampire.

Callahan lingered in the doorway, his mouth dropping open when I finally turned to face him.

"Please believe me when I say I have absolutely no desire to see you harmed. I know you're a decade into yours—but I am currently living my worst fucking nightmare. If I can't rescue them or hand you over by Tuesday, my family's dead.

"I thought I was looking for some vile, dangerous assassin that I didn't know if I was even capable of catching. But now, I'm faced with the impossible decision to either put my family at risk and try to save all four of you, or save them and condemn you to death and live with it on my conscience for the rest of my life." He covered his face with his hands, rubbing at his temples and then dragging his fingers into his hair to pull on it.

It was strange to feel broken for someone who held the power of my life or death in their hands, but I couldn't bring myself to hate him. He looked utterly devastated, and I was certain that many in his shoes would have just tied me up, gagged me, thrown me in the boot of their car, and handed me over without question. He slumped against the bathroom wall and sighed.

"We'll take you back to the farm with us in the morning. Fletcher and Isla live on-site with their families. We can all put our heads together and try to come up with a plan that keeps everyone safe."

I felt weak with relief at his words. "Thank you for at least giving me a chance," I said softly.

He grunted and headed for the door, but before he left the room he turned to say, "You shouldn't have to thank me for giving you the chance to live."

Shortly after, Isla and Fletcher left with the promise of being back first thing in the morning and apologetically locked us in the room so that I had no easy way to escape. Callahan looked lost when they left. He stood in the centre of the room, head in his hands. After mumbling a string of curses he went to collapse on the bed, groaning as he shifted onto his back and stretched out, one arm bent over his face and his feet nearly reaching the end of the mattress. I edged closer, perching on the other side—at the foot of the mattress, still cradling the remnants of my drink.

"Can I ask you a question?" I said cautiously. He shifted onto his side so he could look at me and gestured for me to speak. "At what point did you know I was in the club?"

He frowned. "I didn't. Not until I was in there and then I had this gut feeling." At my puzzled expression, he continued, "I spent the last two days wandering around the city getting nowhere, but I figured—it's Friday night, maybe whoever I was looking for would be out with friends. It was a bit of a stretch given you were supposed to be an assassin but I was running out of options. So Isla and Fletcher were looking in every bar and club this end of the city, and I...well obviously I found you."

"Lucky me," I mumbled under my breath. "How did they get your family?"

He chewed on his lip, one hand fiddling with the cross around his neck. "Mum and Dad took Caitlyn to the theatre. It was her birthday a couple of weeks ago, so it was a belated gift. I got the call late, so it was after the show finished when they were probably on their way back to the car that they must have taken them. I don't know the specifics of how they did it. They called from Caitlyn's phone first, but I was asleep, and then I picked up the second call expecting my mum. They told me they needed my particular skill set to track down an assassin and gave me a week to do it. You said earlier we have the same eyes—I couldn't figure out before why they targeted us or how they knew what we were, but I guess that could have given us away. I don't know much about them."

I drained the last of my now very cold drink and with unsteady feet, got up to place it on the bedside table.

"It's a big enough bed, you can sit and talk to me and at least make yourself comfortable," he said, reaching across to pat the other side of the mattress.

I was so exhausted, I agreed without argument. I propped the pillows up against the headboard, slid my flats off and slipped my legs beneath the covers.

"They're not like you," I said, fiddling with the edge of the duvet.

"I should fucking hope not," he snorted. I glanced at him and gave him a wry smile. "They don't look like you, is what I meant. You have the same eyes, but they always seem to look malnourished. Pale and sickly, and their teeth are different. They slice through my skin without leaving bite marks. I think there's something in their saliva that makes me feel sicker and weaker, and it does something to the wound to seal it. Your teeth don't look sharp enough to slice skin."

"They're not. Well, if I bit hard enough they would, but so would your teeth."

He ran the edge of his thumb along the point of a canine, pressing it hard enough to leave an indent. My fingers tightened around the edge of the duvet keeping them in place. I still felt compelled to check for myself, to know with one hundred per cent certainty they were not the same, that there wasn't something sharper hidden behind them.

He laughed softly. "You have a very expressive face. I feel like I can hear your thoughts out loud."

I could feel the flush creeping into my cheeks, and to my surprise, he shifted onto his elbow and held out his hand between us.

"You still want proof that I can't slice open your neck when you least expect it. Not that I would. It's disgusting, and I wouldn't be stupid enough to go anywhere near your blood."

I hesitated but then gave him my hand. His fist closed around my fingers, and he placed the point of his tooth on my thumb and pressed down, proving it was completely dull and unable to puncture skin without brute force. The fact that he was willing to risk it was proof enough. As he let go of my hand I asked, "Did you mean you think blood is disgusting?"

He grimaced and nodded his head, settling back down on his pillow. "I hate it. Even after all these years of drinking it."

I shimmied down in the bed, keeping a healthy distance between us and shifted onto my side facing him. My bones felt grateful to be relieved of their duty.

"How old are you?" I asked sleepily.

His eyes were closed but he smirked. "Twenty-seven. I'm human, remember?"

"Can you read minds?" I asked after a moment, fighting to keep my eyes open with little success.

"I swear, I am just a normal mortal human. I can't read minds or…or do anything remotely magical or superhuman."

I heard his answer, but the heavy pull of sleep made it sound distant. My eyes felt as if they were glued shut, and despite the potential danger, I could not find the will to open them again. As the silence stretched on between us, I drifted to sleep, listening to the steady cadence of his breaths.

10

SUNLIGHT

Consciousness slowly bloomed in the morning, my thoughts groggy and incoherent, like a dream you know you've had but can't quite grasp or explain. I pried my eyes open to find myself pressed up against the expanse of Callahan's chest. We were facing each other, as we had been when I'd drifted to sleep, only now his arm rested over my shoulder blades. He was sleeping on top of the duvet, his head above mine, and I guessed by the slow rise and fall of his chest he was still in deep sleep. I had no idea how many hours had passed or when Isla and Fletcher were due back. I was debating whether to try and move without disturbing him or to fall back asleep just to forget what was happening when Callahan whispered, "Olivia, are you awake?"

"Just," I croaked, groggy with sleep.

He slowly withdrew, shifting onto his back to stretch out and then rubbing the sleepiness from his eyes. My stomach twisted when it struck me that this could be my last morning. Whatever happened today, I had to make it count.

"What are you thinking?" Callahan asked.

I fidgeted with the string on the hoodie he'd lent me and took a long breath before answering. "That this could be my last morning. Which is pretty ironic as I went out last night for the first time in weeks because I was lonely and wanted to feel alive again."

"You wish you'd gone home with blondie from the bar," he said quietly.

I snorted and looked across to find his expression wholly serious as he stared up at the ceiling.

"Well, Blondie wouldn't want me dead so that would have been the wiser choice."

"I don't want you dead. Far from it." He glanced over at me, his face contorted with sadness. "You know, I haven't slept the last three days, but I couldn't fight it last night. I think the way your scent affects me must have helped." After a pause, he added a quiet, "Thank you."

I laughed darkly. "Glad to be of service." I scoffed. "Of all the superpowers I could have—that! That's what life throws at me?"

He snorted with amusement as he pulled his phone from his pocket and his thumbs danced across the screen. After a moment he stopped texting, turning the phone over and over in his hand before peering at me. "Isla and Fletcher are ordering coffee and food; what do you want?"

"Where are they ordering from?"

"Anywhere that delivers," he said with a shrug and sat up, swinging his legs over the edge of the bed.

If it was my last morning, I was going to make the most of it. To hell with being healthy. "I'll have a large vanilla latte and any salted caramel cake, doughnut, or brownie they can get their hands on. Please."

He grunted in acknowledgement and stood up, pacing about the room as he relayed my request, and I took the opportunity to slink off to the bathroom.

Thirty minutes later there was a soft knock at the door and the sound of the key clicking in the lock. Isla and Fletcher strode into the room, Isla scanning me from head to toe. She offered a shy smile and handed me a small paper bag. Inside it was a hairbrush, deodorant, and a new toothbrush.

"If you want to shower before we go back to the farm you're welcome to use my hair stuff too. I can grab it from our room. I would offer you a pair of jeans but..." She looked down at her legs, considerably shorter than mine and loosed a sigh.

"Thanks," I said.

She gave a sympathetic smile before plonking herself into one of the chairs and digging into a croissant.

"I was wondering if there would be time to detour to my apartment?" I spoke loudly enough that Callahan and Fletcher could hear, and they stopped unpacking the food to look at me. "I can grab my laptop with all my research on it; maybe there's something on there that's usable?"

And I could get out of this dress into something more appropriate. They glanced at each other but said nothing in response. I guess not then. Fletcher stalked over to where I perched on the bed and wordlessly handed me my coffee and a cake box before commandeering the other leather tub chair. He unfolded a sizable breakfast wrap and took a bite. This was surreal.

"Do you think vampires eat normal food?" I asked as I removed the cake box lid to find a salted caramel brownie and a cupcake with salted caramel-infused frosting. My eyes widened at the bounty and I pulled out the cupcake and took a bite, savouring the sweetness. The mattress dipped as Callahan sunk onto the bed and settled himself against the headboard.

"I don't see why they couldn't," he said, pulling out his own wrap and taking a bite.

"Do you think they can go out in sunlight like you?" I murmured between mouthfuls of cake.

He swallowed, wiping the grease from his lips with the back of his hand. "Do you seriously believe they're some all-powerful supernatural being like from the movies?"

I flinched, not appreciating the insult to my beliefs. I'd had little opportunity to disprove any of the mythical theories so far, and my blood was, by all accounts, supernatural.

He seemed to catch the hurt in my expression and sighed. "If they're similar to us, as you seem to think they are, then the only thing different about them is that they need human blood or they'll get sick. So, yes. I think they probably can."

It took a moment for that reality to settle, the very possibility that they could be walking around in public was utterly inconceivable to me. Callahan leaned across the bed and gently prodded my shoulder. "Are you alright?"

The room snapped back into focus, and I turned to stare at him, my mouth still hanging open. "I was attacked in a multi-storey a few months ago when it was late afternoon, and I thought it must have gotten trapped in there at dawn. It caught me off guard because it was daylight, and I couldn't understand why that was possible. Then in the summer around dusk...This whole time I thought..." I trailed off, mentally checking off all my theories that relied upon superhuman abilities and released a string of curses under my breath. Most of my assumptions were now void, and I had even more questions than ever. A shiver rattled down my spine, and I set the cupcake back into the box and clutched my coffee with both hands.

"Olivia?" Isla's tone was full of concern. She sat down at my side, her long curtain of light blonde hair swayed as she leaned forward to draw my attention. "What are you piecing together?"

I swallowed and met her gaze. "This is going to sound ridiculous now, but I'd always assumed that the vampires must be able to wipe people's memories. So they would take blood but leave the person who supplied it alive and unaware. But if they can't do that...then either they're finding willing volunteers or they really are killing people. I don't understand how they're getting away with it. How much blood do you drink a week?"

Her mouth twitched to the side, and she glanced at Fletcher warily. "About a litre and a half minimum," she said as she stared at her hand and spun the rose gold ring adorning her thumb repetitively.

I started to work out the maths. "Humans need several weeks to regenerate red blood cells. If you go to a blood bank to donate they will only take what— half a litre max? Then you can't go again for a couple of months. So let's say they require a similar amount of blood each week. If they were doing this with willing suppliers, and without risking people dying, each vampire would have to use three different people each week. So that would be twenty-four different people over eight weeks.

"I've killed thirty-two. If I hadn't, those thirty-two vampires would have needed..."

"Seven hundred and sixty-eight people over eight weeks to not put them at risk of losing too much blood." Callahan stared at the number on his phone, biting his lip.

"If they needed that many people, there is not a chance in hell the whole city wouldn't know about them," Fletcher said gruffly.

My stomach twisted, and dread settled over me.

Callahan chucked his phone on the bed and rubbed his eyes with the heel of his hands.

"Assuming the average person has five litres of blood in their body, they could feed three vampires comfortably for a week before they died," he said despondently. "Thirty-two vampires would need at least nine people to feed them for a week. So your very existence—your blood killing those thirty-two vampires—has potentially saved over four hundred lives in the last year alone."

That knowledge certainly made my life more valuable.

The room fell silent. I glanced at each of them, noting how healthy they looked. Their skin was soft, supple, and tanned. Full of life. They were all beautiful and all exuded a vibrance that set them apart from the vampires.

"I don't think they're drinking enough blood. That's why they all look so pale and sickly. They're only having enough to get by," I mused, staring at the cake box in my lap and wondering if I could stomach eating my treats.

Fletcher shifted in his seat, leaning forward and bracing his elbows on his knees. "Probably to avoid suspicion. Olivia, can I take a look at your research?"

I nodded, setting the cakes aside and gulping down my coffee instead.

Callahan stood. He looked pale, the conversation had leached the colour from his face and his eyes betrayed the weariness he no doubt felt. He rifled through the tangle of things in his suitcase, gathering an armful of clean clothes. When he straightened he looked to Fletcher. "I need a quick shower, and then we'll go to Olivia's on the way home."

He didn't wait for a response, but solemnly made his way to the bathroom, and the door softly clicked shut behind him. My heart ached for him, for the impossible position he'd been put in.

The three of us sat in silence, sipping our coffees and processing the enormity of what we'd theorised. Now more than ever I wished there was a way for me to question a vampire. To learn the truth directly.

Isla set down her empty coffee cup and blew out a breath. "If they're only taking enough blood to get by, how are they managing to beat you up if they're that sickly?"

"Adrenaline mixed with desperate hunger probably," Fletcher answered for me.

I sat stewing on the numbers, feeling sicker by the minute as I considered how many people may have died as a result of the vampires over the last ten years. How many more could I have saved if I'd been brave enough to be proactive? If I'd figured out a clever way to kill them or found someone who would believe me and help. They certainly had to be getting help from somewhere to get rid of the bodies.

My tirade of thoughts was cut off as Callahan emerged from the bathroom. He was flicking his fingers through his damp hair and grabbed the tub of wax off the side. He gave me a knowing look as he unscrewed the lid and began teasing it through the longer strands, settling it into his dishevelled style. He seemed less sombre, with a steely determination about him that had hope rising in my chest. He grabbed socks from the suitcase and sat down next to me, crossing an ankle over a knee. As he slipped the sock over his toes I noticed a large yellowing bruise spreading from his ankle.

"How on earth did you do that?"

He huffed a laugh and gave me a sidelong look. "Hazard of the job. A cow stomped on me. I'll probably have a similar bruise on my other shin in a couple of days," he said with a wink and a sly grin spread over his face when my cheeks flushed hot.

"Well, maybe the cow thought it was in danger of being dinner," I retorted, and he snorted a laugh.

"I'm pretty sure that's not what that particular cow was thinking," he said, swapping feet and pulling the leg of his jeans up to show me the purple mark I had caused.

I winced. "Yeah, that looks sore. And I want to apologise, but you did deserve that! You could have said right at the start that you didn't plan to eat me."

He huffed, covering his leg and sliding the sock over his toes. "It's so disturbing when you say it like that, and in my defence, I was trying to make sense of who and what you were, and I'm not sure we would have believed each other anyway."

He had a point. I might have been more suspicious if he'd

openly told me he wasn't a threat. If I hadn't been hoping he would bite me, I wouldn't have let him get close to me.

I brushed my hair and teeth while he finished getting ready. Before we left, Callahan took my hand, tightly lacing our fingers together as he had the night before, and he took a deep breath before tugging me forward.

11

OFF THE RADAR

The first step onto the flagstone path outside the B&B I held my breath, staring wide-eyed and open-mouthed, as the morning sunlight doused Callahan in all its brilliance and had absolutely no ill effect on him. He paused to retrieve the pair of shades dangling from the collar of his T-shirt and nonchalantly slid them onto his sun-kissed face with his free hand. I almost tripped when he abruptly started walking again and dragged me forward.

"You totally thought I was gonna burst into flames didn't you?" he said mockingly over his shoulder.

"One hundred percent!" I said as I half-skipped to fall into stride with him. "But it's hard to rewire a whole decade of beliefs."

We caught up to Isla and Fletcher. The height difference between the two of them still amused me, and the pace slowed to accommodate her much shorter legs.

We located Callahan's farm-muddied Dacia Duster a little way up the street. A haphazard pile of emptied Dorito bags, receipts, gloves, half-empty water bottles and blue paper roll littered the seats. Callahan stared at the mess, assessing, almost letting go of my hand but then clamping down tighter while he thought.

"I won't run," I said with as much reassurance as I could squeeze into my tone. "If you give me a chance, I promise I'll help you. I won't run."

Slowly he released my hand, though his handsome face looked hollow and pale with terror at the prospect of me fleeing and jeopardising the chance to gain back his family's freedom.

I folded my arms and leaned against the car. Isla had gotten in the back—driver's side. Fletcher hovered nearby ready to give chase as Callahan gathered all the litter precariously under one arm and brushed some dried mud off the seat before gesturing for me to get in.

~

When we pulled into the multi-storey around the corner from my building, I could see the anxiety churning in Callahan's eyes. I waited in the car until he'd made his way to my door and offered him my hand when I stepped out—a sign of good faith that I wouldn't betray his trust. He'd taken it gratefully, though his fingers stayed loose. It was my hand that tightened when we walked through the multi-storey, as for the first time in ten years, the safety of daylight was lost to me and I was on edge the whole walk to my building, as if seeing everything with fresh eyes for the first time.

When I unlocked my apartment, Callahan looked around wide-eyed and lips parted.

"How long have you lived here?"

"About four months" I replied as I headed to the kitchen area, realising how hungry I was and wishing I'd remembered to bring the cakes with me.

"Where's all your stuff?" He meandered around the near empty front room, stopping at my bookshelf.

"This is all my stuff." I watched as he perused my books, came across the photo frame I'd hidden and pulled it out. He stared at it pensively but didn't ask who it was, and when Isla spotted him she clipped him across the shoulder and told him to put it back in a hushed voice.

He very gently slotted it back between the books then turned to take in the eerily empty room once more, shaking his head as he did so. I turned before he could catch my eye, grabbing a selection of fruit and preparing it, placing it in a bowl. The mix of citrus and berries was pungent and refreshing, and my stomach gurgled in anticipation.

"Make yourself at home," I said and strode down the hall, bowl of fruit in hand.

Callahan caught up as I got to my bedroom. I opened the door and hovered on the threshold, staring at him. Could he enter if I didn't invite him in? "Are you planning to guard my bathroom door while I shower?" I edged into my room, my eyes drawn to his feet as they stepped towards the threshold even though I knew it was ridiculous. Did they have to be invited into every room or were they free to roam once they were invited into your house?

I shook my head, irritated with myself for still obsessing over these myths when he wasn't even a vampire. Not in the traditional sense anyway. When I looked up, his arms were folded, and he watched me with a raised eyebrow. One corner of his mouth curved.

"I don't need your permission," he said, stepping onto the threshold, once again anticipating my thoughts. "But…to put my mind at ease, can I please take a quick look around?"

Did he still think I was capable of violence or escape or that I might harbour weapons in here?

"I don't care if you stay." I turned on my heel, hurriedly stuffing strawberries and blueberries in my mouth then yanked open my wardrobe doors and thought about what to wear.

My skin prickled at his approach. He eyed my fruit. I offered him the bowl, and he obliged, picking out a slice of nectarine and popping the whole thing in his mouth as he took in the neatly ordered clothes. He inhaled a sharp breath. "Your apartment"—he winced as he tried to find the words—"is very…"

I glared at him with raised brows, daring him to echo Noah's accusations about why I lived like this.

"It's very organised." He refused to meet my eye, stealing the last piece of nectarine. He kicked off his shoes and hopped on my bed, sprawling out, tucking his hands behind his head like he'd been here a thousand times before. At least he felt more comfortable in my presence now that neither of us was expecting the other to kill us!

I pulled out a black vest top and ripped jeans by the hangers and draped them carefully over my bedroom chair. I tugged off his hoodie and dumped it on his lap before heading to the bathroom.

Once inside, I finished the rest of my fruit, taking a moment to breathe, to feel at peace in my familiar space. As I was about to undress, there was a knock. I pulled the door open and leaned against the door jamb, waiting for Callahan to speak. He was holding the clothes I'd picked out.

"You might need these," he said, offering them to me. "How long will it take you to get ready? Are you planning to do hair and make-up?"

My eyes narrowed on him as I took the hangers. Was he saying I needed it? His hands dragged through his hair, and he shifted uncomfortably under my glowering gaze.

"I…we don't have a lot of time and I think you look better without it, for what it's worth." He worried his lip, taking in my unflinching expression.

"I like your freckles," he said softly. "It's criminal covering them up."

I retreated and shut the door on him, pausing at the mirror on my way to the shower to look at the smattering of dots over the bridge of my nose and cheeks. Against my olive skin and dark hair, I supposed they made me look a little wild and raw. Unrefined. The opposite of my mother.

∽

It felt good to be clean and in comfortable clothes. I left my face bare and my hair hung in damp unruly waves down my back, soaking into my top.

I found Callahan and Fletcher sitting on my couch, Isla perched delicately on my coffee table as there was nowhere else to sit. Callahan's head was resting in his hands, but he looked up and gave me an approving smile as he noticed the freckles still visible on my face.

"Other than my research, what else should I bring?" I asked.

"Why don't you pack an overnight bag, just in case?" Isla suggested.

I nodded and went to my spare room to grab a rucksack, Callahan hot on my heels. "Pack something you can move easily in. And something warm to sleep in. We heat the house mostly through our wood burner and it won't have been lit since I've been gone."

It was reassuring that he assumed I'd still be alive tomorrow. He sat on my bed, staring vacantly at the floor while I flitted about. I packed a few general items of clothing along with my yoga pants and a pair of trainers better suited to running, it was my usual method of dealing with the vamps. Run and run fast. I figured I should be prepared for that eventuality. I grabbed toiletries, carefully packing them in a plastic case and tucking them in the top of the bag. Callahan was so consumed by his thoughts, he barely noticed me. I zipped up my rucksack and nudged him gently on the shoulder. "What are your parents' names?" I asked softly, trying to draw him back to the present.

"Jodie and Martin," he said hoarsely, fidgeting with his hands.

"Well, if we can work together on this, I look forward to meeting them."

He finally looked up and gave me a half-hearted smile, his eyes shadowed with exhaustion. As I grappled with anything I could say to make him feel more at ease, more optimistic about what lay ahead, I had a sudden revelation. I held my arm up before him to display my smooth skin. "Look, you're off my vamp radar."

He gave a quiet laugh and stood up, those icy eyes holding mine captive, and he took a long deep breath.

"Does being closer to me help you?" I whispered into the small space between us.

He swallowed, his eyes flickering to my neck. "I don't know. I was frantic before I found you—out of my mind. But today I just feel…heavy."

My chest tightened. He was still wrestling with that decision. The innate fear of losing his family was pressing in on him as he considered a new and uncertain pathway to their freedom—to mine.

My skin prickled, and I took a step back. His hand darted to my wrist to keep me from moving further away. He shook his head slowly, a line forming between his furrowed brows.

"I honestly don't want anything to happen to you." His thumb swept over my uneven skin where he still held me, and his gaze shot to my arm, noticing the goosebumps flaring across my body. He released me and stuffed his hands into his pockets, his lips drawing into a taut line as he looked anywhere but at me. Finding my rucksack zipped and ready, he grabbed it and hoisted it onto his back then gestured to the door.

12

WILLING TO FIGHT

The car was quiet as we left the city. Each of us lost in the swell of our thoughts. As we battled congestion, the only sound that filled the silence was Fletcher muttering with vehemence under his breath, *"I fucking hate the city."*

As we got past the outer ring road, traffic eased and his grumblings ceased. I drew my knees up and watched the landscape whizz by, gradually transitioning from rows of white terraced houses, to trees, and then to stretches of land filled with rows of solar panels and seas of giant vertical greenhouses looming on the horizon.

I glanced at Callahan. He was worrying his lip, deep in thought. I felt a sharp pang of regret that we hadn't all met sooner. I'd finally found people that I could be honest with, that accepted the truth, and were living it in their own way. Circumstances aside, I actually liked them. Enough to want to befriend them. I twisted in my seat and peered behind me. Fletcher was staring blankly out the window, his hand was clutched in Isla's, their tangle of fingers resting on the seat between them. Isla tore her gaze from her window and met my eye, giving me a small cursory smile. I reciprocated and turned my attention back to the road ahead, it felt wrong to disturb them when they looked so peaceful.

Isla leaned forward. "So, how many vampires have attacked you in the last year?"

"Only four, but I was lying low for about seven months of that."

"How does that work?" she asked, her brows knotting together.

I shrugged. "I become even more of a hermit. I don't go out after dark if I can avoid it, I never open my windows, I use pretty potent cleaning products, and I keep myself, my clothes, and sheets washed obsessively so they hold as little of my scent as possible."

Her eyes widened. "That's why you keep your apartment so… uncluttered? Because it's easier to clean?"

I nodded, grateful that she was so insightful. She stared at the edge of Callahan's seat, her frown making those bright eyes appear more predatory.

"Did you grow up in the city?" she asked.

"No. I was tutored at home privately. For a chunk of my life, we lived in a country house in Brockham. Then after I was attacked, we moved to a tiny place called Rowsham when I was fourteen. It was very isolated."

She nodded thoughtfully. "So what made you want to live in a city? I imagine it makes your life harder?"

I snorted a laugh. "It does. But…after university, I didn't want to go back to that isolation." I let loose a sigh. "It's ironic, really. I live with a different kind of isolation now, and in some ways, it's worse."

Isla's mouth quirked to one side, and she glanced at Fletcher. "I can imagine. We're so lucky to have each other. Seeing Callahan and my brothers navigate dating has been *hard*." Her eyebrows raised pointedly as she said it, and Callahan briefly glared at her in the rearview mirror.

"Thanks for that," he muttered and turned his attention back to the road.

Fletcher shifted in his seat, a smirk on his lips. "Tilly made it hard for himself when he chose to date those shallow fucking trolls," he said casually and instantly found something to stare at out the window as Isla's face whipped towards him with a murderous expression.

Tilly? Did he mean Callahan? "Why do you call him that?"

"Because his last name is Tilbrook and Callahan is far too long a name. And it's pretentious as fuck."

"Why were you laying low?" Callahan asked, expertly steering the conversation away from himself.

I winced, rubbing at my face, it had been four long months since Noah. Somehow I'd pulled myself through it, but it was still difficult to talk about.

"Ugh. I was trying to date someone. It did not go well, so let's leave it at that."

Callahan glanced at me with a wry smile. "Picture frame guy?"

"Why do you say it like that?" I challenged.

He looked over at me, his eyes flickering over my face before turning back to the road, and after an awkward silence, he finally spoke. "I wasn't…sorry I shouldn't have asked." He loosed a long sigh. Isla smirked as she watched the countryside fly by, Fletcher mirroring her on his side.

"Do you both work on the farm?" I asked them. Isla laughed and shook her head.

"God, no. I work for a florist," she said and then pointed at Fletcher, "and he's a mechanic, but my brothers both work with Callahan. You'll meet them both shortly." She fiddled with her thumb ring, still smiling and asked, "Is teaching as bad as people say it is?"

I could sense Callahan glancing at me as my face scrunched in thought.

"I think...if you go into it expecting it to be this magical experience where you spend all day inspiring kids, yeah, you're gonna be disappointed. I'm quite a logical, organised person"—Callahan snorted, and I ignored him—"so I knew I'd excel at all the planning, and obviously I have a lot of time on my hands, so working at home in the evening doesn't bother me. But I get why a lot of people might struggle with it. The government expects more and more from us when the schools are overcrowded and underfunded." I huffed a laugh. "My parents hate that I chose to be a teacher. They work in the corporate sector, and they had grandiose dreams of me becoming a solicitor or an accountant and joining them in their company."

Callahan frowned. "What do they do?"

I shook my head. "Honestly, I don't know the full ins and outs of it, but let's just say power and money are at the centre of their universe, so I don't really pay attention."

"You're not close then?" he asked quietly.

"I think my mum expected me to be her clone, and when I wasn't and I rebelled at every decision they forced on me, I was just a bigger and bigger disappointment. My Dad's nicer. But he's away a lot more than she is."

"I can't imagine having parents like that," Isla chimed from the back.

I'd known from Callahan's devastated expression that his parents were the good kind, that this whole situation was so much harder because of how good they were. But did that mean he'd be more likely to betray me to get them back or that he was more compassionate because of them? Would he try to find a solution to save us all simply because of the person they'd raised him to be? I hoped it was the latter but I needed to be prepared to escape, I wouldn't make it easy for him.

As we followed the gentle curve of a quiet country road, the atmosphere in the car changed, and I knew we were approaching the farm. Callahan, Fletcher, and Isla came to attention as one, all shifting to sit straighter in their seats.

On the crest of the hill to my right, the barns and farm properties emerged. They sat nestled amongst neat lines of hedgerow and looming oak trees. They overlooked sloping fields of muted green that stretched out beneath them. Intermittent splodges of rich warm brown dotted the land where their herd was busily grazing.

As the Dacia slowed ready to turn down the farm's understated drive, Callahan loosed a heavy sigh that had my stomach twisting in knots. The feeling travelled up into my chest, and I fidgeted nervously in my seat. Being here brought everything into sharper focus. Every thought became a worst-case scenario and threatened to swallow me up in unbridled fear.

We came to a stop outside the main farmhouse. It was a formidable red brick building with a central pitched-roof porch and imposing black wooden door. If the circumstances had been different, I might have felt excited to venture into Callahan's home; I could picture the solid form of the house being a steady comforting presence when everything was as it should be. Seeing it now, I felt sick. It should have been filled with his family's exuberant presence as they busily went about their days, but it was quiet. The emptiness foreboding.

Isla gave me a hesitant smile and then opened her door. "I'll go find my parents," she said and scurried off up the drive, disappearing around a bend in the track.

Fletcher stayed with us until we'd opened the farmhouse door and then he departed to rally his parents. We shucked off our shoes inside the porch and entered into a central hall with flagstone flooring. A chunky oak staircase spanned across the left side of the hall, and to the right, was a sitting room.

The farmhouse kitchen was a light, airy room with traditional cream shaker units and oak worktops. A central island and breakfast bar sat proudly in the centre. The walls were painted white and thick solid oak beams ran at intervals across the ceiling. The far left of the room was dominated by a vast oak dining table. Candles lined the centre of the table, hoodies were draped over the backs of chairs. Various photo frames were placed across the window sills, and the sides were cluttered with cake mixers and other appliances and paperwork. It was lived in, and it was loved, a functional place people could breathe in. Not a room purely to be admired that sapped all the sanctity of home. I dropped my rucksack on a chair and peeked out of the patio doors. The view was breathtaking. At the end of their simple lawned garden were rolling fields as far as I could see, the horizon dotted with clusters of trees.

I was used to the countryside, but I'd grown up surrounded by manicured gardens—gardens I didn't get to spend much time in because my studies were deemed more important. This was wild and free.

"It's beautiful," I said.

He leaned against the worktop, his eyes narrowing as he took in the room, no doubt feeling the potent absence of those who usually brought it to life. I took a deep breath as I faced him.

"We're asking a lot of each other. But let's make it count. Let's not let them win. I know you're facing an impossible dilemma; you have a lot to risk, and maybe I don't know what it's like to be loved like this"—I gestured to the photographs, to the space around us—"but I am willing to fight for it. For your family and all the others they've taken and used. I'm willing to risk my life to save them…but not to be handed over like a sacrificial lamb."

I stared into those bright eyes as earnestly as I could. He held my gaze, sucking in his lower lip; his breaths were so shallow and quiet that I wondered if he'd stopped breathing. Before he could answer, the front door sang on its tight hinges, and I heard Isla's muffled voice as several sets of footsteps drifted through the hall.

Nerves erupted in my stomach; my whole body seemed to fizz with energy and an uncomfortable chill spread over my skin.

A young man with neatly trimmed facial hair framing his mouth and jawline hesitantly stepped through the door. He looked me over in quiet assessment and gave me a nod. A strand of honey-blond hair fell loose and he tucked it behind an ear, the rest was pulled back into a bun at the crown of his head. He clapped Callahan on the shoulder affectionately, offering a sympathetic smile before turning to offer me a hand. His fingers were invitingly warm as they enclosed my icy skin.

"I'm Rory," he said softly.

Isla followed with another slightly younger man who I assumed was also her brother. She gestured to him, and he smiled broadly offering his hand.

"Hey. I'm Finn." His hair was the same light blond as Isla's, and it was neatly trimmed, longer strands falling over one-half of his forehead. He was angelic-looking with those icy-blue eyes.

"My mum and dad will be here soon," Isla said, laying a soothing hand on Callahan's arm. "I had a message from Fletcher, he's currently arguing with Ava and James, so they might be a few more minutes."

Callahan leaned back against the side, his arms folding across his chest as he stared vacantly across the room.

Rory snorted. "We'll be waiting for bloody ages. Anyone for coffee?"

I gratefully accepted, needing something warm to wrap my hands around while we waited. I rummaged in my rucksack and pulled out a moss-green hooded sweatshirt. I was tugging it over my head when Isla's parents arrived. I could hear their hushed voices in the hall and seconds later they appeared together, holding hands. Like Isla, her mum was short and petite, though her silvery blonde hair fell in waves that sat just above her shoulders. She gave Isla a cursory smile, and when she didn't acknowledge me, Isla cleared her throat to draw attention.

"This is my mum, Maddie, and that's my dad, Stephen," she said. "This is Olivia."

Maddie nodded and mumbled hello under her breath as she retreated to the table. I couldn't decide if she refused to look at me because she felt guilty for wanting to hand me over to my would-be murderers or that she didn't trust that I wouldn't try and harm them.

Stephen hovered in the doorway, he gave me an appraising stare and then turned to nod at Rory, his hands raised to form a T-shape in confirmation that he wanted a drink. He joined Rory at the side nearest the sink, arms folded while he waited patiently for his tea. Isla joined her mum at the table.

It was Finn's voice that was the first to break the silence. "Tilly, do you want us all to sit at the table or are we going in the living room? I can build a fire quickly if you want. It's freezing in here."

Callahan straightened, his fingers dragged over his face as he tried to collect himself. "I think we'll stay in here…but yeah, can you light the fire?"

Finn nodded and disappeared out the door. Stephen collected his drink and headed for the table, pausing on his way past.

"Have they sent you any more updates? Are they all still okay?" he asked, his face pinched in concern.

Callahan shook his head. "Nothing since Wednesday morning."

Stephen inhaled sharply and nodded at me. "Do they know you have her?"

Again Callahan shook his head. "As far as they're concerned, I'm still looking."

Rory joined us, two steaming mugs in each hand, and he nodded towards the table. "Go sit down, they'll be here soon."

We followed his lead and sat around the table. Callahan patted the seat next to him. I sat down hesitantly, I would have preferred to hide away in a corner.

Rory plonked himself next to me, passing along our drinks. My fingers melded to the cup and I stared at the still-swirling liquid trying to breathe through the rush of anxiety. I hadn't noticed how much my leg was bouncing until Callahan's hand landed on my knee to still it, making me startle.

"I'm sorry," he whispered.

"For what?" I asked in a hushed voice, my heart rate spiking.

"For making you jump."

I nodded, relieved it wasn't for an upcoming betrayal, though I supposed it still could be.

Rory nudged me from the other side and leaned in to ask, "How old were you when you discovered the vampires?"

My fingers tightened around the mug to keep them from tapping nervously.

"Fourteen. I went out with a friend to a disco and needed to er…go to the shop for something so I left on my own and it found me on the way back. It died on top of me." I shivered at the memory.

"That's rough," he muttered, running his fingers along the neat lines of his facial hair. He leaned back in his chair, his gaze raking over me before turning to Callahan. "Are you ready for this?"

My mouth dried out. Callahan exhaled long and slow and only nodded in response. From across the table, Isla's phone buzzed and she peered at the screen.

"They're on their way," she announced.

13

THE RANSOM

As her words rang out around the room my first instinct was to run. My mind, being on high alert, had immediately conjured a worst-case scenario—that I was about to be handed over to the vampires and that Fletcher was bringing whoever was responsible for my death.

I looked to the patio doors just beyond the end of the table; the key was in the lock but I'd have to escape Callahan's clutches and make it past Rory. If I made it past the door I'd have to rely on stamina and endurance to get across the fields and back to the road.

As if sensing the direction of my thoughts, Callahan closed his hand tightly around my forearm, locking me in place as he leaned in close.

"She meant Fletcher's parents," he whispered, one of his eyebrows arched high as he waited for me to cease my panicking.

When my pulse stopped throbbing through my entire body, and my muscles relaxed, he finally let go, then placed his elbows on the table and buried his face in his hands. The room fell into an uncomfortable silence and beside me, Rory pulled out his phone and began scrolling. Finn sauntered in from the hall and took his place on the other side of Callahan but still nobody spoke. It felt like we were in a bubble on the verge of popping.

When the front door finally clanged open, Isla pushed back from the table and went to flick the kettle on. Fletcher appeared first, his lips drawn down in a stony expression, his eyes sharp and murderous. He headed straight to Isla, and the two of them exchanged pointed looks and frantic whispers before he took a seat opposite me. Isla abandoned making drinks and sat back down. That was not a good sign.

His parents walked through shortly after. They didn't speak, their lips were pursed and their matching dark brows furrowed as they joined the table. Ava sat next to Fletcher, her short dark hair swaying across her face as she tucked herself under the table and James took the end seat. I could sense him eyeing me from the other side of Rory, but I stared into the dregs of my coffee and tried to ignore their bristling presence.

James cut right to the chase. "Callahan, Fletcher has filled us in on some developments, and I have to ask, is it really a good idea for her to be in here right now?"

Ice crept over my skin, tracing the path of my spine, and I forced myself to look at Callahan and stay still. He glanced to Fletcher first, then James. His knee brushed up against mine and mercifully kept it from bouncing.

"What are you suggesting? That we tie her up and lock her away?" He shook his head incredulously and continued, "They lied to us. Olivia isn't some dangerous assassin—"

Before he could finish James cut him off. "Did they lie or did she? And if they lied, it makes even less sense to not use her for ransom. She has no combat skills to help us so she's a liability. If you plan a rescue, you and whoever else is involved will likely end up dead. It's too big a risk; you're not thinking about this objectively."

Callahan's eyes narrowed on James. "I am thinking objectively.

I love my family more than anything, but I have to ask myself, is the 'potential risk' to three lives not worth it for all the lives she would save by being alive? Not to mention what it would do to my soul if we handed her over—knowing I would be complicit in someone's murder."

Ava scoffed and interjected before James had the chance. "She might not save any lives in the next ten years. She might disappear to an island where there aren't any vampires and leave the population to their fate. Is it worth it then?"

"If all of us survive a rescue mission, then I don't give a fuck what she does with her life for the next ten years. She fucking deserves to live on an island if she wants to," he said sharply.

"Callahan. Watch. Your. Mouth," Stephen warned from the other end of the table.

Maddie's face was white as a sheet, and Callahan dutifully apologised. Stephen nodded appreciatively and cleared his throat, ready to take advantage of the pause and speak his piece. He glanced at me briefly, then directed his words to Callahan, his expression one of pity. "I understand where you're coming from, lad, but what you're suggesting is the sort of thing that takes trained professionals. You don't have the skills. It's a suicide mission."

There was a strained silence. Ava and James eyed Callahan smugly, pleased that theirs was not the only voice of reason. Fletcher was drumming his fingers as he stared at me. One eyebrow raised thoughtfully, and he abruptly turned his attention to Stephen. "They don't know we have her yet. What if tonight we pick up a vampire and see what information we can shake out of it?

"They want her dead because they know she's killing off their kind. For them to be aware of that, they have to be in communication with each other, and like us, I would bet they probably live in close-knit communities to keep each other safe. So there's every chance we might pick one up that knows where they're being held or knows who might be responsible." He turned to his mum and dad. "We'll soon find out who's lying."

James stared at his son with fiercely cold eyes, his bearded face propped on his clasped hands in a villainous fashion.

Chills cascaded down my spine and rattled my shoulders. Callahan cast me a concerned glance and his knee nudged against mine, tethering me to a fragile state of calm.

"How are you planning to abduct a vampire without them all realising and retaliating?" James asked his son curtly.

I saw my opportunity and seized it. "They'll use me to draw one out. They don't know I've been captured, so it won't seem out of the ordinary."

James looked at Callahan, his eyes flickering to me briefly before he declared, "It's too dangerous. If she escapes, then they're all dead."

There were murmurs of agreement from Stephen and Maddie, although they sounded less convinced.

"I've had opportunities to escape, yet I'm still here," I retorted and then took a breath to calm my tone. "I promised Callahan that I wouldn't run if he's willing to work together, and I meant it." I glowered at James, waiting for his next argument.

"How exactly would you draw one out?" Ava asked, surprising me with her willingness to hear my plan.

"There's a multi-storey I have to avoid because it's pretty close to their territory. We'd use that as our base point, and then I'd lure it back to the car. I don't have to do anything, I just need to be in relatively close proximity to one of them. Once they catch my scent, they don't have a choice but to follow me. We'd have to knock it out so we could load it and get it out of the city. Then, hopefully, I can stay inside far enough away that when it wakes up and it can't smell my scent anymore, it will be able to speak to them." I had no idea if it would work but it was the best damn idea I'd probably ever had.

She shook her head, eyes narrowing. "What if it doesn't know anything? It would be a waste of time we don't have." She looked to Callahan. "And in what world would you be willing to trust her? To let her run around the city where she could so easily escape. You're not thinking clearly if you think that's a good plan."

"For fuck's sake, Mum. Do you even hear yourself right now?" Fletcher was seething beside her, shocked by her lack of compassion, and he continued his scathing rant. "When did we become people who refuse to even try? How are YOU thinking clearly when you're so set on handing someone over to die without lifting a finger to stop it?"

"Because Caitlyn, Jodie, and Martin need us to come through for them. I don't know her, neither do you, and I'm not willing to risk their lives over hers," she spat back at him, her fingers curled into fists, and she clenched them so tight her knuckles paled.

I drew a breath, ready to defend myself, but Callahan knocked on the table in front of him and every set of ice-blue eyes turned to look at him.

"For ten years this girl has endured the absolute shit show that is her life without anyone to shoulder it with her." He turned to me, his brows narrowed and asked, "Why did you stay in the city? Why not go back to the countryside and hide away from them?"

I swallowed, and my lip trembled. "Because, even though I wasn't brave enough to fight them head-on, I hoped that if I kept surviving and taking them out one by one, someone out there would be safer because of it." I bit my lip, willing my tear ducts to block or dry up completely.

"You hoped people that you didn't even know would be safer because of your sacrifice," he said softly.

"Being bitten a few times a year isn't the same as losing your life," James said acidly.

"And yet, she doesn't know Caitlyn or my parents but she's willing to risk her life to save them. She was willing to risk that before she even knew she was the ransom," Callahan countered, the tension in the room more volatile by the second.

Rory was bristling beside me, staring at Ava and James in disbelief.

"Have either of you ever had someone die on top of you when you've just been attacked and bitten?" Rory asked them. When neither spoke, he raised his brow and said flatly, "Didn't think so. The fact that she went through that as a teenager, stuck it out all these years without ending up in a mental hospital, is a bloody miracle. I think it shows the strength of her character."

"Agreed," Isla said fiercely. She sat straighter in her seat, piercing James with such defiance, the room seemed to take a breath as she launched into the debate.

"She deserves a chance. She cares about people. She's denied herself for ten years to protect her secret —technically our secret as well. If the world knew about her or vampires, it wouldn't be long before they found out about us too. She has every right to be bitter, angry, and hateful. She could have worked for her parents, earned a hell of a lot of money and stayed far away from the city, but she didn't! Because she wanted to do something meaningful with her life. I think we should trust her to help us," she said resolutely. She dipped her head towards me, acknowledging the gratitude rippling across my face.

Rory sat forward, his face trained on Ava with a challenge in his eyes.

"Isla's right. Her sacrifice has allowed us to stay hidden. What you're suggesting—this is not the kind of people that we are. We don't just condemn people to die when there might be another option. Why are you so against trying? At the very least, all of us should be willing to try and get more information out of a vampire."

The silence was heavy. Ava stared back at Rory, her eyes alight with emotion, though the rest of her face remained serene. Then she nodded ever so slightly and turned to look at Callahan, her body tensed as she spoke.

"I have a friend that went through a similar experience. A lot of people died. Including the one like Olivia. I don't want that to happen to us."

Around the room, mouths hung open. Callahan inhaled sharply, and his hands balled into fists.

Fletcher stared at her in disbelief. "You didn't think to tell us that this has happened before?"

She stared at the table, unwilling to meet his eye. "A rescue mission was attempted. The minute they started fighting, the parents were killed, the children left for dead. Their son was murdered trying to save them, along with a friend who was helping him. So forgive me, but I don't want to see history repeated."

I sat forward, hiding my face behind my hands, dread spreading through my veins as I considered the implications. Everything else turned to background noise as I tried to comprehend it—the confirmation of the thing I'd always wondered. There had been someone else out there like me. Another soul on this earth who understood the horrors of having this blood—and they were gone. Murdered before I ever had the chance to meet them. But if there had been one other like me, that left the possibility that there could be more. I couldn't die. I couldn't let them win. Not again.

Around me, the argument had escalated, Callahan stood up abruptly, his chair scraping across the tiles, setting my teeth on edge.

"Then we learn from their mistakes; we do things differently," he bit out.

"James, the lad's twenty-seven. He's not a child anymore. He runs the farm, for Pete's sake. You have to give him a chance.

They're our friends, yes, but they're his flesh and blood. I think he gets the final say in this. And if that involves getting whatever information they can from a vampire, we need to let 'em try." Stephen folded his arms and stared back down the table at James, the two of them locked in a battle of wills. Isla cast a proud glance at her dad, and Maddie sat nodding her head in silent support.

After a moment of tense silence, Ava laid a hand on James' forearm. "We've said our piece."

They both rose from their seats. James leaned on the table, glaring at Callahan. "Let's see if you can even accomplish this tonight, and then we'll discuss what happens after."

He didn't wait for a response, they both made a swift exit. Maddie and Stephen followed shortly after, muttering quiet goodbyes.

Rory sat forward and glanced around the table. "It must be someone else's turn to make a bloody coffee," he declared, instantly easing the tension lingering in the room.

Relishing the prospect of doing something normal, I stood up quickly. "I'll make it." I grabbed his mug and started collecting the others before anyone could argue.

Finn sat staring at the table deep in thought, and I couldn't help but wonder if he agreed with Ava and James—he hadn't spoken the entirety of the meeting.

I filled the kettle, and Callahan appeared at my side as I rinsed the cups.

We stood shoulder to shoulder in amiable silence, leaning against the kitchen island while we waited for the kettle to boil. I eyed Finn across the room. "He's not said a word the whole time. Is he okay?"

Callahan glanced over and then leaned in to whisper in my ear, "He'll be fine. He hates arguing, and he struggles to get words out in situations like that. Always has. He started doing MMA when he was about nine to give him some confidence…and so he could stand a chance against us."

"What's MMA?" I whispered.

His lips curved into a smile and he leaned in again "Mixed Martial Arts."

Noted. Finn was not someone to cross. "Thank you for not trading me the minute you found me. And for defending me."

He gave me an incredulous look and shook his head. "You give me far too much credit. I had to be sure you were the one they wanted. Nothing was adding up when I met you, and I couldn't understand how you could ever be a threat to them. It's hardly something to be thankful for," he said with a sigh. "I keep hoping I'm gonna wake up and this is all just a shitty nightmare."

"You're not the only one."

He rubbed his hands over his face, his eyes deeply shadowed with stress and exhaustion. It was going to be a long day for him.

I stirred our coffees. The bitter scent invigorated my senses, already clearing my mind for the critical hours ahead. "Come on, we've got an abduction to plan. If you're lucky, I might agree to be your nap buddy later so that you don't fall asleep mid-interrogation."

He chuckled briefly in response, some of the tension easing from his face. Hopefully, we could all learn to trust each other to get this done.

14

DAIRY MILK CHOCOLATE

The six of us spent an hour firming up the details of our plan. With little experience of vampires beyond what we'd speculated, the group bowed to my expertise. The plan would require an enormous amount of trust on their part, and trust was a fickle thing for us all, but I wouldn't betray them so long as they gave me a chance. I wanted answers just as much as they did, and we'd agreed I could watch the interrogation via video call. I had specified questions that I wanted them to ask on my behalf, aware that the more invested and helpful I was now, the greater the chance this could be a success. The greater the chance that all of us would come out of this alive.

Rory and Finn left us soon after the plans were firmed up to keep on top of work on the farm, and Isla had taken the car back to the city to collect all their belongings from the B&B, making the most of daylight hours. The three of us remaining pulled together what was needed to accomplish our plan. Well, Callahan and Fletcher were. I was just tagging along.

Birds chortled and called their happy songs as we trudged wearily down the drive towards a brick outhouse.

The building was neatly swept, clean, and tidy but rustic with exposed brick walls. One side contained a long stainless steel worktable and an L-shaped kitchen area with an industrial sink, stainless steel cupboards, a deep chest freezer, and an industrial-sized fridge. The other side was lined with storage racks housing various tools, buckets, and farming equipment. I hovered in the doorway and watched them flit around locating various supplies that they piled on the worktable: thick white cable ties, rope, pliers, a set of knives, and a tarp sheet. They retrieved a box of medical supplies from the fridge and another from a cupboard and then deliberated over a set of instructions.

They were planning to use a sedative meant for cattle, and they were trying to decide on an appropriate dose that wouldn't kill our future hostage. I edged around the room and found myself in front of the freezer. Curiosity had me clutching the handle and tugging it upwards, my skin prickling.

"Do you trust us?" Callahan's voice startled me, and I whirled to find him standing two feet away. His eyes were soft, his face relaxed as he waited for my answer.

"I wasn't looking for bodies, I swear." My voice came out more strained than I'd intended, and his eyes flickered to where my hand still rested on the freezer lid. His lips twitched into the beginnings of a smile.

"Technically there are body parts in there," he said wryly, "but they're from sheep and cows. There's cow's blood in the fridge in the steel canisters, but I wouldn't recommend it."

He held up a syringe sealed in a sterile packet. "We want to try injecting our hostage with your blood when we bring it back here later. We thought it would be useful to see if we can get rid of it without it having to bite you." He winced and continued reluctantly. "We'll need to collect enough blood to coat a knife and fill a syringe. We don't have a plan for a rescue yet but, if the poison in your blood works when it enters their bloodstream without them having to ingest it, then we could arm ourselves with your blood."

I nodded. "I've always wondered that. I hope it works; the last thing we need is a dead body to dispose of as well. And…it would be nice to not feel so sick."

"I bet. I've only ever taken blood from a cow so I don't trust myself not to hurt you. But Rory has all the training so he'll be the one to do it." My brows quirked as he continued. "We've always avoided doctors where we can. We have insurance—it's not that we can't afford it, we'd just rather stay under the radar. Rory finds it all really interesting, he wanted to be a paramedic when he was younger."

He stared at the floor for a moment but then his gaze found mine, those sharp eyes were hard to look away from, and my heart picked up a more intense beat.

"Do you avoid doctors?" he asked after a moment. I leaned against the work table, my hands stuffed in my pockets to keep me from fidgeting under the intensity of his stare.

"I guess I do. Since living in cities, I've just learned to live with whatever injuries I've had, but more because it's hard to explain how I got them. But I do have yearly check-ups. With my parents' position, they have to have high-level level insurance coverage, which involves a pretty invasive check-up each year to make sure they're competent. They do so much flying, and the position is so high stress, it's apparently necessary so I've always been included in that." Thankfully the blood tests I'd had over the years had never been flagged. I'd come to the conclusion that the tests they ran would be looking for specific indicators rather than anomalies.

Fletcher had picked up a wooden chair from the far corner of the workshop, he stopped and pointed at me. "You're not allowed near the cow shed. We don't want your scent anywhere near it, so you might as well go to the house." He gave Callahan a pointed look and then was gone.

"That was Fletcher's way of saying I look like shit and need to try and get some sleep as we'll be up most of the night." Callahan picked up the cable ties and syringes. I was drawn once more to the fridge, and I opened the door. There were two metal canisters on the bottom shelf, each holding about a litre of liquid. Surprisingly, they didn't unnerve me. I sighed, not quite sure what to make of my lack of revulsion. I closed the door, my curiosity satisfied.

When I turned to leave, Callahan was slouched against the door frame. His head leaned back against it, and his eyes were closed. I playfully nudged him as I passed, hoping it would alleviate some of the tension. I wasn't judging him or repulsed by the sight of those canisters, and I didn't want him to feel self-conscious. He gave a tight smile, and we walked back to the house shoulder to shoulder.

As we deposited our shoes on the porch I asked him casually, "So, am I providing nap time assistance or is someone going to be babysitting *me* in your absence?"

He chewed on his lip, mulling over his options and then cleared his throat.

"I'd rather you stayed with me in the house," he said delicately. "It's not that I don't trust the others but…Ava and James surprised me with their reaction. I get it, but…I told you I'd give you a chance, and if they decided to go over my head…" There was no undoing that.

I nodded. "Lead the way."

We headed up to his room. I was surprised to find it relatively tidy and his bed made. I was unsurprised to find that it was an enormous *oak-framed* bed that dominated the room. They really liked their oak. The wall behind it was painted navy blue and above his bed was a large print of a smooth chestnut-coloured cow within a simple bronze frame.

"Can't get enough of these guys, huh?"

He cocked his head and raised an eyebrow. "That's my favourite cow, and it was a gift."

"Do the other cows get jealous?"

"You tell me—does it make you jealous?"

When I gasped sarcastically, his stern face fractured into a smile. He edged around me and dragged the curtains closed. The room fell into shadowy tones, not quite dark but an in-between that felt strangely intimate. He emptied his pockets onto the bedside table and sank onto the bed with a slow exhale. I sat on the edge and swung my legs up, settling on my back and trying to master an air of nonchalance.

"So what's its name?" I asked, to break the increasingly awkward silence.

He smirked. "*Her* name…was Dairy."

"You named your cow Dairy?" I sniggered.

He turned his head to glare at me. "I was eight! And I did it so that when she had her first calf and we milked her, if I had a hot chocolate I could say it was Dairy milk chocolate. I thought I was an absolute genius."

I chuckled, shifting onto my side. "So *did you* have Dairy milk chocolate?"

"I did! And it was fucking delicious. I actually think there is a photo of me drinking it in the kitchen," he added with a wry smile. He rolled onto his side, still smiling. "Did you have any pets growing up?"

I laughed, shaking my head. "I barely had any friends growing up, let alone pets! I always wanted a pet—even if it was just a rabbit, but because we travelled a lot when I was little, I wasn't allowed.

"When I was about six, I started collecting cuddly toys. I didn't go anywhere without at least one. That was as close to a pet as I got. My favourite was a fluffy tiger I called Rajah. I left him on the plane once, travelling back from New York. Fortunately, I realised pretty quickly and we hadn't long got off the flight. Of course, my mum was ready to leave Rajah to teach me to look after my things better, but I was so hysterical, Dad couldn't handle the meltdown and went back. He had to fight through all the passengers and argue with the attendants to get onto the plane to search for him—they almost didn't let him, but he managed it. I think Rajah and a few others are still in my room at my parent's house." I met Callahan's eye, his smile faded to a frown.

"Do you have any good memories of your mum?"

"If ever I had a cold, which was rare as I didn't really mix with enough people to catch one, that was when she was the most attentive and concerned. Sometimes I'd try to fake being ill just to get her attention but she rarely fell for it." I saw his expression and tutted. "Don't look at me like that. It is what it is; life was easy before the attack. I'd sell my kidney to go back to that part of my life."

"Why fourteen? Why not all the times you travelled? Surely you must have come across a vampire before then if you were travelling to places like New York?"

My cheeks flushed scarlet at his question, and I wondered which of us would be more embarrassed when I told him.

"That first attack…happened when I started my first period."

He winced, and a hiss escaped through his teeth. "That's why you left the disco? You told Rory you had to go to the shop?" He swore viscously under his breath when I nodded, secretly impressed with his attention to detail. Nothing got past him. "How do you deal with that now?" His hand instinctively slid towards me but he seemed to realise and pulled it back, balling it into a fist.

"I don't. I'm on a pill that stops them," I said dolefully. His stare was so intense, I forced myself to look away and rolled onto my back.

"I didn't mean to make you uncomfortable," he murmured.

I stared at the ceiling and smiled. "It's just strange, being able to tell the truth. I'm still adjusting. And you're supposed to be getting some sleep." When I looked back, he was pulling the longer lengths of his hair through his fingers.

"Does it not bother you? Lying all the time?"

I tried to swallow down the lump that stuck in my throat. "I don't see it as a black-and-white construct, I learnt that very quickly when I was fourteen. The morning after the attack, I woke up to find a psychologist in my living room. God knows what would have happened to me if I'd told her the truth. I told her that I'd been in shock, that I had blacked out, but that I'd been so scared of getting into trouble about the 'hickey' on my neck and being where I shouldn't have—the lies just tumbled out before I knew what I was saying. I was punished, but it felt a hell of a lot safer than the alternative. Don't you ever lie?"

"You got punished after being attacked? Surely that was punishment enough?" His tone was biting, and his mouth hung open as he waited for my response.

"I was never allowed to see or speak to my friend Penny again, and my phone was taken away, all her details deleted before I got it back. Oh, and shortly after, we moved house."

He stared at me, anger simmering in his eyes. "I'm not sure I could be in the same room as them without losing my shit," he said with quiet disgust.

"Oh, I find lots of subtle ways to aggravate them. Well, my mum anyway. But you never answered my question. Surely you've had to lie in relationships?"

He didn't look at me as he answered. "I do my best not to. I don't like being lied to. No one's ever asked me if I drink blood, and I doubt they ever would, which I know is an omission of truth, but I've never felt like I've needed to address it before. You're the only person who's outright asked me if I'm not human. Which I am."

I fiddled with the strings on my hoodie. "So, in all your past relationships, you never felt like you should tell them those deepest parts of you? How long did you think you could keep that going?"

He turned to look at me, one brow raised incredulously. "How many relationships do you think I've had? And yes, things never got serious enough that it was an issue."

"More of a casual dater, huh?" I teased.

He gave me an irritated look and sighed heavily. "No, unfortunately, Fletcher was right. I have a terrible track record of falling for the wrong sort."

"And what sort is the wrong sort?"

"You're doing a terrible job of helping me sleep." He held out his hand and formed a circle with his thumb and finger. "Zero stars. Do not recommend."

I grinned mischievously. "Come on, what sort is the wrong sort?"

He rolled his eyes and huffed. "The shallow, flirtatious sort that didn't like getting their precious heels dirty."

"So, basically they wanted you for arm candy? And...other things you might be good at?"

His mouth fell open momentarily, and if the room wasn't in shadow, I wondered if I'd have seen his cheeks in full flush. "Well, this is definitely not conducive to sleeping."

"I'm assuming neither were you," I said with a smirk.

He slid both arms under his pillow, partially hiding his face and ignoring my comment. There was barely a foot between us now.

"I don't regret protecting myself, but I am sorry for lying to you," I admitted. Knowing that it offended him so much had been gnawing at me, and despite the situation, I still found myself wanting his respect and his trust.

"Do I even want to know how many things you've lied about since I met you?"

I tutted. "It's not that many things!"

He lifted his head, one eyebrow arched high as he appraised me. "You said you ran from the bar because you thought I was going to murder you, when the truth was, you expected to murder me!"

"Oh, let's not pull at that thread." I took a deep breath, embracing being able to share the full truth. To let some of the walls crumble.

"No, the lie that I'm genuinely sorry for is that…that when I hit that vamp with my car, I was going through a stupid vigilante stage, and I actually cut my arm deliberately because I was freaking out about them biting my neck—"

"Did you just say vigilante?"

"I did…but it was pathetic and didn't last long. After that night I went into hiding. It utterly terrified me. I fell behind at university. I would get hysterical anytime someone touched my neck, and I was a fucking mess. So, now you know the truth."

He was silent for so long I wondered if he'd drifted to sleep, but then he cleared his throat. "Thank you, but I wasn't trying to make you feel bad—I get that it's very different for you." After a pause, he added, "I'm sorry, I probably made you uncomfortable at the B&B in the bathroom."

"You did. But to be honest, the first time you caught my scent, I still thought you might bite me and die, so I wouldn't feel too bad about it. If anything—*I feel bad* for misjudging you."

His breath whooshed out. "Wow. That is brutal!"

"Too much truth?"

He snorted a laugh but didn't respond. His eyes were closed, and despite my unfiltered revelation, he looked peaceful.

"Callahan?" I whispered. He grunted in reply but stayed still. "Am I allowed to leave your room? While you're sleeping?"

"To go where?" he said sleepily.

"The kitchen—to make a drink?"

"Oh, sure. Help yourself. Just promise you'll stay in the house okay?"

"I'm pretty sure we're locked in, but yeah, I promise. Sleep well," I whispered.

He hummed a response, and after a few minutes, his breathing grew deeper. I lay there in the dim light of his room, listening to the sound of his steady breaths and the chirping birds outside his window, and my breathing gradually steadied. The tension in my body started to release, and very slowly, I extracted myself from the bed and tiptoed out of his room. It scared me how much I wanted to stay, which was precisely why I made myself leave.

15

TRUST ME

I made my way downstairs, keeping my steps light to avoid creaking floorboards, and headed to the kitchen. I flicked the kettle on and briefly scanned the photographs dotted around the room until I found what I was looking for. Sure enough, sat on the far windowsill, was the picture of Callahan holding out a mug topped with whipped cream and grinning ear to ear. A chocolatey moustache framed his lips, cream tipped his nose, and the sheer joy in his expression was both captivating and contagious. I found myself smiling fondly back at this little snippet of his memories. The smile still held as I made my coffee and considered if I'd get to see one of those infectious grins when he was reunited with his family. The thought was warming and perhaps it was a little naive, but I hoped it wouldn't be the last we saw of each other.

With a coffee in hand, I crossed the hall to the sitting room, the flagstones cold on my feet. The room was vast, spanning the entire width of the house, but despite its grandeur, it had a cosy atmosphere. The large inglenook fireplace in the centre of the room was rustic and homely. The wood burner within was radiating considerable heat even though the flames were gradually dying down. It had been a while since Finn lit it, and likely no one had tended to it since. Logs were neatly stacked on custom shelves on either side of the burner, and I grabbed one, cautiously opened the door and dropped the wood onto the dying flames.

Sparks floated out as I shut the burner door, winking out before they settled and dissolved into an ashy smudge on the flagstone hearth. In front of the fire, was a U-shaped formation of sofas, blankets folded and draped over the ends of each one, warm and inviting. I could imagine a family gathered around the coffee table playing board games, or quiet Sunday evenings where they each curled up with a good book, content to just be together. At the back corner of the room was a TV and a worn leather sofa for viewing. I liked that the TV came secondary to the company. I'd grown up with very limited time watching TV, and it was one of the few rules my parents instilled that I was grateful for. It always astounded me how obsessed my class was with technology, and it was hard to get children excited by books when TV and game consoles beckoned.

To the right of the fireplace stood a large oak sideboard, adorned with an impressive array of photo frames. I was drawn there, filled with anticipation for what stories they would tell, and there were many. Pictures of a little Callahan stroking a cow with a big grin stretched across his face. One of him giving a great big bear hug to a girl I assumed was his sister and planting a kiss on her cheek—smushing her face against his. She was smiling, and her eyes were tightly shut—delightedly happy. There was one of him, Isla and Fletcher sitting in a row on a paddock fence, Isla in the middle. A group photo with six pre-teens. Fletcher, Callahan, and Isla were at the back of the group, and in front of them was Callahan's sister. She was posed with plenty of attitude, folded arms and a pouty face—far younger than the rest. Rory and Finn were on either side of her looking mischievous.

Another frame contained a teenage Callahan on a tractor; he was wearing shades and grinning, his hand flung out in a rock and roll sign. In the centre was a family picture with his parents; they were in a paddock, the cows dotted behind them unawares. His mum's arms were draped affectionately over Callahan's shoulders where he stood in front of her. His sister was clinging to their dad's leg, and he looked immensely proud. They all had the same bewitching eyes. Eyes that I realised I no longer hated.

A silent tear streaked down my face. These happy memories didn't exist in my house. Any images my parents had framed were formal. Even the few holiday photos we had were heavily staged. Cold and forced. They never displayed love, not like these. And there were so many of them. I knew I would probably find them proudly displayed in every room—little snippets of their stories, frozen in time. It made me excited to meet them in person. The images portrayed them as warm, inviting, and loving—the kind of family I would dream of having.

I curled up on one of the sofas, drawing my knees up to my chest. I thought I would be able to relax, but despite the room's cosiness, the quiet felt suffocating; the space around me seemed to hold its breath waiting for its family to return. My thoughts were complicated and unsettling, and when I could stand the silence no longer, I slunk back to the kitchen, needing something physical to do. I conjured up enough ingredients to cook a half-decent curry and found solace in the rhythmic motions of preparing a meal. When I'd chopped all the meat and vegetables and organised all the spices, I left them to sit, not willing to disturb Callahan's sleep even with the smell of cooking.

∽

I stood at the patio doors staring out across the pastureland. It was soothing compared to the view from my apartment of crowded streets and never-ending tarmac. I'd loved the city when I first arrived, but lately, it was grating on me.

"Well, you've been busy!"

I leapt back from the door with a quiet shriek, startled by Callahan's voice when I hadn't heard him approach or even felt the warning prickle on my skin. He was stood by the breakfast bar, hands in pockets and a bemused smile on his face.

"Sorry. I didn't mean to make you jump. Again."

I shook my head and made my way to the cooker, the click-click-click of the gas ignition the only sound echoing throughout the room. I was starving, all I'd eaten beyond a couple of bites of my meagre breakfast was biscuits while we planned, and I doubted Callahan had eaten a decent meal in days.

"Thank you," he said. "I have to be honest, when I woke up and you were gone, I half expected to find an empty house, not you cooking us dinner."

I glanced at him as I grabbed freshly chopped garlic and ginger and scraped it into the pan. He looked genuinely humbled. He reached for the spoon and started stirring, making sure it didn't burn.

"You assume I'm sharing?" I said, grinning slyly. I danced around him and grabbed the chicken, adding it to the pan as he continued to stir.

"So you're a thief and a liar?" he teased. "But if you could eat all this by yourself, I'd be seriously impressed."

His eyes roved pointedly up and down my body, bringing a flare of heat to my cheeks. I turned away, hoping he wouldn't notice, and washed my hands, hiding behind my curtain of hair and trying to think of anything other than how much I liked those eyes on my body.

Tapping the spoon on the side of the pan he set it aside and hoisted himself up onto the breakfast bar. He looked the calmest I'd seen him. Like this moment could be any other normal day when nothing was threatening his family or my life. I picked the spoon back up and stirred absentmindedly, the motion and aroma soothing away some of my tension.

"I found the picture of you and your Dairy milk chocolate," I said, eager to keep the silence at bay. "It's very cute."

He sighed wistfully. "Maybe I can show you around the farm sometime. Make you a hot chocolate with proper organic healthy milk. Not the shite you probably get in the supermarket full of God knows what."

"I'd like that," I said over my shoulder. Especially when it sounded like he didn't plan to hand me over to murderers. I popped the lid on the pan and turned to face him. His eyes flickered over me and then narrowed.

"What? What's that look for?"

Before I could dismiss him, Isla and Fletcher appeared, both appraising the casual scene in front of them with conflicted expressions.

"Your stuff is in the hallway," Isla told Callahan. "The room is checked out so you don't need to worry about it." Callahan thanked her, sliding off the island and leaning on the counter next to me. She investigated the simmering pan. "Damn this smells good, I'm assuming this is your cooking, Olivia? "

Callahan threw her a wounded expression as I nodded. "I figured it would be a long night and we needed something decent in our bellies. And I had nothing better to do," I added dryly.

She gave an appreciative smile and glanced back at Fletcher where he hovered by the door, he seemed to read something in her expression and cleared his throat.

"Finn will be here in a moment. I need to go over a couple of things with you," he said pointedly to Callahan.

So Finn would be my babysitter. With his martial arts experience, I supposed he was probably the most qualified, despite his angelic appearance. I wondered if Fletcher would be advocating for his parents or if he still disagreed with their opinions. Regardless, I would continue to endear myself to all of them, to make it difficult for them to betray me. Though, in truth, I wanted them to like me legitimately—not be manipulated to do so.

As soon as Finn arrived, Fletcher and Callahan disappeared. Finn looked filthy and dishevelled and quickly peeled off his scruffy fleece, dumping it in the hall and then scrubbing his hands, arms and even his face in the sink. Isla made him a coffee while he cleaned up but there was little in the way of conversation. When they joined me at the table Finn seemed more relaxed, and he gave me one of his warm smiles as he sat down.

"Are the cows behaving?" I asked him, trying to avoid more awkward silence, at the very least it made him smile as he sipped his coffee.

"Mostly. It's the chickens that are the mardy ones."

"I believe you. So, have you named any cows, or do you try not to get attached?"

He pushed his fingers through his hair to tame it and offered me a wry smile. "Tilly told you about Dairy then? I bet he didn't tell you how much he balled his eyes out when she died," he said with a mischievous grin. "But yes, I do name them." He nudged his sister. "Even Isla has named a few. The cows we breed from we know will likely be around a good while, so they tend to be the ones that get named."

I nodded. I knew little about farming beyond all the negative media coverage. "Believe it or not, I've had kids in my class that live in the city centre and have never actually seen a living cow."

His eyebrows quirked. "I shouldn't be surprised. I would bet money some of Tilly's ex-girlfriends hadn't ever been around animals the way they acted." He glanced at Isla and shook his head. Callahan's past lovers seemed to be a bone of contention for all of them.

"How did he end up with these people?" I asked bewildered. Callahan was astute enough to figure me out, so it seemed odd that he would make such poor choices repeatedly, especially when he came across as a genuinely nice guy.

Finn scoffed. "Because he's a sucker for a pretty face, that's why. He'd get approached in clubs and get caught up in all the attention they'd give him. Which is fine if you're gonna bed someone and leave it at that, but Tilly doesn't do things half-arsed. He goes all in and then regrets it later."

Isla slapped him on the arm, defending her absent friend, and turned to me with a fierce look in her eyes. "He learnt his lesson, believe me. I don't think he's been on a date for over a year. I think he genuinely thought the last one was different, and it put him off when it all crashed and burned."

I thought back to our brief conversation about Noah—the 'picture-frame-guy' he'd called him—and I wondered if he'd been surprised that I wasn't too shallow to date someone who wasn't a muscled poster boy. Hopefully, his opinion of me was improving. It was unnerving that I even cared so much. It wasn't like me to willingly let people get close enough to matter. *These weren't just any people though.*

I pushed my chair back and went to monitor the food, busying myself with clearing up. Isla joined me after a while, pulling out cutlery and plates and readying the table. We worked in comfortable silence, preoccupied with thoughts of what was to come.

She would be staying behind—Fletcher was unwilling to take the risk of her being with us in the city should things go wrong. Rory and Finn were also staying, as too many of us would likely complicate things and they would be responsible for me while the interrogation happened.

The front door slammed and I heard footsteps dashing up the stairs and a door slamming on the first floor. Fletcher stalked into the kitchen and gave Isla a subtle nod before heading to the sink to wash his hands.

She helped me portion out the food and just as we were setting things on the table Callahan emerged and swiftly headed for a seat. He kept his head down, avoiding all eye contact, and he looked decidedly pale.

I grabbed a loaded dinner plate and pointedly took it to him. As I placed it in front of him, I leaned in close.

"It's going to be fine," I whispered.

He stared at me in surprise, and as I turned to walk away, I caught a hint of peppermint fragrance on his breath. When I glanced back at him, he was staring at his plate like it was Everest. I wondered if I'd mistaken his demeanour for something other than fear of what might happen when he had to let me out of his sight. Fletcher had taken him out to get blood. It made sense given he'd been in the city prior without access and he'd explained how much he hated drinking it.

Fletcher was not so affected. "Thanks for this. I'm supposed to let you know that Rory is having dinner at home. Maddie had already made him food, and he didn't want to upset her."

I nodded, a little stunned at his politeness and his comment seemed to pull Callahan from his quiet bubble of shame and disgust.

He took a bite, his eyebrow twitching up. "It's really good thank you," he piped up, giving me a fleeting smile from across the table.

Finn was the one to drive the conversation forward. He and Fletcher asked me endless questions about my experiences with the vampires and about my research. When Isla could get a word in, she asked more lighthearted questions about my love of cooking and reading, and by the time we'd finished eating and clearing up Callahan was in a slightly better mood.

As the others headed for the comfort of the living room, he caught my wrist and beckoned for me to stay. I leaned against the edge of the breakfast bar waiting for him to speak. When he was certain the others were out of earshot, he stepped closer, his hands bracing on either side of me as he eyed me intently.

"Are you planning to run?" There was a rough edge to his voice, and underneath his calm but intense façade, I suspected he was filled with sheer terror.

"I should run," I whispered, not taking my eyes from his for a second. "But I won't. You can trust me to do this."

"Do you trust me?" he asked quietly, his eerily bright eyes searching for any hint of deception and piercing right through to my soul.

Despite the uncertainty of everything we had to face, my lips curved into a devious smile. "I shouldn't. But against my better judgement, yes—I do."

16

GET READY

When 11 p.m. rolled around there was a collective sigh as our stilted conversation and fretful pacing was finally over. We all stood, said our goodbyes to Isla, Finn, and Rory, and made our way to Callahan's car.

On the drive into the city, my feet and hands tapped constantly, earning me several concerned glances from Callahan.

"Can you save your energy for the vampire?" Fletcher had snarked from the back, agitated by the repetitive sound. Eventually, he convinced Callahan to give him control of the music, and the car was filled with enough drum and bass to drown me out. Nerves aside, I felt strangely excited to be doing something purposeful. With the backing of Callahan and Fletcher, it was far less terrifying.

Soon enough, we pulled into the basement car park of a shopping mall on the outskirts of the city centre. There were no streams of people this far out, and it was now blessedly quiet. We headed to a handful of spaces that seemed to be out of CCTV range and easy enough for me to run back to as I lured our prey.

I waited in the car until Callahan lowered the back seats in the Dacia, and then got out once he was ready.

He handed me his phone and an earbud, his eyes wide with fear. "This will be connected to Fletcher's phone, you need to stay on the line at all times."

I nodded, sliding it into the pocket of my yoga pants and popping the earbud snuggly in my ear. "I'll be back shortly," I told him and set out to familiarise myself with the car park layout. I reached the entrance and jogged back to the car, they were both perched on the bonnet waiting expectantly. Both of them were tight-lipped and tense.

Satisfied I would know the route, I turned back and briskly walked to the entrance again. I walked further out and waited for the telltale signs to swarm my body, but there were only nervous jitters. I was closer to the bus station, which was now mostly empty and quiet. A set of flats towered over the station. Businesses on the ground and first floor and residential flats on the floors above. Most had their curtains drawn, a few lights remained on, but most were dark, the occupants tucked away in bed, unaware of the danger nearby.

I saw a flicker of red in my peripheral, and noticed a camera hidden in an alcove and turned back to distance myself from it. I paced down to the corner of the flats and headed up the other street towards shops, but it was mostly empty, only a few people in the distance. I didn't stay long before returning to the dark mouth of the car park. If a vamp came from the bus station side it would cut me off before I reached the entrance and ruin everything.

I loitered by the front of the building, keeping to the shadows and leaning against the black bricks that helped keep me concealed. I smirked at the irony of the situation. Usually, I hated breezy days, but tonight would have been the perfect time to utilise a light wind to carry my scent, and yet the air was impossibly still.

"Typical," I muttered under my breath.

"Are you okay?"

I flinched, forgetting that Callahan was still in my ear and had muted his mic so he didn't distract me while he was talking to Fletcher.

"I'm fine," I told him, keeping my voice low. "There's nothing here yet. I'll yell when there is."

The line went quiet again, and I edged away from the wall. I was getting impatient. I didn't want the trip to be a waste—we needed this. I needed this.

I headed towards the bus station entrance which was tucked away behind the car park. Running past it was an alley leading parallel to the shopping centre and out onto a busy main street behind. I hurried through it and stood for a moment, scanning the area, a few cars passed by, but there was not a being in sight anywhere else. Frustrated, I spun on my heels and headed back again. I slowed by the bus station gates and peered in, but it was so heavily watched by CCTV, it was hardly the place for crime to be rampant, and of course, my working theory was that vampires gravitated to criminal activity. Fuck. The one time I was actually eager to lure one, and they were nowhere to be seen. I kicked the wall childishly and decided to try closer to the shops.

I jogged up to the end of the street, my breaths slow and even. I stopped and let my heart rate recover, paying attention to my skin, and every slight emotion that I felt. As I turned to jog back, the hairs on my neck raised, and I stopped, scanning up ahead and then behind for movement, praying it wasn't at the bus station. Goosebumps raised along my arms, so I set off at a brisk pace but still walked, scanning all around to figure out where it was but finding nothing in the shadows. As the nausea crept in I sprang into a leisurely run, my focus on the entrance ahead. As I reached the connecting corner of the streets I saw movement in the alley by the station entrance.

"Fuck. Get ready," I yelled and sprinted hard.

It reached the edge of the car park just as I slowed to squeeze through the barrier, almost tripping in my haste to beat it through.

It was sprinting almost beside me, and I gulped down as much air as my lungs could hold and urged my legs faster and faster, cutting across it to take the first turn back to the car, I refused to look back, all my focus was on running as hard and fast as I could to the next turning.

I could hear its footsteps pounding the tarmac behind me—I needed to be faster. The next turn was a sharp right and sloped down to the lower level. I waited until I was halfway across to turn, hoping the vamp would slow to avoid overshooting, and bore right again onto the last straight, pushing my body to the absolute maximum.

I could see the car now. The back doors were open and Fletcher was standing against the wall waiting. I murmured a plea to God as I slowed my pace and then hurtled into the back of the car, crawling frantically across the seats, Callahan was ready waiting in the front with the syringe.

As expected, the vampire lunged through the car door after me only to find itself restrained by Fletcher. In the momentary confusion that passed across its face, Callahan plunged the syringe into its neck, and I scooted out the other door, slamming it shut behind me.

The vamp was no longer my problem, and I bent over, forcing the air back into my burning lungs and hoping the running didn't cause me to vomit. I walked to the front of the car, stretching my legs and trying to calm the pounding in my chest and ears. I was hot, pure adrenaline ripping through my body, making my thoughts a jumbled mess as I tried to focus on what was happening.

Callahan and Fletcher were watching through the back passenger window. There was some movement in the car but the sedative was taking rapid effect. I leaned on the bonnet, appreciating the cold metal under my sweaty palms, a private smile creeping onto my face as I realised we had actually done it. Now we just needed it to stay alive and for the sedative to reset whatever spell I put them under.

I let out a long shaky breath and peered over my shoulder. They had opened the door and they were rolling it's body back towards the boot so the seats could come back up. We'd decided it was less suspicious if the vamp got itself in the car, rather than risk Callahan and Fletcher being witnessed carrying and dumping a body into the boot.

Movement caught my attention, and I turned to see a second vamp stalking towards the car. We weren't prepared to handle two vamps back at the farm and on instinct, I pushed myself up, legs wobbling like a newborn foal as I jogged away from the car.

Callahan shouted my name, and Fletcher shouted at Callahan, but I ignored them. Its footsteps were loud and assertive behind me, and as I turned around I was unceremoniously shoved, staggering back until I hit the cold brick. Its cold fingers gripped my throat, digging into my skin, and I clawed at its hands, desperate to dislodge them and take a breath. The pressure was mounting in my head, the pain excruciating and my vision began to swim. There was a slight reprieve when the vampire's teeth tore into the delicate skin on my neck, forcing it to loosen its grip. My head throbbed, my chest burned with the effort of trying to breathe and then finally air rushed painfully and fully into my lungs when Callahan jerked the vampire away, sending it flailing to the ground as it began to choke.

The world spun, and my legs disappeared from under me. I expected to feel the jarring bite of concrete on my knees but a heartbeat later, arms grabbed me, keeping me upright, and supporting me as I wobbled forward.

Callahan's voice cut through the disorientation. "A few more steps. Just a few. You're okay. Deep breaths."

I was carefully lowered onto a seat, and when my breathing was more controlled and my vision cleared, I noted Callahan leaning in the passenger doorway. His face pure anguish as he took in the angry bruises no doubt emerging around my throat.

"We need to get out of here," he said. "Will you be okay if I start driving?"

I nodded and he tugged at the seatbelt, leaning across me to clip it in place. Before he pulled away, my shaking fingers clutched at his hoodie, and I nestled my face into his shoulder, fighting back a sob. He held me while I hurriedly pulled myself back together. With his towering height, he must have been uncomfortable, but he braced the seat with one hand and the other cradled my head with such gentleness it was hard to let go. But I had to—we had no idea how soon the sedation would wear off.

Fletcher was watching the dead body intently from the back as Callahan slid into the driver seat. Even Callahan was momentarily transfixed as the beginnings of deterioration had started stripping the flesh from its face.

"Well that's fucking disturbing" Fletcher mused.

Callahan shook his head, a grimace still adorning his features, but he put the car in gear and we lurched forward, leaving the vamp to disintegrate as we raced to get out of the city.

17

REFRESHING

I sat huddled against the passenger door, hugging my knees as if that would somehow hold me together. I was cold, trembling, and struggling not to gag. I'd never been in a confined space with a vamp for such an extended period.

We were almost out of the city. Soon I could open my window and fill the car with fresh, untainted air. Its rancid smell was clogging my nostrils. Metallic, greasy, and ashy—it felt like every breath was taken through a cloud of second-hand smoke blown directly in my face. As we exited a roundabout I felt particularly peaky and swatted Callahan's arm, managing to mouth 'pullover'.

The car was barely at a stop when I threw open the door and launched myself out. I landed on my knees a few metres from the car and retched. Callahan quickly appeared at my side. He held my hair out of the way as I violently hurled up the entire contents of my stomach.

When I was certain nothing more was coming back out, I crept back to lean against the car, mortified that he'd witnessed it. The only consolation was that it was dark. He disappeared to the boot and returned with a chunk of blue paper roll and a half-filled water bottle.

"I definitely wouldn't swallow this; it's probably been in my car a couple of weeks, but you can at least rinse your mouth."

I took it gratefully and he leaned against the wheel arch while I cleaned myself up.

"I'm sorry, I'll be all right in a minute" I rasped. I tried to stand but I felt so sick I couldn't straighten and slouched back down to sit on the cold tarmac.

"Do you always throw up after they bite?"

I shook my head. "It's the smell. Making it worse. Once I can open a window, I'll be okay."

"The vampire or the smell of my car?"

"The vamp. Can't you smell it?"

He crouched down next to me. "What does it smell of?"

"Grease, metal, and—" my hand clamped over my mouth, and I tried to breathe through the queasiness, swallowing desperately to keep the bile from rising. Every breath in was laden with violent shudders. Callahan's hand rested gently on my shoulder. His thumb offered slow, reassuring strokes. I focused on the cadence of his quiet breaths, and the queasiness gradually passed, allowing me to throw out the rest of my sentence. "And breathing in smoke."

He dwelled on this for a while. "Do I have a specific…smell?"

His face was heavily shadowed, but I could see a glint of blue watching me intently. "You smell…refreshing."

"And what exactly does refreshing smell like?"

I leaned my head back against the car and remembered the shock of his scent when he'd pinned me outside the club. It felt like a week had passed since that moment. More than a week. "Like…the forest after it's rained."

Other than a surprised "oh" he was silent at my words.

I braced my arms against the car, heaved myself upright, and took a deep breath. I could do this. As I opened the door Callahan handed me his hoodie. I stuffed it against my face as I shut the door, taking long soothing breaths against the soft cotton fabric.

Callahan's rich scent did a surprisingly good job of filtering out the unbearable smell permeating the car, and as we picked up speed, I opened the window and relished the flood of fresh breathable air.

Ignoring the ache in my throat and the stiffness in my legs, I curled up and closed my eyes. I was relieved we had achieved what we needed, despite the brutal assault. I let my mind empty and focused on my now steady breaths, feeling myself drift, lulled by the motions of the car and the comfort of Callahan's hoodie.

∽

When I was gently shaken awake, we were already back at the farm, and all the car doors were open except mine. Callahan was waiting patiently beside me.

"We need to get our bloodthirsty friend down to the barn before he wakes up and smells you again."

I nodded sleepily, trying to swallow and wincing as my ravaged throat reminded me why I felt so weak.

"Can I see it first?" I rasped.

"Yeah, it's still in the boot. I'll come round and help you out, but you need to be quick." He was at my door seconds later, supporting me as I unfolded my stiff body and straightened with a shiver. I wrapped myself up in the hoodie and took a deep breath.

Fletcher was waiting by the boot, shining a torch on our oblivious hostage. I suppressed a gasp. Now that it wasn't spellbound for my blood, the vamp looked peaceful as it slept, completely unaware of its fate or what it had tried to do less than an hour ago.

"He's young," I whispered.

He was pale and scrawny with long dark lashes that matched the black wavy hair falling haphazardly around his sleeping face. Without the sneer and scowl and murderous rage, it was not so scary.

I rested my hand subconsciously against my raw, bruised

throat. It wasn't this vamp that had inflicted the damage to my body, and looking at him like this, it seemed impossible to imagine him being capable of such violence. I couldn't remember much about the other vamp, but did it look as young as this? I was anxious to know what it would be like when it woke up.

Isla appeared at my side, resting a hand on my arm. "Are you ready to go?"

I turned to follow her, my steps still a little unsteady and Callahan was quickly at my side holding out a steadying arm which I gratefully took.

When we reached Isla's front porch, she went in ahead of us to give us a moment alone. He tilted my chin up to look at the marks, pushing his hoodie aside to get a better look. His mouth formed a tight line and there was a deep crease between his brows as he took in the extent of the bruising under the porch light.

"I'm fine," I croaked.

He went rigid, his eyes filled with rage. I took that as a good sign. If he didn't like what happened to me now, he'd really be upset about whatever the vampires had planned for me.

"I'll check on you before I shower," he said resolutely, before jogging back to the car where Fletcher was leaning against the bonnet, staring up at the stars.

"About fucking time" he growled as Callahan climbed in.

His abrasiveness made me smile, and I wondered what Fletcher was like when only Isla was around.

Isla's family were waiting for us in the kitchen, sitting at a circular dining table, all nursing freshly made drinks.

Maddie, bundled in a fluffy blue dressing gown and looking every bit as harrowed and exhausted as I felt, gasped when she saw the marks on my throat.

"Maddie, get the poor lass some painkillers, looks like she's had a rough night," Stephen said.

As Maddie hurried out of the room, Rory examined me, his brows drawn together as he carefully tilted my chin up.

"Did you get strangled?" he asked quietly.

I nodded, trying not to breathe on him after my earlier vomiting ordeal.

"Did the one you brought back do this to you?"

I shook my head.

"How many vampires were there?" Finn asked, his typically angelic face taken over by an intense scowl as he eyed my neck.

I held up two fingers, my throat too sore to speak much.

Rory placed a glass of water in front of me just as Maddie came rushing back in and handed him a basket of medication. She hovered by my side looking increasingly more worried as he rifled through the contents.

"Do you have any allergies?" he asked. When I shook my head he picked out two sets of medication and pushed the tablets into my hand.

"Can I get you anything else?" Maddie asked once I'd choked down the pills.

I wanted to feel clean. I wanted to sit in the bottom of my shower at home and wash away the horror of everything I'd experienced and then crawl into bed, but there would be hours before that could happen.

"Is…is there any chance I could shower and change?" My voice was tight and gravelly, and I grabbed for the water, my hands were still trembling.

"Of course you can. Isla will take you up and get you towels," she said kindly.

"Did you leave your stuff in the farmhouse?" Isla asked.

I nodded, and she pulled her phone out and called Fletcher.

It wasn't long before there was a knock and Callahan let himself in, my rucksack slung over his shoulder. "Come on, I'll carry your stuff up."

I let him shepherd me upstairs, Isla leading the way and grabbing fresh towels which she draped over the side of the corner bath. There was an awkward pause between her and Callahan, but then she cast a brief smile my way and excused herself leaving the two of us alone.

He stood, eyeing my bruises and fidgeting with his hands. "I'm sorry I didn't get there fast enough," he said, his voice broken and gruff. I took a breath ready to brush off his apology but he cut me off. "And I'm sorry I found it hard to trust you. Thank you for not running at the first opportunity."

I dipped my head in acknowledgement, pulling his hoodie tighter around me as the trembling escalated with the effort it took to stand. His frown deepened. "Is this normal or am I making it worse?"

"It's normal. Well, worse given the strangling, but it's not you," I assured him.

"Are you okay?" he asked softly.

"No. Are you?"

He huffed a laugh and shook his head, his eyes holding mine and then darting to the floor. I took a tentative step closer and laid my hand lightly on his arm.

"We can be 'not okay' together then," I rasped.

We were, after all, two sides of the same terrible coin. He blew out a breath and closed the gap between us, his arms enveloping my shoulders and drawing me against his chest. I sank into the embrace, locking my arms around his waist and holding him tight, and after a few deep breaths, I could feel some of the tension leave his body, my trembling subsiding.

"Fletcher is going to roast me alive," he murmured against my hair. "I'm supposed to be showering right now," he added with a sigh.

Reluctantly, I released him. "Until the next bathroom rendezvous," I teased.

He left with a hint of a smile on his face, and I wasted no time getting cleaned up. I showered, scrubbed my teeth multiple times, applied copious amounts of arnica, changed into fresh clothes, and finally felt human again.

I found Isla waiting in her room. She was cross-legged, leaning against her headboard, staring intently at her phone. I glanced around her room as I tentatively perched at the end of her bed. She had a simple botanical theme, white walls, white furniture and several plants giving pops of calming colour. Some plants were trailing from wall-mounted geometric pots and others inhabited the window sill and the dressing table, and there were even larger plants on the floor that stood over a metre tall. It was peaceful, and I felt instantly at home.

"Nice room."

She dropped her phone and gave me a shy smile. "Thanks. You look a bit better. Do you still feel sick?"

"Yeah. But I'll be fine by morning."

She frowned and scooted forward to get a better look at my throat. "Has that happened before?"

"That and worse."

She grimaced. "Have you ever taken self-defence classes?"

"I did when I was younger, my parents made me, but I stopped practising, and in all honesty, it doesn't help with the vampires. If they bite me they die, so I make it easy for them. Fighting them only makes it worse. Especially if I end up bleeding in the process."

"But why did it hurt you tonight then if you didn't fight it?"

I shrugged. "Who knows? Maybe it was because I was jogging away from it to start with."

She sat back, her expression perplexed as she stared at the leaf print on her duvet cover.

"Tell me about you and Fletcher," I whispered, hoping to shift the conversation to something lighter.

She smiled coyly. "What do you want to know?"

"Why him?" I asked, genuinely curious.

She chuckled to herself, and her eyes held onto her smile; they seemed brighter and more captivating as she considered how to respond.

"He's always been the quiet brooding one, even when we were children. I think I liked his mass of dark waves," she said with a wry smile. "I suppose being surrounded by annoying blond brothers, I was naturally drawn to him because he was different. But I always liked that he's so smart, and he's always been protective of me."

"So did you not ever see Callahan as an option?" I asked cautiously.

She fixed me with her narrowed eyes but then shook her head. "No. By the time Callahan realised he liked girls, I was head over heels for Fletcher. But Callahan always seemed to go for tall, leggy girls anyway." Her eyebrow raised pointedly, but I ignored her baited comment.

"Is Fletcher a secret romantic?"

This made her laugh. "Hmmm, I wouldn't say he was romantic as such. It's all the practical things he does that show how much he cares. The way he makes sure my windscreen is clear on a frosty morning, the way he brings me coffee without being asked, the times he has come into work and volunteered when we're frantic on Mother's Day or Valentine's Day. He is passionate too." She blushed realising the implications of her words but then turned the conversation deviously full circle—asking me about Noah.

I told her how we'd met, how I'd tried to ignore his attempts to pursue me but ultimately gave in. I told her about the night we broke up and how much lonelier the city had felt since. How it had led me to go out the night I'd met Callahan.

It was incredibly liberating to open up and divulge every facet of my life to someone, even if it was physically painful to talk. As time wore on, the conversation shifted to less serious subjects, Isla doing most of the talking to preserve my throat. It made the situation that much more bittersweet. I was aching to be a part of this life, even though stumbling across Callahan could have meant forfeiting mine.

18

A FAVOUR

Two hours later the call finally came. The vamp was groggy but awake. It was secured to a chair, its head lolling from side to side, and it groaned repeatedly. Callahan had placed his phone in the pocket of his jeans, the camera lens just peeking out so that I could see what was happening. He also wore a discreet earbud so that I could relay any questions to him that he might miss.

Isla sat shoulder to shoulder with me on her bed, full of jittery nerves as we stared at the screen in my hands. There was so much hope attached to this moment.

The vampire was lit up by portable floodlights, its skin even paler against the black void of the cowshed behind it. It was more coherent now and squinting against the light. It looked panicked, struggling against the ties that bound it.

Callahan stepped forward, drawing its attention, and it stilled, anxiously licking its lips. "What do you want? Where am I?"

"You're here because I hope you can help me solve a little problem," Callahan replied. His voice was low and sinister, without any hint of fear or uncertainty.

"Oh, really? Why would I ever help you?" it sneered.

"Because I'm the one holding these. And I can either use them to cut *you* loose or cut *some* of you loose. And believe me, I'm desperate, so don't underestimate what I'm prepared to do to you."

It was silent. Its eyes flickered between whatever Callahan was holding and his face, trying to ascertain just how serious the threat was. His voice was cold, vacant, and I had no doubt he was capable of everything he promised.

"What's the last thing you remember?" Callahan asked.

The vamp flinched, its brows creased together as it frantically tried to recall what had happened. "I was walking down Cairns Street—that's the last I remember. What did you do to me?"

"It doesn't matter what I did to you. It matters what I will do to you." He paused and the vamp grimaced as Callahan stepped closer, its shoulders bunching protectively and its face contorting with fear.

"What do you want?" it pleaded.

"I'm looking for someone. An assassin"

I scoffed, forgetting Callahan could still hear me and Isla turned to glare daggers at me before muting our mic.

The vamp's eyes widened, and then it smirked. "So they finally found a mediator. What did they take from you?"

Callahan remained silent, drawing something else that had the vamp cringing in terror.

"I don't know where the assassin is. If I did, I'd be dead," it stammered.

I gasped. "Holy shit, they actually refer to me as the assassin?"

I laughed incredulously, and Isla shushed me, digging her elbow into my ribs, and she hissed at me to be quiet.

The view on the video call dipped as Callahan crouched next to the vamp and it started pleading, "No, no please no!"

We could see one of its bare feet bound to the leg of the chair. It strained unsuccessfully against the cable tie, its toes curling as the pleading became more panicked.

"Stop, stop, STOP," it shrieked. There was a pause as the vampire fought to get its ragged breaths under control. "I swear I don't know where it is. I don't even know what it looks like, none of us do. That's why they've got you involved."

"How do you know it exists if you've never seen it? Why should I waste my time with a fucking urban legend?"

"I promise you it does exist. It's killed about a third of our kind. They literally disappear, and we can't find them or reach them at all. Some of our kind started wearing trackers and we'd find their tags with a pile of their clothes. No blood. No trace of them. Just gone."

I'd wiped out a third of their kind? That gave slightly more weight to their motive for getting rid of me. It also meant the sixty-ish remaining vampires required a lot of blood to keep them alive.

Callahan stood back up, and the vamp came back into view. It was sweating profusely, still terrified and eyeing Callahan, watching every move and glancing at whatever instrument of torture he still held.

"What makes you think I can capture it, if it's killing all of you?"

It was quiet for a moment, weighing its answer, and then it released a slow breath.

"There's a rumour that it's been done before."

Beside me, Isla let out a shaky breath at the confirmation that Ava and James were being truthful.

The camera swung around as Callahan walked in a wide circle. He stopped at close quarters to the vamp, and it shrank back as much as it could while being tied to a chair.

"You're gonna have to give me more than that if you don't want to crawl out of here holding your toes in a fucking bag."

It nodded quickly in response, pledging its compliance.

"One of our elders met another vampire by chance. He was from India, and he told our elder that something had been hunting their kind, and that they'd realised the older blood drinkers in the community, the ones like you that have been around longer than us, weren't affected by the assassins' scent. They were still drawn to it—as you should be—but because you don't drink human blood, you're unaffected, so you make the perfect go-between, hence why I called you a mediator."

"What happened to that assassin?"

The vamp scoffed. "I don't know, but I imagine it was put down. Obviously."

"By who?"

Its brows knitted together in confusion.

"Who killed it? I was tasked with finding them only, and I want to make sure I understand the assignment."

"Why would I know who killed it? It didn't happen here. A lot of us want vengeance, though. I doubt they'd want you to do it. I'm lucky that my parents and brother haven't been victim to it yet, but we all want the freedom to go out during the day again. All of us. We've had no choice but to avoid going out in the day for years in case we get caught and draw attention to ourselves, and it's fucking tedious. Not that you'd understand. It's not an issue for you."

"You're sure they would do it themselves? Why not get a regular human involved to do it?"

"Fuck no! That's far too much of a risk, and they'd want to know with absolute certainty that it is the assassin. Our lives depend on it."

Callahan was silent for a moment, and the vamp, who had visibly relaxed, looked emboldened enough to speak. "I don't know anything else. Please. I've helped you. Let me go."

The camera angle dropped to the floor again.

"I'm not done yet. This next question is particularly important, so I want to make sure you answer truthfully."

We could hear the laboured inhale and exhales of the vamp as it struggled against the ties, becoming overwrought at the imminent threat of losing a body part.

"One of you took my family. My parents and my sister. Your family is safe, but mine is not. I want to know where they are, so that if I fail, I have the chance of getting them back. Where would they keep them?" His voice was icily cold and full of menace, and the vamp cried out in desperation.

"I DON'T KNOW. I don't know. I'm sorry they took them, but I have no idea who did or where they would be. Please, you have to believe me. The only reason I know what I do is because we've all been told that finding one of you would be an opportunity to get rid of the assassin. We all keep a lookout for your kind. You could saw off my fucking arm, and I still couldn't tell you who has them, because I don't FUCKING KNOW."

He was a desperate creature, and I believed him. Chances are he wouldn't be able to go to a hospital, so the loss of any of his digits could be catastrophic to him if he got infected or bled out. Callahan remained crouched so we couldn't see anything, but we could hear the vamp whimpering to itself.

"How do you get away with killing people when you feed off them?"

"Why do you even care? Fuck, no, please don't. I'll tell you, I'll tell you. We mostly target immigrants, homeless people, sex workers, the ones who won't be missed and who would likely wind up dead anyway. We're doing society a favour."

Callahan's only response was a tsk in revulsion at what it had revealed.

"How do you avoid the police?"

"As far as they're concerned, we don't exist. There is no murder weapon; we're not registered so our prints aren't in the system. What would they charge us on? There's no DNA evidence to link us to a victim, and we take only enough blood that it wouldn't be suspicious or we leave them as a suicide to cover it up."

Which meant they could be killing more than we thought.

I felt sick, wondering just how many people had fallen victim to their so-called 'societal favour'. I was angry at myself for not doing more. I'd been kidding myself all these years, believing they weren't killing their victims and that was why I hadn't found any reports to say otherwise. I was stupidly naive and selfish. Five minutes ago, I would have felt guilty about killing this vamp. Knowing it had a family. Knowing that just as I had been traumatised by their existence, I had been traumatising theirs. But now I felt nothing but pure obliterating hatred.

I unmuted our mic. "I have no further questions. Is it time?"

Callahan was still at the outer edge of the cowshed composing himself. He hummed his agreement. I grabbed my jacket and left Isla sitting on the bed looking utterly sickened and speechless.

"I might enjoy seeing this one rot," I said on my way out the door.

∼

Rory was sitting in the kitchen cradling a coffee. He hastily stood when he caught the look on my face and nodded as we both headed for the door.

"I'm guessing it didn't give a location?"

I shook my head. "No, and the whole thing is worse than I ever thought."

Rory muttered a curse as we stepped out into the frigid night. He grabbed my arm gently.

"Is Callahan still on the line?" I nodded. "Okay, let's slow down. We need to see at what point it catches your scent."

I handed him the phone, and we both watched as we took slow deliberate steps, helpful given the sudden burst of movement had brought back another wave of nausea. We paused every few steps to see if there was any noticeable change. The vamp had started pleading incessantly with Callahan for its release, but he ignored it completely. Waiting just as we did for the moment it changed.

Just before we reached the outhouse, the pleading stopped, and its head whipped towards the open door. It strained against the bindings, its nostrils flaring as it scented me. We stopped, and Rory looked around with the torch for something to mark the spot we stood in. He strode forward into the outhouse and came back with a fork which he laid parallel to me and out of the path so that no one would trip on it.

We stepped inside the outhouse and sure enough, needles and sample bottles, a bowl, a knife, and a first aid kit sat waiting on the worktable with a chair tucked underneath. I pulled it out and took a seat, shucking off one sleeve of my jumper. Rory donned his gloves and grabbed the tourniquet. Once in place, he sterilised the area, then loosened the band on my arm once the needle was prepped.

"You ready?"

I nodded, and with steady hands, he inserted the needle. He loosed a sigh once it was correctly in place and clipped the sample tube in, my blood bubbled into it, a deep, rich red.

"Callahan said you wanted to be a paramedic?"

"I did for a bit. Mostly because I wanted to keep our family safe." He paused as he released the second tube and carefully removed the needle, placing a cotton swab firmly in place.

"I did all the upgraded health and emergency response courses so that I could treat all our minor injuries and the certificates I gained entitle me to send off samples to certain testing labs with our insurance company. So if one of us ever had something like strep throat I could do a sample, send it off for testing, and if confirmed, they'd send out the right antibiotics. It only covers a few very specific viruses, but it's handy when you're trying to avoid visiting the GP."

"Was it expensive?"

"Hell, yes! I get why the government created these extra courses, but there is no way the people who can't afford insurance are gonna be paying that." He filled a syringe with the blood and grabbed the knife and bowl, beckoning me to follow.

Callahan met us outside the barn door. "Fletcher's experimenting."

I raised my eyebrows, conjuring all kinds of twisted images. They weren't far wrong. When we stepped through the doors, Fletcher was crouched behind the vamp, crunching its fingers between a large pair of pliers. It barely flinched, its focus entirely on me. It narrowed its eyes, lips curled back in a snarling grimace, as it strained against the ties, desperate to get to my blood.

Fletcher straightened as we neared. "I'm not sure it has any awareness of pain whatsoever. It's fucking freaky as hell." He eyed the knife and syringe in Callahan's hand. "Dibs on the knife," he said and reached for it before Callahan could argue.

"Are you using the knife first?" I asked. The image of the dead vamp I killed with my car churned in my mind. I didn't want to have to dispose of a body. The thought made me feel almost as sick as the prospect of being bitten.

Fletcher nodded, testing the sharpness of the blade against his thumb before responding. "I think it needs to be the knife. It will slow them down in a fight even before your blood takes effect. But we have to know if it works. If it does, I can't see why the syringe wouldn't. I think the syringe would only be useful in close combat or in a covert attack. Something you could hide easily."

I nodded, trusting his rationale.

The vamp was still grunting and straining, spittle flying from its mouth. Its eyes remained locked on me with its insatiable bloodlust. He turned to face it.

"Wait," I squeaked. Fletcher looked at me, surprised at my panicked tone. "Don't stab it anywhere fatal. It might take longer to react than usual, and if it bleeds out and dies of natural causes, it won't decay."

My heart pounded, the insurmountable fear of them being responsible for a murder and facing prison was too much.

"Let me do it," Callahan said.

Fletcher grumbled but passed him the knife. I stood fixed in a state of panic as he crouched next to the vamp, holding the knife over the bowl and pouring the tube of my blood over the blade. Then, without any hesitation, he plunged it into the vamp's outer thigh and left the blade in.

I counted in my head. Four seconds passed, ten seconds, then at fifteen agonising seconds, the vamp started to shudder, and its glare finally moved from me to the knife still sticking out of its leg. It started gasping for breath, the white skin of its face turning a purplish blue, its eyes bulging. I turned away, rubbing my face, not wanting to see anymore.

"Hey." Callahan pulled me into his chest, tucking me protectively in his arms, and I almost collapsed against him. My mind was a whirlwind of chaotic thoughts and fears. We had no location, no place to look for his family, and therefore no plan for a rescue. Where did that leave my life?

One arm unfurled from around me as he dug through his pockets and pulled out his earbuds. "Here, put these in."

I took them gratefully, and he selected a song on his phone while I stuffed them securely in my ears. He pulled me back against him, his hand trailing up and down my back and tangling in my hair, providing a very welcome distraction.

Shortly after, I felt his chest rumble as he spoke, and I twisted to see Rory staring openmouthed. Fletcher watched the process intently. I closed my eyes again, content to miss this part after the horrors of the last few hours.

In the moment of silence between one track ending and the next beginning, I heard a crack that made even Callahan flinch.

"Fuck that was loud," he said.

He squeezed me tighter, and I felt his chest expand as he drew in a deep breath. Just as the third song ended, he relinquished his hold on me. The three of them were in front of the now impossibly empty chair. They nudged the clothes away and stared in disbelief.

Fletcher finally broke the silence. "Drink?"

"Fuck, yes!" they chorused.

I nodded my approval and headed for the door. Callahan caught up to me and slid his fingers into mine. I wasn't sure if it was to stop me from running since we had no usable intel for a rescue plan, or if it was a simple kindness, but the gesture made my stomach flutter even amidst the lingering nausea. We trudged back in heavy silence. The drink couldn't come soon enough.

19

FLIGHT OR FIGHT

It was 3:30 a.m., and the five of us who were still awake were slumped dejectedly in Callahan's living room. Rory was stretched out on his back, commandeering the sofa facing the fire. His whiskey was resting on his chest, and he stared blankly at the ceiling. Fletcher's feet were propped on the coffee table, and Isla was curled up against him, using his shoulder as a pillow, her eyes fixed on the flickering flames of the fire. Callahan's head lolled back against the sofa. His eyes remained closed, dark shadows forming underneath like a brewing storm. He was so still, I wondered if sleep would finally overtake him, but his whiskey would periodically find its way to his pursed lips. I was curled up in a ball at the opposite end of the sofa, bundled in a blanket, but still shivering.

We were together, yet separate, our thoughts churning. Oblivious to the time seeping away from us all as our hopes were crushed.

The single thought that *I was not the only one*, replayed constantly in my head. I had assumed there would be more vamps somewhere in the world, but to think someone else had suffered all the same harrowing things as me, and had then been so hideously snuffed out, left me reeling. It was like discovering a long-lost sister or brother much too late.

I had so many questions. How long had they survived on their own? Were they braver than me? Had they been fighting the vampires proactively with strategic weaponry? Had their families been equally as dismissive? Perhaps we could have helped each other, supported each other, and shouldered the loneliness for each other. I couldn't help but think there had to be more of us out there. The possibility brought a little courage creeping through my veins.

If I survived, I was going to do things differently. I knew too much to go back to my old way of living—to go back to being a coward. Not when innocent people were being targeted, used, and murdered. The vampires had to be getting help from somewhere or someone higher up was turning a blind eye.

Eventually, we all succumbed to the call of our beds. I changed into my pyjama shorts and vest top in the bathroom, glad to exercise my bedtime routine just for some sense of normalcy.

I padded across the hall and peered into Callahan's room. I would be staying with him again as I was considered more of a flight risk now. He was sprawled out like a starfish on his bed but sat up when he felt my presence and beckoned me in. He gave me a sad smile and scooched over, kicking the duvet back and then pulling it up over his long muscular legs—which I tried not to notice. I settled myself delicately into his bed, breathing in his familiar scent and wondering how things would change between us now we were out of options. Well, now he was out of options. Would I become a means to an end?

We lay on our sides facing each other. The position dredging up memories of Noah I'd sooner forget, adding to the dark storm of emotions I was already feeling. I closed my eyes to stop them from welling up, and Callahan reached across, nudging my arm.

"Are you okay?" he whispered. When I didn't answer he

scooted closer and pulled me against his chest, tucking me into a protective embrace. His fingers entwined in my hair, and I hated how easily it calmed me. I hated how much I wanted to be here right now, his warmth reaching out and drawing me in, making me feel safe and settled. I hated that I had to question my sanity for caring about him.

"Are *you* okay?" I mumbled into his chest.

"No. I have no idea what to do now, and the delay will cost my family. They'll be starting to feel rough soon without blood. I doubt the vampires will be providing anything for them." He paused, letting out a frustrated sigh. "I feel like I'm failing everyone. I should be doing something. I just don't know what." His arms tightened around me and he rested his chin on top of my head. Sharp, spiky stubble grazed across my scalp, and I could feel his heart racing in his chest.

"If you don't rest, you won't be able to think clearly enough to help anyone, and we aren't out of time yet, so you're not failing at all," I told him in my croaky voice. "If anything, you're exceeding expectations," I added and mentally rolled my eyes at myself.

He snorted. "That's debatable."

I tried changing the subject to pull him out of his self-doubt. "Do you think it's true that your kind has been around longer than the vampires?"

His breath stuttered as he exhaled. "I don't know. Maybe Ava and James would have an answer for that." There was a bitter edge to his tone, well deserved given the information they'd withheld until this morning. I fell silent, not knowing what I could say to ease his anxiety.

"You were right. About their eyes. Not that I thought you were lying, but it was really fucking disturbing seeing it first-hand."

"So now do you understand why I ran at the bar?"

"I always worried that people would be suspicious that we all had the same unusually bright eye colour, but I never hated it. Not until tonight."

My fingers traced a soothing path across his ribs. "I've gotten used to them now. I quite like your eyes."

He tilted my chin to look at him. "Sometimes, when I look at you in a certain light, it seems like the blue in your eyes is just as bright as ours. But it's not all the time. They're quite captivating. I've never seen eyes like yours before. Do either of your parents have blue eyes?"

I shook my head, and his hand fell away, the spell between us broken. "Both my parents have deep-brown eyes, but apparently my grandmother on my mum's side had blue eyes. I never met any of my grandparents."

Conversation ceased under the weight of our fatigue, though I willed my hand to keep tracing its gentle path along his ribs until I was lulled under sleep's dark and comforting embrace.

~

When I woke, my eyes were painfully sore and hard to open. I was pressed up against Callahan's back, my arm clutched around his warm, bare midriff. His hand was clenched around my knuckles, holding me in place.

Daylight streaked through his curtains, but I had no idea what time it was. I tried to stay still, not wanting to disturb him, and guiltily revelling in the feel of his warm skin against mine. I had no recollection of him taking off his T-shirt but the intimacy was a comfort, especially knowing what I potentially faced today.

Just as I was drifting back to sleep, I felt him tense, and a groggy moan reverberated through his chest. The sound brought a traitorous smile to my lips. I tried to slide my hand back, but he grasped it tighter then pushed his fingers between mine and squeezed.

"Not yet," he moaned.

My pulse quickened and my stomach dipped as if I'd just plummeted down the steepest drop on a rollercoaster. I pressed my cheek to his shoulder, trying to keep my breathing even, and allowed myself to savour the moment. A minute later his head jerked up, and his fingers loosened.

"Shit. I'm sorry I was half asleep. You can...you can move if you want to. I shouldn't have made you—"

"I'm fine," I said flatly, slightly irked at the dismissal, but my mood lightened when I caught sight of his erratic bedhead. Part of it was plastered to his face, and several strands stuck out at odd angles.

He saw my expression and looked indignant. "Oh you can fuck off, this is mostly your fault!" he said, pointing at his hair. "I felt like I was in a sauna half the night."

He ran his hands through it, trying to force it into submission without much success while I grinned obnoxiously at his failed attempts. He reached over and frantically mussed my hair, dragging the tangled mess over to cover my face.

When I didn't move or rise to his bait he huffed, muttering under his breath as he scraped a cluster of crazy, tangled hair to one side, tucking it behind my ear. His eyes narrowed and he slowly shook his head.

"It's utterly sickening how well you can pull off bedhead."

He recovered his T-shirt off the floor, his cross dangling as he reached down, and with concerted effort, I averted my eyes before he caught me staring. I wasn't ready to leave this bubble of lightheartedness. I didn't want to think about what happened next.

He glanced at his phone. "Shit. Ava and James are on the way over here. They've organised a meeting. We've got five minutes."

I clambered out of bed and grabbed clothes out of my rucksack. He blocked the door with his arm as I tried to pass him, his face still tight with fear. He swallowed and finally met my eye.

"Olivia, I need you to trust me today. Say it. Say that you trust me," he implored.

"I trust you."

Unease stirred in my stomach as I threw on my clothes and swallowed down painkillers.

In the kitchen, a multitude of ice-bright eyes stared at us as we took our seats around the table. Fletcher cleared his throat and very succinctly relayed the entirety of our evening. When he was finished a hushed silence fell, making my skin prickle. My eyes darted to Callahan and I watched his expression closely, he stared at the table, tracing the wood grain with his finger.

"So it was a waste of time," Ava eventually said, cutting into the silence with her sharp tone. Callahan said nothing.

"So are you going to listen to us now?" she said icily.

My breathing ceased and every muscle tensed as I waited for him to speak.

"We don't have a choice, do we," he said gruffly.

Beside me, Rory inhaled sharply, and he stared at Callahan in disbelief.

My chair flew backwards as I stood, my heart beating against my ribs as I started moving. The room seemed to distort and time slowed as I sprinted for the front door.

It was locked. I dashed to the living room and tried the windows but they too were locked. Callahan cut off the only exit, so I retreated to the fireplace, grabbing the first thing I could to defend myself. Hot, angry tears streamed down my cheeks. Callahan shut the door, his hands held up in surrender.

"Olivia, please put the fucking poker down. I have a plan" he hissed. "Remember when I asked you to trust me?"

The conversation flashed through my mind, though it did nothing to calm my hysteria. He edged closer, and without a second thought, I slashed the heavy metal poker through the air in front of me.

He dodged, and before I could swing a second time, he darted across and grabbed it, twisting it from my grip, and wrestling me to the ground. One minute I was defending myself with the cold iron bar in my hand, the next I was on the floor, utterly powerless with Callahan straddling me to keep my legs from kicking out. His long fingers pinned my wrists to the floor, and we stared at each other for a moment, both in shock.

"When we get through this, Finn is going to teach you how to protect yourself," he said breathily.

The living room door swung open, and without taking his eyes off me, he bellowed, "Get out!" His voice was so loud, I flinched under him, and goosebumps spread out over every inch of my skin.

"For fuck's sake, Tilly, it's me." The door slammed shut, and Fletcher crouched beside us. He held his phone above me. "You need to read these," he said flatly.

"*Please* read them," Callahan begged.

I focused on the screen. The messages were sent in the early hours of the morning and were between Callahan and Fletcher. With a lack of better ideas, Fletcher suggested they set up the exchange but take the risk of fighting their way out of it. The vampires were malnourished and weak; they wouldn't risk exposing themselves or their community, so it was unlikely they would set up the exchange in a public place. They would probably take a small group to the exchange, giving us better odds at winning than if we attacked them on their territory where they had the advantage of numbers. They discussed arming themselves with my blood, and depending on the location, they would even be willing to utilise the shotguns they owned—even if it meant leaving bodies behind. The messages talked of Ava and James and how they would never support the decision, so it was easier to go along with the original plan as if they intended to hand over the ransom. When Fletcher was satisfied that I'd read to the end of the messages, he stood up and headed for the door.

"I'll deal with everyone else. Good luck," he said over his shoulder.

Callahan's fingers slid over my palms and threaded between mine, interlocking our hands. He shuffled back and pulled me into a sitting position. My legs were still stuck beneath him. "I didn't have time to tell you this morning, but it's nice to know that when I asked you to trust me, you did the exact opposite."

I winced. He'd trusted me last night even though the cost would have been his entire family if I'd betrayed him.

"I expected you to run," he continued, "but trying to stab me with a fire poker?"

"I'm sorry. Apparently, I have a strong flight or fight response, and when you don't tell me the plan, what the fuck am I supposed to think? You could have said something more specific than just to trust you?" I rasped, still hoping his trust in me was not completely broken.

Voices echoed through the hall and he stood up, dragging me to my feet.

"Go sit down," he told me, nodding to the sofa.

I did as he asked, grabbing a blanket and draping it around my shoulders. Although the panic was beginning to subside, I was still shivering. Callahan perched on the arm of the adjacent sofa, listening intently to the snippets of conversation. When the front door finally slammed shut he watched out the window, waiting until the figures had retreated further down the drive before he dared move.

"God, I need coffee," he muttered as he headed out of the room. I followed him, still reeling with the knowledge that he and Fletcher were willing to fight for my life and equally terrified of something happening to one of them in the process.

Rory and Fletcher were in the kitchen, the kettle already on and as we made our way to the table Fletcher handed Callahan his phone.

"I've told them we're ready to complete the exchange and requested a time and location."

Callahan nodded, dragging his hands through his hair and then slumping into one of the chairs, exhaustion marring his handsome face.

Rory passed us both our drinks and as we sat in silence around the table, Callahan's phone chimed. He picked it up, his mouth falling open as he read the text.

"They want to do the exchange tomorrow at 4 p.m. but they won't give us a location until forty-five minutes before. I don't understand…" He trailed off, furiously typing. "I thought it would be tonight." His phone chimed. "They say they're not ready to deal with the assassin until tomorrow."

There was a stunned silence, and my stomach twisted with apprehension. Whatever they had planned, it probably wasn't going to be quick and painless.

∽

The rest of the day passed with quiet angst. It had mainly been the four of us, Rory and Fletcher were supposedly staying overnight to help Callahan 'guard' me. They had retired early to their assigned rooms, wanting as much rest as possible before our coming ordeal.

Callahan had showered and readied himself for bed and when I headed to the bathroom, I took one look in the mirror, grabbed my brush and headed back out.

"You did this!" I said pointing at the bird's nest on top of my head. "So I think it's only fair that you should fix it."

He chucked his clothes in his washing basket and grabbed the brush from my hand without complaint. He sat on his bed, patting the space in front of him with the brush. I had fully expected him to protest, but his quiet acceptance added yet another thing to the already robust list of his likeable qualities. A list that seemed to get longer by the hour.

"Oh. Thank you," I whispered as I sat in front of him. "Just, start at the bottom, it's easier to get the knots out."

"I know! I have a younger sister, remember?"

Very gently, he took a handful of hair and brushed methodically from the tips, careful not to pull at my scalp. My skin prickled with pleasure, and I felt my tension working its way out along with all the knots.

As he continued to work on the tangles he laughed breathily and started to tell me a story. "When she was younger, Caitlyn went through a stage of stealing anything and everything important to me, and she would trade my stuff back for time spent playing with her hair. She even had a timer that she'd set to make sure I fulfilled my end of the bargain."

I chuckled, enjoying the sweet moment of vulnerability. "I assume she was smart enough to demand you pay up front?"

"Yep. And she never hid my stuff in the same place twice, so I never managed to track it down myself without a trade."

I snorted at the thought of him being bested by a little girl. "Did you not get Fletcher to help you?"

"What, and admit to him of all people that a little girl could get one over on me? I would never have heard the end of it." He ran the brush through one last time and chucked it beside me. "Now hurry up and shower. I need sleep."

20

DON'T DIE

Sleep enveloped me swiftly, and when I woke, it was to the pre-dawn chorus of birds, with Callahan's arm draped around my waist. His warm breaths tickled my scalp, and I resisted the urge to stretch and fidget.

It felt good to be held, to feel warm and snug against another's chest, and I could even pretend a little that it was genuine affection that held him there and not because I was a valuable ransom. I waited until I felt a change in his breathing and started shifting delicately, desperate to rid my legs of stiffness from laying still for so long.

He groaned and mumbled, "You are such a fidget when you sleep."

"Is this another zero-rated review?" I asked, twisting to look at him over my shoulder.

"Mmmm no," he said sleepily. "I'd still give you a four."

He relinquished his hold on me all too quickly and stretched out onto his back. I followed suit, stifling a yawn and stretching out every part of me, my toes making a satisfying crack that made Callahan grimace. I missed my yoga mat. My body and mind relied on it to carry me through the day, and I was starting to feel the clawing of unreleased nervous energy, pent up from the past two days.

Callahan sat up, rubbing his eyes and then reaching for his watch. He turned to me as he wrapped it around his wrist. "I need to occupy myself today, or I will not be a nice person to be around. Which means you're coming to work with me on the farm." He was already sliding out of bed, not waiting for me to reply.

~

We stood, some fifteen minutes later, in the outhouse looking at various charts. Rory and Finn were already there when we arrived and had made a pot of coffee which we were all blessedly enjoying.

They'd been explaining to me how much farming revolved around consistent year-round routines as well as seasonal routines. Each month had its own set of specific chores that related to the progress of their cattle so they had to assess and plan their day every morning.

Most would find their ramblings extremely dull, but it was a surprisingly systematic and calculated workload and much more complex than most people probably gave it credit. It was the kind of structure and level of planning that I very much liked, and I found their animated explanations fascinating.

I helped them load trailers with hay, a necessity for the cows at this time of year, which Finn and Rory went to deliver while Callahan and I were on fence duty. Not quite so interesting.

We spent almost two hours travelling the length and breadth of the farm checking all the fences for signs of damage or weakness, checking the water troughs were freshly filled and recording the pasture quality of each field so that they could keep on top of rotational grazing. All the while, I kept Callahan talking with endless questions about farming, trying to keep both of us from plummeting into a spiral of panic.

The beautiful countryside and fresh air certainly helped keep my mind more peaceful, and I deliberately pushed away the intrusive thoughts that had plagued me while we'd been getting ready. I'd imagined the creative ways that the vampires would kill me without succumbing to my scent. I suspected they would remain in their car and have Callahan tie me down so they could run me over, my head squishing like a melon. Or they'd lock me in a car and set fire to it or explode it or perhaps even let it roll into a lake to drown me. All things I wanted to discuss with Fletcher later. He was the sort of rational, pragmatic thinker who could devise a rescue plan for every scenario, and put my mind at ease. But for now, I was determined to enjoy the moments of freedom, even if at the back of my mind I felt like each could be my last.

At the crest of a moderate hill, with the farmland stretching out serenely below us, I made a very reluctant and sceptical Callahan stop work and take off his boots and socks to stand barefoot with me. I scrunched my toes into the lush grass; it was dry and refreshingly cool underfoot.

"This is the perfect spot for yoga," I said wistfully.

By this point, my throat was hoarse and aching from all our talking, and my voice was back to being a quiet rasp. The arnica gel had already started to improve the bruising, but my neck was still an ugly mottled purple, and I wore a light scarf I'd borrowed from Isla to keep everyone from staring at the unsightly marks.

"Oh, God, really? You want to do yoga right now?" He was staring at me open-mouthed and his reluctant expression had a smile brightening my face. He grimaced. "You're going to make *me* do it aren't you?"

I didn't give him the chance to argue, I just instructed. "Stretch your arms up over your head, palms facing in toward each other, and take a slow, deep breath in. You need to feel the stretch all the way to the tips of your fingers." To my delight, with a resigned sigh, he did as I asked.

"Not a word of this to Fletcher or Rory," he warned.

∽

Thirty minutes later, as we donned socks and shoes, my mind felt blissfully stable—all things considered. I would have liked to spend an hour at this beautiful spot, letting my body work through all the powerful stretches that came as second nature, but Callahan was not so enthusiastic. He was not as flexible as he imagined, and while his balance wasn't terrible, it was a new way of directing and shaping his body. Watching him wobble like a newborn colt had set me giggling more than once. But he wasn't a quitter. Despite his reluctance, he'd mastered the basics of each pose with dogged determination, and the sight had stained my cheeks crimson on more than one occasion. As we started the walk back to the yard, he quietly admitted that he did feel better and even thanked me for forcing him to take a moment to breathe and refocus.

We were almost back to the outhouse when he nudged me with his elbow. "Thank you for coming with me this morning. I think you've taken more interest in the workings of my life in the last two hours, than all my previous girlfriends combined over the many months I wasted dating them." He winced and added "A different context, obviously. I know you were just keeping us busy."

His confession brought a swell of sadness, and I stopped him, yanking his wrist so he turned to face me. "I genuinely wanted to learn. And you deserve so much better than that, so maybe you should let your friends vet potential girlfriends in the future."

His eyebrows sprang up in mock offence. "Brutal," he retorted and then steered me to the outhouse where the others were already gathered around the metal workbench.

Rory pointedly looked at his watch as we walked in. "You took your sweet time."

Before either of us could respond, Fletcher pulled out the chair still left tucked under the table from the day before. "Take a seat, Olivia."

I stared at the battered wooden chair, wondering if I was about to be bound to its frame—wondering if all of this had been just too good to be true.

"If it's okay with you, I'm going to take more blood," Rory said diplomatically as he moved to stand by the chair. "Fletcher is severely lacking in people skills. He doesn't care if he sounds like a creepy murdering bastard—but I do. I promise we're just trying to prepare for later. Nothing sinister."

I nodded, removing my arm from the sleeve of my jumper and plopping myself down. Callahan hovered nearby as Rory took several vials of my blood, and Fletcher explained they were preparing ways to expose the vampires to it by any means necessary. They wanted to fill more syringes for close-range combat too.

Hearing Fletcher speak so frankly brought our harsh reality screaming back into focus and fear squeezed me in a vice-like grip. Over the last sixty hours, I had very quickly grown attached to these people. The unexpected kindness and friendship they'd all offered, even in the face of their turmoil, was more real than anything I'd ever experienced before. The thought of any of them being hurt or losing their lives while trying to save me brought a wave of hysteria that ripped tears from my eyes before I had a chance to blink them away. Callahan noticed and his hand fell to my shoulder giving a reassuring squeeze. I heard the scuffling of feet between sobs, and then silence.

Callahan crouched by my chair. "You're not going to die," he said softly. I shook my head, my hands covering my face as my shoulders shuddered and I fought to keep myself in check. He dragged me to my feet, tucking me against his chest and anchoring me in his arms. He stayed quiet, letting me unravel while he held me secure.

"It's not that. I can't..." I started but I couldn't push the words out and took a deeper breath, forcing my body to still as I needed him to understand I wasn't afraid just for my life. "I've never had people to talk to, and...I just can't bear the thought...of anything happening to you," I managed to say around the tears.

He squeezed me tighter. His fingers winding soothingly through my hair.

"I get it. I feel the same," he mumbled. "I wish we'd met a different way. But we didn't, so take a breath—don't make me have done yoga for nothing."

A laugh bubbled out of me, and I clung to him a moment longer, feeling his chest swell with a deep inhale as he waited for me to wrangle my fears and get them under control.

"You good?" he asked when my breathing quieted.

I laughed nervously. "I think so, I'm sorry, I think I've snotted all over your hoodie."

His hands moved to cradle my face, his thumbs sweeping the remnants of my tears away.

"Believe me, I can handle a little bit of your snot." He studied me, his eyes flickering between mine. He drew a breath to speak but blinked, stepping back to put distance between us as he cleared his throat.

"Do you think you can manage to eat anything before we leave for the city?" he asked, his face betraying none of the vulnerability we'd just shared. I shrugged and followed him back to the house.

My thoughts were chaotic and bleak and the minutes ticked by in haze. Conversations drifted over me, food without flavour passed over my tongue, and my body felt distant and detached.

All too soon my feet were crunching over gravel, and I found myself in front of Fletcher's truck.

Isla squeezed my hand and whispered, "Good luck," then darted over to Fletcher. Her worry was written clearly over her face.

Rory stood by my side, his arms were folded and he chewed on his lower lip. "You're coming back," he said resolutely. "No matter what happens, breathe through it, and tell yourself you'll find a way. Don't give in to the fear. You won't be able to think straight if you do."

He clapped Callahan on his shoulder and stalked across the yard without looking back.

As I climbed into the truck, Finn appeared at my side, arms folded across his chest and his expression carefully guarded. "Don't die."

I arched a brow, my head tilting as I glared back at him. "Inspiring."

His mouth twitched at one corner, fighting a smile. "Glad to help. I'll see you later," he said and pushed the door shut.

So this was it.

21

STAY WITH HER

We were waiting at my apartment when the text came through at 3.15 p.m on the dot. It was a location pin to an area of woodland northeast of the city. They sent instructions about the entry point and reiterated that Callahan was not to bring backup, only me.

While Fletcher studied the satellite images online, Callahan hastily loaded me with small concealable weapons should they have to hand me over. I had folding pocket knives hidden in various pockets to cut through the cable ties they might have to bind me with and we were carrying multiple other weapons in the car: bricks and stones to shatter glass would send my blood hurtling into their vehicles as a deadly bio-weapon; crowbars and tools to get me out of any vehicles quickly should I be trapped; knives, syringes filled with my blood, and two shotguns.

Fletcher had prepared us as best as he could for every eventuality. Not that it helped ease the sense of helplessness and terror, which had spread through my body like a fever, causing a constant tremble. I'd barely spoken a word.

I had offered up my car for the exchange. They were already risking so much, and if the vampires planned to destroy me and a vehicle in the process, I didn't think it was fair for Callahan to lose his. If my car survived, I could at least drive myself home and have my freedom back.

After driving the appropriately sized Duster, it amused me to see Callahan squeeze his solid six-foot-two frame into a tiny city car. Even for me, it wasn't entirely comfortable.

"How the fuck do you drive this thing? It must be a squeeze even for your legs?"

My nerves hit a moment of hysteria, and I grinned at him, my lips trembling even as I tried to suppress the inappropriate giggles bubbling up—particularly when he ground the gear trying to push it into reverse. He turned to look at me, the crease between his brow beginning to deepen as his eyes narrowed in silent challenge.

"I never said a word," I squeaked.

He shook his head, the tension in his face releasing. "Next time, we're taking my fucking car."

I laughed. "Next time? God, I hope this is the last time you ever plan to drive me to a hostage exchange."

He snorted. "You know what I mean."

If I hadn't been so consumed by nerves, I might have blushed at the prospect of there being a 'next time'.

Fletcher was waiting for us in his much larger and formidable Warrior truck. We followed him, driving in convoy through the city and out onto the smaller country roads. The location took us to a single-track lane, and a few minutes before we reached the gate they'd directed us to, we pulled into a passing place and got out.

Fletcher opened his boot, handing Callahan one of the shotguns. "Just remember, these fuckers have countless deaths on their hands. They will not think twice about killing you, so if you have to pull the trigger, don't fucking hesitate."

Callahan nodded, laid the gun across the passenger seat, and turned to me. With a remorseful tone, he told me it was time to move to the back of the car. Fletcher approached and handed me my phone and an earbud.

"You can hide this under your hair—you have to be the one to keep me in the loop, as Tilly will be communicating with them. Give me as much detail as you can, and don't panic. As soon as Tilly's family is handed over, we'll be throwing everything we've got at exposing them to your blood."

When I nodded, he turned on his heel and went back to his truck, ready to part ways without so much as a good luck or goodbye.

Callahan dipped so that his forehead rested against mine and the tips of our noses were touching. The rush of emotion had my teeth chattering. I was shaking so violently. He cupped my cheeks, steadying me.

"Don't be scared. I won't let them take you," he whispered. "We're not going to let them win. And please, listen to Fletcher—do what he says, okay?" He pulled away and gently turned me around, placing a cable tie loosely about my wrists then he helped me climb into the back of my tiny car.

We found the gate less than five minutes later and drove up a winding farm track towards an area of dense woodland. The leaves were still thick and green, even though we were on the cusp of autumn. It wouldn't be long before we were completely hidden from sight. As instructed, we followed as the track forked to the right, routing us between the trees and isolating us further from the road.

It was an ominously dark afternoon, the sky heavy with thick grey clouds; the further into the trees we drove, the darker it felt. There were no other vehicles to be seen, and it wasn't until about two hundred metres further down the track that a tall wiry figure emerged from the shadow of the treeline. My skin prickled ferociously.

They were dressed in black from head to foot, wearing a

strange black headpiece or helmet. As we neared I finally understood what I was seeing. It was wearing a gas mask, and hanging over the crook of its arm was a shotgun raised in our direction. It signalled for us to pull over.

"Fletcher. It's wearing a fucking gas mask. And it has a gun," I whispered.

"How many can you see?"

I scanned the treeline and realised there were two more dark-clad shapes partially concealed just off the path.

"There are three in total on our left side. One is maybe thirty metres from the car. The other two are in the treeline. One is in a mask but not the other. I think it's...tied up. Oh, God. They're going to use it to make sure I'm their target."

It made sense, otherwise Callahan could have tried to deliver any random person to get his family back.

"Tell Fletcher I can't spot any on the right so they must be well hidden if there are more.

"I heard him," came his reply before I could speak. There was no sign of any of the Tilbrooks.

"Fletcher, they're not here," I hissed, trying not to fall into full-blown panic. I took a carefully controlled breath in, letting it out again slowly and started working a knife out of the back pocket of my jeans.

Callahan's phone buzzed in the front. "There's a message. They want you out of the car. But they can fuck off. You're not going anywhere until I see my family."

The closest vamp raised his gun at the car in warning.

"Fletcher, there's definitely a fourth vampire hidden. I didn't see any of them look like they were texting."

"I reckon they'll be on your right side, covering every angle. The masks are a weakness in some ways as they can't communicate with each other very well and it will partially obscure their vision. Tell Tilly to sit tight."

I looked to the right once more, but I still couldn't see our mystery vamp. "Fletcher said you need to stay put."

He didn't move, instead picking up the phone he started texting. The closest vampire took a few steps towards us, gesturing for us to get out, but we didn't move, and Callahan held his phone up pointedly. The masked vamp at the treeline answered a call and then stalked towards us, withdrawing a knife.

"The vampire near the treeline is heading our way," I whispered to Fletcher.

"Good." He sounded out of breath and offered no further comment, running somewhere discreetly through the trees.

The vampire detoured and trudged towards its comrade with the shotgun, and they conferred. Callahan used the moment of distraction to slip a syringe from his jacket pocket and discreetly reached back to slide it into my lap. The vampire bent down to retrieve something from the long grass and continued towards us. It was a length of rope. It began to swing one end as it walked, and as it neared the car, I realised that the end it was swinging was fashioned into a noose. A noose meant for my neck. A truly sadistic execution. But one that wouldn't spill my blood.

"Fucking animals," Callahan muttered under his breath.

When it was close enough to see me, I scooted back, scrambling into the corner as far away from the door as possible. Keeping my thighs clamped against the syringe to conceal it. The vampire dropped the noose and wrenched the car open, beckoning me to get out with its knife. I scrunched further back, shaking my head profusely. Its eery, round eyepieces lowered, giving me a glimpse of icy blue eyes filled with malicious rage and it growled in frustration, the air hissing out of the mask unpleasantly. The other vampire had edged its way further around the front of the car and was aiming straight at Callahan.

"The gun is pointed at Callahan," I told Fletcher in a shrill small voice.

From the front of the car Callahan spoke sternly, his voice low enough that only I would hear. "Don't you dare move yet."

I reminded myself of Rory's words and thought about Caitlyn and what it would be like to hug her for the first time. I thought about the horrendous things the vamps had done and how they needed to be stopped. The anger smothered my fears. I flattened myself against the door. My fingers carefully pried the blade open, and I prayed it would get close enough for me to stab it.

It tapped on the passenger window, signalling for Callahan to put his hands on the wheel. He reluctantly obliged given that he was being monitored by the masked vampire holding the shotgun. I was grateful Callahan's gun was hidden behind a bag and coat.

The vamp at the door peered in again, hesitating to put itself at risk. It braced one knee on the seat, the knife coming in first, and it stretched the other hand towards me, ready to drag me out.

I squirmed, sitting more upright so it had to reach just a little further, and the second its balance was slightly precarious, I pulled my wrists free, one hand grabbing the syringe from between my legs, my right hand sweeping out and striking at the vamp quick as an adder with my knife.

My blade barely scraped its skin and instinctively it grabbed for my wrist, my knife falling onto the seat between us under the pressure of its vice-like grip. It didn't matter, as my other hand swung out, the syringe sinking into the flesh on its shoulder, plunging my blood into its body.

The vampire jolted back, startled for a heartbeat before angrily retaliating—swinging its knife. My arms raised automatically to shield the blow, and the blade sliced, cleaving into the flesh on my forearm, warmth instantly seeping into my sleeve. I clutched at the wound, my hand wet with blood. I needed more time, it was all happening so quickly. The vampire pulled back to strike again, and I lunged forward, smearing my bloody hand across the eyelets of the mask, obscuring its vision and I reclaimed my knife, ramming it into the vampire's thigh.

A deafening boom split the air, and my scream permeated the moments after. Callahan was ducked down over the seats, and I was screaming his name, relieved when he lifted just enough to look out over the dash, seemingly uninjured.

"I'm okay," he choked out with a ragged breath. His hands were finally free of the steering wheel, and he wrapped them hurriedly around his gun, pulling it onto his lap.

The vampire beside me was choking, the poison in my blood finally unleashing its deadly effects. The other vampire was heading towards us, gun aimed at Callahan and holding all the advantages. It didn't matter that Callahan had a gun clutched in his hands, he would never be able to raise it and aim before the other fired.

"I'm going to distract it."

I threw open my door to the sound of Callahan viciously cursing and Fletcher's hushed voice in my ear asking for updates, but I ignored both and cautiously stepped out, my legs wobbling with fear. I kept myself low so the door shielded me and then…I ran.

I ran faster than I had ever pushed myself before, ignoring the pain in my arm as my feet pounded down the dirt track, back the way we had come. I hoped that my escape would give Callahan enough of a window to take a shot, and I was counting on the gun only holding three shells, one of which had just been fired.

Another deafening boom cracked like thunder, and several bits of dirt flew up to my right, missing me by only a metre or two. A second crack thundered and then a third, deafening in my ear and off to my left.

Time slowed. I longed to turn back and see if Callahan was alive, but a gruff voice shouted in my ear for me to run right. I veered towards the treeline, gunfire echoing through the forest behind me and so loudly in my ear that I had to rip out the earbud. Just when I thought the firing had ceased, and I was slowing down, more shots fired. The sound of metal hitting metal brought me to a stop, and I whirled around to see Callahan taking shelter against the car. A vampire was running out of the opposite section of the forest, reloading and taking another shot as he ran, the boom splitting through the air and adding more holes to my car. Thankfully Callahan was unhurt, ducked down by the front passenger door.

I didn't know how to help him. Anxiety tore through my body, so savage it felt like it would rip a hole through my chest. The vampire veered to the right of my car, aiming to skirt around the rear and fire once Callahan was in sight. But Callahan couldn't see it. He was stuck there, unsure of which side his enemy was approaching from, and about to get shot. As it neared the edge of the boot, I did the only thing I could. I screamed and ran forward, the vampire's attention snapped to me, and as it raised the gun in my direction, I darted right, away from Callahan.

Another piercing boom shattered through the forest, and I stumbled, my face scraping over dirt and grass as I hit the ground, jarring my neck and landing on my wounded arm. Distantly I could hear footsteps pounding towards me.

"OLIVIA." Relief cut through me when I heard Callahan's desperate voice, and I started to sob as he reached me.

"Where are you hurt?" His hands stroked across my back as I slowly forced myself upright, spitting out mud, grass and blood. I could feel more blood trickling down my face where the impact sheared off a layer of my skin. My arm throbbed and my neck was stiff but I was otherwise intact.

The forest was silent and still. The birds had hushed their songs amidst the gunfire, and I slowly looked around, taking in the carnage. The only sound was the ringing in my ears and Callahan's ragged breaths. He was staring at the lifeless vamps, his mouth hanging open as he processed the surreal scene in front of us. He shook his head, finally turning to me, his eyes wide as they traversed the mess of my face and landed on my blood-soaked hoodie.

"Oh Shit." He tore a strip of fabric off his T-shirt, bound it tightly around my forearm, and tied it in place. "I'm sorry," he whispered as he caught my pained expression. He got to his feet, peering around before offering me his hand and gently pulling me up.

There were two bodies around my car, a third had disintegrated already and mercifully none of them were our friends. We had survived.

"We need to find your family," I murmured. I spotted the vamp still tied up to a tree a little way along the treeline. It was straining against the ropes, desperate to get to me. I diverted towards it and Callahan followed, handing me a syringe.

"I'm going to get all the weapons and shit from the car. I think we're going to have to part ways with it; it's full of bullet holes, and I'm pretty sure a tyre exploded."

I nodded, and he strode away, leaving me to deal with the writhing creature ahead. I tried not to look at its face as I punched the needle into its neck and spun around without another thought, intent on getting back to my friends and starting our search. It was over.

As I neared the car, movement from the forest ahead caught my attention. It was Fletcher, striding out of the trees, his gun slung over his shoulder. He winced when he saw my face. "You survived. That's the main thing."

I laughed, slightly hysterical and lightheaded.

"There were two in the forest," he told us, picking up some of the knives that were piled next to my car. "One of them is just a little into the tree line. I reckon we leave them as they are and it will look like they were shooting at each other."

Callahan nodded, his eyes scanning the trees on either side.

"Rory is looking for them." I turned to Fletcher in surprise. I thought Rory was staying at the farm to make sure the others were protected. Fletcher smirked. "I sent the location before we left. I thought we might need the help. He distracted the vampires in the forest until I could get close enough to take a shot. He hasn't found them on that side though."

We turned to face the trees at our back.

"Let's split up, I'll take Olivia. We'll go left," Callahan said.

Fletcher grunted in agreement and stalked off.

Looking a little apprehensive, Callahan picked up his gun, laced his fingers through mine, and tugged us forward.

He was quiet as we crossed into the boundary of the trees, stopping every so often to listen, constantly scanning.

"Do you think there will be more?" I whispered. I still had a pocket knife in my jeans and was tempted to retrieve it for good measure.

"You'd think so. But if there were, surely they would have come to help when there was gunfire. Something doesn't feel right." His jaw clenched, worry etched into the lines of his face, and my skin prickled. It was eerily quiet out here. Too quiet.

Blood had seeped through the roughly made bandage and trickled down between our palms making Callahan flinch. He wiped my blood on his jeans and tore off another strip of fabric, the sound carrying out into the trees, then tied it over the top of the blood-soaked one.

"Keep your arm elevated if you can," he whispered.

A tingle of dread crept up my spine as I wondered if his family were even here. We might spend hours searching this place only for them to be locked up in an abandoned building somewhere. We pressed on, pushing our way deeper into the tree line, hoping we'd soon hear movement or muted screams indicating they were somewhere close, especially given that we would lose the light soon.

We were cutting diagonally across our section of forest, hoping it would be the most efficient way to check the area, each of us taking a side of our search path to scan. We clambered through ferns and over fallen trunks, and I was beginning to feel weak, growing more despondent, but then, amongst the sea of muted greens and browns, a pop of colour snagged my attention on the left. It was there fleetingly and then gone again. I stopped, furiously searching, hoping my mind wasn't playing tricks on me.

Then I saw it again—a line of purple peeking past the trunk of a tree. I stayed quiet, creeping closer to get a better view and hiding behind a thick trunk, terrified I might come face-to-face with another armed vamp.

I pulled my knife out, and not seeing any sign of a vamp, I darted closer and thought I saw a glimpse of long brown hair. The flash of purple came into view again, an arm hidden from view behind a tree, definitely female. I thought about screaming for Callahan, but the threat of risking our position and putting him in danger stopped me. Instead, I broke from my cover, rushing between the trees as fast as I could, hoping I wouldn't make too much noise.

As I ducked under a partially fallen tree, it was Caitlyn who finally came into view, stopping me in my tracks. It was all wrong. She was too tall, taller than even Fletcher, and she twirled around with the breeze just as I felt it blow strands of hair across my face. It took a few seconds for my brain to make sense of what I was seeing. To notice that above her head, a rope stretched up and over a higher branch.

"No," I sobbed. My knees threatened to collapse, but I stumbled forward, blurry-eyed as tears streamed down my mud-stained face. I staggered from tree to tree. Callahan shouted my name, his footfalls snapping twigs and rustling through foliage as he raced after me.

By the time I reached her, I was hysterical. All I could think was that I had to get her down before Callahan saw her. The end of the rope was tied off on a slightly lower branch, and I began sawing at it with my pocket knife.

My hands were slippery, slick with my blood, slowing me down. Seconds later, Callahan's heavy steps crashed into the space behind me. I couldn't turn to face him. Instead, I kept frantically sawing as my heart shattered for him. I heard him sob, and as the last threads were beginning to fray, I ran to her body, clutching at her legs and taking the weight as the rope finally gave. I collapsed with her to the floor. She was much lighter than I'd anticipated. I sat up and immediately started to untie the rope around her neck, it wasn't tight. Her face was tense and strained but calmer in death than I would have expected, which didn't make any sense given the brutality. As I slipped the rope from around her I saw the bruising on her throat. The familiar red-purple hickey-like splodges on either side but not the whole way around.

"She was already dead," I mumbled.

I moved as Callahan fell to his knees beside her, and I turned and pushed further into the forest. Dragging my tired body forward. I went back to searching, clinging to the hope that his parents might be okay. The only sound I could hear was Callahan's muffled sobs.

Hope was dwindling and snuffed out when I caught sight of another body. Jodie Tilbrook. Swaying gently as she hung, suspended from the canopy above.

It was too much. The world was spinning out of control. I wanted to curl up in a ball on the forest floor and cry into the earth below. I wanted to fall asleep right there and pray that when I woke, I would be someplace else, waking from the very worst nightmare I would ever have. I looked at my blood-soaked hands and arm. Felt the dull ache of the knife wound. It was so real. Why was this real?

I thought of Callahan and forced one foot in front of the other, finding the rope and sawing once more, barely able to focus through the exhaustion and unceasing flow of tears. It broke before I could catch her body, but I repositioned her in a more dignified manner, telling her over and over again how sorry I was as I worked to remove the noose. The same bruising was visible just as it had been on Caitlyn's neck. They had drained them both. Used them as food and lied to Callahan about the exchange. It utterly disgusted me, though it was a more merciful death than a hanging.

I wanted to stay with her, but with trembling legs, I fought to get myself upright and staggered on. It was mere metres away that I came across Martin. He was slumped under a tree and for a brief moment I thought he might still be alive. A noose hung around his neck and was tied loosely to a branch above him. His face was heavily bruised, his eye swollen and his lip split open, but the blood on his face wasn't fresh. Red-purple bruises around his throat sat starkly against too-pale skin. He'd put up a fight, but he was gone. I wanted to kick and scream, but I was too exhausted. I didn't know why, but I couldn't bear the thought of Callahan's mum being alone. I dragged myself back to her body and dropped to the floor, taking her cool hand and waiting with her. How could I ever make this right?

It could have been hours, it could have been minutes before Callahan's slow and deliberate steps halted the other side of her body. I still couldn't look at him. I was numb and empty on the inside, but the sound of his keening sobs as he dropped to the floor beside her tore apart what little of me was left.

I heard movement from the path ahead and another set of feet strode towards us. Fletcher dropped down beside me. He rested a hand gently on my back.

"Martin?" he asked quietly.

I pointed to the place I'd left him, my hand shaking violently. He stood and followed my direction, leaving me and Callahan once more.

"Is he...the same?"

I was staring at my red-stained hand, clasped around Jodie's long, soft fingers as they remained cold and lifeless in mine. I nodded without looking up.

He got to his feet, squeezing my shoulder as he passed. "Stay with her," he told me, his voice thick with grief.

I was an empty shell. Barely awake, barely capable of speech or emotion by the time Rory found me, still clutching Jodie's hand. He knelt beside me. He carefully lifted my wounded arm, pulling my fingers away from Jodie's, inspecting the makeshift bandages now sticky with congealed blood and crusted on my skin and clothes.

"Are you okay?" he asked.

"It doesn't matter," I whispered back.

Callahan and Fletcher reappeared, Callahan gently scooping up his mother's body and carrying her off into the forest. Rory tipped my chin towards him, but I couldn't look him in the eye, I couldn't look at any of them. "It does matter."

Fletcher's arms wound around my waist, and he hoisted me to my feet. Before I could protest, he scooped me up in his arms and set off after Callahan. I closed my eyes. The forest felt like it was shifting around me, the ground tilting unnaturally, shapes swirling about my head and then, I was swallowed up in a sea of black.

22

THE BEST

It was like swimming through tar, everything sticky and distorted, thoughts slowly reviving, leaving me scared to open my eyes.

I was in pain, a dull ache that seemed to spread out over every limb, made worse by sudden jolts. We were moving.

"I think she's awake." It was Callahan's voice, my cheek was cradled in his lap, and his hands were running up and down my arm reassuringly.

"Do you feel sick?" I shook my head, my eyes staying firmly shut. I felt weak in every sense of the word. I was heartbroken for him, wracked by guilt and shame, but I wasn't going to be sick.

"Stay still. Just rest. We think you've lost a little too much blood."

I could hear the pain in his gruff voice, and my chest ached unbearably at the sound. His hand continued tracing a path up and down my arm and shoulder, occasionally stroking my hair, and I tried to concentrate on the sensation of his touch, pushing away all the grief clawing to take hold and shred me to pieces.

Soon the car slowed, and my body tugged to one side as we took the turn leading down to the farm. The crunch of gravel under the tyres rumbled through my body and filled me with unease, my wounds protesting as the car jostled down the drive. There was only so much longer I could pretend this wasn't happening. I wrenched my eyes open, embraced the sting as they worked to refocus, and attempted to sit.

"Easy." Callahan shifted in his seat, one arm sliding under my legs, the other around my waist, and then gently, he pulled me from the car.

"Where do you want her?" The detachment in his tone was like another knife wound slicing between my ribs. I stifled a sob, clamping my eyes shut as I clung to him.

"Where are you staying?" Rory asked solemnly.

Callahan didn't answer, and the pause stretched on until Rory decided for him.

"Let's put her in my bed. I'll sleep on the floor or the sofa." I heard hurried steps racing down the drive as Rory shouted, "Isla can you grab towels, warm water, and all the first aid stuff."

Callahan carried me upstairs tucked against his chest, and I desperately wished I could find words that would bring comfort or peace, but the image of Caitlyn twirling on the end of the rope like a sadistic wind charm choked every word from my mouth. Silent tears were the only thing that would seem to come out, creeping down my face unbidden.

Callahan carefully placed me in a chair and started tugging on the damp, sticky sleeve of my hoodie, working my arms free and pulling it gently over my head. He knelt in front of me, removing my trainers, and untying the makeshift bandage. Blood had dried and crusted against my sensitive exposed flesh, and I couldn't stop the gasp of pain as the fabric was incrementally tugged away, fresh blood dribbling out as the wound was disturbed. The room distorted and tilted, a strange warm rush buzzing around my head, and my hands flung out trying to right myself.

He gripped my shoulders, keeping me upright. "Shit. Not

again. RORY!" Callahan bellowed as I tried to steady my blurring vision.

"I'm so sorry" I whimpered through the haze. My shoulders trembled, fighting back sobs and he squeezed my hand and stood as Isla came in, Rory on her heels with a medical kit. She placed a folded towel under my arm, laying another stack on a nearby leather ottoman, and after flitting back out, she reappeared with a large bowl of water.

Rory lowered to his knees in front of me and cast a glance at Callahan. "Go clean up. You can borrow one of my shirts. The last thing we need is an infected wound."

With a grunt, he disappeared and Rory dipped a fresh cloth into the water and began cleaning and inspecting the slash. "We figured you probably wouldn't want to risk a hospital, so I'm gonna clean this up, and then it's going to need stitches. It's too deep to leave it. You're bloody lucky it wasn't worse than it is. "

Isla handed me a glass with a good measure of whiskey, which I downed. I leaned back into the chair and waited for the alcohol to dampen my pain. It didn't take long given my head was already spinning.

Callahan stayed while I was cleaned, stitched, and bandaged, and before he left, he tipped my chin up, forcing me to meet his eye. I fought the instinctual desire to look away, though tears still swelled and slithered down towards his hand, and he wiped them away with his thumb.

"I need to go. I'll be staying at Fletcher's, but Rory will make sure you're safe. I'll speak to you tomorrow." He lingered a moment, like there were more words to say, but he swallowed them down and retreated.

The silence he left behind hollowed out my chest, and not wishing to dwell on the horror of the last few hours, I didn't fight the overwhelming tug of sleep.

Images of Callahan, revolving on the end of a bloodied rope, his body riddled with bullets while I was powerless to stop it, catapulted me awake the following morning. I sat up gasping, tears renewing their worn path down my cheeks. There was a dull ache in my forearm, the burn of blisters across my right palm, and my face stung as salty tears streamed across the raw edge of the newly forming scab—all a painful reminder of the reality which was every bit as horrifying as anything I could have dreamt.

There was movement in the corner. Rory was dozing in an armchair, his feet propped up on the ottoman. He stretched his stiffened limbs and sat up with a start. His thick golden hair was loose, sitting just at his shoulders, and the waves fell around his cheeks as he tried to rub away the weariness so evident on his face. It made me wonder what state Callahan would be in this morning, and my chest pinched at the thought.

I remembered seeing Callahan pick up his mum and carry her away, but everything after that was unclear.

"Where did they go?" I asked. "Where are Callahan's family?"

Rory was hunched forward, elbows on his knees and hands in his face. He sighed deeply before looking up, tucking his thick wavy hair behind his ears.

"They're here at the farm. We're gonna bury them this morning in the orchard." He checked his watch and slowly eased to his feet. "I should already be there helping, so I'll check in later." He paused in the doorway and turned back. "You probably realise this but, it was a trap. They never meant for Tilly or his family to walk away once they had you. What you did yesterday was brave, and both of you are still here because you were willing to risk your life for him." He paused, the echoes of yesterday assaulting him, the horror of it glazing his eyes. "His family was already gone before you all arrived. So thank you. We might have been grieving for one extra were it not for you."

He dipped his head and was gone, and my protest died on my lips—because they wouldn't be grieving at all if it weren't for me.

∽

I stayed tucked up in Rory's bed, the events of the previous day pushing into every thought no matter how hard I tried to block it from my mind. Rory was right, they had to have murdered them well before we arrived. Why was I even shocked? Knowing they feasted on what they considered the dregs of society, without a shred of guilt. They were vile, selfish, disgusting creatures. While I could never atone for all the lives that were already lost, I was damn well going to figure out a way to keep people safe in the future. It would involve a lot of planning and require a lot of help, but this couldn't go on. I had to do something.

Finding my rucksack at the bottom of the bed, slowly and painfully, I managed to change into clean clothes. My limbs and back ached from my fall, and the large ugly scab on my face made it difficult to wash, but I made the best of it and made my way unsteadily downstairs.

Maddie was sat in the kitchen, her elbows on the table and hands steepled in front of her face, a pile of discarded tissues in front of her. When she noticed me hovering in the doorway, her face cracked into painful sobs, her shoulders heaving and she got up and turned away, making her way outside. My chest was expanding too quickly, too painfully, and I retreated to Rory's room and shut the door, planning to stay hidden so that I could allow them space to grieve peacefully without an ever-present reminder of their loss. I'd lost my phone in the chaos; when Rory checked in later, I would borrow his and organise a way home.

With nothing else to do and in desperate need of a distraction, I inspected Rory's bookcase. There were lots of medical journals and a smattering of fiction, mostly thrillers. Picking one up, I settled in his chair and tried to force my eyes to take in the words jumping off the page. I read and reread sentences and paragraphs multiple times before laying it aside, resting my eyes as my head began to pound.

~

"Olivia."

I woke with a start, stiff and sick with hunger, to find Callahan staring at me with empty eyes and pale skin. My hands were reaching for his face before I could stop them. He closed his eyes as my fingers drifted down over his stubble. After a moment, I dropped my hands to my lap, not quite sure how to behave around him now. He exhaled, long and slow, like he was preparing for something momentous, and I waited, giving him time to find the words he needed. He swallowed, looking down and fiddling with my fingers where they rested on my lap.

"We're all going to the orchard in a little while, to pay our respects." He sniffed, a tear began snaking down his cheek. "Will you come?" His voice was so soft, so quiet, I almost didn't decipher the words.

"If that's what you want, then yes, of course."

He nodded, squeezing my fingers and then stood with a groan. "Can I ask a favour?"

Slowly, I got to my feet and waited expectantly. He pressed a key into my palm. "Can you please find me a shirt and jeans or whatever you can find that's smart from my room?" I nodded and relief flooded his face. "I'm going back to Fletcher's. Ava and James are preparing some words, and I need to go through some stuff with them." He spun on his heel and left the room, leaving me clutching his key, the emptiness suffocating in his absence. Forcing my feet to move, I carefully descended the stairs, slipping out the door unnoticed.

The air was cool and crisp, a brighter day than yesterday, which seemed disrespectful. It did not reflect the heartbreak and despair that orbited each person here. The atmosphere was so heavy, you could feel it settle on your shoulders and seep into your soul, crushing you from the inside out.

My legs wobbled, forcing me to stop and take a breath. It wasn't that far, but my body felt as brittle as my mind. I made it to the front door of Callahan's home, my stomach spinning unhelpfully as I turned the lock and braced my shoulder against the heavy door. I took a breath before stepping inside and heading straight to his room. A quick investigation revealed most of his clothes were folded neatly in his drawers. I found two shirts in his wardrobe, one midnight blue and one grey, both immaculately ironed, and I wondered if this was Jodie Tilbrook's mothering touch. At his hotel room in the city, his belongings were haphazardly cast about the room, and I had expected to find his clothes similarly arranged here, shoved in drawers and hung complete with their creases. Settling on the blue shirt, I laid everything carefully on the bottom of the bed and then climbed into it, breathing in his familiar scent for a few moments before dragging myself back out.

I knocked on the Moores' door and waited, nerves still dancing around in my stomach. Fletcher answered, pulling the door shut behind him and retrieving the clothes from my unbandaged arm.

"Thanks, I'll pass these on to him." He turned to go back inside, opening and closing the door like I was a stray dog that needed to be kept out. Ava and James' loathing opinion of me had clearly tripled in intensity. Terrific.

~

Back at Isla's, I heard hustle and bustle in the kitchen and hoped I might find Rory. He at least, was a friendly face. I peered in from the hallway. Isla was at the sink furiously scrubbing her hands. Rory and Finn were leaning against the side next to her. They were both covered in dirt. Rory was staring at the floor, hands shoved in the pockets of his jeans, and Finn was half-heartedly munching on a sandwich.

My feet stuck. I wanted to walk in and speak to them, find comfort in their friendship and be a comfort to them in return, but I couldn't seem to find any forward motion or remember how to even speak. Flattening against the wall, I closed my eyes and concentrated on long inhales and exhales, forcing my body to calm and reset.

"Are you okay?" Rory was staring at me, concern knitting his brows together as he eyed me pressed up against the wall like I was trying to disappear inside of it.

I took another breath. "Yeah, I just dropped some clothes off for Callahan, and I'm worried about him."

His lips pursed as he nodded. "Why don't you grab some food; your body needs it after all the blood you lost. I was going to shower and get into some clean clothes, so I could do with having my room back for a bit, if that's okay?"

"Of course. It's your room—you don't have to ask me."

"I won't be long. Go, get some food. Finn will make you a sandwich, or you can just help yourself to whatever you can find."

He grabbed my shoulders and propelled me into the kitchen. Isla gave me a polite smile as she dried her hands and then inspected her nails.

"How are you feeling?" she asked.

"I'm...I'm okay. I'm more worried about everyone else. How are you all doing?" I reached for her hand. "I'm so, so sorry. I can't even imagine how hard this must be." They were meant sincerely but the words still seemed empty in comparison to the loss they were facing. Her eyes were red, shadows circling the pale skin underneath. She nodded slowly, her eyes scanning over my scabbed face and the bandages on my arm.

"I can't imagine how scary it must have been running from a gunman or finding…" Her voice broke into a sob, and I pulled her into a hug.

"I'm so sorry I couldn't save them."

She released me and wiped her face with the heel of her hands. "Handing you over wouldn't have saved them, you do understand that, don't you?" She gave me a fierce look, and I nodded. It didn't change the fact that I could have done so much more leading up to this. Or that my existence was the catalyst for all that had happened.

"I need to get cleaned up. I think Ava was hoping we would all wear something a bit smarter. Do you want to borrow something of mine? I have a long winter skirt that would fit, even if it's a bit shorter on you. I know you didn't bring much."

I gave her a grateful smile, and Finn cleared his throat.

"I made you a sandwich," he said, passing me a plate.

I took it, thanking him. Hearing my stomach rumble at the prospect of food, I realised it was probably almost a day since I'd eaten anything substantial.

"Sounds like you need more than a sandwich. Just help yourself to snacks, okay?" He eyeballed me until I nodded appreciatively, then headed back to the side to clear up.

Isla tugged my arm gently and motioned for us to go upstairs.

∼

We walked to the orchard together in procession. Ava and James led the way, dressed in black, heads bowed. I had no idea what to expect. There would be no coffins. It was an unwritten rule that the circumstances of their deaths were far too suspicious for the authorities to be involved. It would provoke too many questions, so a private burial on their land was deemed safer.

Ava and James had already been spinning a story—that the three of them had been on a family holiday and had been involved in a tragic and fatal accident. That was to be the official party line and they had contacts that were working on a forged death certificate. It would hopefully keep all of them safe.

I walked with Callahan, following behind Ava and James, and as we reached the bottom of the orchard my hand flew to my mouth in surprise. They hadn't been buried in typical graves, side by side. Their bodies rested beneath a mass of beautiful plants and shrubs. A large square flower bed lovingly tended. I hadn't seen Isla all morning and now I realised why; she had been making beauty from ashes. Her dedication to these beautiful souls I had only known in death. Tears rolled down my cheeks despite trying so desperately to be strong for Callahan.

We gathered to one side of their grave, and Callahan grasped my hand, his fingers trembling as he entwined them with mine. James cleared his throat, moving to face us and give an official address. He was not quite as tall as Fletcher, and his dark hair was cropped shorter and gelled neatly unlike his son's longer waves, but the resemblance was unmistakable. He fiddled with his tie for a moment, collecting himself before he began.

He shared fond memories of his friends and deep respect for the community they had created here. He spoke of their boys growing up together and having adventures, and how they had been such an example in their commitment to working hard and raising a family. All of which I tried to take in—tried to remain strong while being hypervigilant of Callahan and all his grief. My heart nearly burst open when James asked Callahan to say some words, and I felt his body tremble against me.

He retrieved a slip of paper from his back pocket, focusing entirely on unfolding it as he made his way to the front, eyes only on the words he'd written in preparation. His jaw clenched, I could see the paper shaking in his hands, and I willed my strange calming scent to reach him from where I stood. He took a deep inhale, releasing it slowly through his mouth, and then he seemed to find his courage and began.

"I think, the only way for me to sum up my family is to say that they were...the best. They always *gave* their best, and they *made* the best of everything this life threw at us. Despite our... differences, they wanted us to live, not just a normal life, but an incredible one. They worked damn hard to give us a magical childhood, to make up for everything that we might have missed out on. We had so many adventures here on the farm, so many memories I will never, ever forget. They gave us a community so that we'd never be alone. They gave me room to be who I wanted to be, they loved me through all my mistakes, all my disappointments, and they believed in everything I could be."

He drew in a long shuddery breath and wiped his eyes. My heart was shattering into a million even smaller pieces for him.

"I still can't believe I'll never hear Caitlyn laugh again; she was infectious, tenacious, full of joy, and the best sister I could have asked for. She should still...be here. I wish...I wish I could have more time."

He stared at the words on the page, his jaw clenching as he fought against the emotions wracking through him so viciously his whole body was trembling. Then he crumpled the piece of paper in his fist.

"There are no words that will ever make this okay," he choked out. "I'm sorry."

And then he was walking, skirting around the group, and heading to the outer edge of the orchard, sagging over the post-and-rail fence as if he had no strength in his body to keep him upright. I followed quietly.

Behind us, Ava had taken his place, a poem at the ready. I

hovered a couple of feet away, wondering if perhaps he needed space, but I couldn't abandon him knowing my unique scent was a source of comfort if he needed it.

Hesitantly, I stretched out my hand, placing it lightly on his shoulder. I could feel his body shuddering, grief prowling like a wolf, ready to devour him the minute his guard was dropped. Edging closer, my hand slid over his back in a soothing motion. Gradually, his body stilled and he was able to stand upright, pulling me into his chest as he leaned back against the fence.

"Thank you," he whispered into my hair.

~

We were the last to leave the orchard. It was dusk by the time we made our way back to the houses. Neither of us spoke, just drifted together, lost in our sorrows. There wasn't anything I could say that wasn't cliched or an attempt to fill the silence, and I didn't want in any way to undermine what he was feeling. As we neared the turn to Isla's drive, we came to a natural stop, a goodbye looming over us.

I wasn't welcome at Fletcher's. I hugged him, giving him one more opportunity to find comfort before we parted ways, though it seemed to have the opposite effect. He clutched me tighter and sobbed into the crook of my neck, his tears sliding over my skin and further bruising my fragile heart. I could feel him losing control, and abruptly, he yanked himself away from me, wiping his eyes.

"I'll see you tomorrow," he said as he turned and hurried away.

Maddie and Stephen were consoling each other in the living room, Finn was nowhere to be seen, and when I reached Rory's room, I found him perched on the end of his bed, staring dejectedly at the floor. He stood as I walked in. We stared at each other, our emotions fragile and loosely held together.

"Come here." He beckoned me and my feet instantly responded, finding my way into his waiting arms where my resolve finally broke.

"None of this is your fault," he told me as I sobbed against his shoulder, but it did nothing to satiate the guilt eating away at me. After a few moments, we relinquished our grip on one another and he checked my wounds. "Do you remember when you last had a tetanus shot?"

"When I was a teenager. Why, do you think it's infected?"

"No, but you were filthy, and it's a deep wound, so it could definitely be a risk. If it feels hot or itchy or painful or you start to feel achy or feverish, that's a really bad sign."

"Ok, Doc. I'll keep an eye on it."

His lip twitched, fighting off a smile as he unravelled a clean bandage and started re-wrapping my forearm. "I'll grab some stuff in a minute and leave you to rest."

"No, don't. I should probably go back to my apartment and leave you all to grieve in peace."

He gave me an unsettled glance. "I think you should stay for a bit. You're wounded, exhausted, and now that they've figured out a way to deal with you, I don't think it's safe right now. They could be hunting for you as we speak. If I were them, I'd have teams of two prowling the streets—one in a mask and one without."

"Well, thank God you're not them!" I muttered shakily. "I don't know, Rory, I feel like I'm intruding here and upsetting your parents, and I need to figure out how to make this right. I have to do something about them."

He grabbed my shoulders, tilting his head to catch my attention. "If you die stupidly in the city, Tilly will be destroyed. We all took risks to keep you alive, and if you die now, it will have been for nothing. And if we hadn't, I already told you, I think Tilly would be dead as well. So please, will you just bloody stay put?

We can figure out what to do about them together. Just give us a few days to wrap our heads around it all."

Together. I liked the sound of that, but I didn't want my presence to be a burden. Everything had changed.

"I have a key to the farmhouse. Can you please ask him if I can stay in his room? At least then your parents don't have to see me, and you can sleep in your bed. I would ask him myself, but I don't have a phone."

He nodded, sliding his phone out of his pocket and relaying my request. We stood waiting, unsure if Callahan would even look at his messages. Just as the silence was stretching beyond awkward, his phone buzzed, and his eyes darted to the screen.

"He's fine with it," he said, relief melting away the tension in his face.

I grabbed my bag and hoisted it over my shoulder, flinching as the muscles in my back jarred with the effort.

"Thank you for taking care of me," I said appreciatively, turning before he could see the pain in my expression.

"I'll swing by in the morning," he replied as I slipped out of his room.

23

OVERTHINKING

My night was plagued by harrowing dreams of gas masks and lifeless bodies. They left me with a chill that penetrated down to my bones and stuck there, gnawing at my sanity. I had never been happier to see the glimmer of dawn seeping past the curtain edges.

Rory stopped by briefly in the morning, and I sat huddled in the duvet feeling enormously self-conscious as we spoke. He hadn't seen Callahan, but Isla was with him and would no doubt report back.

Once I'd reassured him there were no signs of infection, he left me to rest. It was needed—the tension and lack of sleep caught up to me like a tidal wave I couldn't outrun. It was late afternoon before I woke after a pleasant dreamless sleep. My stomach gurgled viciously as though it housed a starving wild cat. I ventured down to forage for food, nibbling on cheese and over-ripe fruit like a lost stray.

～

In the evening, I was lying awake in the dark, wondering where and what Callahan was doing, when I heard the front door slam and voices echoing up the stairs. The lights went on, the warm glow creeping up the stairwell and faintly illuminating the room. I listened to the footsteps cautiously ascending and then a whisper-shout across the hall.

"Olivia??"

"I'm awake," I called, sitting up and switching the lamp on beside the bed, my eyes blinking away the shock of light.

Rory leant against the doorframe, hands in pockets, waiting for me to compose myself. "Finn and I brought you some dinner, so get dressed. We'll eat together."

I cringed, thinking about how long it had been since I'd showered. I looked and smelled like a stray by this point.

"I might put you off your dinner—I'm kind of disgusting right now ..."

"Then I'll run you a bath and put lots of bubbles in. You'll just have to keep your arm dry." He was already moving towards the bathroom, and I heard the taps twisting and the splash of water against the tub echo across the hallway. Doors opened and closed, and then he reappeared, poking his head around the door. "Come on, I've got you towels, and it's nearly ready."

There was the sound of swishing and swirling as I neared the bathroom and found Rory sitting on the edge of the tub, his wrists and forearms dusted with foam which he shook into the steaming water.

"Enjoy," he said as he slipped out of the room, quietly closing the door behind him.

Typically, I preferred showers, but this felt like a luxury. The heat was divine and the rising steam drenched me in the smell of vanilla and citrus. I felt both bonelessly relaxed and invigorated. I carefully sank into the water, letting the lengths of my hair float weightlessly under the surface, tickling my back and shoulders. I did my best to scrub my scalp and body while trying to keep my forearm dry, failing miserably, but at least it wasn't fully submerged. The wound was itching incessantly, but I hoped that was more to do with the skin knitting back together again than infection.

I borrowed one of Callahan's T-shirts and zip-up hoodies and slipped my pyjama shorts back on. I smelled and felt so much better. Good enough to face company.

Finn was setting food on the table when I walked in. The kitchen smelt deliciously spicy, and my stomach rumbled loudly in anticipation when I eyed the plates of steaming chilli and rice. Finn pulled out a chair for me at the head of the table, only leaving my side when I was tucked in and appreciatively staring at my food.

"This is amazing, thank you," I told him as he slid into the seat on my right, opposite Rory.

"It's pretty much the only meal I can cook that actually tastes like food," he said sheepishly. I loaded my fork and groaned when the flavours ignited in my mouth.

"Steady on—it's not that good," Rory muttered beside me with a smirk.

"I've barely eaten the last two days. Believe me, it is that good. Finn, honestly this is amazing, thank you again."

Finn smiled, a tinge of light pink blossoming over his cheeks. "Have you heard from Callahan?"

"Nope. I'm officially in the Stone Age. No car, no phone, no laptop. I might have to go old school and write him a letter."

He looked thoughtful for a moment, and his lips turned up in a half smile. "Maybe you should. Does he know you've lost your phone?"

I actually hadn't considered that, and now my mind was a tangle of worries. "Maybe I should write to him," I muttered under my breath.

"I'll deliver it for you if you do. I need to speak to him about work stuff anyway," Rory offered.

"How is work going? I'm sorry it must be harder at the moment since Callahan has been away."

He finished his mouthful and pushed his plate aside. "It's okay. There is a lot to sort, but we'll manage. There is no way Tilly is ready to be at work right now. He *would* work if we let him, but I think he needs time for it to sink in." He stared at his hands. "It's hard for all of us but…" He fell quiet, and I noticed Finn was staring at his plate, his knife and fork still in his hands though the food was all gone. I gently touched his shoulder and he jumped. "Sorry, I was miles away, what did I miss?"

"Nothing much, I just wondered if you could teach me what to do with the fire at some point?"

He nodded. "We'll do it now," he said, rising from his chair and heading out the kitchen. "And when your arm is healed, apparently I'm supposed to be teaching you self-defence."

"Right. That. I guess it will come in handy now that they're running around in fucking masks. I really wish they hadn't figured that out. Never thought I'd appreciate being hunted by mindless monsters so much."

He snorted. "I honestly can't believe you're still sane. Rory had nightmares after what happened in the cowshed."

"Oh, I've had plenty of those. And I'm pretty sure my ex thought I was either batshit crazy or dealing drugs on the side," I said as we settled in front of the hearth. My eyes stared fixedly at the wood burner, refusing to acknowledge the dresser full of memories that now felt like a shrine.

He explained how to build the fire and how to use the damper to start and control the flames. It was brief, but it gave me the confidence to attempt it if needed. He made his excuses and left shortly after, promising to tell Isla I missed her, leaving Rory behind to wait while I wrote my letter.

It took me fifteen minutes, much to Rory's amusement. It was so difficult penning words to paper and several sheets were scrunched and discarded before I finally settled on a simple message and folded it in half, passing it to him. He opened it and much to my embarrassment proceeded to read it aloud.

"Callahan,

I just wanted to say I'm thinking of you. I am always here for you if you need me.

Olivia xx

Ps My phone is lost, hence the note."

"It took seven attempts to write that?" he said incredulously.

My eyebrows inched their way further up my forehead. "It's not that simple."

"Then you are definitely overthinking it. Bloody hell, how many trees did you waste for this? If you needed help you could of just asked."

"Oh, fuck off."

"I've been trying to! If I'd known how long you were going to take to write one sentence, I would have made another coffee."

I considered punching him, but my weakness would no doubt fuel him further. "Goodnight, Doc."

He shook his head. "Please stop calling me that."

I shrugged. "Then don't be so annoying."

He chuckled, refolding the note and tucking it into his pocket. "I'll deliver your pitiful excuse for a letter in the morning. Get some sleep, I'll see you tomorrow."

~

I lay staring up at the ceiling; with no streetlights nearby, it was as pitch black as the back of my eyelids, but I couldn't bring myself to close them yet.

My thoughts drifted back to Callahan no matter where I tried to steer them. I wondered how long it would be before the sheets started to smell more of me than they did of him. I wondered if he was sleeping and if he'd actually talked to anyone—whether he would ever want to see me again. I totted up the hours since we'd met and realised I'd known him for one hundred and ten hours and spent a considerable amount of them stuck by his side. The last twenty-four hours without him had been particularly arduous.

How ridiculous was it to be so attached to someone after so few days? There was something wrong with me for sure. Maybe I *was* batshit crazy. Although, it was about more than just him. I was attached to this place, where I felt like I could breathe. To these people who knew my secrets and didn't treat me or the world any differently. I dreaded going back to the city. Going back to isolation, fear, and constant lies.

It was time to try something new. One way or another, I was going to find a way to stop the vampires from hurting anyone else.

24

KISS ME

By 7 a.m., I was wide awake, my body tense and tightly coiled with energy that was desperate to burst out. Pulling back the curtains and unwrapping the gift of a new day, I discovered it was disappointingly bleak and grey outside. The clouds were thick and heavy, an impenetrable shield against the sun's rays, and a light mist had settled over the farm.

I stepped out into the frigid, damp air, needing movement in my limbs and fresh air to fill my lungs. Making my way down the farm track, passed the barns and the cowshed, with its ugly memories, and along the pasture land, I finally saw the rich brown bodies of a herd.

They were all bustling around a crown-like feeder containing fresh hay. Their tails swished back and forth, and their hot breaths fogged the air as they snorted and grunted at each other while snatching mouthfuls of their breakfast. Occasionally their bodies would shake from head to hindquarters—dislodging mist and dirt from their coats in a cloudy haze. The odd one or two watched me as they chewed. Their ears flicked back and forth, and their nostrils flared, as if trying to place my scent. Assessing whether I was friend or foe.

Further down the track, I came across another herd and spotted a well-placed fallen log ripe for contemplation, and my legs appreciated the moment to rest. Rory's comment about the vampires hunting me was still churning in my mind. Every time I thought of going back to the city, unease expanded in my chest, crowding my lungs, and making it difficult to breathe. How would I ever sleep there again? I sincerely fucking hoped they were not that bold—that walking around in a gas mask would draw unwanted attention and be too risky.

It was time to reconsider my living arrangements and find somewhere on the outskirts of the city. Maybe closer to here. My bank account might disagree with that plan, but with the addition of the gas masks, things had changed. However much I dreaded it, I'd have to go back soon, regardless of the threat. There was a whole list of issues fighting for my attention.

My musings were cut short by the roaring of a quad. It was carrying Rory, an empty trailer bobbing along behind it. He pulled up a few metres away and strode over looking remarkably smug.

"Have you finally figured out that cows are better company than Tilly?"

I shook my head and gave him a perfunctory smile as he sat down, not in the mood to joke. "No, he probably doesn't want to see me. I can't really blame him; they'd still be alive if it weren't for me."

He picked at the long blades of grass growing up against the log, flicking them out in front of him absentmindedly. "Nobody blames you for this. Least of all Tilly."

I scoffed. "Well that's hardly true, I'm not allowed in Fletcher's house, and I'm pretty sure Ava and James wholeheartedly blame this on me."

He stopped picking and turned to me. "Martin and Jodie were always close to Fletcher's parents. They might not be dealing with it very well, but I'm pretty sure they realise they were wrong. They love Tilly, and they will be doing their best to look after him. He and Fletcher were inseparable as kids." He paused, letting out a wistful sigh. "It used to make Isla so mad because they were always having sleepovers without her. Especially once Caitlyn was born. So don't take it personally. It's not that he doesn't want to see you, it's that he doesn't want you to see him. He's a mess, he's vulnerable, and Tilly doesn't like being the vulnerable one. He's the one that protects and takes care of everyone else. He and Fletcher both. They're two peas in a pod, only Tilly is actually fun. Well, under normal circumstances he is."

I was quiet, digesting everything he'd said, morosely wondering if Ava and James were right to want to hand me over.

He leaned towards me and playfully jostled me with his elbow. "Come for a ride with me on the quad."

I hesitated. I wanted to go, but I couldn't help but feel it would be a betrayal. To do something fun on *his* farm with *his* friend while *he* was hurting. Rory pulled out his phone and frantically typed a message. When he got a response shortly after, he handed it to me to read.

He'd messaged Callahan: *Hey, can I take your girl out on the quad? She's pretty blue. Thought it might cheer her up to see a bit more of the farm.*

Callahan had replied: *Please keep her safe. I know I'm being a dick. Please tell her I miss her. But I can't face the house yet.*

I choked out a sob. I was both heartbroken that he was in so much pain he felt completely unable to face his home and selfishly relieved that he wasn't avoiding me.

"See, I told you, he's not avoiding you at all. He's avoiding the house."

"Okay, fine, maybe you were a little right. But I'm not his girl."

"Sure you're not," he said with a smirk.

"Seriously. We're just helping each other through a hard time,

217

and we barely know each other anyway," I said a little too defensively.

"Remind me, how many dates do people have to go on before they're allowed to have feelings for each other?"

I rolled my eyes and kept my lips sealed. Picking a dried stalk of grass and wrapping it around my finger.

"And can you date someone if you've only just met them?" he asked with a cocky tilt of his head.

"I'm not particularly well versed with the rules of dating, so maybe you should ask Callahan if you're rusty and need advice."

He snorted a laugh and then stared at me with one brow quirked dubiously.

"I've only ever had one relationship—and that was a disaster," I supplied before turning my gaze back to the cows, finding the closest one staring at us while swiping a long narrow tongue over its pale pink nose.

"You've seriously only been with one dude?" I didn't miss the shock in his tone and turned back to see his mouth hung open.

My lips curved into a sly grin. "I've only had one relationship," I corrected.

"Arh, gotcha," he said with a wink, the smile on his face growing ever wider. "I actually heard you have a thing for blondes."

I rolled my eyes and ignored his baited comment.

He slid a little closer, and his smile abruptly vanished as he eyed my face. "Here, let me see your cheek." Concern gouged a divet between his brows, and I turned so he could see the messy scab. He pushed a strand of hair back behind my ear, his fingers lingering.

"Hmmm, I don't think it will scar too badly," he said softly.

I nodded, staring at his shoulder until I realised he was leaning in closer. My eyes flicked up to meet his, and the moment shifted into awkwardness. What was he implying about my preference for blondes? That I would like him? He looked at my lips, hinting at his intent or desire to kiss me. Surely he wouldn't do that?

His tongue swept teasingly over his bottom lip, and I watched in shock as his lips sailed directly towards mine. Fuck, this was seriously happening.

I abruptly sat back out of reach with a gasp, my heart pounding in panic. "Rory, what the fuck are you doing?"

His face exploded into a wide grin. "Proving a point," he said, looking decidedly smug. "Admit it, you won't kiss me because you like him."

"What makes you think I'd want to kiss anyone right now? I've been attacked, shot at, and I've seen things..." My stomach was suddenly a sea of nausea. Memories assaulting me that I couldn't seem to suppress.

His grin vanished when he saw the distress sweeping over my face, and he gently squeezed my shoulder. "Sorry, I was...you're lying to yourself if you think there is nothing between you two. And if you genuinely don't have any sort of attraction or feelings for him, then I don't want to see him hurt. I know him. I see the way he looks at you."

"Er, have you forgotten that he was ready to hand me over to the vampires a week ago? He needed me, and yes we've become friends, but I doubt he has feelings for me. It's probably just that my scent is comforting to you guys. I'm a crutch I guess."

I wasn't even that at the moment. My heart felt like it had been squeezed with an iron fist. Yesterday had been so much harder without him. I was already far too attached but equally too weak-willed to do anything about it.

"That's bullshit. What, you think just because you smell good, Tilly would risk his life to keep you alive? He thinks highly of you —he believed pretty bloody strongly that you were worth fighting for."

"If that's true, why the hell would you try and kiss me just to prove a point? What if I'd kissed you back?" I was staring at him open-mouthed and angry.

He shrugged. "I was ninety-five, maybe ninety-seven percent certain you would never kiss me. And if you had, I would have enjoyed it for a moment and then prayed to God Tilly didn't shoot me when I told him. The fresh air and exercise would probably do him good when he hunted me down, actually."

I shook my head, utterly dumbfounded by his ridiculous rationale. "You're unbelievable."

"But I'm also right."

"No, you're stupid."

He laughed. "Answer me with one hundred percent honesty. Do you think I'm an attractive guy?" He raised his eyebrow, waiting in silent challenge, so confident he already knew the answer.

"I think you're an arrogant bastard, which is not an attractive quality. But I suppose you do have a somewhat pretty face if I really had to think about it."

His face stilled, the confidence no longer spilling out. "You know I'm not arrogant."

I glared at him, refusing to agree. He generally was not arrogant—I wouldn't consider him a friend if he was.

"I think if you didn't know Tilly, and I'd tried to kiss you, you *would* have kissed me, because at times like these, we all look for comfort and escapism and connection. So stop lying to yourself. None of us are stupid. We all see it."

"I think you're a dick."

I stared at the floor, wishing it was that simple. Scarily, perhaps even unhealthily, Callahan had become the centre of most of my waking thoughts. No matter how hard I fought it—my mind succumbed to his gravitational pull, like the tide inevitably making its way back to the shore. But I had first been a necessity to him, and now I was the cause of his biggest heartache. How could he ever look at me and not feel grief and anger and despair?

Rory nudged my shoulder. "Give him time."

I stared at him, my expression hard and serious. "Kiss me," I told him. His eyes grew wide, and he shook his head, leaning back in case I launched at him like a rabid animal. I couldn't help the grin that swept across my face, wiping all my seriousness away.

"You bitch," he said, sucking in air and then laughing with relief.

"What? I was ninety-eight percent certain you wouldn't actually kiss me." I got up, feeling smug and headed for the quad. "Come on, I thought you had work to do?"

∼

I spent the day shadowing him. I wasn't allowed to get involved or even too close—God forbid my wounds got dirty—despite the worst of them being bandaged. For good measure, he reassessed them again before dinner and changed the dressings.

While we ate leftover chilli, he told me numerous tales about Callahan. How he'd always been enamoured with the farm since they bought it when he was seven years old. How he'd worked alongside his dad from the beginning. He told me of the adventures they'd had learning how to farm well. How it was hard for him to stay detached and unemotional when they were old enough for slaughter. I listened with rapt fascination, lapping up every word like it was the most delicious morsel, and slowly, realisation dawned. I was fighting the inevitable. I could keep denying it but there was a spark between us that I didn't want to smother, and the longer Rory talked about him, the more desperately I longed to see him and make sure he was okay. To know if he could ever look at me again and be a part of my life.

"Rory. I know Ava and James don't want me in their house, but do you think you can sneak me in? I just want to speak to him for a few minutes?" I asked as he stacked plates in the dishwasher.

He blew out a breath. "Tonight?"

I nodded, staring at him with pleading eyes and joining my palms in supplication. He sighed, running his hand along the neat facial hair bracketing his lips.

"Stop with the puppy dog eyes. Look, I'll message Fletcher and see if he can help you," he said, pulling out his phone, "but I'm not getting involved."

25

POWERLESS

"Right, they're in the living room with the dogs, so be fucking quiet," Fletcher hissed as he dragged me into his hallway. I was no sooner inside than he was propelling me towards the central staircase.

"Quickly up the stairs, then the first door on the left is my room. Wait in there, and I'll be up in a minute."

I paused on the first step, glancing at him over my shoulder. "Why your room?"

"Because they'll assume it's me and Isla talking in there, and you can hide in the en-suite if you need to."

I nodded, wondering why I'd even bothered to question him, and resumed tiptoeing up the stairs, grateful that it was carpeted. The frantic beat of my heart pulsed loudly in my ears, and it was an effort to keep my breaths steady by the time I reached the top.

The room smelt distinctly boyish, and I couldn't help but notice it was entirely monochrome. Even if he hadn't told me this was his room, I would have known. It was quintessentially Fletcher. The walls, carpet and curtains were varying shades of grey, the dominating king-size bed had a black leather frame with a dark grey cover, and even his furniture was grey. He had just enough space for a wardrobe and a small desk—where a TV stood amidst piles of magazines—thankfully none of them incriminating. He had one bedside table which was stacked with books—all car-related—along with a reading lamp. I'd expected to see some minor feminine touch somewhere in his room, a small hint of Isla, but there was nothing. Not even a picture frame. I heard Fletcher's heavy feet thudding up the stairs a few moments later followed by a knock on the guest room door where Callahan was staying.

By the time Fletcher coaxed him out I was wiping away a sheen of sweat from my hairline. My breath caught as Callahan was pushed unceremoniously into the room. He looked groggy and wore only black pyjama shorts. I secretly applauded myself for keeping my eyes and thoughts respectful and purely on his face.

Fletched reappeared a moment later and draped a T-shirt over Callahan's shoulder, pressing his phone into his hand. As the door clicked shut Callahan finally saw me and registered what was happening. His mouth fell open as he took me in, his brows pinching together, causing my stomach to undulate with nerves.

"I understand if you'd rather not see me. I'll leave if you—"

"I don't want you to leave," he said quickly, his head shaking as he watched me. "I'm sorry…I'm just surprised, and I haven't showered or brushed my teeth. I feel grotty."

"Like I give a fuck about that," I said closing the space between us and pulling him into an embrace.

Underneath the salty scent of his sweat, which was surprisingly not unpleasant, was his usual, comforting woodsy scent. When I closed my eyes and breathed him in, I was transported to the forest, surrounded by the steadfast towering pines glistening with freshly spilt rain. It felt like home.

I shuddered. I was definitely crazy.

Only when his arms settled tightly around me, pressing me against his bare skin, did my heart begin to settle. We stood locked together, the seconds ticking into minutes as I focused on the rise and fall of his chest, listening to his deep inhales, hoping that my scent was dampening the edge of his pain. When he started to shiver, I stepped back, allowing him to slide his T-shirt on. He looked so pale, his eyes were red and bloodshot and his lips were sore and chapped—the sight caused a painful jolt in my chest and words stuck in my throat.

He drew closer, his fingers gently brushing hair away from my scabbed face, eyeing the wound.

"Just a scratch," I whispered.

He shook his head, his eyes narrowing as his gaze travelled to the bruising on my neck and then lingered on my bandaged arm.

"I've never felt more powerless than when I was sitting in the front of that car," he confessed, his voice whisper-soft.

A tear escaped before I could blink it away, and I bowed my head trying to hide it.

"I've never felt more terrified than when I thought you were going to get shot. Both times," I admitted, holding back more tears, grateful that he was even speaking to me.

"And you decided to run screaming away from and then straight towards a gun. Fuck, you scared me. What if I had been out of shells?"

"I don't think I cared," I said mournfully. I fidgeted with my hands, trying to keep the worst of my storming emotions locked away. "I'm sorry you had to do that. If any of it leads back to the farm, I'll confess that I did it and make it clear you were no part of it. My parents have money and connections, and they'd make sure I had a good lawyer."

He stared at me open-mouthed. And I hurried to add, "I don't think it will come to that. For a long time, I've been in denial about there being someone higher up covering up the deaths. If this gets covered up then I guess it will just confirm my suspicions. If it doesn't, there is not a chance in hell I'm letting the police anywhere near you and that's non-negotiable." I tipped my head up, braving his reaction. He was rubbing at his eyes with the heels of his hands, and I cursed myself for adding a layer of worry to his overburdened plate.

"Do you wish—"

"Don't even," he retorted curtly, giving me a sharp look, knowing where my question was headed. Yet some psychotic part of me wanted to ask him, I wanted to hear his answer. Did he regret not handing me over at the first possible second? Did he believe it would have made a difference? Would he even hesitate to go back and make a different choice if he thought there was any small possibility his family would have survived?

"Can we sit?" I asked instead, needing to ease the trembling in my legs and the awkwardness stacking up between us. He released me and clambered across Fletcher's enormous bed, settling against the headboard. He pulled up the pillows and stuffed them behind his back. I waited, watching him adjust until he was comfortable, uncertainty turning my muscles to stone. Seeing my hesitation, Callahan swiped the air towards him, ushering me to his side. When I obliged he tucked me under his arm, the awkwardness between us at once dissolving, and he rested his cheek against the top of my head. The heat of each of his breaths warmed my scalp, and I could feel his pulse steadily thrumming beneath my fingertips. My whole body seemed to thrum in response.

"I'm so sorry," I whispered, "for all of it."

I didn't know where to start. Whether he needed my silence, apology, acknowledgement or reassurance. His chest shuddered as he took a shaky inhale, and my fingers flexed, digging in as if I could hold him tighter.

"Whatever you need from me, it's yours," I whispered. "In whatever capacity. Whether it's a shoulder to cry on, a listening ear when you want to reminisce, a hand to hold when you're facing all of the firsts, a warm embrace when you need comfort, or maybe vengeance. Anything you need, I'm here. If you want me to be."

The ensuing silence had panic smothering my breath, my throat drying out at the possibility that he might need my absence above anything else.

"I just need you to be patient with me. I don't know what I'm feeling from one minute to the next. I'm a mess." He wiped away a tear, and when I shifted to look at him he closed his eyes, tipping his head back against the leather bed frame, avoiding my gaze. "I still keep thinking I'm going to wake up…"

My heart cleaved open at his painful admission. Oh, how I wished I could take it all back. That I wasn't the epicentre of his brokenness. Moving down the bed and stretching out, I motioned for him to join me, cradling his head against my chest and teasing the lengths of his hair through my fingers.

"I'm so sorry, I wish I could make it right." After a time, a hot trickle of tears saturated my hoodie as his breaths became more stuttered. He was trying so hard to keep himself from breaking, and I held him tighter, anchoring him as he had anchored me.

The sound of footsteps trudging up the stairs had my heartbeat rapidly accelerating, and Callahan shifted to look at me. His eyelashes still harbouring tears that had yet to spill down his cheeks.

"They don't know you're here?"

I shook my head, wiping his face with my sleeve, and he groaned quietly. "Did you just wipe my snot on your jumper?"

I pressed my finger to his lips, my heart kicking wildly against my ribs in warning as I debated dashing for the bathroom. There was a soft knock that had Callahan scrambling off the bed and dragging me with him. I hid behind the door and stopped breathing.

It was Ava. There was surprise laced in her tone as she greeted him, and Callahan told her he was about to use Fletcher's shower. After a brief conversation, he bid her goodnight and was quickly across the room, slipping through the bathroom door and twisting the shower on.

"I'm sorry," I murmured. "I know you don't like lying."

Yet another thing I had forced him to do, along with torture, murder, and of course the most recent, secretly burying his parents and sister. How was it even possible he wanted me here?

"It's fine. I need to shower anyway," he said resolutely, rubbing his eyes and then testing the temperature, the spray of water dusting my skin.

"If I can borrow your phone, I can text Fletcher and get him to sneak me back out?"

He shook his head. "Might be better to wait until they've gone to bed. I won't be long and they definitely won't come in here now so just sit against the shower. I trust you."

I did as he said, folding my arms over my knees and resting my head on them, pleased that he wasn't ready for me to disappear. My mind was occupied with so many things, I barely noticed when he stepped out of the shower and flicked me with water. Only when he'd dried off and wrapped himself securely in a towel, did I finally move.

"Callahan, at some point soon, I need to go back to the city. I need to figure out what to do, and I want…" I trailed off. Not knowing how to put into words all the things I was feeling and facing now that our worlds had collided so chaotically, the effects devastating and life-altering.

"What do you want?" he asked quietly, his expression guarded.

The truth twisted uncomfortably in my stomach.

"I don't want to leave you. I want to help…"

"Help fix me?"

My mouth fell open, the hurt at his suggestion tugging my eyebrows together, and I took a breath to level my tone, knowing I needed to tread delicately—that he was speaking from a place of brokenness.

"No, I want to help on the farm because I care about you. Believe me, if I could go back in time and alter the outcome, *whatever* that entailed—I would."

The hard edge of his expression tempered. "I'm sorry. I'm…"

"You're grieving. I can take it—if you want me to. I can also leave. You have every right to be angry at me, and I would understand if you didn't want me here."

"No," he whispered, "I don't want you to leave." His head bowed as he blanketed his face behind his fingers. His shoulders rose along with the deep breath that swelled his chest and finally, he lowered his hands to look at me. "I'm not angry at you—I'm angry at myself. I failed them."

"But you didn't. The scales were always tipped against you. It was never a fair fight! You and I should both be dead right now, but we survived. And I plan to hunt them down and fucking end them. Something I should have already done. I have so much blood on my hands."

He closed the distance between us, lifting my chin, his usually bright eyes dulled with sorrow and exhaustion as his gaze met mine and held it steady.

"Your blood doesn't make you responsible for them, or for the lives of anyone they've killed. My family included," he said pointedly. "I don't blame you—if that's why you keep saying you'll leave if I want you to?"

I held his stare, searching for any hint of falsity in his words, but his expression didn't give much away, shadowed by the permanence of grief.

"I mean it," he whispered, reading the suspicion in my eyes. I gave the slightest shake of my head, bewildered by his ability to sense the direction of my thoughts and wondering for the hundredth time if he really could read minds.

His eyes narrowed, flickering over my face, and he cupped my cheeks, his thumb sliding over the freckles breaking up my olive skin, sending my pulse spiralling.

"Please can you just trust me? I haven't got the energy right now to battle this out with you. I am so fucking tired."

My eyes snapped shut, and my bones felt like they crumbled under the weight of sorrow in his voice.

"I trust you," I choked out and dislodged myself from his grip to fold my arms around him, my fingers swirling in a trickle of water that had descended from his hair.

"I should probably go before we get caught," I muttered against the warmth of his bare skin.

"Yeah, I guess so. Stay here," he said as he squeezed past me back into Fletcher's room where he headed for the door and slipped out into the hall.

He returned fully dressed and with Fletcher in tow.

26

SAVE IT

"I'll come find you tomorrow. I need to try and get my head around work, and I'll help you sort a replacement phone or whatever." His phone buzzed, and the screen lit up with a message from Fletcher. He nodded, his brows tugging down towards his nose. "Fletcher said his parents are in bed. It's all clear, and he's waiting outside."

"Okay, sleep well. I'll see you tomorrow."

Not daring to look at him in case my emotions disabled me, I edged past him into the hall. I could feel his gaze lingering on my retreating form. Inflating my lungs as if it could somehow make me lighter, I carefully positioned each foot, easing myself down the stairs one step at a time. Having descended without so much as a creak, I took a step towards the door, towards Fletcher's silhouette, framed by the gentle kiss of moonlight as he waited for me outside.

"How. Dare. You. Trespass in my house."

My breath rattled out. Well, this was fucking peachy.

Slowly, I turned. My skin stood to attention with an abundance of goosebumps that had infuriatingly arrived seconds too late.

There, in the pitch-black hall was the faint glimmer of James' ice-blue eyes slicing through the darkness.

The hall lights snapped on, momentarily blinding me.

"Is it trespassing if you're invited?" I grimaced as the words parted with my lips. Invited was a bit of a stretch; manipulated was much closer to the truth. Fletcher stepped into the hall behind me, cursing under his breath, and the stairs creaked as Callahan flew down them to stand at my side. James didn't take his eyes off me, hatred stirring in his expression.

"I'm sorry. I was just worried about Callahan, and I wanted to check—"

"You should be sorry. You're the reason Callahan is hurting. You're the reason we've lost our best friends, and you have absolutely no right to be anywhere near this farm." He spat the words, imbuing them with every ounce of hateful emotion he could muster, and each one lodged itself bitterly in my brittle heart.

I was so swept up in the tidal wave of self-loathing that my vision hazed as tears flocked to spill out over my cheeks. Callahan tugged my shoulders, spinning me around and steering me towards the door.

"Why are you so intent on having her here? She's ruined your life," James seethed as we stepped towards freedom. Callahan's touch disappeared from my shoulders as he swivelled around to face him.

"I wouldn't fucking be here if it wasn't for her."

"You're right. If she didn't exist everything would have continued on as normal."

Callahan snorted at the twisting of his words. "I'm not doing this, James. My heart is fucking broken, and this is not helping. Seeing as you don't seem capable of facing reality, and apparently wish me dead, I'll find somewhere else to stay."

He almost choked on Callahan's words. "I would never wish you dead. That's absurd. But if you insist on seeing her, then by all means, stay elsewhere. I don't want her around—she manipulated you and it cost us all dearly. I can't believe you don't see it for yourself."

My jaw dropped with a sharp inhale, but before I could wade into the battle, Fletcher's calloused hand barricaded my mouth, and he dragged me back towards the door.

"Not the fucking time," he mumbled in my ear. I tried to dislodge him, but his grip tightened, and four steps later we were emerging from the war zone into the pitch black of the drive. When I was unpinned, my fist launched at Fletcher's arm and my knuckles screamed on impact.

I shook my hand, cursing profusely under my breath and shaking with rage. When I finally righted myself, Fletcher was eyeing me smugly, arms folded across his chest, and I bit my tongue, reining in my fury.

Callahan stood a little further up the drive, his fingers pulling at the longest strands of his hair as he stared at the farmhouse. Its dark foreboding form stared right back at him, the challenge stretching between them, and I cautiously approached, the familiar edge of guilt shredding through my veins.

"I'm so sorry," I told him, frustrated that the words were rolling off my tongue yet again.

"Save it," Callahan said curtly, stealing my breath and driving the guilt deeper like a blade between my ribs. I sucked in a breath and turned away, my feet refusing to move. Even Fletcher remained a statue metres away, waiting for Callahan to collect himself and make a decision.

Hanging my head back in exasperation, I found the night sky glittering with a vast blanket of stars, more visible out here than in the city. I'd never realised how much I'd missed them until now, when the beauty of it momentarily blotted out the cutting silence that stretched between the three of us.

"You said you wanted to go back to the city. Would you mind

if I crashed with you for a few days while I get my head straight? I can't stay in the house. I'm not ready yet."

"I don't mind at all," I answered quickly.

"I don't think I unpacked my stuff from the B&B, it's probably still in the hall. Can you grab it and I'll drive us back to the city?"

"You sure you're alright to drive? I can take you over and drop your car off tomorrow when Isla finishes work?" Fletcher suggested as he made his way towards us.

To my immense relief, Callahan nodded, and I launched into action, my limbs released from their rigid protest.

∼

After an uncomfortably quiet drive to the city, Fletcher pulled up on the street outside my apartment, dropping us as close to the building door as he could physically get and minimising the risk to our safety.

Our overburdened limbs thudded heavily against each wooden step as we ascended to my apartment. Neither of us spoke. I unlocked my door, stepping over a pile of colourful junk mail, as the light dutifully flickered on when we crossed the threshold. It did not feel good to be home.

"I forgot how depressing this place is," Callahan muttered as he passed and headed straight for my room.

Swallowing down my guilt, I locked the door, pacing through my apartment to make sure everything was secure. When I entered my room, Callahan was already in my en suite, his suitcase propped open against my wardrobe. I grabbed pyjamas and changed in the main bathroom, rustled up a spare blanket and pillow and dropped onto my sofa. Scrunching my body into a ball to keep my feet from overhanging, I hoped sleep would find me quickly.

It did not.

My chest was burning with rage. Fucking Ava and James. I understood their anger, the guilt I personally felt was overwhelming, but they were willing to let me die. They wanted me to die. They'd felt my life was a perfectly acceptable sacrifice for their friends, without a sliver of remorse, so they were hardly fucking saints. I didn't ask to exist like this. How could they not see that the majority of their wrath was misplaced and should have been directed at the perpetrators of this whole situation? The murderers who were still out there using and abusing vulnerable people.

"What the fuck are you doing?" Callahan's voice exploded through my thoughts, and I sat up with a wince, surprised I hadn't heard him approach.

"I'm trying to sleep."

"I can see that, but why are you out here? You have a king-sized bed. If you're that desperate to stay away from me, build a pillow fort between us, but don't be ridiculous and sleep on that. It's not even long enough for your legs." He sighed heavily, his fingers massaging his temples. "I didn't come here to turf you out of your own bed."

Gritting my teeth and taking a breath to soften my reply, I said, very respectfully, "I assumed you needed space, and I fit on the sofa a hell of a lot better than you would."

"Well, I don't need space," he grunted in response. "Will you please come sleep in the bed?"

He waited for me to stand then grabbed for my pillow, tucking it under his arm and gesturing for me to move. When we reached my room he flung my pillow on the bed and dropped onto the mattress like a felled tree, groaning as he adjusted until he was comfortable. I followed with slightly more poise, turning out the light and settling on my back leaving an arm's length between us. Despite knowing the tension wasn't entirely aimed at me, it was hard to know how to respond to it. On about my third sigh, Callahan broke the silence.

"Liv?"

"What was that? Did you just call me Liv?"

"I'm guessing nobody's ever called you that?" he mumbled against his pillow.

"Would you be surprised to know my parents aren't the sort of people that use nicknames?"

He snorted a laugh, and the sound eased the strain between us and dragged a smile across my lips. "What did…actually never mind," he said and puffed out a frustrated breath. "Earlier tonight, you said you'd be here for me in whatever capacity…"

"I did."

"I believe you might have mentioned something about a warm embrace…"

He cleared his throat, and just as I was about to scoot closer, his voice floated across in a whisper. "Olivia, I need you."

"You've got me," I replied, sliding across the bed at breakneck speed. He shifted onto his back, and I nestled into his chest, draping my leg over his to bind us, not caring what lines we blurred.

"I've got you," I reiterated. "Don't bottle it up. I'm here for you, whatever you need."

"I know," was all he said as he clutched me to his chest like a life buoy.

Oh, God. He was freshly orphaned and currently relying on me to help him. Me. The bringer of chaos. Me. With the big fat crush on the grieving man who took her hostage not quite a week ago. What a mess. And yet I still hoped Rory was right and I wasn't going to get my heart broken. My conversations with him cycled through my mind on repeat.

"What are you thinking about so seriously?"

"What makes you think I'm thinking anything?"

"I can feel your lashes fluttering against my skin," he answered softly, "so I know you're not trying to sleep."

"Really? My lashes are the reason I'm getting the third degree?"

"I'd say it's your defensiveness that's currently fueling it," his voice carried a hint of playfulness, and after the last few hours, it was like the first heavenly drops of rain falling over parched land. If it didn't require me to move I'd have considered turning the light back on just to see the hint of a smile on his lips.

"Tell me," he demanded, squeezing my shoulders.

I swallowed frantically, my heart travelling up my throat ready for me to spit it out along with my dignity.

"Just tell me, it's not like anything you say could make my life any worse right now is it?"

That was debatable. "What if it's something wildly inappropriate that would make you feel extremely awkward?"

"Oh. Were you thinking about someone else?"

"No," I spat, shocked by the direction of his assumption. "I was deliberating how likely it was that my heart would end up broken. I told you it was inappropriate."

"By me?"

"No by fucking Santa Claus. Yes. You. Who else am I currently sharing a bed with?" My blood simmered with embarrassment and utter horror at spewing those words to him when he was only two days into grieving for his family. "I'm so sorry. That was so insensitive. Fuck. Do I need to build a pillow fort or am I banished to the sofa?" I tried to sit up and give him some space, but his arms tightened like a snare and held me in place.

After a brief, somewhat stunned silence, he snorted a laugh. "Neither," he said and loosed a resolute sigh. "Thank you, for being honest with me—"

"But you don't want me like that," I finished for him, recognising the gentle rejection within the cadence of his voice and preferring to drive the blade in sooner rather than later.

"Why would you think that? Olivia, *wanting you* is the only thing keeping me from completely falling apart." He cursed under his breath, his body tensing beneath my fingertips. "I can't...I can't do this now though," he eventually whispered. "At least, I can't handle more than this. I need time to process and I don't want *us* to be a distraction that stops me from sorting my shit out. And..." His breath stuttered and a shiver vibrated over his skin. "Then I'd eventually ruin everything, and I can't deal with more failure."

Well, that was a delightful emotional rollercoaster. For the briefest of moments, my heart had soared euphorically before plummeting to tragic rocky depths. I couldn't catch my breath, let alone speak.

"Please say something," he pleaded. His every exhale danced across my lips, taunting me.

"You. Are. Not. A. Failure," I finally said, infusing my words with as much authority as possible. "And I completely understand where you're coming from. So, friends it is, and maybe next time, please listen when I tell you I was thinking about something awkward that I didn't want to share." Dropping back against my pillow, I put a respectful distance between us. The darkness thankfully veiled my disappointment.

"I don't want to lose you," Callahan said gruffly. He was still propped on his elbow, and I could just see the faint glow of his eyes—highlighted by the street light creeping around the edge of my curtains.

"I don't want to lose you either. We'll just take each day as it comes."

He sighed, long and heavy, and settled back down, reaching for my fingers and entwining them in the hollow space between us.

27

WHAT DO I DO?

Sleep came and went in the blink of an eye. Callahan was shirtless when I woke, sprawled across his half of the bed and still sleeping, so I left him be.

My morning was filled with mundane tasks: ordering a new phone, arranging a food delivery, cancelling my car insurance, and informing the DVLA that I'd sold it then inwardly freaking out about the implications once my car was found. So far nothing had been reported. I scoured the internet for possible replacements, though the options were few given my meagre savings. After many coffee interludes and serious deliberation, I emailed my agency and told them I was taking some time out for at least the next week, clearing my schedule to devote time to Callahan. However he needed me, I would be there.

By lunchtime, he still hadn't stirred, and it was unnerving. This was a man who woke before sunrise every morning in readiness for a day of hard graft. After researching grief extensively online, general exhaustion seemed to be a standard physical response which was a mild comfort. The endless list of distressing emotions he was yet to feel was not. I saved links to various sites, ordered a couple of books to help me navigate the long journey he had ahead, and hoped we could weather it together. Having spent a decade doing life alone, I would not give up on him easily.

There was still no movement by dinner time. This whole situation had me feeling extremely out of my depth. I'd never had family die. And family was a somewhat loose concept to me. It certainly meant something far less important to me than it did to Callahan. I'd lost friendships, which entailed a form of grief, but I knew they were off finding happiness somewhere else, and I was familiar with death, but only the kind people rooted for. That was justified. Not this.

When I entered my room, he was curled up with the covers heaped on top of him. Sitting on the edge of the mattress, I pulled away the duvet and found his skin clammy and overheated. He stirred when my cool palm pressed against his forehead, absorbing some of the heat.

"Caitlyn?" he mumbled as he slowly pried apart his eyelashes and his focus resettled on me. I swallowed, trying to hold off my sadness, when a look of pure pain flashed in his eyes, and he promptly closed them again.

I gave him a moment to recalibrate. "Hey, are you hungry? I'll order some food if you can manage something?" I ran my hand over his bare arm and down his shoulder blades, soothing and gentle.

"What are you ordering? And can we eat it in bed?" He rolled onto his back and stretched out, his athletic frame flexing beneath my stare.

My eyes flew back to his, the tell-tale warmth of a flush creeping over my cheeks as I realised I was caught out. He didn't seem to care.

"I'm not fussy. I'll eat whatever you can manage," I told him.

An hour later I was pulling pizzas out of a delivery robot, feeling my typical guilt for not ordering food from Piccolinos when it was just downstairs. The last time I'd ordered pizza had been in the summer when all the outdoor tables and chairs were heavily utilised. The little white robot had struggled to navigate through all the obstacles to my apartment door and I had to meet it on the edge of the street. The shame I felt when carrying my pizza box past all the restaurant eaters, was stifling. Made worse when I had to shuffle past a waiter who had eyed my box with flat-out contempt. But the heart wants what it wants.

I was slowly making my way through my fourth slice when Callahan pushed his meat feast away and wiped his mouth with a serviette. He'd eaten only three slices and looked decidedly peaky. His skin was dull, and I noticed a fine sheen of sweat at his hairline, I hadn't thought it was that spicy. With a huge sigh, he shifted back and propped himself up against my headboard, giving me a tight-lipped smile when he caught me staring.

"Tell me something about you that nobody else knows," he said, his eyes sparking to life with the extended challenge. I tapped my nails across the lid of the pizza box in front of me, scouring my memories for anything vaguely light-hearted.

"That's surprisingly hard when you already know my biggest secrets! When I was in my late teens, for about a year, I used to carry garlic cloves in my pockets if I went out at night. Nobody knows that."

One side of his mouth curved into a vague smile, and he shook his head slowly. "I'm guessing you found out the hard way it was completely useless?"

"You would be correct. What's the wildest thing you and Fletcher did when you were younger?"

He tipped his head back against the wall and blew out a breath between pursed lips. "God, there are so many. We did a lot of stupid stuff on the quads. And we used to set up obstacles with hay bales and wood and any other shit we found laying around the farm so that we could do stunts with our bikes. When I was about eleven, Fletcher dared me to get on one of the bulls. That was probably the stupidest thing I did as we were on our own, and it could have gone so, so badly."

"Did you get hurt?" I asked, trying to imagine an eleven-year-old Callahan based on the photographs back at the farm.

"Just a few sore muscles," he said with a smirk "I fell off pretty quick and narrowly avoided being trampled. It was close, though. What's the worst thing you did growing up?"

"You were lucky," I said, shaking my head but not particularly surprised. "Oh, that's easy. I called child services and told them I wanted to go to school but my parents wouldn't let me. I got in a shit tonne of trouble for that!"

Callahan's eyebrows flew up. "That's like every parent's worst nightmare!"

I grinned sheepishly and stretched out my legs before crossing them again, my elbows resting on my knees. "It didn't get very far. I don't remember them visiting or anything. I think my parents were so wealthy and so well-connected it wasn't hard for them to prove that they were paying obscene amounts for all my private tutoring. But I begged them to let me go to school. It was all I wanted—just to be around other children."

"I thought you said that was the better part of your life?" He frowned.

"It was," I replied quickly. "I liked the travelling we did. We'd be gone sometimes a month at a time, and while Mum and Dad were working, I would still have my lessons but at the weekends; there would be other children around for me to play with. We didn't always speak the same language, but we could still understand enough to play." I smiled. Hazy though they were, those memories were the fondest of my childhood and some of the only ones that remained. "That's how I met Penny, actually. I was in New York with my parents, and she was staying at the same hotel. I was at breakfast, and I spotted her playing with a doll that I'd put on my birthday wish list, and I ran to their table to see it. I introduced her to Rajah, my tiger, and we just started playing right there at her table. Our parents didn't know each other, but rather fortuitously, it turned out they only lived forty minutes from us, and so they exchanged numbers." I sighed wistfully and Callahan leaned forward and squeezed my knee, his touch igniting my skin on fire. "That's probably the cutest thing you've said about your childhood, but it still makes me feel sad."

Pressure built in my chest, I didn't know why his pity seemed to snatch all the air from my lungs. Perhaps it was the realisation that even the good parts of my childhood weren't good enough. That I had been robbed of even more than I could comprehend. He seemed to read my expression and changed the subject. "What was your favourite subject?"

"Science!" I said without any hesitation. "It was one of the few things my Dad used to help me with. I had one of those science subscription boxes for Christmas one year, and we used to set up the experiments together every month."

He smiled and tipped his head back against the wall. "Your Dad sounds halfway decent. How the hell did he and your mum end up together?"

"God knows. I'm not even sure they like each other. At all. I don't think I've ever seen them kiss." I looked up from fidgeting with my nails to find his eyes were closed and his face looked painfully tense. Placing my palm on his forehead, my stomach dropped when I felt the unmistakable burn of a fever, clammy against my skin.

"Are you un—" Shit. When did he last drink blood? "Have you not had blood since Saturday night?"

"How do you know I had it then?" he asked quietly, his eyes remaining shut.

"You disappeared with Fletcher, then brushed your teeth when you got back—right before dinner. You looked like you were struggling to eat any of the food. That was six days ago. I thought you needed blood every three days?"

"I do," he sighed, "but I don't want it."

"Callahan, you can't—why are you doing this?"

He was quiet, his breathing becoming deeper as sleep tugged him away from me.

"Callahan!" My voice jolted him awake, and he rubbed at his face with a look of contrived innocence. "Why won't you drink?" I said again more forcefully, wondering if he was punishing himself or embarrassed to drink it in front of me.

"Many reasons."

"Which are?" His eyes twitched with annoyance. "The sooner you explain it to me the sooner I'll leave you alone. I just want to understand."

His body was trembling, and worry knotted in my stomach.

"What do I do?" I asked shakily.

"Nothing. I'll send for it when I'm ready."

28

FOR YOU

For three wretched days, I nervously paced my apartment while Callahan's condition grew steadily worse. He refused to call Fletcher or Rory, refused pain relief, refused to unlock his phone so that I could contact someone, and he even refused food. We barely spoke other than his vague reassurances that he knew his limits and that it was his way of coping. That I needed to trust him. The majority of his time was spent asleep, and when I wasn't wearing grooves into my wooden floors, I tried to keep his fever from reaching dangerous heights. My fear grew agonising while watching him suffer—as he tempered the ache of grief with physical pain. I assumed that his blatant self-harm was also a form of control and punishment for his perceived failure. So much of the last two weeks had left him vulnerable at the mercy of others, and it had terrified him. It had cost him more than anyone should have to pay, so I could, in part, understand his desire to control the narrative.

But today I was done.

I wavered between despair at the prospect of losing him and anger that he would do such a thing. The pendulum swung back and forth by the minute and each time anger rose, it was doused by the relentless guilt that overshadowed my every thought.

He was like this because of me. Because I existed.

I knelt at the edge of the bed, my cheeks salty and damp from the constant flow of tears, pressing cold cloths over his forehead. When he finally stirred, he looked frail and disoriented, and I crumbled, terrified that blood wouldn't reach him soon enough. I slumped against the bed, burying my face in my arms, overwrought and crying.

"Please don't cry. I'll be fine." His voice was husky and raw, and he ruffled my hair with shaking fingers. "Can you pass me my phone please?"

Lifting my head to scrutinise him, my face puffy and my eyes raw, I asked if he was calling Fletcher.

"I'm gonna message him," he said with a nod. My body dropped some of the tension coiling tight within every muscle, and I shuddered as I reached for his phone.

Satisfied that he was finally putting an end to his grief-stricken self-sabotage, I climbed into my shower and wilted like a spent flower, slithering to the floor. Steam filled the room—gathering in swirling clouds beneath the spotlights and my finger traced a triangle on the misted glass. There used to be just me and them. But now there were three factions. All connected somehow. How many others like me were out there? How many more like Callahan? And what was at the centre of it all?

I pressed my thumb pointedly in the middle and it left an eye-shaped imprint. I scoffed. Who was watching the vampires and cleaning up their messes? It had been a whole week since it happened, yet there was no mention of the murder scene anywhere. It seemed too auspicious to think that it hadn't yet been found. Perhaps my belief that we were somehow a natural phenomenon was far too naive after all. The thought chilled my veins, and even the heat of the shower couldn't thaw the sense of foreboding. I swiped my hand over the glass, wishing I could erase the perpetual niggling feeling that sat at my core just as easily.

∾

When Fletcher arrived, I shook with relief.

"Thank you for coming," I said as more tears streaked down my face. "I'm so sorry, I should have thought about it before we left. I'm such an idiot."

He shook his head, handing over the thermos flasks, which I held as reverently as precious crown jewels.

"It's fine. I would have come tomorrow anyway, it's not the first time he's done this. He knows what he's doing; it's really not your fault. But I should warn you, he's very sensitive about this." He gave me a pointed look, and I nodded, fully aware of Callahan's distaste and shame over this part of him. "He'll need the second one in a few hours. If he's still weak tomorrow, let me know, and I'll drive more over, but he should recover pretty quickly after the second lot."

"Thank you," I said again. "How is everyone?" I asked, unable to resist requesting news. I'd missed them all so damn much.

"All right. We drove through the city the last couple of nights. Didn't see any masks. Doesn't mean they aren't using them though, so don't go out alone. And we left Callahan's car in the multi-storey. Here's the key," he said, pulling it from his pocket and dropping it on top of one of the flasks.

He turned to leave, the conversation brought to a swift close, and he pulled the door closed gently behind him.

Callahan was very unsteadily heading for the sofa when I reached the living room. His usually golden complexion was a dull grey, his jaw shadowed with several days' worth of stubble. He looked as hollow as I felt. He eyed the flasks in my arms, his expression darkening.

"I need you to leave," he said stiffly. Despite being prepared for it, his dismissal stung, and I set the flasks on the table and strode into my bedroom, slamming the door behind me.

The tenuous peace I'd cultivated in the shower shattered. A spark of anger transformed into a furiously burning rage, and with no other way to express it, I stripped my bed, viciously yanking the sheets off, ripping open poppers, and wrestling with my duvet while letting loose an endless stream of cursing. It was surprisingly therapeutic. Emotionally and physically exhausted, the lull of fresh sheets was entirely irresistible, and I slunk under the covers. For the first time in days, I drifted into a deep sleep.

∽

A gentle knock at my door roused me several hours later, and Callahan let himself in. He perched on the bed, a blanket draped around his shoulders. His skin was no longer coated in a sheen of sweat and some colour had returned. He still looked like hell and desperately needed a shower, but it was a vast improvement.

"I didn't mean to upset you," he said, his voice quiet and filled with remorse.

I sat up and hugged my legs, resting my chin on my knees. "I know. I was emotional because I thought…" I couldn't even bring myself to say the words.

He stared at his hands and took a deep breath before looking at me. His face was mostly expressionless but the pain, the all-consuming, heart-wrenching sadness was displayed so vividly in his eyes.

"I'm sorry," he mumbled under his breath.

My chest felt raw. It was agony—watching someone I cared for be so profoundly broken and yet being powerless to fix it. I dragged him further onto my bed and settled against his chest, needing the steady beat of his heart to reassure me everything would be okay. His hands wound through my hair, and he took long comforting breaths against the top of my head.

"Fletcher said you needed to drink both flasks. Maybe you should have the other now before you fall asleep again?"

He tensed, and his hands paused, it was several seconds later before he relaxed and resumed pulling the strands through his fingers. I sat up, giving him room to move.

"Please. I'm seriously fucking worried about you. I can't do that again."

He pinched his temples and groaned before sitting up, bringing his forehead to mine, his fingers brushing loose hair back behind my ear.

"For you," he breathed. Pushing himself off the bed, he moved steadily across my room and grabbed a handful of belongings from his suitcase before exiting.

I collapsed back onto my bed, a trembling mess. The pent-up emotion, the longing, the need for him felt unbearable. Taking a deep breath, I picked up the book I'd left on my bedside table and immersed myself in another world.

∼

An hour later I dared to venture out and found him in the main bathroom shaving. Half his face was still covered in foam, and I perched on the closed toilet seat to watch him. He was wrapped from the waist down in a towel, freshly showered, and I had to fight to keep my eyes from roaming. His chain hung around his neck, and every time his razor reached the underside of his jaw, the chain seemed to beckon for attention and tempt me to explore him.

I swallowed. I was torn, very much wanting to stay. There was something so soothing about the way his razor cleared a fresh path across his skin with each swipe, and the methodical splash as he dipped it in the water and tapped it against the side of the sink. But he'd embargoed our relationship, and now I was sat guiltily, fighting my instinctual desire to run my hands across his back and kiss that sweet dip between his shoulder blades. I was a bad person.

"You do realise your face is pretty damn expressive?"

Shit. My face was immediately scorched with shame, and I forced myself to stand and quietly headed for the door.

"Olivia, wait!"

I stopped, turning my body but keeping my eyes on the floor.

"Look at me," he pleaded. His beautifully straight brows were crunched together, almost meeting in the middle, his jaw clenched. "Please don't distance yourself from me. I'm sorry, I never meant to scare you. I'm trying to—" He sucked in a breath, frustration straining his features as his head tipped back.

I sighed and took a step closer. "Can you do me a favour?"

"What?"

"Can you stop punishing yourself? You're not the one who deserves it. They are."

His lips formed a tight, unbreachable line, and his shoulders tensed as he looked away. I left before I could make anything worse.

～

After a very basic dinner, I sat staring at my laptop, a throbbing ache pulsing incessantly behind my temples. I blinked, then scrunched my eyes trying to clear the blur just edging around my vision. I'd been scrolling through various news reports, crime statistics, and even social media for the last two hours, desperate to find even one mention of 'the incident'.

Callahan was stretched across my sofa on his front, braced on his elbows and trawling through a selection of cars Fletcher had sent over, in between going back and forth with Finn about farm issues. He was still shirtless, a blanket around his shoulders as he wavered between hot and cold flushes, though he was mercifully awake and in better spirits.

I sat cross-legged on the floor, my body numb from the lack of movement, and I silently cursed my lack of furniture. Callahan repeatedly offered to share the sofa but I refused, I didn't want the object of my attention to weigh on him. I was getting nowhere.

I dragged myself towards the kitchen to make a drink, and just as I reached the kettle, a heavy knock at the door made my stomach clench. I took a deep breath and headed to the hall, visions of police officers waiting to question me assaulting my mind. I swallowed and cautiously cracked the door open. My breath caught and my stomach plummeted as I pulled it wide and stepped aside.

29

YOU'RE LYING

"Good God, Olivia, I've been trying to reach you for a week," Mum said as she shoved past me into the apartment. She turned to appraise me, taking in my bedraggled appearance and the wound across my forearm. "What happened to you?" She stared, eyes narrowing suspiciously as she reached up to move aside my mess of hair and take in the graze still steadily healing high on my cheek. "Start talking."

Perfect. An unsolicited visit from my mother. Of all the times for her to take a sudden interest, she had to pick now. She was in her usual business attire. Her face was perfectly made up, not a single hair out of place. Her dark-brown eyes were wide and alert, calculating and cold—she never missed a thing. Beyond having dark hair, there was very little of my mother in me, and I wasn't disappointed by that at all.

"Can I interest you in a coffee, Mum?" No doubt she'd take it black and scalding, like her heart. She nodded, but her expression remained deadly.

"What have you gotten yourself into?" she asked venomously. "When you didn't return my calls, I had to enquire with your supply agency, and they said you haven't been in for over a week. What's going on?"

"Nothing, I lost my phone on a night out. I haven't gotten round to sending out my new number yet," I said with a weary sigh. If I'd known she'd end up at my door on a rampage, I would have sent it to her two days ago.

Her eyes twitched. "Does the truth ever find its way out of your mouth?"

"Wow, tell me how you really feel!" I folded my arms and held my ground. "Look, whether you believe me or not, that is the truth, not that it's any of your business. I took some time off to help a friend through some stuff."

My words were slow and deliberate, and I struggled to keep the edge of irritation from my tone. She shifted on her feet, the silence between us growing sharper.

"You're lying to me. Look at you, you're a state. I've never seen you look like this. What have you gotten yourself mixed up in?" Her eyes flickered distastefully down my body and back to my unmade face and tousled locks. Even at home she would be perfectly put together. I was practically feral in comparison. Her eyes darted past me to the living room as Callahan cleared his throat, and I heard his quiet steps approach.

This would be interesting. Callahan was wearing jeans and little else other than the blanket draped around his shoulders.

She looked him up and down and flinched, taking a step back. For a split second, I saw fear—an emotion I had never once witnessed on my mother's face—and then just as quickly it was gone again, replaced with disdain.

"So this is what you've been doing? While I've been worried sick that you were lying in a ditch somewhere, you've been shacking up with *him*? I thought you were done with relationships after what happened with Noah?"

"How fucking dare you," I spat. "You don't get to march in here and pretend you give a shit, and you certainly don't get to speak to my friends like that. Now get out. I don't have time for your shit today."

With a sharp intake of breath, she took a half step back, rage simmering in her eyes, and her hand instinctively rising in retaliation.

"Oh, I wouldn't." Callahan was at my shoulder, towering over her and staring at her with hard, predatory features—her rage mirrored right back at her.

She didn't shy away. Instead, she met his gaze, eyes scrutinising him unapologetically.

"I am not scared of you," she whispered. She turned to me. "Fine, you want to behave like this? So be it. Don't come crying to me when it falls apart and you find yourself packing up again. I will not be guaranteeing your next apartment. You're on your own." She turned on her heel, pausing as she reached the door to give me one final look of distaste over her shoulder. "Did you lose your car the same night as your phone? That's two this year, isn't it?" Her expression was smug as she noted my surprise, but she didn't wait for me to respond. She walked out, slamming the door behind her.

Of course she would leave with the upper hand. Every single fucking time. She probably expected me to crawl after her, begging to know how she knew about my car. I exhaled. Slowly. Reining in my temper.

"Callahan, allow me to introduce Mrs Diana Blake."

"She's quite charming. It was a pleasure." He retrieved his fallen blanket from the floor, wrapped it around his shoulders, and pulled me through to the living room towards the sofa.

"Did you see how she looked at you?"

"What, like I was a drug-dealing hobo? Yeah, I did catch that." He was fighting to keep the smile off his face, eyeing my frown as I tried to make sense of what had just happened.

"No, she...maybe I'm imagining it but I swear when she noticed your eyes she looked scared. I seriously have never *ever* seen her afraid of anything. Obviously, she is generally the scariest thing in any room, but maybe I'm just overthinking it."

"I can't say I noticed anything but complete and utter disgust. So what happened to the last car? Should I be worried about letting you drive when you get a new one? Remind me never to put you on my insurance."

I arched a brow, tilting my head as I glared at him. "My driving is fine. I got attacked in my car, and it was traumatic, so I got rid of it instead of having it repaired."

He winced. "Shit, I'm sorry. I'm assuming *it* died though?"

I tried to suppress the unwelcome memory, the terrifying moment my head collided with the car, rendering me utterly defenceless. Something that could happen a lot more if they did use the masks.

"Yes, it did eventually die. I just—I wasn't ready for it. It happened during the day, and at that point, I didn't think that was possible."

"Right, the days when you thought people burst into flames—B.C." He smirked but then his expression quickly shifted into something serious. "What happened with"—he cleared his throat as if it pained him to say the name—"Noah?"

I sighed, expecting that it would come up after my mother's outburst. "Well, funnily enough, those two things are linked. After I was attacked in my car, he happened to be waiting for me at my door earlier than we had planned. Long story short, he misunderstood the situation. We got into a fight, and he left me when I told him I could never marry him or have children."

His eyes widened and then he frowned. "How could he possibly have misunderstood that situation?"

"Oh, there was more to it than that. He put two and two together and made 100. Well, I suppose that's not totally fair—I had to lie to him by omission. A lot. So he had plenty to be mistrustful about."

The crease was still between his brows. "Do you still feel the same way?"

"About him?"

"No, about why he left?"

My heart was suddenly in my throat. Cold panic sending a shudder down my spine. "I don't know how to even answer that." I swallowed, my throat constricting. "Would you leave someone? For not being able to give you those things?"

Oxygen evaded me as I watched him consider. Mere seconds went by, but waiting for his answer felt like waiting for the swing of an axe coming down on my neck.

When he looked at me, his expression was calm. "I wouldn't leave *you*. I'd be content without those things."

Air rushed back into my lungs, and I flopped back against the sofa, closing my eyes, the sheer swell of relief almost painful. I willed my lungs and heart to settle back into a steady rhythm.

"Do you want those things though?" I asked cautiously, my eyes staying safely shut. He scooted closer and began fiddling with my hair.

"I like the idea of marriage. I like the idea of children, but it's always bothered me that my child would have to live this way, so I don't think I've been set one way or the other. But my decision to be with someone wouldn't depend on that. I understand why you wouldn't make that decision with him, but do you want those things for yourself? You work with children, so you must like them?"

I finally dared to open my eyes. His elbow was resting on the back of the sofa, propping up his head. His tousled hair was sexily dishevelled, my eyes dipped to the slither of bare chest where the blanket gaped open. My heart sped up—a slightly off-kilter rhythm. This was beginning to feel like a mild form of torture.

"I do love kids. I love working with them—they accept the small part of me that I can offer them and never expect more. They're content with that—they know I have this whole other life outside the classroom, but that's okay with them. Having one of my own is not something I've ever let myself dwell on, but I suppose I have nothing against either of those things in principle. I just wouldn't want a child to ever experience what I've experienced."

I wrenched myself away from the sofa and headed for the kitchen, grabbing fruit to prep. I needed routine, a simplistic task while I processed.

"Did I upset you?" Callahan leaned against the wall, his eyes worried as he watched me organising.

I smiled with as much sincerity as I could manage. "No, I'm just starving."

"We only ate dinner forty minutes ago?"

I shrugged. "Apparently, dealing with the wicked witch of the west gave me quite an appetite."

He laughed and started walking away. "I'm just grabbing a shirt."

"Thank God," I muttered under my breath. There was only so far my self-restraint stretched.

30

PROMISE ME

I'd worried that Callahan would need more blood to get back to full strength, but today, his grief was a raging beast. He'd woken up before me—the first time since being at my apartment. Before I'd even laid eyes on him, I could tell his mood had shifted. His body was tense beside me and after fidgeting relentlessly, he'd thrown back the covers and stalked from my room without a word.

Being open and vulnerable about his emotions was not something that came easily to him, so I partitioned off my heart, preparing myself for whatever he might throw at me and quietly went about my day. There were still things to research, ideas for me to plot, apartments to look for, and cars to prospect.

He worked out, got showered and fully dressed, silently helped me make food, and generally remained a prisoner of his tumultuous, grieving mind. I'd convinced him to walk through the city with me in the afternoon, but we were both on edge, unsure if the vampires were still dormant during daylight. It had not been the spirit-lifting excursion that I'd imagined.

He was no better by the evening. Burying my head in a book, I respectfully kept my distance. His anger may have been difficult to watch—and never directed at me—but it was infinitely better than the previous few days. While I debated the merits of reading in bed, he inhaled deeply and turned to face me from his spot by the window.

"I need to vent," he said before prowling out of the living area and heading for the door.

I grabbed my sharpest knife from the kitchen, wrapped it in my jacket, and hurried after him.

"You'll need me to find one," I said preempting his probable speech about why I should remain behind.

"I'm not planning to use you or put you at risk."

I shrugged. "Well, it just so happens, I had hunting vampires down in the diary, so I was planning a trip out anyway. I need to keep them in line. And no matter what you say, you won't change my mind."

He huffed, his mouth forming a hard line. When we found his Dacia and scrambled inside, he finally paused to look at me, his eyes flickered to my neck and his brows pinched together.

"Do NOT let them bite you, just please stay in the car."

My mouth dried out. "But the body…"

With a clenched jaw he turned the key in the ignition and the engine roared to life. "I don't want to see those marks on your throat. Not now. Not ever." He shook his head and turned his attention to driving.

I stayed quiet as we drove out to the more secluded, seedy spots in the city where the vampires could usually be found. My stomach roiled with dread. Sweat beaded on the back of my neck as recent memories resurged in my mind.

Callahan quietly simmered beside me. His lips pursed and eyes harsh and unforgiving. Every time I glanced at him, his body was rigid and tense, murderous intention etched into every muscle and every taut line on his face. Most people wouldn't usually get to take their anger to this extreme, and I desperately hoped it did not make him feel worse. He slowed to almost a crawl as we neared the more notorious areas on the outskirts of the city centre. Areas where foreboding buildings were boarded up, iron bars at the windows, and metal gates padlocked to keep squatters out. My skin was crawling with goosebumps, and my stomach twisting wretchedly with unease. This did not feel safe. We were definitely in the right territory.

We passed crumbling buildings hemmed in with masses of towering scaffolding and cranes looming in the darkness. Some of these places had been sectioned off from the public for at least the last two years, maybe longer. No doubt being on the edge of the city centre and out of the immediate public eye, it was low on the council's agenda to fix. It was certainly eerie at night. The mix of deep-red and black-brick buildings sucked the vibrancy out of the streetlights, casting everything in sinister shadows.

We parked and left the engine running for a swift exit. The street was dark and empty, looping around to join another street. There were no visible cameras or any signs of life. It was the ideal location to come across one of them, although slightly unnerving how close to the abandoned buildings we were. If they had such things as lairs, I would bet money on those buildings being one of them.

Before he got out of the car, I grabbed Callahan's arm. "If more than one shows up, promise me we'll drive away."

His face was stony—harsher than I'd ever seen it before, the sharp edges of grief pressing in and pushing out the darkest parts of him. He nodded and reached for the handle.

"Promise me you won't let it bite you," he said gruffly.

"I won't."

I opened my door and stepped out into the crisp, cool autumn air. The seconds stretched on unnaturally slow as I paced back and forth. Callahan stood in the middle of the street, hands hung loose and ready at his sides, and his face was set with grim determination.

After a few minutes, we heard hurried footsteps, and our heads snapped toward the sound. I hovered by the open passenger door, watching as the figure emerged—a dark outline against the distant glow of streetlights. Its eyes locked on mine as it paced directly towards me, a sneer across its face.

"Get in the car." Callahan was behind me, waiting for me to duck safely inside, pushing the door shut behind me. He wasted no time, meeting our enemy with a powerful right hook to the jaw that sent it sprawling backwards.

Before it fully recovered, Callahan had already landed his next punch, crushing its nose, splattering blood as it broke beneath his fist. He swept out his leg and knocked its feet from under it, sending it hurtling to the floor and out of my view.

I swivelled in my seat, making sure nothing else was coming, and when I turned back, Callahan was no longer in sight. Fear crept up my spine, sending ice-cold tendrils down my limbs and bile rising in my throat. I reached for my jacket, my hands shakily unravelled the knife, and I clutched it tightly. Cautiously, I nudged my door open just enough to see what was happening. The sickening thuds of Callahan's fists meeting flesh echoed around the empty street. Glancing back to the rear, the vamps legs were all that could be seen, poking out from behind the car, unmoving while the assault continued. I wasn't even sure if it was dead or unconscious as it lay limply on the tarmac beneath him.

Movement caught my eye further down the street, and I edged out of the car, creeping forward with my knife hidden by my side. The fury of Callahan's fists had slowed and he snarled at his lifeless enemy, his breaths ragged.

"Callahan," I said, keeping my eyes on the approaching vampire. This one was a tall female—tall enough to tower even over me. It was no less sickly and pallid than its male counterparts, and its attention was solely on me.

"Shit," Callahan mumbled, dragging himself to his feet. His eyes were wide, his mouth hung open as he stared at the oncoming vamp. His fists were bruised and split, blood dripping onto the floor at his feet.

I suspected he'd never seen a female before, and the turmoil was written all over his face. He was not expecting to fight a woman tonight. I turned and ran, putting more distance between me and the vamp, then took a deep breath and sliced the knife across the edge of my palm, my teeth clenched tight as I coated the blade with my blood.

The vamp was on me sooner than I'd anticipated, the scent of my freshly spilt blood quickening its steps. I swung the knife between us, but she reached me first, and cold fingers dug into my shoulders. My left foot buckled on a rock, and with my heart in my throat, we plummeted to the ground.

My promise to Callahan was screaming at the forefront of my mind, and I brought my hands up to block the needle-sharp teeth. We landed with a crack, my back hitting the concrete, knocking the air from my lungs, crushed further by the vampire's weight. When I wrenched my eyes open, I found it had been impaled on my knife. The blade protruded from the side of its neck, and blood was dribbling down the hilt onto my fingers.

Seconds later Callahan dragged the body off me and warmth sprayed across my face as the knife ripped free with a squelch that made me gag. I squeezed my eyes shut, my body trembled and I pressed my lips tightly together as rivulets of blood meandered down my face, coming dangerously close to my mouth. Distantly I heard the thud of its body hitting the tarmac, the sound of my knife clattering to the ground by my face, and Callahan calling my name. I couldn't move. His hands forced their way under my shoulders and pulled me upwards until I was kneeling on the ground, shaking violently.

My mind was full of white noise, my ears ringing. Maybe this was the moment that finally broke me. A car door opened behind me, and then I felt Callahan's presence in front of me.

"I'm going to help you just hold still."

I heard the splashing of water and then damp tissue dragged across my face repeatedly. There was a pause, and then I heard the tear of fresh paper towel from the blue roll he kept in his car. The paper was wetter this time and cold water dribbled down my cheeks, dripping onto my chest.

"It's nearly gone, I just need to dry your face."

The towel sucked away all the moisture left on my skin, and then he pulled my hands out in front of me and tipped the rest of the bottled water over them. My stomach violently lurched, and I realised my hand was still bleeding, most likely attracting more vamps.

"Fuck, we really need to leave. Now. I promise there is nothing on your face. Can you please open your eyes?"

I nodded and reluctantly peered out past Callahan. There was movement in the darkness.

"Is that one dead?" I asked, pointing at the bloody body sprawled on the floor. The female had begun to disintegrate, and I tried not to look at it as I assessed our situation.

"It's still alive. Barely."

I staggered to the body and squeezed my palm, encouraging blood to drip from my wound into its mouth, hopefully finishing the job. I ignored the swollen lumps of its flesh, mottled blue, purple, and red where Callahan had pulverised it with his fist.

"That's enough, Olivia. Let's go."

He was panicked, and one last look over my shoulder revealed three vamps now only thirty metres away. All of them in masks. All of them running. I raced to the car, throwing myself in and Callahan hit the accelerator just as they reached us. One grasped at my door handle, pulling the door ajar, but Callahan jerked the steering wheel back and forth, throwing it off balance and knocking it aside. Another got close enough to grab the rear windscreen wiper and ripped it off as we built up enough speed to send it tumbling across the road in our wake.

31

BE BRAVE

My pulse was so frantic I worried it might explode out of my veins. My clothes were sticky, and I didn't want to touch them, knowing what was likely all over me.

Callahan passed me his hoodie. "Here, to help with the smell and the bleeding."

I took it gratefully and pressed it to my face, taking in deep grounding breaths. His lingering scent calmed my nerves and kept me from retching, though I still shook uncontrollably.

It was several minutes later before I finally felt some semblance of control and realised we were on the outer ring road travelling away from my apartment.

I peeked over at Callahan. The rage was gone, and in its place was sheer exhaustion. He gave me a tight-lipped smile.

"You're bleeding. I'm not risking leading them back to your apartment."

I breathed a sigh of relief and leaned my head against the window, forcing myself to think of anything other than what just happened. When we pulled up at the farm, he parked in the middle of the drive, in front of the main house.

Fletcher's dogs were outside, and they crowded around the car, sniffing around Callahan's legs while he stared blankly at his empty home.

I heard the crunch of gravel, and Fletcher's voice carried loudly across the drive. "What the fuck did you do?" He stopped beside the car and peered in at me, eyes wide as he took in all the blood on my clothes. When Callahan didn't move or deign to answer him, he carefully opened my door. "Are you okay? Are you hurt?"

I held up my hand and showed him the slash across my palm. It had mostly clotted, though parts still oozed and trickled down my wrist. His eyebrows furrowed, and he let out a long steady exhale. He undid my seat belt button, carefully pulling it away from me. "Are you steady enough to walk yet?"

I nodded.

"Callahan, she's still fucking bleeding. What do you want me to do with her?" His shout finally roused Callahan from whatever stupor he was in and he came marching over, the dogs still trailing him and sniffing at his clothes in earnest.

"I'm taking her inside, and I'll deal with the wounds." His face was stern and resolute, and Fletcher stepped back nodding, calling the dogs to heel.

"I'll go find our first aid kit and drop it in the kitchen."

Callahan nodded in thanks and extended his hand to me, helping me out of the car until I was steady enough to follow him to the house. Fletcher stalked away without another word, the dogs obediently following, leaving us in silence. He hesitated at the door but then he rolled his shoulders, and with a heavy breath, he turned the lock and pushed through into the house.

It was cold and deathly quiet inside, but he shucked off his boots and helped me out of my blood-spattered trainers. He flicked on the lights in the hall and gently took my hand leading me to the stairs. I watched him intently, taking note of every minor shift in expression, hoping he was coping with being here again. It was the first time he'd stepped in the house since it happened. He wrapped his arm around my waist and we took the stairs slowly. I was still trembling and nauseous, still doing everything I could to put aside the events of the evening, concentrating all my efforts on him.

He led me to the bathroom and turned on the shower, letting it heat up while he fetched clean towels from the airing cupboard in the hall. When he came back in he pulled his blood-stained shirt off over his head and tugged off his jeans and socks, dropping them in a heap in the bath and then stopped in front of me.

"Let me help you out of these and get you cleaned up."

He waited until I nodded and then gently pulled my T-shirt up and away from my face so the blood didn't touch me as it passed over my head. He pulled it carefully from my arms, avoiding my wounded hand and chucked it in the bathtub with the rest, then stooped to unbutton my jeans and tug them down my legs. I slid a hand into his hair, using him to balance as he eased my jeans off, one leg and then the other, and despite the nausea, I felt my cheeks flush at my brazenness.

When he stood up he was biting his lip, one eyebrow raised pensively, though he avoided eye contact and turned to face the shower, clearing his throat. After an uncomfortable pause, he turned to me with a wince and gestured at the shower. "I'll wash your hair." Then his arm dropped dejectedly to his side. "Sorry, I should have gotten Isla."

I shook my head, knowing I would have felt so much more awkward trying to attempt this with her, and stepped toward the shower. We were both still in our underwear, both trying to keep our gaze politely averted. He took my unwounded hand and stepped in ahead of me, taking the shower head out of its perch, keeping the spray of water away until I'd closed the door.

"Keep your hand up; it will reduce the blood flow to your palm while you're in here."

I nodded, raising my arm above my head, and he retrieved the shampoo and motioned for me to turn around. Slowly he brought the shower head up and let the streams of warm water soak through the lengths of my hair before handing it to me. I let the water soak the rest of my body, relaxing into the warmth while he worked the soap into my hair, the shower filling with the scent of coconut.

His fingers massaged my scalp and created a thick lather that he pulled down to the very tips of my hair, sending shivers through my already trembling body. I sucked in my lower lip, determined not to let a moan escape and make this any more awkward. He retrieved the shower head and the delicious heat cascaded down my back, sending soap bubbles trickling down my legs and swirling about my feet. When it was rinsed through, the water moved away, and I was hit with a fine spray as he doused his own hair and shampooed it rapidly.

I watched, a little mesmerised, as his hands raked through his typically tousled locks and down his face as he stepped out of the shower stream and grabbed shower gel from the shelf, lathering himself hurriedly and then washing it away. His soaking boxers clung to his body, and I tipped my head up to the ceiling before I could glimpse anything that would entrap my wandering eyes.

His fingers encircled my wrist, and he pulled my hand up and squeezed blue herbal-scented shower gel into my palm.

"If you switch with me and turn around, I'll undo your bra and get out, so you can wash while I get a towel ready for you."

I found myself disappointed that he was planning to leave, the closeness was a comfort despite its awkward beginnings. His hands closed gently around my shoulders and guided me to the other side of the shower and then he stepped closer and hooked his fingers around the clasp of my bra.

"Wait"

He removed his hands immediately and I half turned towards him, peering over my shoulder, my voice small and uncertain.

"Before you leave, can I...hug you for a minute? It helps...with the, er, after effects."

All the tension in his face dissolved, and he nodded, a tender smile taking over.

"Can you turn around?"

He did so without question, and I rinsed the shower gel off my palm and stepped up to him, wrapping one arm around his torso and pulling myself tighter against him, keeping my injured palm up high. My head rested in the hollow of his shoulder blades, and I felt myself unravelling as my skin pressed firmly against his, the warmth of our bodies fusing and melting away the last of my trepidation. He sighed deeply, and his fingers slid between mine, clutching my hand tightly against his chest before relaxing, both his arms bracing against mine. It was a while before either of us dared move.

The shower continued to flow luxuriously down my back as I concentrated on the feel of his skin, felt the rise and fall of his steady breaths, and the weight of his head leaning back against mine. The nausea faded, and the trembling completely ceased. I took one more breath and reluctantly untangled myself from him.

He squeezed more soap into my palm, deftly unhooked my bra, and stepped out, leaving me to wash. When I checked over my shoulder his back was to me, a towel wrapped around his waist and another dangling from his hand waiting for me. I managed to shimmy out of my underwear and cautiously pulled the door back. My palm was trickling blood, and I tried to keep it away from my freshly cleansed body.

"I need something to wrap around my hand or I'll get blood everywhere!

He grabbed a small navy towel that was draped over the sink and passed it over his shoulder. When it was pressed against the wound, and the blood was temporarily staunched, he carefully helped me wrap the towel around my body, averting his eyes to preserve my dignity. As I stood clutching my towel with one hand, I surveyed the carnage in the bathroom. Callahan sighed, clocking my despondent expression.

"Let's forget about this until tomorrow. We should fix your hand and find you some clothes."

∼

We climbed into bed a while later, his body curled around mine, wrapping me in warmth and comfort. Contact I'd sorely missed since we'd agreed to be 'friends'.

"Do you want to talk about it?" I whispered.

"Not particularly."

I let out a steady breath. "Well, for the record, I'm sorry I freaked. Thank you for helping me."

He pulled me towards him so he could see my face. "You do not need to be sorry. I'm sorry. I shouldn't have put you in that position at all. And maybe we do need to talk about you repeatedly running towards danger. Did you even hear me tell you to run to the car? I thought you were, but instead, you ran away from it, and I couldn't get to you in time. Again."

"No, I honestly don't think I heard you. I was so worried about keeping my promise."

His face softened, and he shook his head. "I'm so sorry. We never should have gone. I fucking hate that you always end up bleeding because of me."

"Don't be sorry. I don't regret any of it. For the first time in ten years, I felt like someone who could be brave."

32

THIS CLOSE

The thud of the front door closing jostled me from sleep the following morning. My body was lovingly cocooned by Callahan's solid sleeping form. He radiated a warmth that spread beneath my skin and settled deep into my bones. The night had been heavy, but it had contained pivotal moments. An overcoming that stripped the weight from my heart and left it fluttering lightly in my chest. I had made a fumbling mess of my heroics, but I had willingly and even somewhat courageously chosen to bleed for him. To fight for him, instead of merely submitting to the inevitable. For several consecutive seconds, I hadn't been afraid.

"Callahan? Olivia?" Rory's voice echoed through the house. He shouted again, and as I was mustering the will to reply, I heard his feet pounding up the staircase. "Please don't be naked," he pleaded loud enough for us to hear as he stomped across the hall and knocked on the already open door.

Stifling a yawn I said good morning and he leaned against the door frame, arms folded and a suspicious look on his face.

"I hear you had quite a night."

Apparently, news travelled fast around here.

Callahan groaned beside me and slowly uncoiled himself from

my body, stretching his long limbs. Slowly, he sat up and rubbed his face. "Please tell me you didn't wake me up for the sake of gossip?"

Rory shrugged. "Well, I can't deny I'm intrigued but actually, Mum is doing a cooked breakfast and wondered if you wanted to join?"

The mention of food had my stomach complaining, and I sat up, instantly more alert.

"I did try calling," Rory said. "Anyway, Fletcher mentioned you both came home covered in blood. Are you okay?"

His eyes shifted to mine, quietly assessing. I held up my bandaged palm which now had a rust-coloured stain where it had seeped overnight. It throbbed, but the sharp ache was a smug reminder of the mental barrier I had finally broken through.

"Seriously? You're a bloody idiot. You could have lost the use of your fingers. What did you use?"

"Just a knife from my kitchen," I said sheepishly and resigned myself to the scolding I was about to receive.

His eyebrows raised. "Please tell me you sterilised it first?"

I bit my lip. "Yeah, no. There wasn't exactly time to faff."

He shook his head, his eyes narrowed and his lips thinned, filling me with a small degree of shame. "If you get an infection don't come whining to me." He blew out an agitated breath. "I'll take a look at it after breakfast. Now get your lazy asses out of bed; you've got fifteen minutes before I eat your food without a single regret."

He turned and thundered down the stairs, the door slamming on his way out. Without Callahan's warmth to chase it away, the cold air licked at my bare skin, making me shiver. I pulled the duvet up. Callahan yawned, sliding his hands through his wild hair. He gave me a quiet, tender smile. There was something softer about his countenance this morning that made my heart a little unsteady.

"Rory wasn't joking; he will genuinely eat your food if you don't move," he said, flinging back the bedding and pulling open the curtains. He rifled through his wardrobe for a black T-shirt and thick black jumper.

"I'm assuming you need something to wear?" he asked as he pulled the top off that he'd slept in and chucked it on the bed. I nodded, remembering the pile of bloodied garments that were probably staining the bath crimson, and did my best to look nonchalant as I watched him thread his arms through the clean black T-shirt and pull it down over his head. I probably should have made more of an effort to look away. He rummaged through his drawers and tossed an armful of clothing on the bed for me before exiting his room, his jeans and underwear tucked under his arm.

～

We arrived at the house with only a minute to spare, and Maddie greeted us at the door, the smell of bacon clinging to her hair as she fixed me with a gentle hug and a kind smile. It wasn't the reaction I'd expected, and my chest tightened as we hung our jackets on the bannister and followed her to the kitchen.

It was such a deeply dark grey day that every light was on, chasing away the shadows, and the tungsten wall sconces blended with the buttery walls and filled the room with cosy warmth. It was a pleasant atmosphere—even more so when Rory and Finn gave us wide smiles from their spots at the round table. Everyone else was seemingly back at work, and Isla's absence rippled through me. I'd been looking forward to seeing her.

After taking our seats, Callahan loaded my plate, and despite my quiet protest, cut up anything that couldn't be sliced with a fork one-handed.

"So, how was the city?" Maddie asked Callahan, her eyes

darting between my bandaged hand and his bruised and split knuckles in curiosity.

He'd just loaded his fork with crispy hash browns, sausage and baked beans and stared at it longingly for a moment before he pried his eyes away and gave her his full attention. "Well, I spent most of the time in bed," he started, and Finn sniggered from across the table; he was carefully organising his next mouthful, and though he didn't look up, his eyebrows were suggestively raised. He didn't catch the glare Maddie gave him, though he had probably expected it. Finn might look angelic, with his white-blond hair and ice-blue eyes, but I suspected he was far from innocent.

Callahan ignored him and continued, "But we did have a surprise visit from Olivia's mum. That was enlightening."

Maddie smiled politely. "Did you have a nice time with her?" she asked, her tone hesitant as she wasn't quite sure how to take his comment.

I paused from eating, intrigued to hear his response and whether he would divulge that I had fought with her. Maddie would probably have wilted on the spot with the foul language I'd used.

"Well, I wouldn't call it a nice time. I don't think she liked me. Well, that's an understatement. I think she despised me." He was about to load his mouth with food but paused to add, "I was half naked though so that probably didn't help the situation."

Rory choked. "You mean to tell me that the very first time you met your girlfriend's mum you weren't even dressed?" He was staring open-mouthed at Callahan who was politely finishing his mouthful, and an awkward silence ensued between them until Rory tutted. "My bad, didn't realise we were still pretending this isn't a thing," he said waving his fork in our general direction. "So you met your...not girlfriend's mum, half-naked." He turned to me. "Were you half naked?"

I shook my head with a smirk, but it promptly slipped from my face when I noticed the deathly glare Callahan was giving him.

I cleared my throat, choosing my next words wisely. "My mum was so rude, I had to ask her to leave."

Rory whistled and glanced at Maddie who looked positively mortified. She was such a gentle soul. "I don't understand, why was she rude to you?" she asked.

Callahan put his fork down and leaned back in his chair. "It wasn't just me; before she realised I was there, she told Olivia to her face that she was 'a state'. And it wasn't because she was worried about her cuts and bruises." His eyes flickered my way, and he gave an incredulous shake of his head.

"My mum is the sort that won't leave the bedroom without a full face of makeup and a perfect updo."

He scoffed. "I don't care; she had no right to speak to you like that. In fact, she is one of the people in your life who should never say things like that to you."

"Oh, I wasn't defending her. I was just trying to give everyone else context."

His eyes softened. I'd suspected he might have overheard her and come to defend me, his outrage now all but confirmed it.

Finn leaned back in his chair. "So, she was upset with you because you weren't wearing makeup?" He looked astounded even just asking the question. Rory was also staring open-mouthed.

"Well, that was a last-ditch attempt to get under my skin. She was upset because she knew I was lying to her. Somehow she knew about my car, but she only told me as she walked out, knowing it would leave her with the upper hand. I'm pretty sure I notified the DVLA before it was found, so I have no idea how she knows, but I refuse to play her games."

"She pretty much assumed I was a low-life drug dealer," Callahan said dryly.

Rory tried and failed miserably to keep the grin from spreading across his face. "I would have paid good money to see that exchange."

Maddie cleared her throat, our chuckles dwindling as we waited for her to speak. "Ava said they have a visitor arriving tomorrow. She's flying in from Colorado apparently."

"And?" Rory drawled with raised brows.

"I, um, I think she knows more about Olivia's kind."

A poignant silence eclipsed the lighthearted banter from moments before.

Everyone stared at Maddie, while Maddie stared at her plate sporting an uncomfortable grimace.

"Mum, are you planning to elaborate? Or just leaving us to stew on that mood-killing gossip?" Rory said tightly.

She looked up apologetically. "I don't know anything else, Ava only told me out of courtesy in case we saw a stranger milling about the farm. She said…well, I think it was something like 'Em is well acquainted with Olivia's kind' but that's it. It was only in passing. I just thought you should know as you'll probably see her too." She stood and started collecting plates, the clack of porcelain being stacked filling the stunned silence around the table.

Pushing my chair back, I made to help, but Callahan stilled my wrist, his long fingers hot against my skin.

"I'll sort this. Let Rory look at your hand. I probably did a terrible job."

"I guarantee that you did," Rory retorted dryly.

Callahan gave me a tight-lipped smile and gathered our plates. Finn said his goodbyes and headed back to work on the farm, kissing his mum on the top of her head as he left.

Rory washed his hands, grabbed his kit and started unravelling the stained bandage with a resigned sigh.

"Is this where all the blood on your clothes came from?" he asked quietly. When I didn't answer immediately his eyes narrowed. "What happened?"

He rifled through his kit for an antiseptic wipe and a permanent marker and then paused, his brows arching high as he waited for me to elaborate.

"Well, I fought a ridiculously tall female—badly, might I add. I'd coated the knife and tried to use it, but we fell and incredibly, things didn't go as terribly as they could have. She impaled herself when we landed. My knife went straight through her throat."

He blinked. "Where was Callahan while you were wrestling a vampire?"

I frowned, feeling defensive of him. "When I saw her, he was dealing with a different vampire, so I ran away from the car, too far for him to reach me before we fell, but I wasn't supposed to fight."

Rory looked back to my hand and grabbed the antiseptic wipe, the sharp smell of chemicals hit my nostrils as he tore it open, and I hissed as he gripped my palm, holding it in place as he cleansed the area.

"Did you get any of its blood in your wound?"

My shoulders jerked back at his question, the thought of it repulsed me. "I honestly don't know."

His mouth became a tight line, his brows pinching together as he stared at the angry slice of skin. He picked up the marker pen and drew a line across my palm, the sensation sending goosebumps spreading up my arm as it tickled my delicate skin. "If the redness goes past this line, you'll probably need antibiotics."

"Great. You were right, by the way; three masked vampires showed up as we were running for the car. That's why we came back here." I bit my lip, the confession sitting heavy on my mind.

"Shit," he muttered under his breath. "You need to get your stuff and stay here. I know you want to go on the warpath, but it needs a proper plan, and none of us are ready yet."

I blew out a frustrated breath. "I know."

After my wound was securely rebandaged, we all parted ways,

Maddie requesting emphatically that we join them again for dinner, and Callahan seemed happy to oblige. No doubt eager to be anywhere but at home.

It was a truly miserable day outside, it wasn't raining, but the air was thick and damp, the clouds dark and ominous, blocking out the sun's rays completely and leaving the day with a grey tinge. The clouds seemed to gather mockingly above the farmhouse, a hulking mass of steely blue ready to crack open and pour itself out at the most inopportune moment. The closer the farmhouse loomed, the more withdrawn Callahan became, making my heart ache.

"Can you help me make a cup of tea?" I asked him as we neared the door—giving him a task seemed like a good way to distract him.

He tilted his head, his face scrunching in confusion. "I didn't know you liked tea."

"Yep. Not often and usually when I'm craving a little sugar. I like my coffee bitter and my tea sweet."

"Fair enough," he said as he shoved the door open. "I can make you tea."

"That depends. When do you put the milk in?"

He snorted. "After I've taken the tea bag out. What other way is there?"

"Some of my colleagues used to put it in before they added the boiling water, and there should be laws against that, in my opinion."

He shook his head in disbelief. "That is sacrilege."

In the kitchen, Callahan busied himself with pulling out and prepping the mugs. Something simple and routine for him to do as he acclimated to the house without the ones who made it home.

Bracing one hand on the breakfast bar, I tried to push myself up and screeched as I overbalanced and had to fling both hands out to keep me from splatting on the floor. Pain sliced across my palm as I felt the flesh tugging apart where it had only just begun knitting together. The tea canister clattered over the worktop as Callahan spun around in shock.

"What the fuck did you do?" he asked wide-eyed.

I clutched my palm against my chest, willing the sharp hot pain to subside. "I was trying to get up here," I said nodding to the breakfast bar.

"Why the hell didn't you just ask?"

He stepped towards me and placed his hands lightly on my waist. "Whenever you're ready," he said softly, and as my knees bent and I propelled myself upwards, he caught my weight and slid me easily on the breakfast bar.

"Thank you."

He shrugged and turned back to make the tea, the kettle now spitting steam behind him.

"I heard what Rory said about you staying here. I think he's right. We could drive over this afternoon and pick up some of your stuff before it gets dark."

"What about Ava and James?" I asked as he squeezed the tea bags and flung them into the counter compost bin.

"What about them? It has nothing to do with them."

"Won't it make things difficult for you, given that they hate me?"

He rolled his eyes. "They'll get over it, besides, the mysterious Em arrives tomorrow; maybe she'll change their minds."

"Or, alternatively, she might—"

He shot forward, his fingers stilled my lips, and he shook his head, desperation in his eyes as he halted my pessimism before it ruined his fragile state of calm. Guilt clamoured in my chest as he turned away to finish making the tea, sloshing milk in the cup until the liquid turned a mid-beige that reminded me of my previous apartment.

I shuddered. It didn't seem possible that it was only months and not years since I'd lived there, since I'd been so lonely I'd gambled away my heart on someone who gave me a temporary sense of happiness—built entirely upon lies and half-truths. It was destined to crumble. Now, I existed in this niche space that felt so overwhelmingly right, so easy to live in, that my mind battled a constant undercurrent of fear that I was dreaming, that my new world could be ripped away at any moment. It would take time to settle into it, or perhaps that fear would never fully dissipate. The downside of being a survivor, I supposed, was always looking for the worst and having to prepare for it.

Callahan set my tea beside me and leant against the counter, looking uncomfortably about the room, his face paling as he took it all in.

"Callahan."

His eyes flicked to mine, and the deep well of sadness in his stare struck painfully, swelling in my chest until it hurt to breathe.

"I probably have no right to say it, but don't run from your memories, even if they're painful right now. They're a gift. If you don't embrace them, you'll eventually lose them."

A tear streaked down his face, and he swiped it away, closing his eyes.

"The one thing you can do...is make new memories," I said. "Not to replace or diminish your old ones but to let this place evolve with you and be somewhere you feel comfortable in. It's going to feel different for a while, but it will get better."

I scooted off the breakfast bar and dropped my head on his shoulder, tightly coiling my arms around him and pressing myself against his chest.

"I'm here for you," I whispered.

He squeezed me, one hand tangled in the hair at the nape of my neck, the other braced across my shoulder blades. He sighed deeply and pressed a lingering kiss to my temple, just above my scarring wound, his lips delicate and warm against my skin.

I tilted my face up to look at him, to try and understand the measure of his kiss. The ice blue of his irises was swallowed up as he watched me; only a thin band of luminous colour remained, almost eclipsed by the vastness of his pupils. He wanted me. He wanted us, and I could see the decision teetering on the edge, the scales ready to tip either way.

I didn't move for fear that even a blink might snap the exquisite tension between us and push the scales unfavourably. My pulse fluttered like a hummingbird, blood rushing into my cheeks and radiating molten heat between us. He pulled back, and my heart stuttered, my eyes slamming shut to keep the disappointment contained.

I started to release him and step away but his grip tightened; his fingers skimmed along my jaw and lightly cradled my cheek. His thumb softly traced a path over my freckles as he held me captive to his every intention. I waited. Each second fell heavier than the last, the silence expanding until it sucked away my breath —and shattered when his lips brushed against mine with a quiet moan. It was utterly divine—each kiss a slow and gentle caress that sent a tidal wave of heat spreading out through my body like wildfire. His tongue brushed against my lip, and my mouth obediently parted, welcoming each languid stroke with pure unadulterated euphoria. My body was adrift with a heady mix of relief and desire that had my heart running wild and my breaths ragged.

When he reluctantly pulled away, with kiss-swollen lips, deliciously flushed cheeks and erratic breaths, my smile stretched wide.

"Well that's definitely *my* new favourite memory," I told him breathlessly.

He planted a slow kiss to my forehead, his fingers slipping through mine as he eyed me with a steadily growing smile—the first proper smile I'd seen since the day we went back to my apartment.

"If we don't leave now to get your stuff, you'll be stuck wearing my clothes for another day, because I am this close," he said, gesturing the tiniest gap between his thumb and forefinger, "to carting you upstairs and forgetting the world exists."

"That is not a convincing argument for leaving the house," I said, rising to my tiptoes and dropping another kiss on his lips just because I could, my fingers straying into his dishevelled hair, eliciting a stifled moan that had my stomach fluttering.

"You might blush all the way through dinner," he countered.

I wrenched myself away. "Fine, you win. Let's go get my clothes."

33

SAFE

Hours later we were walking back to the Hayes household. The light had completely faded leaving the farm in a thick cloak of darkness. It was the kind of cold outside that clung to your bones and left you shivering for hours. I was grateful when we entered the familiar hall and felt the rush of delicious heat envelop us.

It was a full house. I could hear Finn and Rory antagonising each other in the kitchen, and Isla appeared from the living room when she heard the door. I couldn't help the idiotic grin that devoured my face and she took one look at Callahan and said, "If you don't mind, I need to speak to my friend *alone* before dinner."

My smile grew even wider at her inference, and she dragged me into the living room before he could respond and kicked Fletcher out. He was nursing a stiff drink and minding his own business, but he didn't protest.

The room was square and sizable, painted a buttery cream with imposing brown leather sofas positioned in an L on one half of the room. As with the farmhouse, there was a central fireplace but it was sleek and modern. A simple wood burner and flue stood on a marble hearth in front of the plain painted wall. One corner of the room contained a piano with floating shelves above it, adorned with various trailing plants and books—a little bit of Isla's influence in the room. Further along, under the large window, was a dark stained sideboard. A beautiful decanter and set of crystal glasses sat on top and I could just imagine Stephen pouring a brandy and reclining in front of the fire after a long day at work.

The minute we were alone she guided me to one of the sofas, and we sat down angled towards each other.

"Come on, give me details!" she said impatiently. "I know something's happened between you two."

I tried to tone down my smile enough to speak. "We had breakfast here…"

She waved her hand at me, urging me to fast forward.

"All right, all right! The short version is that he kissed me," I said in a hushed voice.

She smiled excitedly. "And? Was it good? Where did it happen?"

I chuckled delightedly at her eagerness. "Yes, it was the kind of kiss that gives me butterflies just thinking about it, and it was in the kitchen. He was understandably sad, and I tried to encourage him and told him that eventually, he'd make new memories that made it feel more like home again, and I guess he followed my advice!"

Her smile became as wide as mine. "So are you guys official now then?"

"I don't know, we didn't really talk about that."

Her eyebrows flew up. "Busy, were you?!"

"No, not that kind of busy. We drove back to the city to pick up a bunch of my stuff. Did Rory not tell you about last night?"

Her eyes widened. "No, I've barely seen him. What happened?"

I proceeded to fill her in on the previous night's events and had just started relaying the details of my mother's visit, when there was a knock, and Fletcher poked his head around the door. "Can you two stop gossiping? You're delaying dinner."

Isla glared at him. "God forbid!"

He rolled his eyes and swiftly retreated.

Not wanting to irritate her parents, we got to our feet and headed for the kitchen.

I was intrigued to see how Callahan would treat me in front of everyone else. In the city, he'd struggled to keep his hands off me. The minute my apartment door swung shut, he'd cupped my face in his hands and kissed me until I could hardly breathe or walk or think. When I finally dragged myself to my room to complete my packing mission, I'd placed five things in my suitcase before he gave me that hungry, devouring look, and I ended up straddling him on my bed, breathless and aching for more of him. Those moments had been running on replay in my head all afternoon.

We had eventually forced ourselves to disentangle and get the hell out of the city before it got dark and I ended up with a vampire sucking on my neck. That had been the sobering thought that got us moving. Especially given that I had wounds that were healing. He'd confessed to me while we were packing my things that every time he'd seen those bruises on my neck, he'd had vivid flashbacks of me being strangled and bitten and that it made him sick to his bones. We both agreed that finding another way to fight would be a priority once I'd healed and we'd had a little more time to process what had happened.

When we walked in, Callahan and Rory were carrying platters of roast potatoes and Yorkshire puddings to the table, laughing over some unfortunate farm incident. Finn was already at the table engrossed in conversation with Fletcher, and Stephen was washing his hands, chatting happily with Maddie. Seeing everyone together in such an ordinary, normal way made my heart feel full and content. It was a room full of love and slowly reviving joy, and it felt like a dream and a privilege to be included.

When he noticed we'd entered the kitchen, Callahan sauntered over with a tender smile. He placed a hand lightly on my side and leant in to give me a brief, delicate kiss. He began to step away, then turned back to plant a fuller kiss on my lips, smiling as we parted before ushering me to my seat to the chorus of Rory and Finn's wolf whistles.

The meal was spectacular. Maddie was truly a queen in the kitchen. It was the first time I'd had roast beef courtesy of the farm, and it was succulent, tender, and full of flavour. I hadn't thought there would be such a difference to normal store-bought beef, but there undeniably was. It made me appreciate all the more everything they were trying to do here.

There was a mountain of food and it was largely demolished by the five hungry men that squeezed around the table, us women wedged in tightly between them. Not that I minded when it forced me to be so close to Callahan. All the little touches, the little smiles when he thought no one was watching, and the way his hand caressed the inside of my thigh made my pulse a constant cycle of steady to accelerated in the blink of an eye. I was so aware of him, so consumed, that I barely heard the conversation around the table. Thankfully with everyone present, it was less noticeable.

During the flurry of clean-up activity, I managed to corner Rory and pull him aside.

"You seem very…what's the word I'm looking for? Vacant… tonight," he whispered with a mischievous grin.

"I need your help," I whispered back.

His brows narrowed. "Go on."

"Can you occupy Callahan for like forty minutes? I need to do something at the house."

He folded his arms and smirked at me. "I'll be lucky if I can keep him here thirty, but I'll do my best."

It was good enough for me, and I gave him a wink. "You're the best. Thank you."

And with that, I found Isla and promised we'd catch up soon, and on my way out, I mentioned to Callahan that I needed to make a quick private call, and Rory swooped in on cue to divert his attention.

The run back to the house was exhausting. Flinging off my shoes, I raced to build a fire in the living room then hurtled up the stairs to gather a few essential items, brushed through my tangled hair, cleaned my teeth, and then hurtled back down. I dashed room to room locating the candles I'd been spying since the afternoon and placed them around the living room, creating a beautifully soft, atmospheric glow. Once ready, I messaged Rory:

Tell Callahan he needs to meet his girlfriend at home in the living room. She has plans for him.

He replied thirty seconds later: *Gross. Never seen him move so fast. Enjoy!*

Sure enough, not quite a minute later, I heard his footsteps pounding on the gravel outside and the door flew open.

I waited, leaning casually against one of the sofas with my heart beating wildly in my chest. He stopped dead in the doorway, his eyes raking over every inch of me.

"My shirt has never looked sexier."

I highly doubted that. I wore the grey shirt that I'd found ironed in his wardrobe, and with his piercing eyes, the grey would look agonisingly good on him. He moved towards me with slow deliberate steps and it took every ounce of self-control to keep from running to him and stripping him on the spot, patience be damned. My whole body was trembling with anticipation.

His eyes were bright and alert, flickering over me like I was a coveted prize he'd just won and had yet to claim. When he stood before me, he teased me, stooping to bring his lips tantalisingly close, his nose grazing mine, and the warmth of his breath whispering over my skin. When I moved to kiss him, he stayed just beyond reach, and it made me ache in a way I didn't think possible.

My breath was quick and shallow, my heart a beating drum with no sense of rhythm, and I couldn't think of anything beyond how much I wanted him. How much I needed him. The world could have gone to shit around us, and I wouldn't have noticed. Nothing existed but us, suspended in this calm before the storm of desire.

Just as I was preparing to beg him, his tongue brushed over my top lip, and my answering gasp shattered his restraint. His mouth crashed against my already parted lips, his tongue meeting mine with such devotion it made me weak and boneless. He stooped lower to lift me, my long legs wrapping around his strong form, and when his hands skimmed along my bare thigh up to my hip and down the curve of my rear, he stopped abruptly, and moaned.

"Fuck, I didn't realise you were in nothing but my shirt."

I nodded and kissed his grinning lips as he squeezed me tightly against him.

When we broke for air, both of us hot and panting, he finally took in the room.

The candlelight flickered in his eyes as he glanced around and then he spotted the duvets laid out on the floor in front of the burning fire. He was quietly taking it all in, an appreciative smile on his lips that melted me, and made me contemplate all the things I could do to keep that smile from ever fading. He walked us around to the bedding and carefully dropped to his knees before one of the sofas, leaving me perched on the edge.

I needed to see, to feel his skin, and I tugged impatiently at his T-shirt until he yanked it off over his head. My God, he was beautiful. I trailed kisses under his jaw, down his neck, over his chest, savouring the taste of him, while my hands ran over every inch of his bare skin. Pining for his kisses, I brushed against his lip, nipping it as he parted for me and slid my tongue along the blunt edge of his canine.

He groaned in response, and the sound seemed to travel along every nerve in my body, deliciously twisting in my stomach and making me ache for him. He deepened the kiss, his breaths turning desperately ragged, and his hands slid behind my knees and dragged me even closer to him.

"Callahan?"

He pulled away from me, his brows tugging together as he registered my expression. "Are you okay?"

I nodded, feeling guilty that I'd worried him. "I want…"

He tilted his head, waiting for me to explain. His breaths were still erratic, and it gave me a deep satisfaction to know I had that effect on him.

I took a stuttered breath. "I want you to kiss me here."

A shiver rattled down my spine as I tapped a finger against my throat. My currently unbruised, untainted, delicate skin that I'd never willingly let another man near. But he wasn't just anyone, and he deserved to have my trust implicitly.

His face softened in understanding and he kissed me delicately, melting away a little of the tension I hadn't noticed creep up on me.

"Now?"

Pulling my hair to one side, I took a deep inhale and nodded. He planted sweet gentle kisses along my jawline first, and when I didn't stop him, he softly brushed his lips a little further down, pausing to give me time to process, to monitor my reaction. Every tiny hair on my body stood on end, but it was not a fearful response. He kissed lower, holding his lips against my skin a little longer. I had hoped at best that I would feel comfortable and safe, but it turned out the best-case scenario was enjoying it so much I moaned.

He groaned in answer, and his kisses became more intense, his tongue brushing against my skin making me arch into him. My hand was no longer braced on his shoulder but winding through his hair, holding him to me.

I ached for him; there was too much space between us, too much material separating our skin, and my hands travelled to the waist of his jeans, fumbling with the button. I wanted to feel his weight above me, another thing I had never allowed before and yet now craved with such intensity it took my breath away.

"We need to move."

He grunted his approval. His lips trailed over my collarbone, his fingers making deft work of the buttons on my shirt. He got to his feet, pulling me with him and slid the shirt down my arms, letting it drop in a pool of material around my feet. He stepped back to drink in every inch of my nakedness, his lips were parted and his eyes half-lidded. His finger circled, demanding I spin for him which I did slowly, when I completed my turn the hunger in his eyes had my heart pounding so loud I thought he would hear it.

In the space of a heartbeat, he was pressed against me, his mouth meeting mine with such intensity it was dizzying.

His jeans hung low on his waist where I'd managed to get them undone, and I tucked my hands into the band of his boxers to push them down, ignoring my burning palm, desperate to feel every curve, every hard line of him. He released me, sliding out of his boxers and jeans, dropping them on the sofa, and then pulling me against him like he couldn't bear another second without the feel of my skin.

As we kissed, I dragged my tongue slowly across his canine and pulled away to look at him. His face was deliciously flushed even in the glow of candlelight.

"You are absolute perfection. Every. Single. Inch." I slid my palm up his length, his answering groan sending shivers skittering down my body and all the way to my toes, and I continued up his torso, resting my hand against his heart. "Especially this."

His eyes fluttered closed, his forehead resting on mine. One hand wound through my hair, the other trailed a burning path from my hip, up to caress my breast and ended under my jaw.

"It's so hard to put into words everything I feel about you. Honestly, every time I try, it's like they fucking evaporate right off my tongue."

I could feel his heart hammering against his chest where my hand still rested on him.

"I think you're doing just fine."

I made to step away, ready to lay down with him, but his arms drew me back, scooping me under my hips so that my legs wrapped around him, and I clung to him, as he lowered gracefully to his knees and laid me down reverently on our makeshift bed, settling between my thighs.

I could feel every perfect inch of him against me, and fuck, it was everything in life that I'd never known to wish for.

"You're trembling," he whispered against the soft skin of my neck.

"I've never let anyone be with me this way."

I cringed, reminding him that I'd been with others was not particularly smooth. But he didn't seem to take it that way and shifted his weight to one elbow, kissing me while he explored every contour of my skin, driving me insane with want.

"Callahan." His name was a question, a request, a desperate plea and he knew it. He shifted again, ready but not giving me what I craved.

"You do realise we're about to skip a whole lot of fun?"

I nodded earnestly. "I don't care. Trust me, I don't need it, I feel like every inch of my body is craving for more of you. It's fucking agony."

He smiled against my lips, his mouth working down under my

jaw making me arch against him then he stopped to look at me, his expression suddenly serious.

"You have no idea how much I want you to enjoy this. Please, just tell me if we need to move."

I nodded, emotion swelling at the tenderness, the sheer devotion I felt from him. In the next breath, he shifted his hips and my head tipped back in ecstasy.

A thousand butterflies surged through my body, all scrambling frantically for their freedom, and it was the most exquisite sensation. I wasn't sure if anything in the world would ever compare to this moment. The warmth of his skin sliding against mine, the way his hands clutched at my body, like he couldn't pull me close enough. The feel of his tongue as it swept against mine, our ragged breaths mingling together, stifled moans against each other's lips. The satisfaction of dragging my fingers through his hair and down between his shoulder blades. The way his fingers entwined in mine and squeezed tightly with every nuance of pleasure. The way he lifted his chest to gaze at my body moving beneath his, entranced by the way we fit perfectly together. Nothing had ever come close to this feeling. I was utterly lost in it.

The pleasure built, a slow delicious ascent, and I both willed it to finally release but mourned its end. I could feel Callahan's breath hot and growing more rapid against my skin, and he gave an excited moan as he sensed I was on the edge.

My legs wound around him, locking at his hips to keep him deeper, closer to me in pursuit of release. The movement made him groan against my mouth, and the sound was so beautiful my insides felt like they shattered. Then, I was falling. Obliterated. My body arching into him, my fingers digging into his skin then the cushion behind me, anything to keep me tethered as I rode out each wave of exquisite pleasure, and it pushed him over the edge to his release.

He found my unbound hand, clenching it tightly as he drove

into me with each crescendo of pleasure, panting and kissing me through it. When his body finally stilled and his kisses grew slow and tender, he rested his forehead against mine.

"Fuck," he whispered. "That was the most beautiful thing I've ever seen."

I chuckled, my fingers winding through the hair at the base of his neck, enjoying the moment of blissful intimacy, my body a vessel of pure contentment.

"Don't move yet," I whispered. "I've never had this—and I feel so safe with you."

His chest expanded with a deep inhale, his nose brushing the tip of mine before he left a sweet trail of kisses across my cheeks and down under my jaw.

"You have a knack for breaking my heart with the things you say," he said softly, the words falling against the tender skin below my ear making my toes curl.

"That's not my intention."

"I know. I know, I didn't mean it in a bad way. It's more like…" His tongue swept over the bottom of his lip as he tried to find the words. "Don't laugh, but I think the only way to describe it is that it makes me want to tuck your heart away and rebuild the broken parts of mine around it. To keep it safe."

I clutched him tighter, my fingertips creating divots in his flesh —a physical anchor against the surge of overwhelming emotion and my breath rattled out with the force of it.

"I want that," I whispered. "I want that very much."

34

RECONNAISSANCE

Callahan woke me just before sunrise, peppering kisses along my shoulder, and groaning as he wrenched himself out of bed. I would have petitioned him to stay, but he was determined to be back on the farm, picking up the slack he'd left to Rory and Finn since his family had been taken from him just over three weeks ago. It was an important first step, one of an infinite many that he would have to tread. Proud seemed like too small a word to describe the swell of my heart every time I considered the depth of his bravery and endurance; he was astonishing.

Try as I might, sleep did not return to me. My thoughts were giddy and restless, delicious memories of the previous evening on a constant loop, and in the end, I dressed and headed out to explore.

The temperature had plummeted overnight, and with a clear sky, the landscape stretched out in shimmering white, the colours muted by a thick dusting of frost. Much of my morning was spent strolling around the farm, enthralled by its beauty: the enchanted spider webs weaved between the paddock posts, tall frost-covered grasses wavering ghost-like in the cool breeze, the sun's rays gradually thawing everything it touched leaving tendrils of steam dancing within the glowing morning light. It was so peaceful and so perfect after last night. I idled by the paddocks for some time, watching the cows huddle together for warmth, their bodies partially clouded with their foggy breaths, and finally, when my fingers were so cold I could barely feel them, I trudged back to the farmhouse.

Callahan was still out somewhere with Finn, but Rory was sitting at the large oak dining table, a pen dangling from his lips as he scrolled on the laptop. He was organising transport for a portion of the herd heading to slaughter—a thought that made me more uncomfortable than I expected. He'd put it off as long as he could, but there was a substantial waiting list for orders after the disruption in the last few weeks. While he worked, I started prepping a meal for the slow cooker, determined to look after them in one of the few ways that I could. All the while, I tried to come up with a plan to surreptitiously annihilate the vampires.

"You need a whiskey from the sound of it." I turned to look at Rory, my gaze narrowing as I wondered if I'd said my thoughts aloud.

"Did I say something?"

"No. Well, not with words, but you did just release the longest, most depressing sigh I've ever heard." He tucked his pen through the bun at the crown of his head and raised an eyebrow at me. "Out with it. What's on your mind?"

Scooping slices of carrot into a porcelain bowl, I emptied the waiting mushrooms onto the chopping board and sighed, again. "Ava and James have their guest arriving from Colorado today. I was just hoping she might have information that could help us. If it's another dead end…" I started slicing, warding off the anxiety, it was about time something went our way, and it was hard to admit my hopes were currently pinned on a complete stranger that I knew absolutely nothing about.

Rory pushed away from the table, refilled the kettle, and stole a slice of carrot. "What's your ultimate goal in all this?"

I paused mid-slice, my face scrunching into a frown. "I want to stop them killing any other people. Obviously."

He folded his arms and leant against the counter. "I get that, but how? What about all the ones in the other cities—the ones in other countries? How do we fit into all that? Because from my perspective, if you care enough to do something about the ones in our city, it's a bit hypocritical to stop there."

I swallowed back my discomfort and continued quartering the mushrooms. "I don't know," I finally admitted. It was above and beyond me, beyond any of us, and yet I still felt the responsibility of it biting at my heels. Each day was another life that hung over my head. Each day, the mountain grew inexplicably bigger to face in the light of our inexperience and lack of resources. We were severely outnumbered, and my unique DNA was both a weapon and a handicap.

He sighed, turning to pull several mugs from the cupboard. "I'm not trying to discourage you Liv, but it's a question we all need to be able to answer."

He was right. God, he was always right, and I didn't know how to respond. Fortunately, the question was put on hold as Fletcher and Isla arrived, shouting their hellos from the porch and discarding their shoes. Isla was still wearing her work uniform, a deep purple sweater with the floristry branding etched on the back in gold lettering.

"Hey, did you finish early?" I asked as she plonked herself down on the far side of the table.

She gave me a withering look and shook her head. "Work sent me home. There was a funeral order, and I got a bit emotional."

Fletcher squeezed her shoulder affectionately as he pulled out the adjacent chair, crossing an ankle over his knee and blowing out a long breath through pursed lips.

"You want a coffee, Sis?" Rory asked, looking every bit the protective brother as he eyed her staring vacantly out of the patio doors.

She nodded, wiping fresh tears away with the sleeve of her sweater.

With little else to bring her comfort, I retrieved the biscuit tin from the cupboard and offered it as I took a seat next to her. "I'm sorry you had such a rough morning."

"Finn and Callahan were just walking down the drive," she said, as she picked out a stack of digestives, ignoring my sympathy. She caught me staring at her and gave me a weak smile. "I'll be fine in a minute. It was just unexpected—the first order like that we've had since it happened, and it was just a lot to process, especially with all the lies we've had to tell. I don't know how you've done that for ten years." She smiled gratefully at Rory as he popped our coffees on the table.

As the front door slammed she rolled her shoulders, her sorrow shuttered away behind a happy mask, and she smiled brightly when Callahan strode through the door, Finn following close behind. When Callahan spotted me at the table, one corner of his mouth twitched up in a lop-sided smile that had butterflies unspooling in my stomach.

He veered towards me, dropping a kiss on my cheek and whispering hello against my skin, before making his way to the sink to scrub his hands. It was the first time I'd seen him in full work attire. He wore scruffy black jeans, complete with various streaks of mud and other questionable things, with a black T-shirt and forest green fleece which was covered in wisps of hay, his gloves peeking out the edge of one pocket. Even fresh-off-the-farm dishevelled, he was utterly captivating. He and Finn were deep in conversation about separating the herd, but his eyes frequently darted towards the table, though never quite meeting mine.

Isla playfully flicked my arm. "Go see him," she whispered,

her eyebrows raised at my guilt-ridden expression, having been caught staring at him like an infatuated teen. "Don't hold back on my account. I don't care," she said with a dismissive gesture. Giving her an appreciative smile, I slid out of my chair, making a beeline for the counter where Rory was waiting for the freshly filled kettle to boil.

"I'll make the drinks," I said casually.

He eyed my still-bandaged hand with a quirked brow. "It will be quicker if I do it, and we both know you didn't get up just to make the drinks."

I bit my lip, trying to suppress my guilty grin as Callahan tossed the tea towel at Finn and slipped his arms around my waist, plying me with gentle kisses and just enough tongue that my breath was very quickly ragged.

Rory groaned as he picked up the kettle. "Can you two go fawn somewhere else? Unless you want me to hurl in your coffee?"

"If they don't take it elsewhere, I'm going to hurl in the coffees," Finn muttered under his breath as he passed by. He was clutching several bags of crisps, which he dumped in the middle of the table before taking a seat opposite Fletcher.

Callahan chuckled and pulled me closer, whispering in my ear; "If we didn't have a houseful, I would definitely be taking you somewhere."

Kicking them all out was certainly tempting. His fingers tangled in mine as we joined the others, the chair scuffing on the floor as he dragged it out and sat, pulling me onto his lap.

Fletcher rolled his eyes, and Isla smiled as she stared into the dregs of her cup. Shyness was never a problem around Noah. I'd always felt in control, but now my cheeks were most certainly hot and rosy, and my body had a perpetual sort of buzz to it in Callahan's presence—being with him was thrilling in a way I hadn't experienced before.

I reached for the biscuits, trying to appear nonchalant despite the buzzing in my veins and passed him a custard cream, which he promptly dunked in the coffee, popping the entire thing in his mouth.

Somehow, even the devouring of a biscuit was inherently sexy. Aware that we had an audience, I nestled back against him, flinching when needle-sharp stalks of hay bit into my skin. When I started plucking them from his fleece, he stilled my hand and planted a kiss on the tips of my fingers.

"Don't bother. You'll be here all day," he said and unzipped the jacket, shucking it off, and drawing me back against his warm chest. The gesture had my heart thrumming double time. I wished I could bottle these little moments, save them for the dark days, and drink them down like a fine wine when joy was lacking—the pessimist in me never quite willing to believe my luck would last.

Rory slotted back into his seat beside us and took a slurp of coffee, balancing it on his lap as he retrieved his phone and mindlessly scrolled. The room was unusually quiet, aside from the contented munching of snacks.

"What time does your visitor arrive, Fletcher?" I asked, trying to get my mind away from Callahan for at least a full minute.

He shrugged, his face utterly void of any emotion. "Not my visitor. And I've been staying at Isla's. Mum and Dad aren't talking to me at the minute. They think we need to back off and leave the vampires to it," he said, unfurling from his seat and leaning over the table to reach for a biscuit.

He took a custard cream and his long fingers pried it apart. He ate the plain side first, then looked at Callahan, a question brewing on his lips. Just as he was about to ask it, Isla snatched the remaining, better half of his biscuit, and stuffed it in her mouth before he could claim it back. I stifled a laugh as he stared at her for a moment and then retrieved another from the tin, repeating the process in his lap beyond her reach.

He sat forward, pushing a wave of dark hair behind his ear.

"Anyway, obviously I disagree with them. Would you be up for a little reconnaissance trip?"

I wanted to reach across the table and hug him, because I had, admittedly, been a coward the last couple of days. There was so much to discuss, so much to plan, but with Callahan's grief so fresh and raw, no one had dared to bring it up. Least of all me. He tensed, resting his chin on my shoulder while he considered the possibility. Everyone else at the table had conveniently found somewhere else to look, each waiting with bated breath.

"When do you plan on going?"

Fletcher shrugged, taking a sip of coffee. "Tonight? Tomorrow? Whenever you're ready."

Callahan's fingers tightened around mine, and he sat up straighter, squeezing me against his chest. "Can we do tomorrow? If we do extra farm prep tonight, we can have a lie-in as I'm guessing we wouldn't be heading out until pretty late?"

Fletcher nodded, draining his coffee and setting it back on the table. "When we went out at the beginning of the week, it was before ten, and we didn't see anything useful so the later the better."

Taking a breath, I decided now was as good a time as any to broach my most pressing idea.

"I think one of the biggest questions we need to answer is who, if anyone, is helping them cover all this up. Whether it's one dirty copper or maybe even a few who are turning a blind eye. I think we need to know who we're up against. Would you be willing to help me snatch another vamp so that we could question it? If we can manage to get a gas mask to put on it, I'll do it myself." Fuck I wished we'd been the ones to think of that. "I mean, I'd like to do it myself. There are so many things I want to know, and we'd probably get information quicker than just watching them, right?"

"Gas masks are easy enough to order. It's just a question of when it will arrive." Fletcher said, pulling out his phone and opening a search.

Isla was watching me intently. "What if the police are helping them? Doesn't that complicate everything?"

"That would depend on the why," Callahan answered. "If they're helping because there is someone higher up forcing them, then yes that's a fucking big problem. If they're looking the other way because they think it makes their job easier, then no, I don't think it will be much of an issue."

She nodded, her brows pulling together pensively. "But, it might not be the police helping them?"

"Right, it could be other vampires, or someone they subcontract to in the worst-case scenarios. Or someone they work for who isn't connected to the police at all," he said and squeezed my hand before continuing. "Olivia is right, though. We need to find out who else they're involved with. I doubt it was pure luck that the bodies we left behind haven't been reported publicly."

"Liv said there were three in masks the other night. If you do this, I think me and Finn should be with you this time. It could get messy," Rory said.

Finn had been quietly scrolling on his phone, but he stopped at the mention of his name and nodded his approval before popping another crisp in his mouth with a loud crunch.

"I agree," Fletcher said. "We need to be in and out of the city as quickly and smoothly as possible."

I expected Callahan to disagree but he nodded and gently squeezed my knee, which I hadn't realised had started to bounce as my nerves ratcheted up a gear. The more we planned, the more insignificant I felt in the face of all the risks. The thought of anything happening to any of them almost had me backing out. Almost.

35

AN EQUILIBRIUM

"Holy shit! Is it true that cows can smell things up to six miles away?" How would they even quantify that? Callahan's fingers stilled on the laptop, and he turned to me with a curious expression. "What are you reading?"

I uncrossed my legs and shifted across the sofa until my thigh was pressed up against his, showing him my screen. "It's a book I downloaded about farming, did you know this?"

He chuckled and slid his laptop onto the coffee table, draping one arm along the back of the sofa. "I did know," he said and his smile stretched into a rare full grin that showed the blunt points of his long canines. I found them oddly mesmerising. "If I'd known how impressed you'd be, I would have dropped it into conversation sooner. How long have you been reading about farming?"

"Only over this weekend while you were working. I figured it wouldn't hurt to know a bit more, and then maybe I can be of use."

A wave of emotion rippled across his face, and a heartbeat later, his hand was in my hair drawing me into a tender kiss. As our lips parted, deepening the kiss, my tongue brushed against one of his canines, eliciting a groan that skittered down my spine and stole my breath. My lips split into a wide smile, and he drew back, tilting his head.

"What are you thinking?" he asked.

I laughed, silently cursing my expressive face. "That I never expected to be so obsessed with your teeth. I love the noises you make when I touch them."

He didn't speak, his irises reduced to a tiny band of colour as he took a slow inhale. "Fuck," he said and blew out a breath, glancing guiltily at his laptop.

"Sorry, I promised I wouldn't be a distraction. Do your work; I'll read my book quietly. I promise."

I sat back against the corner of the sofa putting space between us and draping a blanket over my legs for good measure. He exhaled long and slow and dragged his laptop back onto his thighs, the silence settling comfortably around us, only the crackle of the fire and steady tapping of his fingers against the keyboard to fill it.

It had been two days since our impromptu group meeting. We were waiting for a gas mask to arrive later this afternoon before we embarked on the next covert mission to forcibly gather information. A plan that had tripped the return of anxious nightmares and had me scrambling for Callahan's body in the darkness, my pounding heart only calming when he was wrapped snugly around my body. It was not ideal when we had a long night ahead of us. Reading had helped settle my nerves and kept my mind occupied, and I suspected Callahan was purposely doing what work he could from home to keep an eye on me.

~

As the hour ticked into lunch, Rory appeared with freshly cooked bacon butties, courtesy of Maddie, and shortly after, Callahan kissed me goodbye and headed back out the door to meet Finn, leaving Rory behind to do farm admin. A steady presence to calm my skittish nerves.

His tasks required less concentration, and he glanced up from his spot on the opposite sofa. "Do you have a plan for extracting the information you need? No offence, but you're not exactly terrifying."

"Thanks for the vote of confidence," I muttered, locking my phone and dropping it in my lap. "I do have a plan. I need a syringe with my blood and a syringe with someone else's. I'm going to be honest and tell the vamp what I am, and that when all its other vampire mates die, they don't usually know what's happening, but with the mask, it'll be aware of every horrible second if it doesn't tell me what I want to know. I figure I can insert the needle which doesn't have my blood so I don't kill it prematurely—a useful threat."

His brows quirked, and he returned his attention to his laptop.

"I can also be creative about where I stab him with the needle."

He looked up with wide eyes and his hand smoothed over his neat facial hair. "If you're suggesting what I think you're suggesting, I'm not sure how I feel about that. Even as a method of torture, I can't imagine I'd want you going anyway near another set of—"

"Rory, there are lots of painful places I could stick a syringe. I was actually thinking that in the skin close to an eye would be quite effective."

"Yeah, that'd work," he said with a shake of his head and went back to staring at his screen with a long sigh.

A loud knock punctuated the silence, and we frowned at each other across the coffee table.

"I'll get it," I told him and hurried into the hall.

When I pulled the door back, my chest tightened. It was Ava waiting on the other side. She was wrapped up in a thick cream coat and emerald-green scarf, her short dark hair swaying in the breeze as she fixed me with bright eyes.

"Hello, Olivia. I was wondering if you'd like to come over for some tea?" she said with a merry tone and stepped aside, revealing that she was not alone. I stood staring dumbly at who I assumed was our mystery Em.

"This is Mahika. I've known her and her sister Neesha for many years, and I think you'd be interested to get to know her. She knows a lot about you and your kind."

The hairs rose on every inch of my body as Mahika stepped forward and held out a dainty hand. I took it hesitantly, taking in her flawless bronzed skin and silky dark hair. It was well past her shoulders, wisps of it being ruffled by the breeze, and she let go of my hand to push it back behind an ornately studded ear. She was perhaps in her mid-30s, with eyes so dark I could barely distinguish her iris from her pupils. Her delicate aquiline nose contained a simple ruby stud, the colour contrasting beautifully with her bronzed skin. She was stunning and not at all who I'd been expecting. She watched me carefully, noting every emotion passing across my face.

"What are you?" I asked. Not the most polite greeting, but I was still shocked by Ava's willing presence and friendly invitation. It was the most she'd spoken to me since the meeting she had condemned me to death.

Mahika's smile grew wider, more cunning, and I noticed the elongated canines, no doubt purposely bared. "I am a blood drinker, just like your friends," she said, strongly accented but not at all American. She inclined her head, waiting for my response. I stared back, transfixed by her impossibly dark eyes—completely unlike any of my friends or any of the vampires in our city and my brain could not grasp it. Why weren't they blue?

"Hello," Rory said over my shoulder, thankfully stealing the attention away from my awkwardness.

She smiled demurely at him and held out her hand. "I'm Mahika."

"Oh," he said, shaking her hand and briefly raising a brow at me, both of us silently acknowledging that Em was, in fact, M. "Oh, and I'm Rory. Sorry, I just wasn't expecting to see Ava on the doorstep," he said pointedly and folded his arms, leaning against the door frame.

Ava drew in a breath, her expression giving nothing away of how she felt about me, or any of our plans. It was as if the previous two weeks had never occurred.

"I was inviting Olivia to have a cup of tea with us. Mahika was keen to meet her." Her eyes drifted back to mine. Rory was silent at my side, the atmosphere charged and uncomfortable.

I cleared my throat, finally pulling myself together. "Perhaps Mahika could have tea with us here a bit later when Callahan gets back?" After my last encounter with James, having a casual cup of tea with them was a definite hell no.

"That will be fine. When will he be home?" Mahika said without even a glance at Ava. Her fingers grasped at wayward strands of hair lifted by the breeze and tucked them back behind an ear.

"I'll get him to message Ava when he's back," I said, stepping further into the house, making it clear our conversation was over.

She nodded. "I look forward to our chat." She turned, and took casual, unhurried steps away from the farmhouse, Ava sauntering dutifully beside her. Rory had a curious expression on his face when I turned and he shook his head before meeting my eye.

"Don't tell me you fell for her pretty smile?" He laughed and disappeared into the house before I could press him further.

∼

An hour later, Finn, Rory, Callahan, and I sat around the kitchen table with Mahika.

Callahan poured her a cup of tea from the glossy black teapot.

"Thank you," she said, flashing a brief smile. She added half a teaspoon of sugar to the steaming amber liquid. We were all strangely transfixed as she stirred in the milk, the tea turning a light sandy colour that was far too weak for any of our tastes.

"So," I said, shaking myself out of her spell and launching straight to the point. "What is it you know about *my* kind?"

She took a leisurely sip of tea, before answering. "I live and work with four other girls just like you back in Denver. Nanda is the youngest; she came from Brazil just before she turned sixteen. Veda and Priya were from India, like me; they've been with us the longest, and then there is Mei. She's our eldest at twenty-three, and she is originally from China." She threaded her fingers together, resting them on the table before her.

Four. There were four others like me. I was not alone, and the revelation had me practically bouncing in my seat. I sat back in my chair and calmly crossed one leg over the other, determined not to let the full extent of my emotions show. Callahan gave my hand a gentle squeeze, grounding me in the present.

"What are you doing with them? And what do you mean when you say 'with us'?" I asked, my head spinning with the dizzying number of questions now dancing about my brain.

"We...are a safe house and a research facility. There are six of us who oversee the ranch. The girls live there, protected and trained by us, and in exchange, they provide blood every four days, which we use in our research and weapons development."

Rory sat up straighter, a frown on his face. "How can you take blood every four days? Their red blood cells wouldn't have time to reproduce in that time."

Mahika's lips curved in a cat-like smile. "Olivia's blood is different. Her RBCs replenish almost as quickly as the plasma.

Technically, it only takes three days for her body to replenish one pint. We've completed extensive research on her blood and ours." She glanced at each of us around the table, a spark in her eyes, as she waited for us to launch into the next round of questions. She seemed to be enjoying this.

"Is my blood poisonous to you?" I asked.

"Not at all." Her confidence was at least reassuring, one small weight off my mind.

"How did you meet Ava?" Callahan asked. His hand was still entwined with mine, and his thumb gently caressed the back of my hand. She took a dainty sip of tea and folded her arms on the table.

"Our grandparents knew each other. They'd always told us that they first met on holiday when our parents were babies. But neither of our grandparents were blood drinkers and in recent years, we've wondered if the circumstances of their meeting were not quite so serendipitous."

That was loaded. And far too big a subject to wade into right now—that sucker needed a whole lot of unpacking judging by the stunned silence around the room. I squeezed Callahan's fingers, and he turned to give me a tight-lipped smile in acknowledgement.

"How exactly did you find the others like me?" I asked, breaking the oppressive silence and steering the conversation back to easier territory.

"Well, that's a question that probably needs the full story." She checked her watch and glanced back at me. "I am expected for dinner soon, but I will try and explain what I can."

I nodded, leaning forward in my seat, resting my elbow on the table and dropping my chin in my upturned palm. I needed this.

"I'm assuming you realise by now that we blood drinkers were on the scene a little before the vampires?" Our heads all gave a collective dip of acknowledgement and she continued. "In India, where I grew up, they started to pop up in the community a few years before I was born—not that their behaviour was overt, just that we had an acute awareness that they were different, and in the interest of keeping our existence off the radar, we had a tentative truce with them. I grew up aware of their presence and was taught to turn a blind eye and keep my head down. When I was ten, something changed. The vampires started to disappear, people in the community reported strange and terrifying behaviour, and it was rumoured that there was an outbreak of rabies or some other horrifying disease that turned people savage. The vampires went to ground, believing they were being hunted, while we remained totally unaffected. We monitored the situation, fearful that it could eventually catch up to us, and about three months after the first vampires started to disappear, one of our kind witnessed what was happening." She paused to take a sip of tea, all of us on the edge of our seats, enraptured by her story. "A vampire was seen chasing a teenage girl through the streets, not the least bit concerned about being seen by the public. The blood drinker who witnessed it followed, watching as the terrified girl was bitten but ran away completely unharmed—while the vampire died a brutal, agonising death. My parents told my siblings and me that it was nature's way of rebalancing. An equilibrium. We kept the knowledge from the vampires but it wasn't long before they connected the dots. They accused our kind—they thought we were somehow involved and extracted the truth from one of our family friends using torture." She checked her watch, her eyebrows raising as she registered the time. "The rest, you can probably gather for yourselves. They tried to force us to track down the 'assassin' using our awareness of your differences, the strange pull we have to you," she said with a nod to me. "As an adult, I started travelling and making more connections, and a small team of us developed a research programme. We realised that the vampires are steadily growing in numbers, some communities clever enough to wipe out the others like you—the assassins—and we decided to do something about it." She made a point of checking her watch again. "I'm so sorry but I don't want to be rude and keep Ava and James waiting. I hope we can chat some more, perhaps tomorrow if you are free? Or another day, of course. I am staying with them for the next twelve days." She rose gracefully from her chair, tucking it back under the table as she gave us a parting smile and turned for the kitchen door, leaving us all speechless.

36

THEORIES

After Mahika was gone, escorted out by Rory, I sat in stunned silence, my head in my hands, turning every scrap of information she'd given over and over in my mind.

Four.

There were four of them. Five of Us. Weapons. Research. There was so much still to learn, and I half wondered if she'd deliberately cut her visit short to keep us all partially in the dark, desperate for more knowledge that only she could impart. She was the sun, and we were her seedlings, bending and stretching for just a snippet of her glorious light that would give us the power to flourish.

"Are you okay?" Callahan gave my shoulder a soft lingering kiss, his fingers trailing a reassuring path down my spine.

"I have so many fucking questions." I pressed my lips to his before launching out of my chair and pacing around the kitchen.

I needed to organise my thoughts. Locating a notepad and pen, I flicked the kettle on as I made my way back to the table, dropping in my seat and tucking myself in. Tearing my tentative shopping list off the pad I set it aside and stared at the blank sheet, questions chaotically spinning in my mind, until finally, I pressed the pen to the page and wrote 'Eyes'.

Callahan snorted and dropped a kiss on the top of my head as he rose and collected the mugs. Finn grunted his approval from the head of the table, quietly scrolling on his phone and not yet ready to speak.

"I assume you want another drink?" Callahan asked, pausing halfway to the counter as Rory returned looking slightly flustered.

"I'll have a tea please," I replied, scrutinising Rory as he hovered nervously at the door. His eyes bounced between the three of us and his hand smoothed over the coarse hair along his jaw.

"I might have to take the truck to the western pastures tomorrow. Apparently, M doesn't drink cows' blood, so I'll have to bring a couple of the sheep in."

M? Well that didn't take long. When I was feeling less highly strung he would receive a proper roasting for his instant familiarity.

"Do you have a preference?" I asked them, realising it wasn't something we talked much about, and I hadn't considered if they drank cows' blood for the flavour or because it was more convenient. Rory shook his head and Callahan's jaw clenched as he stared at the mugs in his hand.

"It's all disgusting. No matter where it comes from," he finally said, turning away and heading for the sink. Finn stopped his scrolling and noticed my patient stare; he tucked his phone in his pocket and covered his mouth as a yawn overtook him. No sooner had he started than I felt the tension building in my jaw, and he laughed as I followed suit.

"They're like dominoes," he said with a lazy smile. "Only takes one to start a chain reaction."

He sat back in his chair, folding his arms across his chest, his lips pursing as he considered my question.

"My only preference," he said, "is that it's fresh. I've always thought it would be so much easier if we all enjoyed the taste, but Tilly's right, it is disgusting. Fletcher is probably the most indifferent."

That was hardly a surprise. I imagined he was the type to eat his steak fresh off the cow and oozing blood.

"What did you think of Mahika?" I asked him. He was so quiet and unassuming in these situations. He might sit and scroll on his phone, appearing as though he wished not to be included, but my instincts told me that he was a deep thinker, a vast well of wisdom if only you took the time to draw it up from the darkest depths.

"Well, aside from her ulterior motive for visiting, the thing that bothers me, is that Mahika and Ava's grandparents weren't blood drinkers. Now I'm wondering if our great-grandparents didn't drink it either, and if they didn't, why the hell did we all start needing blood?" He stared at the table, his brows pinched together. It was one of the many thoughts I'd also been circling.

"Do you think she knows why?" I said.

He glanced up, dragging his tongue unhurriedly across his bottom lip. "I reckon she has theories," he said cautiously.

Rory leant against the breakfast bar, his hands tucked in his pockets. He was alarmingly quiet and his easy smile was replaced by tension. I tapped the pen to my lip as I eyed him, and he clocked the movement and smirked.

"Careful. That's been in my mouth," he said with a devious grin.

I glanced at the pen and shrugged. "You don't want to know what I scratched with it yesterday."

He laughed, pushing himself off the side and taking a seat next to Finn, still sniggering as he did so. A moment later, Callahan set four mugs of fresh tea and coffee on the table and sat beside me, his hand resting on my thigh like he needed physical touch to soothe away the strain of the last hour.

"What are *you* thinking?" he asked, so gently it was barely audible, and I wanted to kiss him, to use my lips to smooth away the tightness from his face. I wanted the warmth of his skin against mine to melt away the worries. I sighed, resigning myself to an evening of being patient.

"I really want to know what their research entails. How much do they know about the vampires? And...I can't deny that I want to meet the others."

Rory's lips were pinched together, and he remained quiet, even though it clearly pained him to do so. Callahan was worrying his lip, I could see his chest expanding more rapidly, and I slid my hand along his thigh, squeezing until he met my eye and gave me a small sad smile.

"Imagine if you'd all grown up separately, not knowing if there was anyone else in the world like you. If you found out there were others, having been alone your entire lives, wouldn't you jump at the chance to meet them?"

He ran his hand through his hair and rubbed his face. "Yeah, I expect I would. But it's much easier for me to travel. There's a much bigger risk to you. Especially now."

"I know," I said with a sigh.

He looked at his watch and planted a kiss on my cheek before getting to his feet. "Fletch and Isla will be home any minute and they're coming straight here. I'll throw the pizzas in the oven."

∽

We retired to the living room after dinner. The fire raged, and half-empty bottles of whiskey, vodka, and Baileys were clustered on the coffee table. All of us sporting a rosy glow courtesy of the delicious heat and alcohol as we tried to chase away the day's demons, recounting every detail of Mahika's visit.

Fletcher confirmed he had at least heard of Neesha, though he'd never met or spoken to her and while we sat around the cosy lamp-lit room with slightly spinning heads, we speculated about their great-grandparents, and what could have started this chain of genetics that required the drinking of blood.

Finn reasoned that there could have been a sickness that caused genetic mutations like common zombie stories often depicted, but we all agreed that it seemed too ridiculous to be plausible.

Isla was convinced it could be a side effect of a vaccine put through human trials with disastrous consequences. Rory and Fletcher argued against it, aside from the general improbability, they claimed it would have been so closely monitored and analysed it couldn't be hidden from the world. Everyone would know. It also wouldn't explain the occurrence of my 'Assassin' bloodline. I still couldn't take that title seriously. Neither Rory nor Fletcher seemed willing to vocalise their own theories, and Callahan listened, occasionally chipping in with logical counterarguments to some of the more outlandish suggestions.

Curiosity burned through my body, all the questions a persistent itch that I couldn't yet scratch. It took effort not to march right over to the Moores' house and demand answers, but I wouldn't give Mahika the satisfaction of seeing how much I wanted her knowledge—how much it ate away at me.

"Do you know what's also strange?" Callahan said, eyeing me. I was sat sideways on the sofa, my back leaning against the sturdy armrest with my legs draped over his lap. His hands were a constant caress, the warmth of his palms seeping through my jeans and sending the occasional tremor down my spine as he teased me absentmindedly. "We all have a family line that shares our genetics, even if it's a short lineage, but you don't have any family members that share your traits that we know of.

"Yet there are girls randomly popping up in other parts of the world of a similar age, completely unrelated to you—even in their living circumstances—with your exact genetic differences. And they seem to appear near communities of vampires."

He was right, and if my parents were like me, I would have expected them to help me. As cold as they were, surely they would give me the courtesy of explaining what was happening to me if they knew. I'd been content to believe that we were a random hiccup in nature, but it seemed far too suspicious to be a complete coincidence, and knowing their great-grandparents were normal, with no requirement for drinking blood whatsoever, I felt this deep dark pit opening in my chest. There was a lingering feeling that something was very wrong, and that I wouldn't want to know the answer. My mind wanted to box up the questions and lock them away, throwing them in the attic of my memory where they could be ignored and forgotten.

"You're going to speak to her again right?" Isla asked from the opposite sofa, her legs tucked under her and a glass of neat vodka resting on her thighs. Finn sat to one side of her, Fletcher on the other with the laptop open—balanced on the arm of the chair. He had been researching genetics as we discussed back and forth.

I stifled a yawn, tired to my bones from the can of worms we'd inadvertently opened, and said resolutely, "I have to. There could be things she knows that would help us here. Things that could help answer some of your questions too."

"I preferred it when I thought we were from some ancient and mysterious bloodline," Finn mused. "Makes having blunt fangs and sipping blood so much more noble."

"I must admit, it always annoyed me that we didn't have any wild superpowers," Rory agreed. He sat up, swinging his legs off the sofa and reaching for the whiskey to refill his glass. "But then, I suppose it's better than having to live with all the pitfalls of vampire mythology. It would be a pain in the arse not physically being able to go out in the day."

I thought of all the ridiculous myths I'd believed before I met them all and glanced at Callahan.

He was staring at a bottle on the table, the glow of firelight pulsed through the glass, turning the contents a deep rich orange. His lips curved at Rory's words, turning into a full mocking grin when he caught me staring. Damn. Every smile was breathtaking, like dark winter clouds giving way to an unexpected blue summer sky, they filled me with a sense of relief and excitement.

"I'm so glad you guys can go out in the daylight, but I really fucking wish the vampires burnt to a crisp," I muttered.

Maybe this whole crisis could have been averted if they didn't see me as the sole reason to hide away. Not that I would say that out loud.

Conversation trickled off, and after a short interlude of silence, Fletcher closed the laptop abruptly and stood, holding his hand out to Isla, like they were important dignitaries retiring to their mansions, nodding towards the door.

Rory and Finn followed, and when the door was locked and the house quiet, Callahan pulled me into a hungry kiss.

"I thought they'd never leave," he said against my mouth, dragging us back towards the stairs. My tiredness and vampire problems were forgotten as the feel of him against me crowded out all other thoughts.

37

BUTCHERED

With a long slow exhale, I raised my fist and forced myself to knock on the Moores' front door. I did not want to be here, but the need for answers had driven my feet down the drive and now it was too late to turn back, the last grains of sand dropping into the bottom of the hourglass as the key turned in the lock.

The door creeped open to reveal Mahika, tungsten light spooling around the mass of dark hair heaped atop her head like a halo. She wore baggy jeans and a thick black polo-neck jumper—understated, casual attire that still managed to exude elegance and sophisticated beauty.

"Good morning Olivia," she said, a bemused smile tugging at the corners of her lips—perhaps she didn't expect to see me grovelling at the door quite so soon.

Her beautiful dark eyes marked every uncomfortable twitch as I stood awkwardly grasping for words. There was something about her that still brought nerves fizzing through my body and the fine hairs on my arm standing to attention. Was it the threat of danger? Or the fact that I found her quite dazzling?

"Hi, I was just heading out for a walk and wondered if you were in need of some fresh air?"

Her head tilted, and a perfectly shaped eyebrow arched gracefully as she scrutinised my invitation. The gesture reminded me of my mother—the way she'd stare back at me when I asked to do something cute as a family like taking a bike ride in the country or travelling to the beach for the weekend—maybe that was why she unnerved me.

"Is that a polite way of saying you have more questions?" Though her tone wasn't unkind, it cut through my niceties and carved out my intentions so precisely I felt my cheeks warming.

"Naturally," I said with a shrug of my shoulders, my eyes flickering upwards as a cold splodge of rain fell from the brooding sky and trickled down my forehead.

She considered it for a moment. "If it's all the same to you, I'd rather talk by the fire with a coffee in my hand. I have no desire to walk around the farm today."

"Fine, as long as it's not here," I said a little too sharply. "No offence, but the Moores and I don't have the best track record."

"Not a problem," she said, sliding her feet into a pair of black and white Converse and stuffing a stray lace back down the side of one heel. "But Ava and James are good people. Perhaps you should consider a fresh start with them?" She grabbed her jacket, and the weight of her stare shrivelled my curiosity, making me wish I hadn't acted on the need to scratch that proverbial itch. Not if it came with the caveat of chumming it up with the Moores. She shrugged on her jacket, slamming the door shut behind her, the lock settling with a loud clunk as she turned it.

"Where are the Moores?" I bet she didn't know the full history of our encounters.

"It's Tuesday. I believe they are at work," she said as if it were obvious.

It seemed rude of them to abandon her when she'd travelled all this way to see them, but I couldn't deny my relief when it had been Mahika's face that peered around the door. We lapsed into silence as our feet crunched rhythmically across the gravel, our pace quickening as the raindrops increased their intensity, the sky darkening as the clouds released their gathered boon. Hopefully, it wasn't a bad omen.

With fire lit and coffee made, we sat on opposite sides of the coffee table, rigid and tense, the sound of crackling wood filling far too many gaps in conversation. I tried to be polite, tried to appear interested in more than just the information I wanted to pry out of her like a stubborn molar, but she gave little away. Her responses were clipped, so I quickly gave up, cutting right to the chase.

"Tell me more about the research," I asked, hungry for the knowledge almost to the point of desperation.

A cat-like smile worked its way across her mouth as if she'd been waiting for me to give in and beg her for the answers, toying with me all along.

"There is only so much I can tell you," she said, setting her coffee cup on the table and propping an elbow on the armrest. "Our aim is quite simple: to better understand the differences in our DNA and how we can use that to our advantage."

Nicely vague. I resisted rolling my eyes.

"For weaponry?" I asked, folding my legs underneath me, settling in for whatever nuggets she would willingly impart.

"Well, that's part of it, yes, but we've made progress in other areas, most of which I can't share with you yet."

My gaze fell to the curling and stretching flames in the wood burner, certain that any eye contact with Mahika would only give away my mounting frustration. Even now, with access to someone who had devoted years to research, there was only so much I would ever know, so many questions left unanswered. I took a breath, shaking off the sinking feeling in the pit of my stomach.

"How do you use the weaponry?" I asked. "I mean, do you sell it? Have you used it successfully to wipe out vampire populations anywhere?"

She stared at the table, the tip of her tongue running over the edge of a canine as she thought, and when she glanced up a minute later her expression was inscrutable. "No, we don't sell it. Our aim is to recruit as many mediators as we can. We try and build them into a capable team, then we find ways to traffic our tech to those that need it most. There aren't as many of us left these days, and a lot of those with young families have fled to remote locations." Her fingers drifted down over her neat row of ear piercings as she paused, momentarily lost in thought. "As for success stories, we have a few. Mostly in smaller cities like this one where the vampire population was less established. The countries that pose the biggest difficulties are Pakistan, Indonesia, Nigeria, and most recently, China. Last year, two mediator families were butchered in Beijing when the vampires were trying to eradicate assassins. We managed to get Mei to safety, but we lost two other girls."

A knot tightened in my stomach, and for once I was glad Callahan wasn't here. I wondered how many more like me had died across the world, girls that even Mahika had no idea existed.

"Have you met more assassins than just the five of us?" I asked, trying to steer us back to the living.

"Yes," she said, giving a brief sympathetic smile as she marked my hands incessantly fidgeting, and the way I hunched forward in anticipation. "I've met three others who chose to stay in their cities, content with their survival methods, and I definitely think there are more like you that we've yet to find. Two members of our team are currently in Indonesia, and they've just made contact with a girl of eighteen. We're hoping we can convince her to come to Denver."

"Why Denver?" I should have been taking notes. My head was a jumble of crumpled thoughts and half-considered questions, and a part of me didn't trust that I wouldn't miss some critical piece of information, too consumed with pulling out as many facts as I possibly could to satiate my greed.

"Gosh, well, it wasn't that we chose Denver specifically," she said, crossing her legs and resting her elbows on her knees. "The ranch was inherited by Alec's husband—Alec is my research partner. But given that it was so remote, Alec and Ryan decided that it was ideally situated for a research site that coupled as a safe—"

"Are Ryan and Alec both mediators?" I said, cutting in before she could finish answering.

"Alec is, yes, but—"

"Woah, hold on, how did Ryan and Alec meet and how did he go about telling Ryan the truth?" This was the first time I'd heard of a normal human being aware of our reality. I wasn't so ignorant to think people didn't know, but I hadn't personally met anyone clued into our secrets.

"That," she said sharply, "is not your business. If ever you meet Alec, you can ask him yourself."

"How is the safehouse and all your research funded?" I asked, changing tack and hoping I hadn't put an end to the flow of information.

"The usual way—grants and crowdfunding, but obviously we alter the project specifics to something desirably mainstream, and some of the labs we've worked in have had breakthroughs that have made waves in the pharmaceutical field. Before you ask, that is all information I cannot speak about. It's tightly bound with iron clad NDA's."

"Right," I muttered under my breath. Speaking with her was like swimming against the tide and a pulsing ache was gnawing at the spot between my brows.

"Look, it's a lot to take in, and I've got some emails to attend to before I leave for London tomorrow, so I think we're done for today. I'll see myself out. Thank you for the coffee," she said, adjusting her jeans as she stood.

I unfurled my legs, pins and needles flaring from my toes and spreading past my ankle leaving my foot an agonising useless lump of flesh.

"I didn't know you were going to London," I said, grimacing as I tried to massage life back into my appendage.

"I didn't tell you," she said flatly, eyeing my foot with a raised brow. "I'm visiting other network members for a few days. While I'm gone, perhaps you could consider whether you'd be willing to come back to Denver with me."

She was already walking into the hall by the time the question fully sank in, and I half walked, half hopped after her, propping myself against the door frame as she pulled on her trainers and coat. She gave me a nod and wrenched the door open, flinching as she found Rory on the other side, and her cheekbones developed a rosy hue that didn't go unnoticed.

"I didn't know you were stopping by," he said with a roguish grin. "I'll walk you back before I have my coffee break." He peered in and gave me a nod. "Stick the kettle on, Liv. We'll all be back in about five." He turned and escorted Mahika as if she were a celebrity needing his protection.

"Wow," I muttered to myself with a long sigh. That did not go down as expected. Denver. I sat on the bottom of the stairs and pulled up a search on my phone, wincing at the nine-and-a-half hour minimum flight time. Surely it wouldn't be logistically possible?

Before I could give it more thought, Callahan arrived, eyeing me curiously as he shucked off his boots.

"What's up?" he asked, dragging me off the stairs and cocooning me in his delicious warmth, squeezing me against his chest and pressing a kiss to the crook of my neck. An involuntary groan escaped my lips, and I nipped and licked at the tender spot under his jaw, enjoying the taste of his exertion on my lips—until I remembered he worked on a farm, and it didn't seem quite so sexy. I booted the thought from my mind and decided I should rip away the bandaid and tell him what was on my mind.

"Er...so, Mahika asked if I would go back to Denver with her."

38

MOTIVES

It had been three days since Mahika invited me to Denver, and the decision shadowed my every thought. I wanted desperately to meet the other girls, but at almost ten hours, the flight seemed too steep a mountain to tackle. The risks were unquantifiable.

Callahan had dutifully talked it through with me, remaining supportive, even though the prospect clearly unnerved him. Mahika had returned to the farm late the previous night and had knocked on the door early, no doubt eager to see if her scheming was falling into place.

We stood shoulder to shoulder, looking out over the farm from the crest of a wooded hill. The leaves were a stunning, harmonious palette of amber, burnt orange, and red, and each bluster of wind sent a flurry of leaves dancing down the hill.

"If you think this is beautiful, Colorado will leave you breathless," she said, turning to face me and pulling the collar of her thick navy coat tighter around her neck. Strands of her hair were whipped up by the wind and thrown chaotically around her face. She turned on the spot until the tendrils of inky black fluttered behind almost superhero-esque, and she tucked it back into her coat.

"How the hell would I get to Denver?" I said checking my messy bun was withstanding the onslaught of weather. "I mean, what if there was a vamp...a vampire?" I amended when I saw her confused side glance. "If there was one in the airport? Or worse, on the plane?"

I was pretty sure the money they procured for research did not extend to chartering private jets. I waited, but her gaze never left the sweeping autumnal landscape, my worries ignored, floating off with the wind, and not a single fuck given.

Then casually, she said, "I have ways around that. I can block your scent."

Surely I hadn't heard her correctly? Because the ability to do that would drastically change my entire fucking life, and it felt like something that should really have come up sooner.

"What did you just say?" I said, staring at her, slack-jawed, my brain dangerously close to short-circuiting as I waited for her to dignify a response.

"It's one of the breakthroughs in our research. A drug that provides a temporary alteration to your pheromones. It's no good if you bleed, there is absolutely nothing that can be done about the scent of your blood, but your general scent will change enough that vampires can be in your presence completely unaffected."

Holy fuck.

I pinched the back of my hand, and the piercing pain proved I was awake. There was a ringing in my ears as first shock, then anger, disbelief, curiosity, and hope rapidly fired behind my eyelids.

"That's just a taste of what we can do. If you come with me to Denver and help with our research, we'll teach you a better way to fight. We'll give you access to that pheromone blocker. Access to custom-built weapons." She watched me like a cat eyeing a mouse before it pounced.

"It sounds too good to be true," I muttered, my voice as raw as I felt.

"It's not. And you don't have a better option," she said flatly.

It was probably true. What we had was sloppy, uneducated—dangerous and unsustainable. I'd sworn off being a coward, but replacing cowardice with recklessness was hardly better. We'd held off on our latest plans in the hopes that Mahika would provide further information about her research, not wanting to rush into something that would risk more retaliation before we were ready for it. There was so much at stake.

"Before I agree to anything, I need proof. There is not a fucking chance I'm heading into an airport without testing that this…stuff you're talking about actually works."

A devious smile played about her lips. "I wouldn't want you on my team if you were stupid enough to let me load you with a random drug and not question it. Which is exactly why I brought several doses."

"But I don't just mean testing the blocker. I want you to show us what *you* can do. Show us how we can fight better."

I needed to see if the gamble would be worth it, because I wanted to hit them hard. There was retribution to be had, a reckoning. They'd gotten off lightly while we waited for Callahan to piece himself back together after they'd so thoroughly shattered him. Their days were numbered.

Her beautifully arched brows pushed together in a frown, her lips bunching as she tipped her head back and stared into the greying sky. Her shoulders rolled and then her face returned to a look of cool indifference.

"Fine. But it will have to be tomorrow. I have plans tonight. I'll need to collect some of your blood—I suppose we could do that now. And then tomorrow, I'll give you the shot two hours before we head out." Her head dipped and she eyed me beneath lowered brows. "But I'll want your decision the following morning."

"Right," I agreed, trying to contain the giddiness crawling beneath my skin. The intriguing possibilities overriding the frustration of her withholding information. "Does the invitation to Denver extend to Callahan?"

I had no idea if he would want to leave the farm, or if he even could leave the farm, but the thought of going without him hollowed out my chest. It was hard enough not to follow him out to the farm in the morning, every time the door slammed shut, I had to convince myself it was all real—that I was alive, very much awake, and that I had not only Callahan but all these other people whom I adored to fill up my once empty life.

She rolled her eyes and huffed. "Yes, if you cannot be without him for even a week or two, then I suppose we have no choice but to accommodate him."

Evidently, her patience was spent, and she stomped back down the hill. My feet slipped in mud as I hurried to catch her up, eyes straining against the biting wind and leaking tears down my cheeks. Not that there was much point in chasing her. Mahika might be beautiful, poised, and probably a certifiable badass, but one thing she was not, was a conversationalist. It was slightly unnerving just how little she spoke—every single word was carefully measured and used only when absolutely necessary to achieve whatever schemes and manipulations she was orchestrating. I couldn't help but wonder if it was incredibly lonely and exhausting being so perpetually insular and self-controlled.

The approaching hum of quad bikes brought us to a standstill. Callahan and Rory drew to a stop on the dirt track behind us looking decidedly roguish. Their faces were winter flushed, their hair wild around the edges and their mirrored bright eyes held mischievous sparks. They cut the power to their quads, the roar of the engines teetering out, giving way to chattering birds and the rustling of leaves being stripped from their lofty branches by the wind.

"Ladies," Rory drawled, his eyes roaming over Mahika, making no secret of his obvious attraction. I half expected Mahika to shred him to pieces verbally, but she smiled politely, seemingly unaffected.

Callahan dismounted, his face lit up with a tender smile, his eyes drinking me in as if he hadn't had my body wrapped around him only this morning.

"Hey," he said, his lips ghosting over mine teasingly, sending my heart rate near instantly off kilter. "Can I interest you in a ride?" His fingers traced over my cheek, wiping away the remnants of wind ushered tears, and he chuckled at my expression. "I meant back to the farm, on the quad!" he said, a tooth snagging on his lower lip as he smiled.

"Have I ever refused you?" I said wryly. "And have I ever mentioned how fucking sexy you are?"

His head tipped back with the force of his laugh, drowning out the disgruntled voices of Mahika and Rory. "You actually have not!" He grinned, pulling me against him, still smiling as he kissed me. The roar of a quad bike spluttered to life behind us and soon became a distant rumble.

"Mahika's been holding out on us," I said as we finally relinquished each other, Callahan leading me back to his quad.

"What do you mean?" He stopped, his feet sinking into a patch of sticky mud, suspicion concentrated between his brows, the line forming a deep crevice as he waited for me to elaborate.

"They've developed a way to temporarily block my scent from the vampires. Which means Denver might potentially be on the table after all."

His nostrils flared as he took a sharp intake of breath, his eyes flickering to the sky and overhead branches that lined the track. "Oh?" His eyes finally drew back to me, and a complicated mix of emotions clouded over the smile from minutes before.

"I'm not considering it as a viable option unless she can prove herself to us," I said placatingly, "but if we felt it would be worth it, would you—"

"—yes," he said before I could even get a question out. "I'd come with you. If you wanted me to."

His face was a mass of tense, hard lines until a relieved smile swept across my face, soothing away the angst in us both.

"Thank God," I groaned, tucking myself against his shoulder. "I'm not ready to say goodbye to you just yet. Even if that does sound clingy."

His arms folded around me reflexively. "It's not clingy," he muttered, "but let's not make any hasty decisions. I'm not sure I trust her yet, and I don't like the idea that she's playing on your emotions with the other girls. I understand why you'd want to meet them, what it means to you and all, but what if you go and they don't want you to leave?" He pulled back to look at me, cradling my face as the concerns rushed from his mouth. "What if they want to keep you for research, and the girls are just a means to get you there?

"I don't know, maybe it's the way Ava and James treated you before, and that she came here through them. It just makes me question her motives."

"That's fair," I murmured, my voice small and almost lost against the wind. Now more than ever, my trust should be guarded carefully and sparsely given. "Let's see what happens tomorrow night. I made her promise to show us what she can do, so we can see if the drug really works on my scent and whether she's genuine about all the things she says she can offer us."

His shoulders loosened, and the crease between his brows disappeared.

"Rory seems to be quite smitten. Would you trust his judgement of her, or do you think his opinion would be compromised?" I asked cautiously as he slid his fingers through mine, tugging me towards the quad bike.

"Generally, I would trust his judgement," he said, sliding his leg over the cold leather and guiding me onto the seat in front of him. He started the engine, pointing out the brakes and wrapping his arms around my waist, laughing as I eased the quad forward at a snail's pace. "Go on, give it some," he encouraged.

"I'm just getting used to it," I shouted over my shoulder, gradually picking up speed and shrieking with excitement as we hurtled down the track, every dip in the rough ground travelling up my spine and vibrating down my arms. The farmland whizzed by us in an exhilarating rush of rich autumn colours and endless muted greens, the wind biting at our cheeks, turning the tips of my nose and ears to ice. The cows raised their heads in unison as we whipped past their paddocks.

My body still hummed with sensation when we dismounted and found Rory and Mahika in the outhouse with all the first aid kits laid out ready. Callahan busied himself making drinks, while Mahika made quick work of taking samples, talking an already knowledgeable Rory through the process. I glared daggers at him and mouthed 'chicken' when he didn't admit to his competence on the matter. He ignored me, lapping up her attention, asking questions he absolutely knew the answers to and offering her compliments. He flicked me on the shoulder on his way out with a fiercely agitated look and the promise of payback. Callahan's chuckle echoed around the empty room when they left.

"Ok, I see what you mean, but honestly, he must have another angle as he's not usually THAT painfully obvious," he said, handing me a tea, sweetened with a spoon of sugar just the way I liked it. It was so cold in the outbuilding, the steam left a fine layer of condensation on my cheeks and some much needed warmth to my painfully chilled skin.

"But when did he last get laid?" I asked curiously, wondering if desperation would have any influence over his actions, watching

Callahan walk a loop around the worktable, glancing at the fridge as he passed.

"The fuck if I know," he said, drawing to a stop in front of me. He chewed on one corner of his lip, reaching for my hand and smoothing his thumb along the jagged edge of my scarring palm. "Listen, can you give me a few minutes? I need—" He stopped short. "I need blood," he muttered in a low rasp, laying himself bare and achingly vulnerable, the shame he felt etched deeply in every exquisite feature.

"Can I please stay while you prepare it and then leave? It's just, I feel like it's an important part of who you are and…" Words stuck in my throat, a lump of emotion lodged thickly as the memory of him kissing my neck for the first time pinked my cheeks. I'd given him access to all of me, and as much as he considered this different, to me, it was one and the same. It was the place he was most vulnerable and one day, I hoped he might be liberated from all the unnecessary shame that tore him up on the inside. It might never be something he wanted to do but he should never have to hide those parts of himself. Not with me.

He swallowed, his chest rising and falling rapidly as his emotions warred within. "It's not that I want to keep things from you, it's just…I struggle to keep it down," he admitted hesitantly. "It wouldn't be a pleasant experience for either of us."

Discarding my cup on the side, I rose to the tips of my toes and brushed my lips gently over his, my fingers sliding through the shorter strands of hair at the nape of his neck. "I'm sorry that it's so unpleasant for you," I said softly. "I honestly don't want you to feel pressured, I just want you to feel like you can be your entire self around me without any fear of being judged, and I want to be there for you like you've been for me—vomit and all."

He brushed the tip of his nose along mine, his breath warming my lips as our brows touched and he held me close. "Sometimes," he whispered, "I can hardly fucking believe that you're mine."

39

VULNERABLE

The night was clear. A beautiful mass of twinkling stars hung above my head, their calming presence dampening the edge of the nerves that riddled my body and mind. The air was so bitter —each breath produced a vivid white cloud of condensation, and my fingers were stuffed deep in my pockets to keep away the chill. I'd spent the last thirty minutes wandering about the farm alone in the dark, my phone clutched eagerly in my hand waiting for the signal that we were ready.

Finally, Callahan called.

"Hey, none of us have any idea where you are. So, as soon as you get back here, I think we'll be good to head out."

"Right, okay. Are you absolutely certain you can't feel anything? What if I've gone too far away?"

"Where are you now?"

"I'm sitting on the log down by the second pasture gate."

He sighed. "If you walk to the cowshed, I'm gonna wait there for you and put my headphones in. If it's worked, I won't hear or sense you coming so you should be able to sneak right up on me."

"Oh, game on," I said and hung up before he could respond.

I used the low torchlight from my phone to guide the way,

keeping my steps as quiet as possible as I hurried down the track. After a few minutes, I rounded a bend and the looming hulk of the cowshed could be seen within the moonlight. It wasn't long before my body was pressed against the cold corrugated metal, my phone light switched off as I reached the corner of the building and held my breath. Peering around the edge I could just make out his outline leaning against the frame of the cowshed, a tiny pinprick of blue light emanating from an earbud, his breath a steady stream of white clouding the air in front of him. He was oblivious to my presence, and when he finally saw me moving towards him in the shadows, he startled, releasing a string of curses that had me giggling despite the situation.

"You knew I was coming. How did I still make you jump?"

"I have a lot on my mind," he huffed, blinding me with the bright spread of light from his torch. When I reached him, his nose grazed the sensitive skin on my neck, and he inhaled long and slow. "I can smell your perfume but other than that…I feel nothing. Not like before."

"You feel nothing?" I asked, a little horrified.

Taking in my expression, he wrapped his arms around my waist and pressed his lips to my forehead, the gentleness of his touch soothing my irrational nerves.

"Well, I don't feel the same pull from your scent that I did before, but it doesn't change the way I feel about you, if that's worrying you? I'll happily prove it to you later if it is." His tone was playfully suggestive, his lips curved in a wry smile as he pulled away, lacing our fingers together as we made our way towards the house.

"I'll definitely need you to prove it," I teased. "Assuming tonight is not a colossal mood killer, obviously."

He squeezed my hand, his smile disappearing as we turned our attention to what lay ahead, it would be a monumental night for me if all went to plan, and fuck did we need a win.

The journey into the city was uncomfortably quiet. Rory was doing his best to appear indifferent to Mahika as they sat stiffly in the back of Callahan's Duster, and her dislike of social chatter made any conversation awkward. My body was on edge, nerves crawling over my skin making me shiver and squirm in my seat, the nausea winding its way into my stomach. It was a relief when we reached the darker underbelly of the city, knowing soon we would be out of the car and my limbs could expel the tightly coiled energy.

The car idled to a stop at a red light, and Callahan reached for my hand, threading our fingers together with a reassuring squeeze, resting them on top of the gear stick as we waited. His head tipped back against the headrest, and he glanced at me from the corner of his eye and smiled. It was those smiles, as small and fragile as they were, that ignited something deep in my chest. Those were the smiles that cost him the most, where in a place of sorrow and stress, he still made a conscious effort to give something more of himself. To show that he cared deeply, offering wordless reassurance and devotion despite his grief.

Words burned on the tip of my tongue as the glow of the traffic light changed from orange then to green.

Mahika leant forward in her seat and peered into the front. "According to your map, we should be coming up to their territory, yes? Is there somewhere we can pull over?"

Neither Callahan, nor Rory had been particularly keen on this part of Mahika's plan, and his hand tightened around mine.

"Go to the rendezvous site, and wait there for us. But give us at least five minutes before you open the lure, okay?" she said.

He nodded his agreement and turned to face me, lips twitching to one side and eyes dark and heavy. "Stay safe," he said roughly, as he removed his fingers from mine with a sigh, and dropped his head back to stare up at the car roof as I exited.

Mahika wasted no time, and we were swiftly out and walking

right through the heart of the vampire territory at a steady pace. Dark, towering buildings hemmed us in on either side, and with the street lights mostly broken we travelled between sparse pockets of hazy Tungsten light, the looming shadows swallowing all the spaces between.

Many buildings were clad with scaffolding and padlocked fencing, and the breeze rattled through the tarp sheets. My eyes darted from shadow to shadow, expecting to see the familiar outline of a vampire ready to give chase, but we continued without issue, barely a soul in sight.

As we neared the end of the street, Mahika pulled us to a stop. She leaned casually against a secured iron gate, watching the road behind me intently.

"Stay behind me when they come past and keep out of the way. The minute your blood is spilt, the plan fails. Understand?"

I nodded, shifting to watch the street, waiting for movement. Headlights slowed at the other end of the road, pausing for fifteen seconds before creeping towards us. It was the Duster, the windows down and Rory in the front passenger seat holding a small canister of my blood, hoping to trail my scent. They passed by, continuing to our rendezvous as planned, leaving us waiting in the heart of vampire territory.

Finn and Fletcher would already be at our chosen spot with a lure of their own. The six of us were armed with syringes filled with my blood—there would be no knives and as little fighting as possible, if Mahika was to be believed.

Movement caught our attention, and out from the shadows between buildings, a figure clad in black emerged, briskly pacing towards us. I pulled out my phone, holding it to my ear as if on a call, and Mahika placed her body in front of mine, both of us stealing covert glances as it neared.

My skin prickled fiercely, nausea becoming more intense as it approached. It was close enough now that I could see a vacant expression and an icy stare fixed at some point in the distance. My breath caught in my throat as it levelled with us, my heart a frantic beat against my ribs, and Mahika shifted her stance, ready to fight. It didn't stop, barely registering our presence, as its heavy footsteps pounded past us on the pavement, biologically forced to hunt for prey it would never find. Only death awaited. My face was flushed with adrenaline, my body trembling with such force, I had to steady myself against the cold iron gate.

It had fucking worked!

The impossibility of it hit me full force, and I doubled over, my breaths heaving out of me in plumes of white.

"We have a job to do. Have your emotional outburst later when we get back, okay?"

Mahika's hushed voice pulled me from my state of overwhelm, and I straightened, forcing another long inhale and exhale before nodding and following her in her steps. We were monitoring the street behind as we walked, keeping a healthy distance from the vamp who was oblivious to our presence.

The rendezvous was soon in sight, it was the rear of the multi-storey car park where we'd taken our hostage, a prime spot for vampires, but just far enough from their territory that it wouldn't attract too many. In the deep shadow of the building, the black bricks sucked in all the light. The construction site was bordered by a line of trees and dense hedging, giving us privacy from the road. Somewhere within the shadows, Fletcher, Callahan, Rory, and Finn were waiting, the small pot of my blood carefully placed somewhere out of reach. As the vamp took its first steps along the access road, Fletcher stepped out of the shadows—a dark wraith intent on his prey—slamming his needle in its neck as quick as a viper. It lurched away from him, stumbling as it tried to recompose, but Fletcher advanced and slung his fist into the vampire's jaw with a resounding crack that reverberated through me even at a distance, the force knocking the vamp off its feet. Its skull met the hard ground with a sickly wet crunch, and it did not move again.

We hung back, tucked away in an alcove a few metres from the entrance to the access road, waiting and watching, the night around us eerily quiet. Just as bones began to crack and splinter, a second vampire appeared across the street. It was tall and lithe, and its cropped black hair made its features look even harsher in the dim streetlight. This time, it was Finn who stepped away from the building like a shadow given life. His leg swung out, expertly timed and positioned, knocking the vamp to the floor. A second later, his knee was pressed between shoulder blades holding it in place while he delivered the lethal dose of my blood. He wrangled its struggling arms behind its back, disabling the vampire until it started to choke, and only then did he slip back into the deepest shadows.

We had agreed with Mahika that after two vampires, the mission would be over. It would draw too much attention if a larger number disappeared, and until we had access to better weapons and could mount a well-considered attack, we had to be sensible. There were too many of them, and with our meagre numbers, it would be unwise to incite an all-out war, especially when we might be leaving the country.

There was movement by the side of the building, a torch flickering on and off in a pattern that signalled the lures were being sealed away in air-tight containers, and Mahika and I joined the others. The bodies were in the later stages of decomposition, and Finn was staring wide-eyed as the rib cage of one caved with a crack, the clothes falling around it, creepily undulating as bones continued to disintegrate beneath them.

A shiver rattled down my spine, and I spun away. Callahan wrapped me up in his arms. We stood entwined, ignoring the carnage around us, my ear trained to the sound of his steady heartbeat as I willed the nausea to calm.

A new sense of foreboding slithered over my skin, my stomach pulsing with a wave of nausea that was almost crippling. A masked figure stared from the shadows of an alcove, the streetlight glinting off the glass eyelets. We watched each other, time stilling, the dark pressing in, chilling me down to my bones, and I swayed. One of its hands was pressed into the wall beside it, the other clutched to its chest. It was small in stature, long lengths of dark hair spilling over its shoulder.

We moved in tandem. My feet propelled me forward, and I sprinted down the access road as the female vamp launched from the alcove heading away from our group. She was fast, even with a mask. My ragged breaths plumed behind me in the frigid air, our desperate footsteps echoing around the street as I raced to catch up with her, my longer strides eating up the ground, hungry for the answers she might provide.

We neared the heart of their territory. I realised another set of feet were gaining on me, and I faltered, checking over my shoulder to find Finn closing on my heels. He pushed harder, his hand reaching to snag my coat, our bodies colliding as my momentum was abruptly interrupted, and we tumbled over each other, rolling to a stop on the pavement.

"What the hell, Liv? What were you thinking?" he said through gritted teeth, panting as he got to his feet, holding out his hand. I took it, my thigh burning with the effort to stand.

"I was thinking—" I doubled over and gagged, fighting back the urge to vomit, swallowing and sucking in the cold air. Another set of feet approached, smaller strides, and I looked up to find Mahika marching towards me with a scowl.

"What. The. Fuck?" she spat, her dainty hands clenched tightly at her sides. "Get moving. NOW."

I staggered forward, clutching my stomach. Finn and Mahika stayed on either side of me as we walked, glancing in every direction and readying for a fight. I just hoped the vamp's escape didn't cost us. I had no idea how long she'd been watching—whether she saw me and Mahika in the shadow of the alcove as the other vampires were executed. My stomach twisted at the thought of her relaying our activity; it could very well ignite the war we were trying to avoid. It wasn't long before Callahan drew to stop in front of us in the Duster, his expression tense with anger as he watched the road ahead, Rory equally fuming beside him. Finn opened the back door, gesturing for me to get in and jogging to the other side of the car, forcing me into the middle seat between him and Mahika. Fletcher pulled up a moment later, offering Finn a lift, but it was declined, so we set off back to the farm, wedged like sardines in the back.

The car was deathly silent until we reached the outer ring road.

Rory turned in his seat to look at me. "So?" he said, his brows raised in question, waiting for me to explain myself, and I noticed Callahan's eyes glancing at me in the rearview mirror. It wasn't an angry look, more intrigued, which was comforting.

"She could have seen everything!" I said indignantly. "It was an opportunity to question her and find out who the hell is helping them AND to stop her blabbering about what we just did. If Finn hadn't distracted me, I was like, two seconds from grabbing her. I had a syringe ready, for fucks sake. I was handling it."

Finn turned to stare at me, his brows rising with disbelief. "You were NOT two seconds from catching it, and you were running straight into their territory. They could so easily have killed you. Without your scent to trigger bloodlust, you're more vulnerable than ever."

Even in the dim glow of passing streetlamps, I could see his face flush, and he turned away quickly, staring out the window, his fingers splaying and clenching in his lap.

Rory cleared his throat, his face softening as he glanced

between Finn and me. "Liv, come on, it wasn't the smartest thing you've ever done."

"What's done is done." Mahika's curt tone cut in and put a stop to the conversation, and an uncomfortable silence ensued.

Rory turned back to face the front, his arms folded across his chest as he stared ahead, biting his lip. After a few awkward minutes, I noticed Finn's hand had relaxed its anxious fidgeting, and I tapped him gently on his elbow.

When he peered at me, his expression still pursed, I whispered my apology, and his body relaxed as he turned away to stare out the window. It was only then that the enormity of it all settled over me in the silence. Emotions crowded in my chest, and I closed my eyes, resting my head back as I counted through each breath. It was a win. For one night, I'd been somewhat normal, and it would change everything.

40

SOMEONE'S BEEN HERE

The decision to fly to Colorado wasn't a difficult one to make. In less than one hour, we had accomplished more than I'd ever thought possible. With my scent strategically weaponised and separated from me entirely, it was so clean and so simple. Isla had stayed home where it was safest, and when we relayed the evening to her, the six of us were euphoric, staying up to celebrate our victory. We paid for it in the morning, but despite the exhaustion, we had hope. How could I pass up the opportunity to learn more and finally meet my sisters in kind?

Fletcher, Callahan, and I, were planning to depart in five days, flying into Denver and spending two weeks at the ranch. For those two weeks, the rest of our little community would stay home. Ava, James, Maddie, and Stephen along with Isla, would help Rory and Finn tend to the farm and stay well clear of the city. We'd needed the demonstration, but it came at a cost. We'd been seen, and although the vampires did not know the farm's location, there was every chance they would retaliate if given an opportunity.

We'd been working on the farm most of the day, and with a couple of hours of daylight left, Callahan drove me to the city to collect more things from my apartment in preparation for our trip.

We parked in the multi-storey around the corner from my building and strode swiftly down the main street, people bustling around us, a sea of winter coats and bobble hats passing us by. The scent of garlic had my stomach gurgling as we neared Piccolino's.

"I've just realised something," I said, a smile sweeping across my lips as I pulled us to a stop outside the restaurant. With a curious smile, he waited for me to voice my revelation. "Now that we have a way around my err...scent," I said quietly, "we could go on a proper date night."

As the words left my mouth, his expression settled into something more tender, and he brushed his nose against mine. "I'd be honoured to take you out on a date, but the candlelit night in front of the fire will be extremely difficult to beat."

His words ghosted against my skin and butterflies swarmed in my belly, my body flooding with warmth and want in their wake. My hands wound around his neck, drawing him in for an unhurried, delicate kiss. We broke away when a tram pulled to a stop ahead of us, the doors hissing open, and the people within were swallowed up by the crowded street. Callahan put his head down as we wove in and out of the rush of bodies, crossing the final few feet to the apartment entrance.

Twisting the key in the lock, I pushed the door open and hesitated on the threshold, frowning at the empty floor where there should have been a pile of mail.

"Someone's been here," I whispered.

Callahan peered past me, a finger to his lips commanding my silence. With careful steps, he crossed the hall and peeked around the corner to check the corridor to the bedrooms was clear, then slid across to the living room door. It was shut when usually I left it open to allow air to circulate as much as possible given that my windows remained closed year-round.

I crept across the hall, positioning myself behind Callahan. The smell of food lingered, and it wasn't from Piccolino's—this was spicy. It had been well over a week since I'd cooked anything here, and the thought of a stranger breaching my home was sickening.

Callahan's fingers closed around the handle, and oh so gently, he pushed it all the way down without making a sound. An inch of light spilled into the hall, and with bated breath, he peered inside.

A moment later, he frowned and whispered, "I think it's your Dad."

My breath hitched. "Dad?" I called, and Callahan's mouth dropped open, his eyes wide, hands splayed in front of him in silent frustration. "Dad?" I ignored Callahan's warning and braced myself when I heard footsteps approaching.

"Olivia?"

I breathed a sigh of relief at the familiar sound of his voice.

"Olivia?" The door swung inward revealing my dad's anxious face. The minute he saw me, he wrapped me in a fierce hug, squeezing me into his chest with a vice-like grip. "I'm sorry if I frightened you," he said, releasing me and giving me a once-over. "I was worried, and I didn't have a number to reach you on. I figured you'd eventually come home."

He turned to Callahan at last, one hand held out in polite greeting, and Callahan took it without hesitation. He looked bemused as he eyed my father, his gaze lingering on the freckles that dusted his cheeks and crept up to adorn his forehead. My father held his steady gaze without any hint of fear or surprise.

"I'm Benjamin. Benjamin Blake," he said, pleasantly. Thank God, this was going much better than it had with Mum. They released hands, Callahan remaining nameless, and my father turned, beckoning us to follow him to the lounge. The coffee table was littered with discarded takeaway boxes, and a duvet sat heaped on the sofa next to an open laptop.

"How long have you been here?" I asked, noting that he wore a fitted dark shirt and smart trousers, but no jacket or tie—this was about as casual as my father got. Even lounging around my apartment wrapped up in a duvet, he didn't deign to wear something more comfortable.

"Three days," he said with a shrug of one shoulder. "Diana doesn't know I'm here. I was ahead of schedule and detoured after she told me about her last visit with you."

Callahan glanced awkwardly between us and cleared his throat. "I'll go find your suitcase." He retreated, allowing my father to speak with me privately.

"You're looking...healthier than I expected after the tales I heard from Diana."

"Well, shockingly, people can still be healthy even if they don't wear business attire twenty-four seven and choose not to wear make-up," I said with a roll of my eyes.

He tucked his hands into his pockets, tilting his head as he gave me a stern glare. "She said you looked like you'd been in one hell of a scrape. And that your car was riddled with bullet holes."

"How the hell did she find my car?"

His mouth twitched at the corner, a barely perceptible smile that he swallowed down before answering. "When she couldn't reach you on your mobile or at work, she panicked and called in some favours. She had someone trace your last known phone location and they managed to pinpoint a stretch of forest. As you can imagine she was expecting the worst, especially when she drove out there and found your car."

"Well, that's...interesting," I said, stalling as I prepared the best lie my brain could conjure in three seconds flat. "I didn't admit it to her because, well, you know what she's like, but I left my phone in the car when I went clubbing, and as if that wasn't stupid enough, I also left the car unlocked. I'm pretty sure you can't claim for stolen vehicles when you practically gift wrap it for the thieves so I just reported the car as being sold on," I said with a grimace. "So however the bullets got there had nothing to do with me. But as I told her, I had a tumble on a night out. Worked out rather well, though as I met my rather gorgeous friend that night," I said, flashing him a devious grin.

His eyes narrowed, lips twitching to one side as he considered my words. He didn't look at all convinced or impressed, but when my grin didn't waiver, he inhaled deeply, the breath released sharply through his nose making his nostrils flare.

"I hope you know what you're doing," he finally said.

My arms folded defensively across my chest, my smile faltering. "More so than you can imagine."

He dipped his head, giving the slightest of nods. "Whatever is between you and Diana at the moment has nothing to do with me. You're *my* flesh and blood. I will always be here to help you if you need it." He pulled a hand out of his pocket, and a card was lodged between his fingers and he held it out to me. "You know I'm always a call away if you need me." I took the card, turning it over in my hands. It was plain, pure white, apart from a mobile number and a line of simple grey text: *In case of emergency. Keep this number safe.*

When I looked up, he'd closed his laptop and had begun sorting the takeaway cartons, piling them up before heading for the kitchen. I pocketed the card, picked up the remaining cans and bottles, and took them to the bin.

"I'll get my things together and leave you to it. I just wanted to make sure you were okay," he said, striding out of the living area without another word.

Callahan reappeared, no doubt avoiding a private chat with my father. "Are you okay?" he asked, leaning back against the counter, his arms folding across his chest.

"Sometimes I wonder if life could get any weirder than this."

He grimaced. "Now there's a jinx if ever I've heard one."

Great. I shook my head, not wanting to consider the possibility, and dropped my forehead on Callahan's shoulder. Maybe in the future, we could have a normal, peaceful life. It was definitely a vision worth fighting for.

It wasn't long before my father emerged with a small black suitcase in tow, his jacket and shoes on ready to depart. He gave me a tight-lipped smile.

"I'm away on business for a couple of weeks in China. I'll drop you an email when I'm back, maybe we could meet somewhere for a coffee?" He nodded to Callahan. "Nice to meet you. Look after her for me, won't you?"

"Always. And thank you, it's nice to meet you too." Given how things went with my mother, I was sure he meant it.

I walked my father to the front door, and he gave me a brisk hug and paused before stepping out.

"Keep that number safe," he said with a pointed look. I nodded, rolling my eyes at his protectiveness. "Dad, he's a great guy, I'm going to be just fine. I know Mum wrote him off immediately, but she caught us on a bad day when he was poorly. He had a fever, which is why he wasn't dressed."

I don't know why I felt the need to defend him, but it would have been nice to have at least one parent on board. Especially since they had both nearly instantaneously approved of Noah.

His eyebrows shot up in surprise and he chuckled. "She didn't tell me that part. But honestly, it's not him that I'm worried about." Before I could question him, he was out the door. "Bye Olivia. Stay out of trouble, and I'll see you when I get back."

I closed the door, leaning my forehead against it and releasing a long weary breath. What the fuck was that about? Shaking my head, I decided my brain did not have the capacity to think about it just yet. It could wait.

∽

After an emotionally exhausting few days of prepping for our trip, with only one day to go, we were tucked up in Callhan's bed in need of a lengthy night of sleep. Callahan was propped up against the headboard researching on his phone, my back nestled against his ribs. His arm hemmed me in, holding me protectively against his body as his fingers stroked the sensitive skin on my stomach. It was the first time I'd felt truly content since Mahika had appeared at the farm, and it felt good to set all the worry and constant questioning aside and lose myself in a book. Even if romance wasn't a genre I would typically read—it was too much of a kick in the teeth. A reminder of everything I would and could only dream of, but my life had drastically changed, and since my books were abandoned on the shelves of my lonely apartment, I was trying something new. That didn't mean I was convinced by it. I couldn't help the exasperated breaths that intermittently rushed out at the sweeter-than-sweet romance. The too-pretty words and cliches—things I might have pined for once, but experience had taught me that it was not what I craved or needed.

After the fourth huff in as many minutes, Callahan dropped his phone.

"What the fuck are you reading?" He shifted so that he could pull the cover of the book towards him. "That's not one of your books is it?"

I shook my head, not for the first time impressed at his attention to detail. "Isla said it was amazing, but I think we have very different tastes in books!"

"Well, I could have told you that. What's in it that you find so irritating?" He ran his other hand up the bare skin on my arm sending a shiver skittering down my spine.

"It's just sickly sweet and flowery. It's old fashioned—lots of 'making love' and other cliches," I said sarcastically as I laid the book to one side and turned my shoulders so I could curl into his chest, wrapping one leg over his.

"Why is that old fashioned?"

I shrugged. "I just didn't think people used that expression any more."

"So, you don't think there's a difference?" His eyes flickered between mine, searching for some emotion, some hint of my truth.

"You do?"

He smiled, a little mischief dancing in those bright eyes. "I do." He leant in to leave a whisper of a kiss on my lips and nudged me onto my back. "I think that sex is something you feel here"—he paused sliding his hand up my thigh leaving the heel of his palm to rest low between my hips, making my breath stutter—"and when you make love, you feel it here." He ground his palm against me for emphasis and then his hand skimmed up over my ribs, over the curve of one breast and rested over my heart. "And you feel it here," he whispered.

My heart exploded, a loud chaotic beat against his palm, my skin flushed hot and, "Oh," was the only sound I could usher out.

His lips parted, his smile gone, but something else in its place —something I wanted to surrender to again and again, and my stomach rippled in anticipation. The feeling travelled low, turning into a familiar ache.

"Have you ever—"

"Other than you? No." His voice was low and rough as he cut me off before I could finish my sentence, and my eyes snapped shut, a barricade against the tears threatening to spill out.

When I peered up at him, he was staring at his hand, feeling the telltale drum against his palm, watching the way my chest erratically rose and fell as his thumb stroked a path across my skin. His breath hitched, and his hand drifted into my hair, his thumb caressing my cheek as he kissed me so tenderly I whimpered.

Our lips parted, and the knots in my stomach ebbed and flowed like the tide with each searing touch. He settled between my thighs, careful to keep his weight from crushing me as our kiss deepened. My legs coiled around him, pressing him against me, seeking out that delicious friction.

He smiled against my mouth. "I plan to kiss you *very* thoroughly before we get to that."

I hummed, content to be patient, savouring every touch, every taste, every moan, until we found our release together, and as the final waves of pleasure subsided he pressed light kisses under my jaw and whispered 'I love you' against my skin.

It had never been uttered to me before, barely even said by my parents, and hearing it then, broke me. A steady trickle of tears cascaded down my cheeks, and he kissed them away—kissed between my brows and down my nose and held me tightly while I pulled myself together.

It was a long while later, when I was tucked up against him, my hand pressed against his heart feeling its steady rhythm, that I could finally bring myself to say, "I love you too."

His fingers paused their soothing descent down my spine and beneath my palm, the tempo of his heartbeat surged.

"I know," he whispered against my hair. "I think I'd know if you never even said the words."

41

THE DEEP END

With Mahika's miracle drug in my system, the airport was easy to navigate. Aside from a heart-stopping moment at customs when it seemed there was a problem with my passport, I breezed through the building without the usual fear of being hunted.

The air stewardess was steadily making her way up the aisle, checking people were secure and the overhead storage safely shut. Callahan fidgeted in his seat to try and get comfortable. He turned to flash me a grin, a hard-boiled sweet wedged between his teeth.

"Are you ready for how annoying I'm gonna be for the next ten hours?"

I chuckled. "You'll be angelic compared to Fletcher. I can practically feel his wrath from here already. Children will be scared to walk past him by the end of the flight."

He gave a breathy laugh. "Imagine if he'd had to sit next to Mahika."

We both sniggered at the prospect, and from three rows ahead, Fletcher turned in his seat and scowled as if he knew we were talking about him. Callahan held up a finger, a devious grin across his face, and Fletcher mouthed something that made Callahan snort.

I had to pinch myself; these small moments of playfulness were becoming a little more frequent, a light growing steadily brighter and beating back the dark. The pain was still raw, it might never fade given the sheer depth of trauma that he'd suffered, but he was a fighter with such a big heart and every day it felt like a privilege to know him. It was a privilege to know all of them.

We would only be away for two weeks, but the goodbyes had hit me hard. I'd wrenched myself away, holding onto the promise of finding my equals in Denver. Those girls might not be related to me by blood, but it felt like they were long-lost family, and every time I considered what it would be like to sit and talk to them, I felt giddy.

Callahan turned to face me, holding out a hand with fingers splayed ready to accommodate mine, and when our palms touched, he squeezed tightly.

"I love you," he whispered.

My eyes flickered to his lips, where those three whimsical words had emanated, those words that started a riot in my heart, and a whirlwind of butterflies in my stomach. I leant across to kiss him just as the stewardess started her pre-flight spiel, demanding everyone's attention and cutting our kiss short.

My focus drifted. Since finding my father in my apartment, I hadn't had much time to dissect our little encounter and the number he'd given me. Something was off; I wasn't sure if things were difficult between my parents, or if they both had suspicions about what was really happening to me, but the number felt like a lifeline, a last resort that I had to protect. I'd saved it on my phone under a pseudonym and committed it to memory, hoping I would retain it while my brain had so many other things to juggle.

With a glance over the headrest, I located Mahika several rows back, staring out the cabin window and doing her best to ignore the family surrounding her, the children arguing over something obnoxiously loud. She'd joined us for dinner last night, still quiet, her words rare jewels kept locked away, though Rory was working hard to coax them out.

"What are you smiling about?" Callahan asked as the plane started its ascent. I'd hardly heard the stewardess, she must have disappeared without me noticing. He handed me a hard sweet, which I took gratefully and started to unwrap.

"I was wondering how successful Rory was with his endeavours last night."

He scoffed. "Don't even. I can't believe he would go there. She's so fucking cold—I still don't fully trust her," he said with a shake of his head.

"Okay, so she might not win Personality of the Year, but she is stunning. I'm sure that has plenty to do with it," I said wryly. "But I have a sneaking suspicion that there's a lot more to her, and I bet she's a fierce badass that could totally kick ass in a fight." I shoved my sweet in my mouth, feeling my ears getting ready to pop.

He chuckled, his eyes bright. "Apparently, Rory isn't the only one stanning over her. Should I be worried?"

I laughed, shaking my head. "Not a chance; you're well and truly stuck with me."

"That works for me. And for the record, I think *you're* stunning."

"Hmmm. I do come with an evil mother, though; think you can handle that?" I replied, scrunching my face in a grimace.

"Oh, God." He groaned, one hand palming his face. "You don't even like her. I don't stand a chance! But I guess I can tolerate her for brief essential appearances." He smirked, handing me another sweet.

Sometimes I wondered how unlucky a person had to be to have both my cursed blood and my witch of a mother. What I wouldn't give for a parent who'd love me as much as Callahan's family had loved him. I sighed, fidgeting in my seat and resting my head on his shoulder, content that we were together even while crammed into this tiny space, stuck with well over three hundred strangers for the next nine and a half hours.

∼

Despite exiting the plane with the body of a ninety year old, bent and crippled after ten hours in cramped conditions, the time had passed relatively quickly. We'd talked about the farm, giggled deviously while making various bets about Fletcher and his behaviour on the trip along with other trivial things, then eventually we'd paused our ceaseless chatter to watch a film. We cleared security without issue, Mahika occasionally offering up tidbits of information about the strangely artistic airport as we moved through it, and finally we stepped outside, relishing the fresh air filling up our lungs.

Neesha greeted us with delighted giggles, throwing her arms around Mahika in a fierce bear hug which was surprisingly reciprocated, and when they stepped apart Mahika busied herself loading the minivan with our luggage. She was several years older than Mahika, but just as beautiful, and the lines on her face that marked her years were those formed from frequent smiles. I liked her already.

When she spotted Fletcher, Neesha smiled broadly. "Oh my goodness, you are just like your father!" she exclaimed, moving towards him and clamping her arms tightly around his towering frame. He stood awkwardly, refusing to return her warm welcome and merely nodded when she released him.

"Thanks for picking us up," he muttered before stalking away to help with the suitcases.

I stifled a laugh at her boldness. Fletcher was not someone I would presume to hug, but she took it all in her stride and didn't seem the least bit offended by his standoffish nature. She turned to me, her hands wringing as she smiled kindly.

"It's lovely to meet you, Olivia," she said gently. "The girls are so excited that you decided to join us."

The mention of them had me grinning ear to ear and Callahan squeezed my hand, his expression doting.

"I can't wait to meet them," I told her earnestly, "and thank you so much for coming to get us."

She waved off my gratitude, shaking Callahan's hand and ushering us to the bus, eager to get on the road.

It had been a while since I'd travelled, longer still since I'd been to the US, and it struck me just how vast the landscape was compared to home; it was mesmerising.

As we cleared the airport traffic, a hulking shape loomed in the distance, cutting into the skyline—a rearing horse, growing more sinister the closer we got. Bright red eyes peered out over the landscape, stark against its cobalt blue body and jagged mane and tail. Mahika was sitting in the passenger seat in front of me and heard my quiet mutterings.

"They call it Blucifer," she said, nodding in its direction.

Callahan sniggered from beside me. "The perfect steed for your mother."

"A match made in hell," I agreed.

He snorted a laugh and sat back, reaching for my hand. "At least your dad is alright."

We fell into contemplative silence, awed by the views: a clear blue sky that stretched for miles, with pockets of vivid amber where autumn was sneaking over the landscape, then distant mountains, shrouded in blue, a jagged horizon that whispered of beautiful things to come.

We travelled through rocky peaks and down through banks of dense conifers and firs and all of it was breathtaking. As the route became little more than a dirt track, my knees started bouncing with anticipation, nerves fizzing in my stomach.

Soon, rolling grassy fields stretched into the distance, the mountains their backdrop and the sky behind glowed like the embers of a fire. It was serene and peaceful, and though it had hurt to leave, I was so happy—so ready for the days ahead. The car veered to the right, a private road climbing into the tree line and eventually we slowed, the trees parting to reveal an expansive drive. The first building we passed was a large, dark stained timber barn, the main door wedged open, revealing trailers and quads. Staggered on the right was a larger set of buildings, the front section of which looked to be a cow shed similar to ours. It was outside this building that Neesha pulled to a stop.

Mahika swivelled in her seat. "Not that I'm trying to throw you in at the deep end, but the shot I gave you will wear off before the morning and since you currently have no scent to trigger bloodlust, I wondered if you wanted to meet our resident vampire?"

42

A CURE

That was not what I'd expected her to say. It or he must be close, by but my body hadn't reacted, and the thought was mildly terrifying. When I didn't answer immediately, she continued, "We keep Rakesh around as a test subject, but when the other girls arrived they found it somewhat cathartic to speak to him, given that they'd never managed to interact with a vampire before."

I understood that desire, that need to see what lurked beyond the monsters that chased our blood. After all, they didn't choose to pursue us, it was instinct.

She glanced at Callahan. "She'll be perfectly safe."

"Okay," I said shakily, my head full of questions that I wished I could write down, knowing they'd flit out of my head the minute I saw him.

Mahika nodded and jumped out, sliding my door open and waiting patiently for me to move. Taking a breath, I gave Callahan a tight smile then swung out, landing with a crunch on the gravel, Callahan joining me a moment later. Fletcher emerged with a grunt, giving Mahika a distrustful stare, shoving his hands in his pockets as he waited for her to lead us.

Neesha appeared before our little group, a warm smile lighting up her beautiful deep brown eyes. "I'll leave you with my sister and get all your luggage taken up to your room. Are you hungry?"

We all glanced at each other, and Fletcher cleared his throat. "Thank you, a decent meal would be appreciated if it's not too much trouble."

"It's no trouble at all. We've not eaten yet. I think everyone wanted to wait for you," she said with a grin. She gave Mahika a nod and climbed back in the minivan, leaving us in stilted silence.

"It's this way," Mahika said, slipping past us with a solemn expression.

Callahan took my hand, and as we set off, he leaned closer and muttered, "I wonder how many more surprises she's going to spring on us."

I squeezed his hand, too nervous to speak, wondering why she wouldn't think to divulge this to us. There were so, so many things I would have asked her if I'd known she had constant access to a vampire. We followed her past the cow shed, into the next timber-clad building, where stacks of hay stretched up over a metre beyond our heads. A small trailer filled with hay stood in the back corner, wedged between the outer wall and towering stacks. She took the break off, pulled the trailer hitch up with a grunt and dragged it forward revealing a padlocked hatch door set in the floor. We watched in silence as she removed the padlock, and wrenched it open, a light flitting on automatically, revealing a metal staircase leading down to a sublevel.

"Follow me," she said, staring resolutely at the bottom of the steps.

I followed first, gripping the side rail tightly, each step taken with careful precision to avoid tripping on the metal tread and scraping my skin. I was very aware that any blood would mark the end of this excursion. The stairs led to a breeze-blocked corridor about two metres wide, a foreboding black door looming at the end. Mahika pulled out another key, the sharp click of the lock the only sound as we waited, steeped in apprehension.

Another long corridor stretched out before us. She strode down it without a word, her boots stomping on the concrete floor until she reached the final of three doors and waited for us to catch up. It opened into a dark box-like room with a large viewing window into the vampire's quarters. Truly a test subject. She knocked on the window.

"Rakesh. You have a visitor," she shouted through the glass.

Rakesh was sitting at a desk. He turned, pushed his dark hair back from his bronzed face and nodded. He was young, handsome even, and not at all sickly-looking. He wore a simple dark green T-shirt and black jogging pants, slippers on his feet, and he stood calmly, waiting for us to enter.

Mahika unlocked this final door and turned to me, nodding to the room. "I'm coming in with you."

I gave Callahan one final glance. His face was tight with worry as he watched me, and swallowing back the nerves and nausea, I turned for the door. Curiosity, the need to better understand our enemy and whatever Mahika was doing here, took precedence in my mind.

I stepped in.

It was a warm, relatively large space, allowing for a small living area, with his neatly made bed at the far end, sandwiched between a chest of drawers and a bookshelf that had my immediate attention. Books revealed something about a person, and I wondered what they would say about him—what kind of picture they'd paint of his humanity. Biting my lip I turned away, glancing about the room, noting the TV, complete with game consoles, and ironically, the myriad of air purifiers and fans stationed about his room that were far too familiar. They helped minimise the usual overpowering stench of the vampires, leaving a mild ashy quality to the air that I could overcome. He seemed at ease with Mahika.

Not scared of her as I would have expected. His bronzed arms were lined with white and pink scars, and when he noticed my attention, he moved his hands behind his back.

His deep brown eyes watched me inquisitively, waiting for my reaction.

"Why are your eyes brown?"

His dark brows rose in surprise and drew together. He looked to Mahika as if she might understand the question better. She cut me a bemused look and shrugged. "Why would they not be? We come from India."

I chewed my lip, folding my arms to keep from fidgeting. "All of his kind have the same eyes as Callahan and Fletcher in the UK. I thought they all had those eyes."

"We'd be like a flamingo trying to hide among geese if we had anything but brown eyes," he supplied, grabbing my attention once more. He had to be younger than me, and he was so calm, while I felt like I was having an out-of-body experience.

"Can you drink animal blood?" I asked him, trying to think objectively while I still had the chance.

His lips twitched together, and he stared at the ground. "I can't survive on it, no. I get sick."

I whirled to Mahika. "Whose blood is he drinking?"

She stared back, unflinching and calm. "With the obvious exception of the assassins, we all volunteer our blood but this is a conversation for another time," she said sharply.

I took a breath and tried to calm myself, surely they wouldn't dream of asking Callahan or Fletcher to contribute given everything they'd been through? The thought was utterly sickening. How any of this could be considered cathartic was beyond me. Perhaps the other girls had had very different experiences.

Turning back to him, I asked, "Why are you here?"

He glanced at Mahika, and I stepped towards him commanding his attention. "I don't want to know why she has you here. I want to know why you are here. What's in this for you? Why are you cooperating?"

His eyes widened, and he bowed his head, staring at his hands, his right thumb pressing into the centre of his left palm as if he were trying to wipe away some invisible stain.

"I don't like being used as a pawn," he said eventually, his eyes slowly lifting to meet my narrowed gaze as I tried and failed to make sense of his words.

"But you're being used as a pawn right now. Being experimented on?"

He must have known what I was and what I could do. Lashing out at me would be his death sentence, and if he were truly desperate, it would be an easy end for him. Which meant, he wasn't desperate, and being here was better than being dead. There was something here worth living for, even when the facility was actively raging a war against his kind.

"Maybe. But I didn't choose to be dependent on blood."

"Oh? And how many did you kill before they captured you?"

"Too many. But they all wanted death."

I shook my head—shook away the 'merciful' bullshit.

"How many have you killed?" He threw back at me. "Did any of them *want* death?"

"Careful. Or I might add you to the number."

He didn't flinch at my poisonous words. Visions of Caitlyn were flooding my mind, her body drained of all its precious life, wasted unmercifully and unjustly to send a macabre message. Neither she, nor her parents, had wanted or deserved to die. It was entirely spiteful—not even careful.

"Do you have anything constructive to say?" Mahika snapped, her hand tugging my arm so that I moved back a step as she glared at me.

My eyes glazed with tears of frustration, and I willed them to retreat and not spill, reining in the tongue-lashing I wanted to launch at her. Why the fuck would she ambush me with this? I could have been prepared, could have used this opportunity to our advantage, and I couldn't help but wonder if it was to purposely get me unbalanced. A show of power?

"Do any others of your kind have a conscience?" I asked coldly. "Would any of them choose to receive donations rather than slaughter innocents?"

He tucked his hands in his pockets, staring at the floor a moment before finally looking up and addressing my question directly instead of seeking out Mahika. "Our family is the only thing we have to live for. Most of us would do whatever it takes to protect them, regardless of the consequences. If slaughtering keeps them safe, that's what they'll do."

"Then why the fuck are you helping Mahika find an easier way to destroy you?"

He flinched, his eyes darkening with rage. "My family is dead," he spat, his eyes flickering to Mahika, and I wondered if she had been a part of that. "If there is any chance that there could be a cure for us, that would stop us being used as the pawns that we are, then I will gladly take being here and being experimented on." He looked to Mahika. "I am done talking to her."

She tensed, her stare deadly. "You are done when I say you are done." She turned to me without waiting for a response. "Do you have any other questions that can only be answered by him?"

"Do you trust her?" I asked, and when he stared at me, I nodded to Mahika whose face twitched with annoyance.

His lips curved ever so slightly, his earlier rage cooled as he took a breath. "She doesn't always make it easy, but yes. I do trust her. Considering what she's been through, she and all the others here have treated me well." He eyed me for a moment longer and then asked, "Are we done?"

Mahika nodded and headed for the door, allowing me to exit first. Rakesh was sitting back at his desk by the time I re-entered the observatory box, and after she locked the door, Mahika moved to a small panel on the wall and flicked off a glowing red button. A speaker system allowing Callahan and Fletcher to listen in. She glared at me before crossing to unlock the next door. "That could have gone better," she said icily.

43

THE BRINK OF DEATH

Mahika barely spoke as she led us up and out of the secret sub-level and across the yard to a large ranch-style house clad in dark stained timber. The back of the house nestled into the sloping landscape and the front was raised and supported by stilted legs. It had an idyllic wrap-around porch across the entire frontage with a wide set of steps in the middle, leading up to an elegantly framed burgundy door. There were three swinging egg-shaped chairs on the left of the steps and two of them were occupied.

Baggy jeans and a manly pair of boots poured from one swing, its occupant shielded from view and paying no attention to our arrival. A young Asian woman was sitting in the other, her body hidden behind a curtain of sleek black hair and as she leaned forward to get a better view of us, the swing tipped, making her startle. She gave us a sheepish wave as she stood, her willowy frame gracefully crossing the porch.

We followed Mahika up the steps, and she paused at the top and gestured to the woman. "Mei, this is Olivia, Callahan, and Fletcher," she said and then pointed to the other swing. "And that brute over there is Dexter."

He gave an answering grunt from inside the swing but made no effort to move.

Looking at Mei and her welcoming smile, all the anger and frustrations melted away, and I swallowed back tears. "Nice to meet you," I choked out, my lip wobbling and control slipping as I arrived at a moment in time that had, up until now, been merely an unreachable dream.

"And you. The others are dying to meet you. I will let them know that you are here," she said, departing with a nod to Mahika.

I stared after her, unable to process the enormity of it all and longing for a quiet room where I could unpack all of my emotions and have a good cry. It had been almost seventeen hours since we'd left the farm, and I was wrecked, especially after meeting Rakesh as soon as we arrived.

We followed Mahika into a large open-plan living area. Delicious spicy aromas drifted from the kitchen area in the far right corner, where Neesha was stirring something wonderful and paused to give an encouraging wave.

Pots and pans cluttered one side, evidence of her hard work despite ferrying us from the airport. We continued, skirting around a central rustic table big enough to seat at least twelve, above it hung a smooth, round, rustic length of wood spanning the middle third of the table. Black pendulum lights dangled from it, their cords wrapped around the wood, sweeping down low towards the table. It was artistic yet homely, and it seemed surreal to think we'd be sitting under the cosy hanging lights incredibly soon, surrounded by people I'd hardly dared believe could be real.

The far left section of the room housed a large fireplace and in front of it were three cream sofas. The arrangement was similar to that of the farm, and the sense of nostalgia had me reaching for Callahan.

As we passed into the hall, Mahika pointed to a door on the

right. "That's a shower room; most of the bedrooms upstairs have en-suites, so it's really more of a downstairs toilet." She nodded to the other doors on the left. "Those are offices. The first door is mine. The other belongs to Alec and Ryan. You'll meet Alec later, but Ryan is away visiting his family." That was disappointing, I'd been wanting to meet him to ask how he'd found out about the vampires and how he'd coped with the knowledge. Hopefully, Alec would be more approachable than Mahika.

With Fletcher and Callahan still suspicious of Mahika's intentions, they'd requested a shared room for the three of us, believing it was safer to stick together. Mahika had been happy to oblige and showed us to a simply decorated guest room with two double beds. If I hadn't been so hungry and eager to meet the other girls, I would have crashed there and then.

Callahan grabbed his rucksack from our pile of luggage and dumped it on the bed. He stood staring at it, shadows darkening under his eyes. "If I lay down. I will never get back up. But fuck I want to lay down."

I wrapped my arms around his waist and buried my face against his back. "If I lay down, I think I might curl up in a ball and cry for a solid hour. Fucking Mahika. I still can't believe she didn't tell us they have a vamp here. And that I could talk to it."

He groaned and I felt the vibrations of it through his body. "I still can't believe Rory might actually have fucked her."

"God. I'm gonna have words with him when we get back," I muttered, exhaustion threatening to hit full force. The comforting solidness and heat of Callahan's body had my eyelids fighting to stay open.

Fletcher sauntered over with his empty rucksack in hand having dumped everything out onto his bed on the other side of the room. "I know this is the last thing you want to do right now, but can you find me your passports and sort a couple of emergency sets of clothing out. This is going to be our go-bag. Mahika might be perfectly trustworthy, but I'd rather be prepared to get out quick if we need to."

I sighed and relinquished my hold on Callahan. "Yes, sir."

∼

Half an hour later the three of us were trudging back down the stairs trying to muster the dregs of our people skills. There was quite a crowd seated around the table. It was Neesha who rose from her seat and came to give me a gentle hug in welcome. I couldn't hide my smirk when she only nodded at Fletcher and made no move to embrace him. She did try her luck with Callahan and smiled broadly when he reciprocated.

"I better introduce everyone," she said and held her palm out, gesturing to the head of the table where a curly, dark-haired man sat. His full lips were framed by a circle of facial hair and his eyes were a rich warm brown. "This is Cleiton. He joined us from Brazil."

He gave a wide and cheerful smile that lit up his eyes and nodded in greeting. Mahika was sat to his left then next to her sat a rugged-looking man, his complexion a rich brown and dark hair cropped short, Neesha gestured to him "This is Dexter. Next to him is Alec." They both put up a hand and said 'Hi'. Where Dexter was rugged, Alec was his opposite. Clean-shaven, wearing a light-blue fitted shirt that made the dark blue of his eyes more pronounced, and his blond waves were neatly swept to one side in a sophisticated style. Neesha moved on. "Then we have Veda, Priya, and Mei." There was a chorus of hellos and Neesha gestured to the young girl sitting to the right of Cleiton. "And last but not least, this is Fernanda."

"Ugh, please don't call me that, call me Nanda," she said with a grin so infectious I instantly mirrored it, and a jolt of excitement travelled through me despite the exhaustion.

"As you will all have guessed, this is Olivia, Callahan, and Fletcher." She turned to us and told us to take our seats. I was happy to find I was next to Nanda. Callahan and Fletcher took up the seats beside mine and Neesha was absolutely beaming as she pulled out a chair next to Fletcher. "Everyone dig in," she commanded.

It was a welcome feast, the table was laden with rustic wooden bowls filled with fresh and vibrant salad, platters of crusty bread, platters of naans, several different spiced rice dishes, and a large pot of lamb curry and another with chicken. The food gave me a second wind and I felt the fog of exhaustion lift. The table was quiet at first, everyone focused on filling plates and satiating the pangs of hunger. Then, from beside me, Nanda turned to me, with a wicked grin on her face.

"So, you and Callahan huh? He's pretty hot!"

To her right, Cleiton's brows arched up to his temple as he tried to ignore her and concentrate on his food. Callahan cleared his throat and was quick to ask Fletcher a question.

"So how did that happen?" she asked, her eyes never leaving mine, a hunger in them to discover all the details. I remembered what it was like to be sixteen, desperate to experience boys, constantly daydreaming of romance and being swept off my feet, and terrified that it wouldn't happen for me.

I chuckled and bit my lip. "Well, we met when he tried to kidnap me." I couldn't help the grin as her eyes grew wide but it quickly faded when I considered explaining the rest of our sorry tale. Still so fresh and painful. "Neither of us knew the other existed until then, but we ended up working together because the vampires in our city were trying to get rid of me and did some despicable things to achieve it." Her expression grew haunted and I forced a smile. "But you're right, he is hot, and I fell head over heels pretty quickly." She smiled and took a bite of food. "How did you come to be here?" I asked her.

She glanced at Cleiton, who was dipping a naan into his curry sauce and keeping his head low. "I was lucky. My parents told me what they thought would happen to me."

My face guttered and I felt my stomach dip and roil with nausea as she continued.

"When it happened the first time and confirmed their fears, they made enquiries and heard that Cleiton had connections outside of Brazil where it was safer, and he and Aline brought me here."

"How did your parents know?" I asked, not for the first time feeling completely short-changed in life.

She shrugged her shoulders. "I don't know. But they knew about the vampires and knew that there were others like me and that the vampires would try and hunt me down." Her lips pursed. "And they didn't want me to go through what happened again. At least here we can help without being hurt in the process."

Callahan settled a comforting hand on my thigh and squeezed, his food temporarily forgotten as he listened intently. When I glanced up, I found Cleiton watching me.

"How did you find out about this place?" I asked him.

He set his fork down and steepled his fingers, his chin resting on top of them. "My grandparents travelled a lot, they knew there were others like us and they spent time trying to find them, trying to build connections." I sat back in my chair, food eclipsed by the opportunity to gain knowledge, and I tried to absorb every word. "They met a few families in Patna, including Mahika and Neesha's parents, before these ladies were even a thought, and they kept in touch, passing those connections down to my parents."

I suspected he was probably only a little older than Callahan and Fletcher and I wondered if his family also knew the Moores.

"About thirteen years ago, we heard about the first 'assassin' in India. It took them all a while to figure out what was happening, then one of the families was taken hostage, and they tracked down the girl and killed her in exchange for their family being released. News travelled through the network, of course, and the majority of us felt the decision was handled poorly. But it turned out there was more than one assassin." He glanced at Mahika, and she gave him a subtle nod. "Mahika, Neesha, and their parents were also taken hostage." I felt Callahan's fingers flex against my thigh, and my hand went to his and squeezed tightly in understanding. "Mohandas, Mahika and Neesha's brother, was responsible for finding the ransom and reached out for help. Sani and his family travelled over from Nigeria, Bashir arrived from Pakistan, and between them, they tracked down the second assassin. A young girl, only twelve years old and already extremely traumatised."

Callahan swore under his breath, and I reached for my water, my mouth already dry at the direction this was heading. The whole table was deathly quiet; no one touched their food as he continued the story. A story that we'd heard pieces of, unaware that Mahika was at the heart of it—she'd been deliberately vague when she'd shared the origin story the day we met. "Mohandas, Sani, and Bashir tracked the vampires, determined to spare the assassin girl, but the vampires caught wind of what they were doing. They retaliated, drained their parents, had almost drained Neesha and Mahika to the brink of death, and Mohandas died as he fought to save them. Sani and Bashir managed to get Neesha and Mahika away, though Sani lost a brother in the fight." He paused to take a sip of wine, his eyes flitting to Mahika who was quietly pushing her salad around her plate. He placed his wine down, glanced at Callahan and took a breath. "The girl got away, they found out later from some of the other families that she had martyred herself. It wasn't safe for Neesha and Mahika to stay in Patna, so they ended up in New York with Dexter's family."

He grunted from his seat next to her. "Mahika's been a pain in my ass ever since."

Alec smirked, his navy eyes glittering. "She's been a pain in everyone's ass ever since." He sat forward, his blond waves falling over his temple as he winked at her, his fingers twirling the stem of his wineglass as he gazed between the three of us. "My family has a long history of working within the sciences," he said. "They were involved with the pharmaceutical companies for many years. When things started to get heated with the vampires, my parents decided to move away from LA to somewhere more rural and started studying the differences in our blood, and in our DNA. When my husband inherited this place, we thought it was the perfect little corner of the world to set up a safe house, and we requested through the network that we start hunting for all the would-be assassins. There are nowhere near as many of us, and we wanted to find a way to protect both assassins and mediators and harness what's in your blood." He nodded at me. "So here we are. Tomorrow we'll take the first donation of your blood."

Callahan was rigid beside me, his skin drained of colour, and he stared at his plate, his eyes utterly vacant. I stroked his arm, trying to ground him, trying to ground myself—my brain felt like it had been dumped in a blender and then poured back into my skull. I downed my wine. My head had begun to throb under the weight of all this information on top of being travel-weary. Exhaling a heavy breath, I looked to Alec. "I'm happy to do it. Just please don't make it too early." I glanced around the table and gave Veda, Priya and Mei a small smile. "I'd love to get to know you all a little better, but I'm going to be rude and ask your leave to go to bed. My head feels like it's going to split open any second."

Neesha stood up at the end of the table. "Of course we understand. Please, go get some rest. I'll bring up a tray of snacks and drinks for you just in case you get hungry later."

We nodded gratefully and said our goodbyes before heading to our room together.

44

ONGOING EXPERIMENTS

When I woke in the morning, it was to a pounding head. I was groggy and confused after our first evening at the ranch. I lay in Callahan's arms, listening to his peaceful breaths and focusing on the faint fluttering of his heart where he was pressed against my back. It was just enough to stay content and chase away the darkest of thoughts circling in my mind.

Fletcher stirred first. He'd barely spoken more than five words before climbing into his bed and tossing and turning for a considerable length of time. Judging by the amount of huffing and tutting that he was doing now, his mood was no better this morning.

It wasn't long before I felt Callahan tense, his arms instinctively tightening around me and then relaxing as he shrugged off sleep and pressed a kiss to the spot below my ear, the gentleness of his lips sending a shiver down my spine. Why the hell did I agree to share a room with Fletcher? He stretched out with a groan and then curled himself around me.

"Did you sleep okay?" he asked quietly. I nodded, relieved that he seemed more himself this morning and hoping we could keep the shit storm that was yesterday from ruining the mood just a little longer.

"I always sleep well next to you, but I do have a banging headache."

He kissed my temple, his lips skimmed my cheek, my jaw, and continued down my neck deliciously.

"I think I know something that might help with that," he whispered. Despite the ache in my skull, a devious smile spread across my face. There was a shift from the other side of the room and the bed creaked as Fletcher stood and gathered his things.

"I will be in that bathroom for fifteen minutes," he said as he headed past our bed and into the ensuite.

I sniggered as he kicked the door shut behind him. "That's oddly specific."

"It's perfectly specific, and it's why he's the best." He gently tugged me onto my back and the sight of his dishevelled hair falling over his temple, the stubble dusting his jaw, and the playful glint in his eye was enough to steal my breath. "Let's get rid of that headache."

I laughed. "You think you can cure me in fifteen minutes?"

He arched an eyebrow and then peered at his watch. "Eleven minutes actually. And the first four"—he paused to kiss me, his tongue brushing against my mouth—"require my tongue."

Precisely fifteen minutes later, Fletcher opened the bathroom door and stalked past our bed without so much as a glance. I was deliberately tucked up against Callahan's chest, facing away from the bathroom. Pink staining my cheeks, still slightly out of breath given that I'd had a minute to make myself presentable. Callahan was replying to a message from Rory, the picture of innocence aside from the wink he gave me when Fletcher was across the room.

"How's your headache?" he asked when my heart had calmed and my breath was steady once more. My fingers drummed against his bare chest. "Hmmm, it's not completely cured, but I have to admit, it's a lot better than it was."

"Then I'll take that as a win," he said smugly.

There was no time to speak to either of them about yesterday's revelations. I'd just showered and dressed when Alec sent for me. Veda, the youngest of the girls from India, knocked on the door and gave me a bright smile when I answered. My hair was still wet, and I quickly pulled my brush through it before following her. She led me downstairs to where Alec was waiting at the dining table. He was sat at the head of the table, his blond waves neatly gelled, and he nodded to the seat beside him.

"How did you sleep?" he asked as I pulled out the chair and settled in it.

"I slept fine." I didn't want to admit how utterly exhausted my body felt and that my legs trembled as I walked down the stairs with Veda.

The room smelled faintly of bacon, and my stomach growled. My hand flew to my navel as if I could muffle the sound, and I wondered how long ago everyone had eaten breakfast.

Alec smiled sympathetically. "Neesha is coming to make you some breakfast shortly. You need to eat a good meal before you give blood."

Neesha's name was an unpleasant reminder of why I had spent all morning trying to keep a lid on my anxious mind.

"Did you all know that Callahan's family had been taken?" I asked.

His eyes widened at my question and his thumb tapped lightly on the table between us.

"Not until it was too late."

I sat up straighter in my chair, my eyes narrowing. "But why didn't they ask you for help?"

He sighed deeply, staring at his coffee as he answered. "I'd like to say it's because they thought you were all more than capable of handling the situation, but honestly, I really don't know. You'd have to ask them," he said gently.

My vision blurred, and I blinked back the tears, my skin tingling with the renewed bristling anger I felt towards Ava and James. When they challenged Callahan and told him to hand me over, they stated that a friend had experienced something similar with a disastrous end, but it was far worse knowing they had an entire network of experienced people who could have come to our aid. In the thirteen years since Mahika's tragedy, their expertise and skill sets would surely have surpassed anything we could have done.

He leaned back in his chair, his face a carefully blank canvas, waiting to see what I would throw at him next.

"You mentioned other names last night. Do they all live here too?"

"Sani and Bashir? No, they've never been here. We limit who comes here to keep the girls protected. The only people not here at the moment are Ryan and Aline. Aline is staying in Indonesia with another mediator called Farel; they've just located another assassin and are trying to negotiate getting her back here to safety."

"And you think there'll be others still to find?"

His lips twitched at this, his dark blue eyes alight beneath his long lashes. "The most populated areas of the world have a higher concentration of vampires, and where the vampire population increases, we find those with the assassin blood invariably pop up sooner or later. The sooner we get to them, the safer they are."

How many had been lost over the years? How many had been like the girl in India and martyred themselves? Unable to cope with the shitty hand life had dealt them but feeling the guilt of not being strong enough to endure it pressing down on them until they felt there was no other choice. I wondered how many they had killed as they did so. Was it worth the absolute horror of dying like that?

He glanced over my shoulder, and Neesha's voice carried across the room.

"Good morning, Olivia. How do you prefer your eggs?"

I twisted in my chair as she approached and I tried to force a smile on my weary face. Her head tilted as she looked me over.

"It's a lot to take in isn't it?"

I nodded, wondering if Mahika had been as caring and compassionate as her sister before their abduction. Was her cold exterior the result of trauma or just ingrained in her personality and magnified in the aftermath?

"Can I please have scrambled eggs?"

She gave a sharp nod and swiftly turned for the kitchen. Alec braced his elbows on the table. "Continue," he said with a smirk.

"What's your plan? Other than finding others like me, what is the end game?" I asked and pulled one bare foot up onto the chair, my arms wrapping around my knee.

"Our goal is to save as many lives as we can. To do that, we have to eradicate the threat. As discreetly as possible."

"How many have you experimented on? Like Rakesh."

He took in another long breath through his nose, shifting in his seat. "Probably fifteen in total over the last ten years. There was a lot we needed to understand. I'm sure you can appreciate that." His head tilted and one side of his mouth curved ever so slightly.

"I'm not judging your methods," I said flatly. "Out of those fifteen, was Rakesh the only one with any sort of desire to help you?"

He stared at the table, his thumb tapping that quiet beat until Neesha's quick steps announced her presence and she set a plate of scrambled eggs on wholemeal toast in front of me and grabbed Alec's empty mug.

"Thank you," I called after her.

"Some of them died quickly in our experiments. So we didn't have the chance to get to know them. The few that were here longer term before Rakesh, were"—he paused—"dedicated to their cause. We were not sorry when they died."

"Why are you keeping Rakesh?" I asked between mouthfuls of food.

Neesha arrived back at the table with a glass of orange juice, a bowl of porridge, and a second bowl of fruit and hurried out of the room as soon as they were placed on the table.

"Would you believe me if I told you Mahika has a soft spot for him?"

I put my fork down. "Mahika? You've got to be shitting me? You're telling me Mahika has a pet vampire?"

I could just imagine Rory's face when he found out that his little sex chum had a dirty secret. It certainly explained why she had chastised me over the way I spoke to him. And why she'd sprung it on us last minute, giving us no time to instigate revenge. Not that I would have.

I stared at Alec. "You can't seriously be holding him here just because Mahika can't bring herself to put him down?"

He chuckled, the sound deep and devious. "We are doing ongoing experiments with him, so he hasn't outlasted his usefulness just yet. He was quite young when his parents were shot by one of our teams. They were using our specialised darts so he wasn't exposed to your blood. The darts delivered the lethal dose, and he watched his parents disintegrate, heard their bones cracking, and could do absolutely nothing to save them. I think having watched her parents die, and seeing all the death and destruction that we do, she has a little more compassion for him. Especially given that he is one of the only ones willing to try and find a solution in spite of what happened to his parents."

Fuck. That was horrific, even for a vamp. Usually, they had no awareness at all, which was a blessing they didn't deserve.

Alec eyed the porridge and fruit and nodded at the bowls. "You need to keep eating."

I sighed; my stomach was full, but I forced myself to take a handful of berries and kept popping them in my mouth while I debated my next question.

"Do you think you can find a solution? A way to stop them needing human blood?"

His lips pursed, and slowly, he shook his head. "I think it's unlikely. We've tried experimenting on ourselves, using protein shakes, iron and amino acid supplements in high doses, while we abstain from blood, and though it slows down the process of us getting sick, we still do. We give Rakesh all those supplements, and fifty percent of his diet is animal blood, but every few weeks he starts to decline, and we have to increase the amount of human blood for a week to stabilise him. We can't reproduce red blood cells as quickly as you do, so we donate on rotation once a week, and we advertise for donors for our research as well. We'll keep trying. Ultimately if there were five vampires out of every hundred that might care about people then it would be worth helping them make a better choice. But Rakesh seems to be an exception." Rakesh's words came back to me—that the vampires' families are all they have and they would do anything to protect them, but who were they protecting them from? The world in general or this entity we were yet to discover? Rakesh didn't want to be a pawn, and it all seemed to come back to this question—who else was involved? Who was covering all this up? I needed more time with him; there were things he could tell me, of that I was certain.

While I forced berries and porridge into my belly, Alec asked me questions about my parents and my experience as one with assassin blood. I told him about my research, the system I'd created, and what we'd learned about the vampires in our city since working together. He told me we were the only large team they'd found outside of their facility working together in an organised way, even if we were only at the beginning of that journey. He said that when they'd found the other assassins, they were terrified, alone, and desperate to escape the monsters hunting them down.

Even Nanda, whose parents had somehow understood what was happening around them and explained it to her, had been desperate to come to Colorado after only one encounter. Living with the wicked witch of the west had made me tougher than I realised.

I'd been with Alec for an hour when he excused himself and requested I send Callahan down to his office so that he could teach him the basics of taking blood samples. It gave me thirty minutes to relax before I would give blood. All being well, Callahan would be the one to insert the needle.

45

BETRAYED

When I returned to our room, Fletcher was staring forlornly out the window, and I found Callahan in the bathroom, hunched over the sink, aggression practically rolling off him.

"Are you ok?" I asked softly.

He pushed himself upright and tapped his fist on the edge of the sink once, then a second time, his lips pursed and eyes narrowed, so angry he was unable to articulate what he was feeling.

I wrapped my arms around his middle, my cheek resting in the dip between his shoulder blades, and stayed quiet, waiting for my presence to take the edge off his rage. Hearing Cleiton tell Mahika's story was heart-wrenching, and it stirred up so many emotions, all still sharp as a blade and twisting deep in his wounds. There was no set formula or timetable for grief; some days it lay dormant and some days it exploded to the surface and knocked you for six, leaving pieces of you on the floor. Healing was a messy, unpredictable business, binding the pieces back together again and again and again until eventually, the glue held fast, even if it was only for some of the fragments.

He slid his fingers between mine and took a deep steadying

breath before shrugging out of my arms. He turned to face me and pulled me to his chest. His grip was tight, the fingers of one hand threaded through my hair holding me against him. When his silence became unbearable, I finally dared to ask him what had happened. He pressed a kiss to my hair and took a stuttered breath.

"I feel betrayed. But I can't talk about it yet. I'm so fucking angry."

I nodded and pried myself away just enough to kiss him, and his hands instantly moved to cup my face, the kiss deepening, his tongue devouring with such intensity, as if he needed to reassure himself that I was his, that I was real and that my heart was still beating. Our breaths were frantic by the time he released me, his forehead resting against mine as we both fought to regain some semblance of control.

My stomach dipped as I remembered why I'd originally come back to the room. "This is terrible timing, but I was supposed to send you down to Alec's office so he can show you how to take blood. He wants my first donation in"—I took a deep breath as I checked my watch and grimaced when I saw the time—"fifteen minutes."

He huffed and brushed his lips to my forehead. "There is no way I'm coming anywhere near you with a needle today." He stepped back, running his hands through his hair, clasping them behind his head. "I just need a minute to get my head right and then I'll go."

After splashing his face with cold water, he kissed me goodbye and hurried out. I stood in the middle of our shared room, staring at the door, wishing I could take some of his pain.

Fletcher was sitting on his bed and groaned as he got to his feet and sauntered over. I hadn't spoken to him since the morning—since we'd had a matter of minutes to enjoy each other and

Callahan had quite spectacularly driven me to oblivion. My whole body heated at the memory.

The taut lines on Fletcher's face dissolved as he stared at me, and he let out a low devious chuckle that had me gaping at him.

"What?" I snapped, feeling the flush on my cheeks burning my skin.

He shrugged. "It just surprises me that you're so embarrassed about sharing a room."

I arched a menacing brow at him. "I'm not."

"Oh, really? So your face isn't glowing because you saw me and remembered what Callahan did to you while I was in the shower?" I couldn't argue with that. Instead, my traitorous cheeks burned even hotter, and Fletcher's eyes lingered on them.

"You're a jerk."

He snorted. "If I was a jerk, I'd have given you five minutes."

My eyes widened, and I tried to swallow my amusement but couldn't stop the bubble of laughter from erupting. Maybe it was the embarrassment, maybe it was residual shock from everything I'd discovered in the last twenty-four hours, or maybe just sheer exhaustion, but I was hysterical. My arms clutched around my middle as I doubled over, failing miserably to stop my wretched giggles from spewing out. Fletcher's unimpressed eye-rolls and mocking smile only encouraged more laughter, and it was minutes later, my face stained with tears before I was finally under control.

Fletcher was still gawping at me, his arms folded against his chest. I blew out a breath, trying not to lose it again and working to keep my face carefully neutral.

"So, did something happen when I was gone?"

His nostrils flared, the only sign that under his carefully schooled composure, he was still irritated. He cleared his throat and nodded to his bed, retreating to sit in the middle of it and beckoning me to perch on the edge.

"I called my parents. I needed to ask them why they didn't reach out for help. Seeing all this, and hearing that other mediators came to help rescue Neeshsa and Mahika, which was thirteen years ago when they didn't have the resources they do now, it fucking bothers me." He cracked a knuckle, his face losing that composure.

"Go on. Why didn't they?"

He loosed a heavy sigh, shaking his head as he said, "They didn't think there was enough time, and they were scared that even if some of them got here, they'd still lose too many people. They wanted to go for the quickest and easiest option even if it was cruel, and they thought we were fully on board with that plan. By the time they realised we weren't, it really was too late."

My shoulders sagged, my lungs depleting in a lengthy sigh. Choosing to ignore such a significant resource seemed like a monumental oversight. I wondered if the anger they directed at me was actually born from guilt. It must be eating away at them, wondering what would have happened if they'd made the call the second they became aware.

There was a brisk knock, and Nanda's face appeared as she popped her head through the gap. Her long dark hair was piled up in a messy bun, her beautiful brown eyes lined with Kohl like Mahika's—her little protege.

"Sorry to interrupt, but Alec is waiting for you." I sighed and got to my feet, jogging across the room to join her.

"Do needles bother you?" She asked as we started down the stairs, our steps in perfect unison.

"They bother me a lot less than teeth ripping into my neck."

She glanced at me, her expression wary, and I wondered if she still felt those phantom teeth ripping into her as I did, that first time, the most haunting of all.

"What about you?"

She gave me a tight smile and shrugged. "You get used to it

after a while." A beat later she asked, "Do you ever wear makeup? You don't need it, you're like, really, really pretty but I just like to practise and wondered if you'd be up for it?"

I grinned, the idea of doing something so sisterly with her was a gift, and I'd savour every second. "I'd love that," I replied and her answering smile stretched wide, lighting up her face, and the sight had my chest swelling with gratitude.

When we reached Alec's office, she knocked, opened the door without hesitating, and headed straight for Callahan. He was sat at Alec's desk, leaning over a rectangular flesh-coloured tray—a phlebotomy practice kit. He was concentrating so hard that the little line between his brows had formed a deep crevice, and he didn't acknowledge us until he'd finished inserting the needle and sighed with relief.

"Good," was all Alec said before his attention turned to me. "Take a seat, Olivia."

He nodded to the reclining medical chair in the corner of his office and I obediently went and settled myself in it, admiring all the shelves of neatly ordered folders around the room. Alec gave Callahan a nod and with another deep breath he picked up a box of medical supplies and approached, setting the box on top of a nearby bookcase and wheeling over a desk chair. He put on a fresh pair of gloves, pulled out a small vial and disposable needle, wiped my finger and pricked it, letting the blood bead before pressing it over the vial which he then handed to Alec.

"So professional," I whispered when he took my left arm and wrapped a cuff around my bicep.

"Shhhh," he smirked and gave me a fleeting glance that had my lips curving in a wicked smile. I noticed Nanda watching him intently too and doubted it had anything to do with learning. Alec joined him to discuss the best vein to use, and once in agreement, Callahan completed the final preparations.

His eyes flickered to mine with a silent question.

"You got this," I whispered.

He nodded, his eyes narrowing slightly as his decision settled in his mind, and he carefully pulled the packet open and positioned the needle. Alec was at his side, quietly observing and offering reassurance.

After a steadying breath, he went wholly still and inserted the tip, watching the catheter intently, and as the needle slid into its final position, his face relaxed.

"Nice work," Alec said and glanced at me. "Anything feel off? Uncomfortable? Achey?" I shook my head, pride swelling at Callahan's achievement, given the anger and frustration he'd had to battle to do this. "Perfect. Let's get her set and we'll see if Fletcher will let you take a sample so you can have another go. Cleiton is around somewhere actually."

"I don't mind volunteering," Nanda chirped from where she was perched on the edge of the desk, her eyes alight at the prospect of being handled by him, even if it involved a needle. Callahan peered up at me as he taped the IV line in place, his expression bemused as I tried to hide my smirk.

"We should have brought Finn," he said under his breath, and the thought had me chuckling wickedly. Finn certainly would have run interference, commanding her attention with his angelic face and silky golden locks. Perhaps he would have had three young girls fawning over him.

~

With my first blood donation accomplished, Nanda led me to the room she shared with Veda, luckily not too put out that her offer to volunteer was denied.

"This is gorgeous," I told her as we stepped inside. "I'd love a room like this."

It was painted sage green, peaceful, elegant and feminine, with white furniture to complement white shuttered windows.

"Thanks," she said with a beaming smile. "Veda and I chose the colour together and the bedding. We loved the monstera design so much we decided to match." She waved me over to her dressing table, her brows pulling together as she glanced about the room. "Would Callahan not let you have something like this?" she asked, turning to pick out various colour palettes and brushes from her mountainous collection.

"I don't know. We don't 'technically' live together," I said hesitantly, although I couldn't imagine not sleeping by his side. "I have an apartment, but it's rented, so I don't get to decorate."

I dropped onto the white wooden chair next to her, and she turned to assess my face, a painter mapping out their canvas, tapping the end of a makeup brush on her lip as she thought.

"Could you leave my freckles visible?" I asked, my face scrunching apologetically. "Or if you want to practise contouring, can you take the foundation off afterwards?"

Since the morning Callahan had pointed out how much he liked them, I'd grown rather fond of my freckles and the wild edge they gave me. The thought of covering them now made me feel uneasy.

"Yeah of course. I can just practise drawing wings and do a smoky look with some blush. Your eyes are incredible by the way! The blue in them is really unusual." She reached for cotton pads and cleanser. As she started to work on my skin, Veda joined us, calmly lighting a scented candle by her bedside table and bringing another chair over to sit with us. She was the shortest of the four girls, and as she sat, she easily brought her legs up and crossed them on the chair, pulling her thick black hair over one shoulder to plait it.

"Did you tell anyone about what was happening to you?" she

asked, delving straight into conversation and surprising me with her boldness.

"The first time it happened, when I was fourteen I did. I told my parents, my friend, and the paramedic, but none of them believed me, and they all thought I was hallucinating." It still blew my mind to think that Nanda's parents not only knew, but did everything they could to stop it happening to her, even if it meant they sent her away. "Did you tell anyone?"

Her hands stilled, her lips puckering as she considered her words. Her fingers eventually continued their weaving but she didn't look at me as she answered.

"My first time, I was walking back from my friend's house, it was only just dusk and a vampire found me as I cut through a quieter street. I was so terrified I couldn't even move my feet to run away. The vampire was quite young, maybe my age, and after he bit me and started to choke, I was on my knees in shock, clutching at my throat when an old lady walked by and saw. When it was clear he was going to die, she started screaming that I was cursed. That I was a Daayan." Her eyes welled with tears and Nanda plucked the box of tissues from her dressing table and passed them to her. "If you are suspected of being a Daayan—a witch—it can disgrace your entire family. Women who are accused are sometimes beaten to death, so I did the only thing I could. I ran. I was lucky enough that Mahika's contacts found me and helped her get me out."

I fiddled with the hem of my T-shirt, the magnitude of her ordeal sitting heavily on my chest. "I'm so sorry," I told her hoarsely.

Nanda had perched on the edge of the dressing table, respectfully allowing Veda to share her story, and in the silence that followed she quietly admitted, "Sani told me that something similar happened to an assassin in Nigeria. The community launched a witch hunt, and Sani didn't find her in time; she was caught by the locals and burned to death."

"Holy shit." My hand flew to my face, covering my mouth, as the shock and abject horror of it all had tears streaming down my cheeks. I'd thought the safe house a necessity to keep the vampires from taking matters into their own hands—not a sanctuary from regular people too. Deeply ironic given our blood was fighting against the real evil. Veda sat quietly picking at her nail polish, her round face pale and sorrowful, and the sight of her had more tears spilling over. Nanda passed me a tissue, squeezing my shoulder before rifling through her draw and pulling out a pack of wipes.

"Here, I can practise another time," she said, passing me the packet. "You're here for like, two whole weeks right?"

I nodded, pitching forward to look in the mirror as I wiped away the streaks of black.

"It gets pretty boring here when Mahika and Cleiton are away. It's been even worse the last few days as Alec's husband went to visit family. And Ryan's really cool."

"How do you know Sani?" I asked curiously. I was under the impression he'd never been here, and his name kept popping up a lot.

"When Cleiton and Aline took me to see my parents in the summer, Sani joined us for extra protection," she said, sucking in her bottom lip and busying herself tidying up her makeup.

"How often have you seen your parents? Have they ever been here?"

"No." She took a breath. "I've only seen them twice since I got here eight months ago. But I love it here. I miss them obviously, but these guys are like family now and I feel safe. And they're teaching me to fight like Mahika so one day I hope I'll be allowed to go on missions with them all."

"On a mission like Aline?" I ventured, distracting myself trying to glean what information I could.

"Yeah, she's with Farel right now. I've never met Farel but I've heard she's pretty badass. And Aline is Cleiton's girlfriend by the way"

"Good to know. So, I hope you don't mind me asking but … how do you both feel about Rakesh being here?" I was surprised when Veda answered first. "I get on well with him. And I feel safe with him, his life literally depends on him being gentle around me. I spend time with him about twice a week. We chat, and sometimes we play games or watch a film."

I tried to keep all my opinions and judgements carefully concealed and looked to Nanda to see if she would answer. She stood upright and stretched, her dressing table now clean and neatly organised.

"I don't go as often as Veda, but I don't mind hanging out with him. He's actually pretty funny. I mean sure, he's eaten his fair share of people, but he's always been very clear that he would rather not."

I couldn't help but snort at her choice of words. How nonchalantly she spoke about him being a murderer.

"Mahika sees him nearly every day," she added.

Well, fuck. He really was her pet, I wondered if she walked him as well.

"And in the summer months, we had dinner outside with him probably once a month," she said with a shrug.

"That's cool," I muttered, trying to breathe through the shock. And I'd thought last night was a lot.

∼

We spent the afternoon chatting about boys, movies, and music playlists, delving into Nanda's nail polish collection and painting our nails in multiple tones. Even Priya came to join us for a while, though she was quiet, content to listen to our idle conversations and carefully interjecting when the need arose. It was perfect. A literal dream brought to life, and it felt like such a luxury to let my guard down, to be with people who truly understood everything I'd been through and who were finally able to give me answers. Tomorrow, or the day after, I would request another visit with Rakesh, and this time, I'd be ready for it.

46

A RUMOUR

"Oh my God, really?" Nanda squeaked, her eyes adoring as she stared at Callahan with a wide and doting smile.

Poor girl had it bad, and Callahan didn't quite know what to do with her infatuation. He shifted uncomfortably, his body inching closer to mine, squishing me further into the corner of the sofa as he steadily increased the distance between them.

She'd stolen Fletcher's seat beside him at the first opportunity, feigning deep interest in farming to keep him talking. His fingers tapped nervously on my thigh, and from the corner of my eye, I noticed Fletcher sniggering wickedly from the sofa to our left.

He'd returned to the seating area with a snack in hand, practically gleeful at Callahan's obvious discomfort and happily plonked himself next to Mei, who was curled up quietly reading.

"Yeah, probably at least ten calves every season we have to get involved with," he said, giving her a tight smile. "It's not a nice experience, though. It's messy, and it's hard work. Sometimes it takes both me *and* Rory to pull them out," he said, squeezing my leg in a desperate plea for help.

Her brows lifted. "Oh, wow. Yeah, I bet it is hard, but worth it?

Do you have to, you know, get in there?" she asked, her hand driving forward to emphasise her question.

Priya was sitting on the other side of her, her lips pulled back in a horrified grimace, mortified by the shameless flirting and intimate questions about cows. Her fingers paused midway through her sleek, long hair, the underside freshly dyed this morning with streaks of blue, still smelling faintly chemical. She was striking to look at, her face was long and elegant with high cheekbones and beautifully arched brows, and her eyes were a rich bright brown that reminded me of autumn—of collecting conkers with the children in my class during forest school trips.

"He certainly does 'get in there'," Fletcher said with a mocking grin. "Poor Tilly over here has had his arm up many a cow over the years."

Nanda's smile faltered, and she plucked her drink off the floor and took a sip, uncertain how to respond to his jibe.

Callahan cleared his throat, a little extra colour dusting his cheeks as he glared at Fletcher. "Fucker," he said under his breath, making Fletcher laugh—a deep throaty chuckle that had me stifling a giggle.

Glancing at my watch, I jostled Callahan with my elbow and pointed out the time. "Weren't you supposed to be calling Rory before we go with Mahika?"

"Shit. Yes, thanks for reminding me," he said, rushing to his feet and pulling out his phone. "I'll see you all later," he said with a vague wave, thumping Fletcher on the shoulder as he passed and hurrying out.

Finding himself alone with four women, Fletcher casually checked his phone and slowly wrenched himself off the sofa. "I'll see you in twenty, Olivia," he said, slinking off without excuse.

When they were both out of earshot, Priya leaned forward, the blue sections of her hair swaying as they tumbled from her shoulder, a smile tugging at her lips. "He didn't really need to call Rory did he?"

"Hell no, just too much oestrogen flying around," I said with a laugh, readjusting my legs and taking advantage of the extra space.

Nanda giggled awkwardly. "I scared him off, didn't I?" she said, her nose crinkling as she grimaced.

"You think?" Priya snorted and nudged her shoulder playfully. "So, how do you feel about seeing Rakesh again?" she asked, her head tilting and fingers twirling through blue strands as she assessed me, perhaps feeling protective of Veda's rather strange relationship with him.

I plucked at the frayed threads of material stretching across my thighs, considering my myriad of emotions before answering. "I'm definitely feeling calmer than I was the first time. I just"—I paused—"feel like I'm always on the cusp of some important revelation that keeps evading me, and I'm so desperate to understand it all."

"What if the truth is insurmountable?" she said cautiously. "The fight is so much harder when you're already beat. Maybe some things are better left in the dark?"

Goosebumps rose across my flesh, and a shiver followed, rolling down my spine and leaving an iciness in its wake that settled in my bones.

"Maybe," I said softly, my fingers tracing my bumpy skin. "But I've spent a decade in the shadows, and I don't think I can do it anymore. So however scary it is, maybe it's time to step into the light, and whatever that reveals, I know we'll face it together."

~

Thirty minutes later, we were waiting for Mahika in the hay barn, the trailer already rolled forward and the hatch door opened wide when we arrived. I picked at stalks of hay from a nearby bale, twiddling them between my finger and thumb, relishing the familiar sweet scent and watching the dust motes flickering in a strip of light, bursting through from a high window.

The quick click of Mahika's heels approaching had us all standing straighter, instantly alert and quickly stepping to the side to let her pass. Her every feature was sharper than usual, eyes cold and narrowed, lips pressed firmly together, shoulders tensed and her dainty hands clenched at her sides. Callahan and Fletcher exchanged a curious glance, their eyebrows silently communicating before they fell in line and followed her.

By the time I'd cautiously navigated each metal tread, Mahika had already unlocked the first black door, and using her body to prop it open, she leaned against it with arms folded and face rigid as she waited for us to pass. Fletcher went ahead. Callahan had waited patiently at the bottom of the stairs and gave me a reassuring smile as my feet touched the concrete floor. Once through, she produced a new key for the first door in the corridor.

The weapons room.

"Holy shit," I muttered as we stepped inside with eyes wide as saucers, taking in the multitude of weapons. On my left, rows of glass-fronted cabinets were stocked neatly with handguns and long-range rifles, and on my right, stainless steel workbenches and industrial fridges. Fletcher gave an appreciative whistle, taking his time perusing each locked cabinet. It was the fridges that kept drawing Callahan's gaze.

"You'll find your typical handguns and rifles as well as tranquiliser guns, which we prefer to use as they are less noisy," Mahika told us as she pulled open one of the fridges and retrieved a black box which she set on the workbench, a key already in her hand. Once unlocked she gently lifted the lid and pulled out a bullet. "This contains blood. We engineered them so that if our targets were too close for the dart guns, we could use these to incapacitate them. The bullet will do enough damage to stop them in their tracks and because they contain assassin blood, it doesn't matter whether we are accurate so long as we hit them somewhere on their bodies. Of course, the bonus is that there is no body to dispose of. They have a soft enough tip that once they penetrate, that tip flattens and the bullet crumples, expelling all the blood." She paused as Fletcher retrieved it from her fingers and twizzled it around between his thumb and forefinger.

Callahan eyed it warily. "I'm guessing the damage from one of these is pretty nasty."

She smirked. "Oh, yes. You don't want to get hit accidentally. There is no clean wound with one of these, the shards will rip your insides to shreds."

Chilling.

She retrieved another box from the fridge, placing it on the bench with the utmost care and pulling out what largely resembled a grenade. "This is incredibly helpful," she said. "It's like a cross between a grenade and a smoke bomb. It atomises the blood. Causes absolute chaos amongst the vampires, but it's safer for our team to get closer and finish the mission with tranquilisers."

"Nice," Fletcher mused, staring as if beholding the rarest of treasure.

"There is a downside," she said quietly. "Even with an anticoagulant, these bullets and grenades have a relatively short shelf life. So every mission has to be well-planned and the timeline strict." She placed the grenade back in the box and gave me a glance from the corner of her eye. "Tomorrow, we'll try and give you some training with the guns. If you insist on being involved, you'll need to avoid hand-to-hand combat. If you bleed, you'll force your team to have to protect you and it could put everyone at risk. Over the next week, we'll teach you how to set up tactical missions. I don't think it will be long before you get your city under control."

I turned to face her, trying to mask the impact of her words, the way they stirred excitement and anticipation. Finally, we would have the means to protect innocent people.

"Will you visit again to help us?"

There was a slight tilt to one side of her mouth, and I wondered if Rory had anything to do with it. "Yes, I think it's safe enough there that I could probably come across with one of the girls. Then it gives us additional blood to get a head start. It's best to hit them hard at the beginning. We don't want to give them a chance to rally in full force."

Callahan sidled up behind me, one hand sliding to my waist and tugging my body against his, I melted into the warmth of his body, relishing the kisses he planted along my neck.

Mahika huffed, rolled her eyes and turned to address Fletcher. "I bet you're wishing you didn't share that room."

"Olivia's embarrassment has been the only highlight," he said wryly, closing the box of grenades.

Callahan grinned, ignoring their jibing and capturing my mouth in a bruising kiss that scorched my cheeks and had both of them muttering profanities across the room. Mahika glared at us as we broke apart.

"Go fuck in your shower if you're that hard up. Nobody else wants to see you letching all over each other."

She turned on her heel, and Fletcher chuckled darkly as he followed her to the door.

Through the viewing window into Rakesh's room, we watched with thinly veiled shock, as he and Veda sat on the sofa yelling at the TV, in the throes of a video game. Veda was on the edge of her seat, her knuckles white, thumbs frantically pressing buttons on the controller, Rakesh dropped his on the floor and threw himself back into the depths of the sofa, his hands clutching at his dark hair in frustration. They were so enraptured, they didn't notice us spectating, eyes wide behind the glass.

Alec was sat at Rakesh's desk, a pile of paperwork visible to one side of him, a safeguard should the absolute worst happen. Mahika rapped on the glass, and Rakesh glanced our way, instinctively waving until he spotted us and dropped his hand, turning away in disgust to pick up his controller. Alec swivelled in his seat and gave us a salute, climbing to his feet and gathering his paperwork. He motioned to Veda, and reluctantly, she handed the controller to Rakesh, their knuckles clashing in a fist pump as she retrieved a hoodie and slung it over a shoulder.

Veda smiled shyly as they exited, walking ahead into the corridor to avoid any judgment while she waited.

"Alec, I'm pretty sure these guys are due blood. Would you mind taking them while Olivia speaks to Rakesh? I'm sure he'd rather not be gawped at like a zoo animal again."

Alec smiled, a dimple appearing on one side of his mouth, his deep blue eyes appraising Callahan's uncomfortable expression.

"Consider it done," he said, nodding to the exit and bidding them to follow. Callahan seemed reluctant to leave, but with a pointed look and a nudge from Fletcher, we said our goodbyes, and I was once again entering Rakesh's room with my heart in my mouth.

Mahika was perfectly at home, perching on the arm of the sofa at his side, her hand held open, requesting the controller Veda had relinquished. I hovered by the sofa, an outsider looking in. Today he wore ripped skinny jeans, a white designer T-shirt, and a grey hoodie that accentuated his rich bronze skin. His hair was soft and fluffy, some sticking upright in the centre of his scalp and the rest falling over his temple, pushed to one side. So unbelievably normal, it was hard to process. Nothing about him screamed predator and other than being nervous, I barely felt nauseous. Fuck. It made me question everything.

When I didn't speak right away, he looked up at Mahika. "What does she want?"

"Rakesh!" she chided, though her lips curved in amusement.

He glanced back at me with nothing but disdain on his face, and I supposed I couldn't blame him. Our first meeting had been full of anger and contempt, the shock of coming face to face so unexpectedly rattling through my bones. He'd approached our meeting so calmly, and I'd been an absolute bitch.

"Are you going to sit? Or just stand there and stare at me stupidly all day?"

His words brought life to my rigid limbs, and I dropped onto the end of the sofa, pulling out my phone with the questions I'd planned to ask him, relieved that it gave me something tangible to focus on.

"How long have you been here?" I asked him.

"Six years."

"And how old are you?"

His brows furrowed and he gave me a fleeting glare, his focus shifting immediately back to the game. "Not really sure why that's any of your business, but I'm nineteen."

I swallowed down my pity, Alec's words ringing in my eyes; he'd been thirteen the day he watched his parents literally break apart at the seams, lost to him forever in the most horrifying way.

"How did you stay hidden when you were a child?" I asked, curious to know why I'd never seen a vampire child.

He stared intently at the screen, manoeuvring his avatar to another position before he responded. "We don't need as much blood when we're younger. If they know there's an assassin in the city, most of us get moved and grow up together on the outskirts in places like this. The ranch I mean, not my prison. Then we move back when we hit late teens so that there's more blood available. It means we're more likely to survive. Some families move around to different cities if they know there is one of your kind lurking around. A few of my friends growing up ended up leaving the city I was in."

"The vampires in my city live in abandoned buildings. How did your family afford to live outside the city in a place like this?"

His jaw clenched, and he didn't answer for a good few seconds. "Sometimes property owners go missing. Particularly ones that have very few family members. I told you, my family would have done anything to keep me safe."

I stared at my list of questions, digesting his words and trying to keep a clear head.

"What about passports? The one we spoke to in my city said they met a vampire from India. Is it common for you to travel to other countries?"

He nodded, still enthralled by the game or perhaps using it as a distraction so that he didn't have to look at me. "Mahika, get the sword!" he demanded, scooting to the very edge of the sofa, his mouth hanging open. "Oh shit! Revive me. Revive me!"

"I'm trying," she muttered acidly.

"Okay. Okay, good. Sorry. Passports. Yeah, if needed, we have forged passports. They're not that hard to get if you know who to contact."

"Would you go back to your kind if these guys were done with you?"

His face whipped towards me, and his lip curled up in a sneer. "No," he snapped.

I held my hands up. "Just curious."

Mahika shot me a warning glare and lightly laid a hand on his shoulder. "She's on her best behaviour today."

He looked up at her, reading something in her expression that seemed to calm him, and he pushed his shoulders back, letting out an agitated breath as he turned to stare at his game.

"Rakesh, when you told me you didn't want to be a pawn anymore, who do you not want to be a pawn for?"

Mahika's head fell back, and she stared at the ceiling, then stood up to pace behind the sofa. My stomach dropped, what the fuck was he going to say?

He paused the game and put the controller down. Something like pity in his eyes. "I don't know who they are, exactly. But I'm pretty sure we were made for a purpose. Not a nice one. One of the girls I grew up with was close to her grandparents, and she told me tales. She said her great-grandparents were paid to have a baby by IVF. They couldn't have children of their own, and it seemed like an opportunity too good to miss. The cost of the IVF was paid as well as extra money on top. The vampires in my community are all incredibly secretive about this kind of stuff; they do not under any circumstances allow a person to walk free if they've fed from them. Regardless of how wrong it might feel, they will not risk it. I always felt like there was this deep, deep fear hanging over my parents and that it was about more than just being discovered. But I can't prove anything."

My throat constricted, my breaths suffocated under the weight of his admission.

"Fuck." I turned to Mahika. "Did your great-grandparents have IVF?"

"I don't know," she said quietly. "All I know is that they weren't mediators like us. If that was how we all came to be, many of them didn't admit it to their children. Maybe they weren't allowed to speak about it, but without any of them alive to question, it's hard to verify."

"Holy Fuck," I muttered, my knees bouncing chaotically, my stomach churning. "So basically, we're all some mad fucking experiment?" I said, launching to my feet and pacing around the sofa coming face to face with Mahika. "Why wouldn't you say something?"

She folded her arms, feet apart in a power pose. "It's speculation. A rumour. Until I have verifiable proof, which we are working on by the way, I have no business filling anyone's head with potential myths from a possibly unreliable source. But in all honesty, where the fuck did you think we came from?"

I turned on my heel, pacing back around the sofa. Naive. So fucking naive to think we'd just randomly evolved. It was most definitely the preferable reason for our existence; this was so much worse. "Oh, God. What's the oldest assassin you've ever come across?"

"Twenty-Six," she said with a sigh.

"Did Nanda's parents go through IVF? Is that how they knew what would happen to her?"

"Her parents denied it when we asked. But I'm not convinced they were being truthful. We've tried to obtain DNA on the sly to run a comparison, but we haven't managed it so far, and I never met Mei, Priya, or Veda's parents."

I collapsed on the sofa, the air whooshing out my lungs as I slumped into the cushions full force, the tension collecting between my temples in a dull ache. I didn't want it to, but it made so much sense. It explained why my parents didn't seem to display the same problematic DNA. Why we were appearing in cities with high numbers of vampires, but were we here to keep their numbers in check, or to get rid of them entirely? I sat up straight, finding Mahika and Rakesh exchanging a look.

"I need some air," I told them, launching from the sofa and hurrying to the door.

When I said air, I really meant the shower, and I found myself jogging through the house and up the stairs, bursting into our room and heading straight for the bathroom. Callahan was sprawled on our bed reading. He rolled into a sitting position when he saw my face and swiftly got up to follow me. The shock had morphed into rage, and I slapped the shower lever on full blast and started peeling off my clothes.

"Rakesh or Mahika?" he asked as he watched me chucking clothes randomly around the room.

I nearly tipped over when I tried to rip off a sock and he stepped forward to catch me and dipped to his knees. He gripped the top of my calf and gently tugged one sock off and then the other. His hands ran up the back of my bare thighs and he kissed my navel before rising to his feet.

"Talk to me," his voice rumbled into my hair as he held me.

I shuddered, and his fingers wound through my long tangled locks, his thumb stroking my cheek as he tilted my face to look at him. Tears trickled and he ducked to kiss them away, the tip of his tongue tracing the salty path towards my eye.

I took a deep but stuttered breath. "You know how Mahika told us that neither she nor Fletcher's great-grandparents weren't blood drinkers?"

His brows pinched together and he nodded slowly.

"Rakesh said that one of the girls he grew up with told him her great-grandparents were paid to have IVF. They couldn't have children naturally. They weren't vampires, but I think he was implying that the baby they gave birth to was. He thinks they were created. On purpose. That the vampires are all afraid, and regardless of whether they think it's right or not, they kill to keep their secret. What if whoever did this is threatening them?"

"What did Mahika say?" he asked after a pause, his breathing growing rapid, his face drained of colour as he tried to comprehend what I was telling him.

"Mahika said it was a theory but she doesn't have proof yet."

The bedroom door slammed, and Fletcher yelled for us, his steps approaching the door I'd left wide open in my rage.

"Shit." Callahan tugged me against his chest and sidestepped us to the closest towel just as Fletcher knocked on the door frame.

"Fucking hell, you know there is a door for a reason," he grumbled as he leaned in and pulled it shut.

Callahan glanced at the shower, the steam so hot and heavy in the air it coated my skin. "Are you getting in? Can I go talk to Fletcher, or do you want me to stay?"

I waved him off, stepping into the scorching stream of water and sliding to the bottom. Bringing my knees to my chest, I let my mind empty and the steamy downpour soak through my hair until it formed a dark sleek curtain on either side of my legs.

∽

The afternoon was spent in Nanda and Veda's room, surrounded by all four incredible girls. We chatted contentedly all afternoon, while Nanda gave us makeovers, and I let my heart be filled with joy and chose to push aside the fears, the anger, and the darkness vying for my attention. Every hour with them was precious and the days were already passing by far too quickly.

Callahan and Fletcher had decided to go for a run and blow off some steam. Callahan was in the bathroom when I returned, freshly showered, shaved and still half-dressed. A sight that made me ache and vehemently regret letting Fletcher share a room with us.

I noticed his gaze flitting over the heavy eye makeup that still adorned my face.

"Do you hate it?" I asked hesitantly. "I made sure she didn't hide my freckles."

He gave me a curious look, his mouth spreading in a wry smile, his eyes, despite their icy tone, were full of warmth and mischief and he shook his head. "No, I don't hate it at all, but if I'm honest, I don't like the way it makes me feel." His voice was low and gruff and it had butterflies taking flight low in my stomach.

I tilted my head, piercing him with a sultry gaze. "How does it make you feel?"

His eyes flickered to my mouth and he brushed the gentlest of kisses over my lower lip, continuing across my jaw. He paused below my ear, the warmth of his breath tickling my neck and making my skin prickle in anticipation of something divine.

"It makes me want to fuck you against a wall," he whispered.

A fiery tidal wave surged throughout my body rendering me breathless and legs trembling. "Why is that a bad thing?" I asked, my head tipping back against the wall as his lips trailed a burning path down the column of my throat, hovering over my frantic pulse."It's not, but, I don't know how to explain it," he murmured against my skin. "I guess, I think your natural beauty is so breathtaking. When I saw you without makeup, the morning after we met, it almost brought me to my knees, and it had nothing to do with where I could put my tongue." I felt his smile against my cheek and his mouth found mine, his lips soft and warm, his kisses tender and full of devotion. "I don't ever want to stop feeling that way," he said softly, his breath fluttering enticingly over my skin.

He'd once told me he didn't plan to use me, and all the intimate moments since then proved that. There was no denying that every time he treated me with such reverence, it was an act of worship. Every time he delighted in pursuing my pleasure, second to his own and it occurred to me that if I wanted to, he absolutely would have me against a wall and he'd make damn sure it was the best experience I'd ever had.

When I couldn't speak, utterly floored by the depth of his admission and all the things he couldn't put into words, he prompted me to get ready for bed. He watched as I cleansed and wiped away every trace of the makeup and then he'd kissed every inch of my face before leading me to bed. We curled up together and despite everything the day had thrown at us, found comfort in the cadence of quiet breaths and steady heartbeats, quickly drifting into contented sleep.

47

NOT RAKESH

I woke with a start, my body tingling ominously and my stomach reeling with nausea. I shook Callahan awake and scrambled out of bed, frantically running across the room to Fletcher and violently shaking his shoulder. He jerked upright, swearing under his breath, his hands rubbing the tiredness from his face.

"What is it?" Callahan asked groggily.

"Get dressed" I hissed, shaking him again and dashing to the wardrobe, using the torch on my phone to locate black jeans and a black sweater. "There are vampires here. And it's not Rakesh because when I saw him today, I didn't feel the dread I feel now."

My words drove them from their beds, both launching into action, darting to their suitcases, and pulling out clothes.

We kept the lights off, hurrying ungracefully into our clothes and shoes, completely forgoing privacy and keeping our voices to a whisper. Fletcher used the light from his phone to check through the go bag, while Callahan grabbed his carry-on holdall and packed extra clothes and toiletries in case we had to escape.

Minutes later, the door burst open, and Mahika barged into our room. Her hair was tousled and her face bare, she wore skin-tight black jeans and a dark T-shirt with a bulletproof vest, which had my heart rate rapidly increasing. She dropped a black rucksack by her feet as she surveyed us, her face smoothing slightly as she noted that we were all dressed and ready.

"We've been compromised," she said, voice low but authoritative. "You need to leave immediately. Get to the utility door and head northeast into the woods. About a hundred metres in, you'll find a black car hidden in the bushes. If you continue northeast through the trees, you'll eventually reach High Road and can get back to the city." She picked up the rucksack and handed it to Fletcher.

My mouth fell open. "You can't be serious? We can't run now and leave you all to fight. Let us help."

"Absolutely not," she said sharply. "We all have our procedures to follow. You are untrained, you've never worked with us as a team, and I do not need a dead foreign national on my hands, so I need you to get the fuck out of here."

"But—"

"I cannot risk it—you'd be a liability, so don't even bother arguing with me." She pulled out a gun from the back of her trousers, double-checked the safety and handed it to Fletcher. "There is an address with a set of keys in an envelope in that bag. It's a safe house that won't be compromised. Get yourselves there, then get on a flight home as soon as you can. There are a couple of doses of ASPB for Olivia and a burner phone. Wipe it, and leave the gun at the address. When we're safe, I'll contact you on that phone."

I grabbed her arm as she turned to leave. "What about Rakesh? What if he gets left down there to rot?" He might be a vampire, but I'd never wish that on him.

"Like I said, we have procedures in place. Now move. You're running out of time."

"Who do you think compromised you?" Fletcher asked as he hoisted the bags onto his back.

She grimaced and took a deep breath—it was the first time I'd seen her anxious since meeting her.

"We haven't been able to contact Farel and Aline for the last five days," she said before turning and slipping back into the hall and down the corridor.

I tried not to think about all the gory possibilities that might have befallen them as Callahan bound my fingers with his, the grip excessively tight as we followed, Fletcher leading the way.

The sound of glass shattering somewhere near the front of the house had my fear spiking to a previously uncharted level, it was hard to catch my breath. The urge to start running was overwhelming. I took a deliberate slow inhale as we reached the bottom of the stairs, and it rattled back out as we dashed across the hall to the sound of gunfire. By the time we reached the utility door, the nausea was crippling.

The gunshots were coming from the main drive, getting closer as we flattened against the back of the ranch. Scanning the trees ahead, Callahan tightened his grip and whispered, "On three. One. Two. Three, let's go."

We darted across the yard on light feet, slipping between the first line of trees and welcoming their shadows, letting the darkness shroud our escape. We followed Fletcher's lead, making slow progress as we moved cautiously from tree to tree with only the moonlight to guide our steps. The sounds of muted gunfire sent jolts of panic trembling down my spine each time they echoed through the forest. I hated myself. I was somehow back to being a coward, ripe with crippling fear and running from the danger instead of saving our friends, leaving behind the girls I'd only just found. As we paused to steady our breath under a large fir tree, I stared back towards the house. My heart hurt with the possibility that one of them might get shot. That I might not get to know them beyond our few precious conversations.

"She was right," Callahan murmured in my ear, and squeezed my hand before pulling me forward to the next cluster of trees.

We had barely covered more than five metres when Fletcher dropped to a crouch before a group of densely packed firs and bushes and signalled for us to hide. Callahan pulled me down beside him, partially covering me with his body. I strained to listen and heard quiet voices beyond the trees we were sheltering behind. Fletcher peered through the branches of a low bush and held up three fingers before ducking lower. Great. Even when we were running away, not even our cowardice could be fucking simple. Callahan started carefully patting the ground around us and stopped when his hands grasped a sizable rock, loose enough to dislodge without making a sound. He nudged Fletcher and gestured his intention to throw it, then moved closer to me, putting his mouth to my ear and whispered, "When Fletcher shoots, we run."

For several, heartstopping seconds we were suspended in time, crouched within the shadows of the forest floor, my raging heartbeat the only noise to fill my ears. Callahan hurled the rock and the sound of it crashing against a distant tree had us plummeting into chaos. Fletcher started firing, the noise bursting through my skull and stealing the breath from my lungs as Callahan dragged me to my feet and propelled me forward, skirting around the trees in our path. Despite the constant crack of gunfire, I followed his lead, running in a blind panic, knocking from tree to tree and stumbling over roots and discarded branches.

Callahan stumbled, grunting as he righted himself, clutching his side with one hand and pulling me forward with the other until the forest lapsed into silence. The only sound was that of our ragged breaths and our feet kicking up leaves and dirt as we ricocheted through the forest.

The car loomed ahead, a black mass camouflaged by foliage, the glint of silver light streaking across the roof marking its presence as it reflected the slither of moonlight that penetrated the towering firs. Callahan collided with it, panting and leaning against the door for stability, his eyes wildly searching for Fletcher.

"Fuck, fuck, fuck," he chanted under his breath.

Fletcher crashed through the trees on the other side of us a moment later, hurriedly removing the rucksack and dropping it on the bonnet to rifle through it. He ripped open the envelope and collected the keys, unlocking the car and shoving his rucksack inside. Callahan grunted as he moved, and it was then that I noticed he was still clutching his side.

"Did you get shot?" I screeched hysterically, grasping his hand and pulling it away from his side to find it wet and sticky. "No, no no."

I swallowed down bile, my eyes flooding and spilling over as I panicked.

Callahan grabbed my shoulder and pushed me towards the car. "I'm fine, get in, we need to get out of here," he told me with a wince.

"It's not fine, you've been shot. Fletcher, get over here," I shouted across the car.

Even in the darkness, I could see the furious look he threw at me as he stomped around the vehicle.

"Keep. Your. Fucking. Voice. Down," he hissed, pulling up the torch on his phone and lifting Callahan's T-shirt to inspect the wound. He turned the torch off and looked at me, his jaw clenching with rage. "Olivia, get in the fucking car, he's fine it's just a graze." He bunched the T-shirt and pressed it against Callahan's side. "Keep pressure on it, the bullet nicked a tiny chunk of flesh out of your side as it passed by, but you'll be fine."

He wrenched the door open and unloaded the pack from Callahan's back. His words were a balm to my rising panic, and I launched into motion, relieved that it wasn't serious, and scurried around the other side of the car.

As I started climbing in, the air split with a thundering BOOM.

The force of it rippled through the forest, and I stumbled back, clutching my head, my ears popping and ringing from the blast and the sheer shock of sound. When I righted myself and looked up, the sky was lit in a blaze of red and a plume of thick smoke swallowed up the canopy of stars.

I stared up at the mass of swirling black, my hands covering my face in disbelief. No. I shook my head, tears trickling over my fingers as I tried to comprehend the enormity of what had just happened. Not again. "Not again," I whispered.

Fletcher appeared at my side, his fingers clenching my elbow. "Get in," he ordered, shepherding me into the car. He shut the door behind me and acknowledged the tempestuous sky for a brief moment before jumping in the driver's seat.

We were all too stunned to speak as the car crept forward, winding its way through the trees, jolting us from side to side as we traversed the uneven ground, creeping steadily away from the carnage. Eventually, we hit a narrow road. It was only then that fear released its grip and sorrow swept in, and I started to sob.

Guilt hit me full force, like being caught in the rolling surf of a stormy sea, the waves relentlessly battered my lungs, forcing the air out until I was choking on my tears, all my carefully tended seeds of hope destroyed so viciously. We had failed them. And by bringing us here, I had put Callahan and Fletcher in harm's way.

48

SIT TIGHT

It was just over an hour's drive to the house on the city's edge. We pulled into a suburban driveway and quietly crept to the porch. We entered cautiously, Fletcher checking every room, drawing all the curtains, and ensuring every blind was down before declaring it safe and flicking on the lights.

The three of us stood in the centre of an open plan room, jaws dropping as we took it all in. The living room was a mix of white walls and bright colours: a fuchsia pink sofa with an orange throw over one end, bright orange curtains, various ceramic vases, and candles in gaudy colours. The kitchen area had lemon walls and sleek white units, and on the counter sat a fuschia pink toaster and kettle. It was so at odds with the peaceful, rustic decor at the ranch.

Fletcher snorted, shaking his head as he eyed the bright sofa. "Fucking hell. It looks like Barbie decorated in here."

Despite the gravity of our situation, a startled laugh escaped my lips, and my hand flew up to smother it. I released Callahan from my grip, his pale face was still a tight grimace, and one hand clutched his bloodied T-shirt, pressing it against his side.

"I'll find a first aid kit," I muttered solemnly, heading for the kitchen, and pulling open each cupboard, my frustration mounting with each door I slammed shut.

"I've got it," Fletcher yelled from the hall. He re-emerged and eyed Callahan apprehensively. "I think we do this upstairs. We need sleep," he said gruffly.

Callahan nodded, retreating to the hall and steadily trudging up the stairs. He'd barely spoken since we got in the car, just tightly squeezed my hand and reassured me that he was fine. But it was not the least bit reassuring, I could have lost him, and the thought was suffocating.

We found three equally garish bedrooms upstairs and a bathroom that made my head spin with its black and white tiles on the walls and floor. Callahan peeled off his T-shirt and braced himself against the basin while I cleaned the wound. He was lucky he was lean—the bullet had literally skimmed his side, leaving a small angry divot of flesh, the skin around it flaming red and bruised.

He was remarkably calm for someone who had just narrowly missed a bullet tearing through his back and abdomen, and I worried he was in shock; it was highly likely we all were. Being ambushed, shot at, witnessing the building we'd just been staying in being blown to pieces, and having no idea if any of the people we'd been with were alive was a fucking lot to process. Guilt was stalking greedily through my mind, waiting to devour me all over again, but I built a wall around it, determined not to let it break me.

"I'm sorry," I muttered when he grunted.

"Don't be. It's got to be done. It just fucking burns, and my skin feels like it's on fire."

With the gauze in place and taped up, I blew out a long, exhausted breath and stood, scanning Callahan's face, wondering if he was just as anxious about our situation and concerned about the wound as I was.

He raised a brow, his hands settling on my waist drawing me closer. "Stop worrying; it's nothing serious." His hands moved to my cheeks as he kissed away the frown line between my eyes, his lips sweeping gentle kisses down my nose and capturing my mouth with a thoroughness that dispelled all thoughts of our last few brutal hours. He withdrew with a frustrated groan, and whispered against my mouth, "I love you," landing a final kiss before stepping back to assess my efforts on his side.

"I'm sorry. Rory would have dealt with it so much better," I said, sincerely wishing we were back home and in his capable hands. God, I missed the farm.

Fletcher knocked lightly before stepping through and packing up the kit that I'd haphazardly strewn all over the floor while rifling through the contents.

"One of the rooms had a single, so I dragged the mattress through to the master. I'll sleep on it and cover the door," he said. "I've messaged Rory and Isla as well—told them we'll be rebooking our flights in the morning."

I nodded, hiding behind my hands as a colossal yawn overtook my face and sapped the remaining energy from my bones. It made me think of Finn and his theory about yawns being like dominoes, and it struck me that my life currently felt like a cruel and catastrophic domino chain.

I'd stumbled into all their lives as the catalyst, the little push that set a chain of events in motion, and now people just kept on falling, swallowed up in the spread of chaos that was too quick and substantial to thwart. What would we do now? If the network was wiped out, if we'd lost those key players choreographing this intricate dance of covert war, we were back to square one. The prospect made me want to scream.

"Hey, don't do this now. Let's get some rest, and we'll figure it all out when we get back," Callahan said softly, dragging my fingers away from my face and carefully drawing me to his chest, wrapping me up in one of his anchoring embraces.

"I love you," I whispered into the crook of his neck, "and it's terrifying—the thought of losing you. I don't think I could do any of this without you. It would hurt so much, I think it would break me in the kind of way you don't come back from."

He squeezed me, swiping the stray tear escaping down my cheek with his thumb. "Good job you're not gonna lose me then, isn't it! Come on, we need sleep. Let's get to bed."

∼

After a nervous wait at the suburban safe house, hearing nothing from Mahika or the others, we were finally approaching the airport under the watchful stare of Blucifer. The giant sinister stallion loomed ominously and I shuddered as we drew close enough to see his soulless crimson eyes. After thanking our driver we hurried inside and checked into our flights, heading straight for airport security given that we only had our carry-on luggage.

Despite having another dose of the miracle drug that blocked my scent, Callahan did not let go of my hand as we queued; his face was taut and leached of colour as he warily glanced around on constant high alert.

Fletcher went through security first, passing through with ease, and hovering the other side of the kiosk, waiting for us. I stepped up to the desk and handed over my documents, leaning on its solid frame and feeling a mix of relief and guilt to be heading home. The immigration officer, a blonde no-nonsense middle-aged lady, opened my passport and scanned it, then glanced at me with narrowed eyes. Her stubby fingers flitted over her keyboard and then she leaned forward, reading her screen intently. Callahan stepped up to the desk, his hand on my lower back as he watched her intently. She typed something more on her keyboard and finally looked up, noticing that Callahan was now beside me. "I need to get a superior to check your details. Your passport has been flagged."

"Flagged? Why would it be flagged?" I asked her, my stomach twisting into a tight ball. Were we once again stepping into a real-life nightmare?

"That's above my pay grade," she answered curtly and then looked at Callahan. "I can get you cleared while we're waiting," she said.

His eyes were tight with worry as he handed the documents over without so much as a glance her way. He laced his fingers through mine and squeezed tightly, his gaze unwavering, his thumb stroking the back of my hand in a quiet attempt to soothe away the anxiety we both felt.

Fletcher squeezed his way back through the press of people to wait with us at the kiosk. The minutes ticked by, and my chest tightened with fear to the point of pain, my breaths and pulse felt swift and disjointed.

Even the most optimistic of people would struggle to find the upside of being flagged by airport security when they'd left a trail of bodies in one country and just bore witness to an entire ranch exploding. Fuck. Fuck. Fuck.

"Olivia Blake?" A tall, suited man approached. He was all sharp jawline and slicked-back dark hair, and if I wasn't so scared, I might have laughed at how stereotypically villainous he looked. Something about him promised he meant business. He smiled at me, but it wasn't a kind smile, and my stomach churned and my skin prickled as he reached us and flashed an official looking badge. "Would you mind stepping this way."

I started to shake and stared up at Callahan, desperate for him to reassure me everything was okay, but he looked equally terrified, and his fingers gripped mine even tighter, as if he could fuse our hands and make it impossible for them to separate us.

"We're travelling together, and we're about to catch a flight. Will this take long?" Fletcher asked, taking charge of the situation and easing my mind a fraction.

"I'm sure you'll all be on your flights in no time," he said with another unfriendly smile.

"Perfect. Are we able to come along and wait for her?" Fletcher asked, his eyebrows raised as he waited for our brute of a chaperone to consider.

He nodded reluctantly and again gestured for us to follow him. "Right this way, please."

We wove through the crowds and slipped into a staff-only area that did nothing to settle my growing angst. We continued down white-washed corridors, stark and sterile, and passed few other people. We took a right turn and our chaperone abruptly stopped, opening a door to a private lounge area. "You two can wait in here," he said, nodding to Callahan and Fletcher.

Callahan didn't let go, his fingers squeezed mine, his jaw clenching as he eyed the man—whose name I never caught—with considerable vehemence. "What is this even about? And where are you taking her now?" he asked, squaring his shoulders as he stared down at him defiantly.

"Sir, this will only take a few minutes," he said with a condescending tilt to his head. "It's just some routine questions; she'll be in perfectly safe hands I can assure you. We'll be just down that corridor in one of those rooms on the left," he said pointing, "I can't leave you unattended out here so please, I'll ask you again nicely, wait in this room." His eyes narrowed, his features tight and beckoning for Callahan to put up a fight.

"Tilly," Fletcher said, levelling him a pointed look. "She's not done anything wrong. They probably just want to make sure she's not smuggling drugs or something—which they won't find because she's not. I know you two like to be joined at the hip, but if you don't stand down, this is gonna take a hell of a lot longer than it needs to, and we have a flight to catch."

"Fletcher's right," I said softly. Not that I felt remotely at ease about the prospect of being separated from them, but the last thing we needed was to escalate this to the point of making it a problem. "I've got nothing to hide. I'll go answer their questions, and then we can get home," I said, squeezing his hand and pushing up onto my tiptoes to kiss him. "I love you," I told him with as much of a smile as I could muster. "I'll see you in a few minutes, okay?"

Fletcher clapped him on the shoulder. With a resigned huff, Callahan relinquished his grip at glacial speed, his eyes brimming with emotion, and he bent to kiss me. "I love you too, see you in a few minutes."

Just as he had informed Callahan and Fletcher, we walked a short distance down the corridor, and our nameless friend unlocked a white wooden door on the left, swinging it open. He followed me in, the door clicking shut behind him. It was everything I hoped it would not be. A small, white, square room without windows, brightly lit with fluorescent ceiling lights and a single grey table with a plastic chair on either side. Taking a deep breath, I lowered into a chair, fidgeting with my hands in my lap and hooking my ankles around the chair legs to keep my legs from bouncing. I checked my watch as he took a seat opposite.

"My flight should be boarding in like, forty-five minutes. I really don't want to miss it," I said in a pleading voice. "Can you please tell me why my passport was flagged and what I need to do to sort it out?"

He smiled, pulling out a phone and setting it on the desk, taking his time before launching into his first question. "What was the nature of your visit to Denver?"

Maybe Fletcher was right. I blew out a breath, trying to ignore the nagging feeling that everything was about to go to shit, before confidently spouting off a list. "Just the usual holiday stuff, eating, drinking, fucking, checking out the scenery."

He raised an eyebrow and looked at his phone. "Where were you staying?"

My mind went infuriatingly blank trying to recall the address that we'd listed on the ESTA for this very eventuality—where the hell was it? A delay would not look good, so I decided to risk our colourful safehouse of the last two days.

"We stayed at a house in Foxfield," I told him, hating my choice to give something away that could link back to the network. "Which, if you need proof, I can give you the receipt for the driver we arranged to drop us at the airport this afternoon."

He ignored my suggestion and moved on. I hoped that was a good sign.

"Your original flight back to the UK was changed yesterday. Any particular reason you cut your visit so short?"

It was a question I should have anticipated. I blinked away the memory of the sky filling with oppressive black smoke and braced my elbows on the table, leaning forward to reply. "Are you actually concerned that I might be smuggling drugs? What do you need to do for me to prove I'm not? I just want to get home, so do whatever it is you need to do, I assure you I have nothing to hide."

He made some notes on his phone and gave me an appraising look. "How long did you stay in Foxfield?" he asked.

I couldn't keep the panic from my voice. "Can you please just tell me what it is you think I've done? I don't understand why you're asking me all these questions. Why is my passport flagged?"

He folded his arms, his lips a tight line as he watched me, then a full minute later he finally spoke. "Why did you cut your trip short?"

Oh, God, what to say that wouldn't drop us all in it. It had to be something that kept the farm out of the spotlight. No matter what I said, we would be doomed if he went to verify with Callahan or Fletcher.

"I just found out that my Dad is sick, and I want to get home to look after him," I said, my eyes convincingly pooling and a well-timed tear slipping down my face.

"Hmmm, is that so?" he said and picked up his phone, dropping it in his suit's inner pocket. "Sit tight. I won't be long." He smirked as he stood up and headed for the door, leaving me in my white box, stewing on the taste of my fear.

Apparently our definition of "I won't be long" was vastly different. When ten minutes passed, I got up and nervously paced the room, checking my watch after every short circuit, my hands slick and clammy as anxiety ran full riot in my mind. After twenty minutes, I forced myself back into my chair, folding my arms on the table and resting my head.

I thought of Callahan, of being tucked against his chest with the steady beat of his heart thumping in my ear, of waking up with his body protectively folding around mine. With any luck, I'd be experiencing all those things and more in just a few hours.

It was thirty minutes before the door finally opened, by which point, all hope of reaching our flight was snuffed out given that I had only ten minutes to get across the airport and down to my gate. My head snapped up expecting to see the dark-haired villain back to ask more questions, but my jaw dropped as I found my mother striding into the room. She looked me over, eyes narrowed and lips tight, shook her head and motioned for me to get up.

"What the hell are you doing here?" I asked, feeling a mix of surprise and suspicion.

"I think you mean, 'Thank you mother, for bailing me out of trouble. Again'. Come on, hurry up, we need to get to the plane," she said backtracking towards the door.

"Hold on," I said briskly, throwing up my hands. "What happened to Callahan and Fletcher? Where are they?" A tremor of panic rattled up my spine.

She looked me over again, her stare so penetrating I folded my arms protectively across my chest. She opened up her handbag and pulled out a bottle of water.

"They're already on the plane," she replied with a dramatic eye-roll. "Here take this, you look frightful."

I took it gratefully, my mouth as dry as a desert after the last thirty minutes of pure panic, and followed her out into the corridor. Another suited brute was waiting outside, stockier than the original, and with mousy brown hair that was cut short to his scalp. He fell into step beside me, not even glancing in my direction.

"We won't make the flight," I said, checking my watch and staring at my mother with a desperation that felt far too vulnerable to expose.

"It was delayed. Stop panicking. You'll be on the plane in the next ten minutes."

Her words brought immense relief, and the tension gradually left my body, my limbs feeling heavier without the adrenaline coursing through them. The sheer terror of the last forty minutes had utterly exhausted me.

"How did you know I was here?" I asked as I willed my legs to keep up with her brisk pace.

Her steps never faltered, sure and steady, as she marched us through the airport corridors, her heels clicking a rhythmic beat that echoed through the near-empty halls.

"Your passport was queried in the UK when you left. I was in New York, and luckily for you, I have friends in high places who notified me there was an issue. I arrived in Denver yesterday hoping to resolve things before they even became a problem. I thought I had a week to sort it," she said, turning to give me a curious look. "But then you booked yourself on an earlier flight, and I had to pull in a lot of favours."

That was unexpected, and given the information that had most recently come to light, I had the sinking feeling her motives were not in the least bit innocent. She was going to great lengths to protect me, which likely meant that if she'd been a recipient of IVF treatment, she was one of the few who must have known the truth about the experiments. She must have known the truth about me and why being in an airport full of people was a huge risk. It also meant she would have known what had happened the first time I was attacked and let me believe I was crazy.

Was she forced to withhold information as part of the arrangement? My skin prickled, nausea resurging, and I opened my mouth to question her, only to feel the corridor spin wildly, and the floor shift under my feet. My legs buckled, and I toppled backwards with a feeling of terrifying weightlessness as consciousness flittered beyond my grasp.

EPILOGUE

When I regained consciousness, my head throbbed, and my stomach was definitely in danger of rejecting its scant contents. I stayed quiet and still, trying to piece together what had happened.

The last thing I remembered was walking through the airport, about to confront my Mother. I recalled the bottle she'd handed me as we left the room and my stomach churned at the betrayal; the pernicious bitch must have spiked my water. Where the hell was I? My eyes pulled apart, sticky with sleep, and I found myself in a reclined leather chair, looking up at a narrow, curved ceiling, dimly lit by neat rows of spotlights emitting a soft warm glow. It was quiet, the only sound, a perpetual white noise buzzing low in my ears.

"What. The. Fuck?" I sat up, my stomach lurching with the sudden motion, and my hand flew to my mouth, stifling the urge to retch.

She hadn't been lying about making our plane, but it wasn't the right fucking plane; this was a private jet. Twisting in my seat, I found her staring at me from another recliner, one leg crossed over the other and a glass of whiskey resting in her lap.

"What the fuck did you do?"

She took a sip and rolled her shoulders. "I got you out of Denver."

I tried to stand, but my limbs hadn't quite caught up to my brain, and I fell clumsily back into the seat, my shoulders shaking with rage.

"Where are Callahan and Fletcher?" I shrieked, angry tears spilling down my cheeks and my jaw trembling.

"I told you, they got on the plane. They'll be landing at Manchester Airport as planned in a few hours," she said calmly, completely unbothered by my obvious rage.

That was a loaded statement if ever I'd heard one. My eyes narrowed on her. "And where are we landing?" I spat.

Her lips pursed in a tight smile, one eyebrow raised. "We'll be landing in London at a small commercial airport where there are significantly fewer people," she said pointedly. Oh she knew. Did she think she was doing me a favour? Was I supposed to feel grateful?

"Fewer people or fewer vampires?" I bit out. Her face remained calm; not a single muscle twitched at my question, and it was all I needed to know.

Getting to my feet, I approached slowly, my rage expanding with each step, flowing hot and fast in my veins, my pulse pounding through my skull, loud and urgent like a war drum.

"How could you not help me?" I seethed. "You threw me to the wolves and then fucking gaslighted me for a decade. How can you live with yourself? You—are a fucking monster, and when I get off this plane, I swear to God, I never want to see your face again." My fists were so tightly clenched I could feel the sharp sting of my nails biting into my flesh.

She laughed, a sound so cold and chilling, it rattled through my bones, and she stood, squaring her shoulders as the distance between us closed. Her eyes were fierce and unyielding, her tone scathing as she responded. "You've always been stubborn, capricious, and naive with all your ridiculous ideals. You always have been, and always will be a risk. So sorry to disappoint you, but when you get off this plane it won't be the last you see of me. You'll be coming home while I figure out how to fix the damn mess that you've made."

"I'm naive? Do you have any idea what you signed up for? Do you know how many people the vampires are killing each week? How much did they pay you to have the IVF?" I said bitterly and snorted an incredulous laugh. "Probably not enough given how disappointing I am right? Well, rest assured I will be cleaning up my own damn mess, so I don't need to spend another minute in your vile presence."

She clasped her hands together, and her chest slowly expanded as she inhaled such a long breath. I wondered if she was consuming the entire oxygen supply in the plane. The bare triangle of skin between her throat and sternum flushed red and blotchy against the contrasting pure white of her shirt. I braced for her eventual eruption, promising to be as devastating as a spewing volcano.

She shook her head. "You will be coming home. But the state you come home in will be entirely up to you. It can be with dignity and full cooperation or unconscious. Either way, you are not going back to Nottingham for the foreseeable future. Your last little stunt in the city has threatened a revolt, and if I don't deal with it, it's going to draw unwanted attention."

My eyes widened. A revolt? The way she phrased it sounded far too personal. I took a step back, piecing together multiple snippets of information and realising that I had given her far more credit than she deserved. The vampires were 'pawns' Rakesh had said, here to do society a favour our hostage had said. All the while I'd been wondering *for whom* when it was right under my nose.

My body became eerily still and empty of thought, my breaths and heart slowing as the truth settled in its enormity.

"Is this the part where you spout some machiavellian shit and tell me it's all for the greater good? That all the people you've been taking advantage of to create your monsters—preying on their desperate desire for a family—is somehow going to save the world?" I asked, wondering if she would deny it or defend her involvement.

She folded her arms, tilting her head as she gazed at me with the usual contempt, her mouth refusing to spill its secrets.

"No? No guilty conscience you want to offload? What about Dad? Does he know exactly what you've been doing? Does he know his daughter was genetically engineered?"

She snorted, shaking her head and though she tried to fight it, an arrogant smile settled on her lips. "Your father was the one who genetically engineered you," she said smugly and looked past my shoulder giving a nod of confirmation. I whirled to the sharp click of a gun, a spike of pain flaring in my abdomen and as I looked down, the last thing I saw as my vision distorted, was my fingers trying to grasp the feathered dart protruding from my skin.

ACKNOWLEDGMENTS

Writing a book is certainly a team effort, there is so much that happens behind the scenes and I am beyond grateful for all those who either helped or encouraged me on this journey.

Firstly, to the God of Angel armies, my father in heaven, rescuer of my bleak and bitter soul, and mender of my broken heart. I would not be here today without the constant assurance of my faith in him.

To my husband. He might not be morally grey, but he treats me like a damn queen and twenty years on, I still pinch myself every day that I got so lucky. He is my rock, my soul mate, and without his unending support, I would never have finished writing this book. Matt, you are quite simply, my hero. Every. Single. Day. I love you beyond measure.

To my mum. My best friend, my reading buddy, and my biggest champion. Thank you for encouraging me chapter by chapter throughout this process. Thank you for believing in me and loving me no matter what. I'm so lucky to have you.

To my girls Angie, Lacey, Kaleigh and Steph. You are the best friends a girl could ask for and your excitement, encouragement, and support throughout this journey have meant the world to me. Thank you for being so patient and putting up with my scattiness whilst my head has been full to the brim with all the intricacies of writing a book. Without you all behind me I couldn't have done it. I love you all so much.

To Lara - I'm not sure I would have believed I could ever do this were it not for your push! Your wholehearted encouragement and belief in my ability made this dream a reality. Thank you for being my soundboard and cheerleader on the hard days. For being the very first to read my work and tell me I had the skill to write something beautiful and compelling. I would never have believed it from anyone else. You opened the door for me to dream bigger than I have ever dared to dream. So thank you.

To Kerry - the friend I never knew I needed. I'm so glad I read a book about Peter Pan and recommended it to you! Navigating this journey has been endless fun since our paths crossed. I love that we're on this journey together - I am so proud of all you are achieving and I cannot wait for the day I get to hold your book in my hand! It's going to be incredible. You are talented, generous and kind, and your enthusiasm and encouragement during this process have kept me smiling on the toughest days. You are the icing on the cake and the cherry on top, of this writing experience! Thank you so much for all your help with this project (it's a big list!), all the endless giggles, the art you've created in honour of my characters and everything else in between. Love you.

To Friel my editor and friend. You are amazing. Your kindness, compassion, and patience know no bounds. You have been such a blessing and so insanely encouraging along this journey. I am beyond grateful you wanted to work with me and you have taken this project and perfected it in a way I never could have. Thank you so so much from the very depths of my heart.

To Caity Farran and Alice Brogan. You are both incredibly kind and talented storytellers and I count it an honour to have your support. Thank you Caity for answering my endless questions, you are so patient and so helpful and you've taken it upon yourself to be my cheerleader in the terrifying final stages before release which means the world to me. Alice, thank you so much for patiently being on hand to answer questions, you are such an encouragement and of course for reading and championing the book ahead of release. I cannot thank you enough and I am so happy you loved it.

To Sandra my cover designer at Maldo Designs. I cannot put into words just how delighted I am with your design. It exceeded all my wildest expectations. You are so talented. Thank you so much.

To my team of beta readers—I cannot thank you enough.

James. Your kind and wise advice helped me hone this story into its very best version and I will forever be grateful. Your influence has undoubtedly left the biggest mark across the pages.

Zoe. Thank you for your relentless enthusiasm and love of my characters, it made this process so exciting.

Kaleigh. Thank you for helping me sharpen the details and for critiquing it so kindly. Your insight was invaluable.

Angie. I cannot tell you the relief I felt when you enjoyed and believed in this story. You are not easily impressed and honest to a fault so to have your approval was everything to me.

David C. Thank you for all the support and input you put into this book and for the ways you helped shape it to its best. You and Liz have been an enormous blessing to me throughout my life. Thank you, I love you guys so much.

Dave L. You are a legend!

Lizzie C. It means the world to me how much you adore this book and how you've taken it upon yourself to be its biggest cheerleader. Your encouragement brightens my days and makes all the hard stuff worth every second.

Glen. Your seal of approval on the final draft was priceless. Thank you for all your encouragement and for all the shared chats about our work and books in general.

Emma, Kev and Lizzie J. Thank you for reading outside of your comfort zone and loving it! It was so exciting to see your reactions.

To the Booksta community - this wouldn't be possible without you all. Thank you so much.

ABOUT THE AUTHOR

Annabella Lowe lives in East Anglia, UK, with her husband, son, two crazy cocker spaniels and an evil cat. Alongside writing, she has a children's photography business and co-owns a wedding photography business, which keeps her on her toes and her creativity flowing.

A born daydreamer, Annabella is drawn to fantasy, especially when seasoned with romance, and is slowly building her beloved book collection. You can find her championing other authors on Booksta and building friendships with the amazing book community.

Her debut novel Find Me in the Shadows, was birthed from a vivid dream she had many years ago and has fulfilled one of her lifelong goals to write and publish a book.

Printed in Great Britain
by Amazon